SADDLEBAGS

SADDLEBAGS

A COLLECTION OF COLUMNS AND STORIES

BY SHELBY STROTHER
OF THE DETROIT NEWS

A&M

Altwerger & Mandel Publishing Company, West Bloomfield, Michigan

Library of Congress Cataloguing-in-Publication number applied for.

ISBN # 1-878005-28-6

Designed by Barry Fitzgerald.

Printed in the United States of America.

First Edition.

For Kim, Tommy and Kenny

I can't explain the feeling, the love, the joy and the constant appreciation of those who have touched me in so many ways. To Buddy Baker, my mentor, to Thurman Strother, my brother and constant companion, to a simple loving sister named Laura, to the State of Florida—imagine that, the world from that viewpoint, the wonderful mixing intangible of love forever and piece of real estate that allowed so much love—I dedicate this book. I cannot explain the unique qualities that tangle the emotion of seeing the two-fisted experience . . .

Shelby Strother
Detroit
Saturday, March 2, 1991

Acknowledgement

───────

Shelby Strother was loved and admired by colleagues throughout the newspaper world. Many of those friends contributed to this volume in important ways.

We are particularly grateful to the Gannett Foundation for its generous support of the publication of *Saddlebags*.

CONTENTS

FOREWORD

Shortly before he became ill, Shelby Strother wrote an affectionate essay about Buddy Baker, a close friend and editor of the Hattiesburg (Miss.) American who was battling cancer. The two had worked together at TODAY in Cocoa Beach; Buddy the boss and Shelby a newcomer on the sports desk. As Shelby tells it, Buddy came to him one day and said, "Let's have some fun; let's learn to write."

Searching for the word that would define Buddy's influence, Shelby wrote, "Mentor sounds too formal. Teacher? Too limited. Creator comes closest to the truth, non-theologically speaking. Buddy Baker created me nonetheless."

Weeks later, the two talked and cried together, linked by telephone and the tragedy of a terrible disease; Shelby in a hospital bed in Detroit, Buddy at home in Hattiesburg.

The idea for this anthology came from Shelby's friends at The Detroit News. When they asked Shelby what he thought, he responded with unmistakable enthusiasm and began ticking off lists of stories and columns that he thought should be included. It was a list of some length, as one would expect from a writer who took great pride in his work.

Shelby was a shy man whose occasional visits to the office

revealed little that would explain the energy and the passion he put into the pursuit of a story. He could be seen sitting quietly at a desk in the back of the sports department, a bear of a man, his eyes shielded by sunglasses, his dress tending toward Hawaiian shirts, jeans and leather jackets.

He argued with his editors. It was often about small things, a period or a comma. He knew that good stories, good columns have a rhythm. His conviction that his own sense of rhythm was often better than his editor's made him a hard man to edit.

Writing, Shelby once told an interviewer, is a constant search for the "truly perfect words that can be necklaced together to make perfect sentences."

This anthology is rich with evidence of the enormous range of Shelby's interests and of his versatility as a journalist. He understood news. He wrote for a generation coming of age. His best work often went beyond the limits of the locker room and the playing field.

Shelby eagerly sought those assignments and they became a showcase for his gifts as reporter and writer. In West Germany to cover the end of the Berlin Wall, he wrote that the colorful graffiti was "scribbled freedom and if put to music, it would be jazz." Later, he said that assignment was "an opportunity to rub your fur in another direction."

Shelby broke away from his coverage of the Super Bowl in 1989 to report on the violence that erupted after a Miami policeman shot a young motorcyclist in a black neighborhood. His account of the shooting and its aftermath ran on page one for several days.

He celebrated the non-celebrated: Joe Don Looney in decline, one-time prep idol Curtis Jones in the prison of his own deteriorating mind, paunchy ex-football great Billy Cannon in court pleading for leniency.

Shelby served with the Air Force in Vietnam for 13 months in 1968–69. The war experience was a theme he often returned to. In 1986, when the movie "Platoon" was getting critical acclaim, he wrote of his impressions. "The vets toted home heavy psychic baggage that is like a Claymore mine. It needs only a trip-wire to bring back to life the lessons that cannot be unlearned . . . Nothing like the pop-pop-pop of fireworks at a Fourth of July party to send someone face down on the ground, hands covering his head."

His personal recollections helped give us a sense of who we are. A piece on shagging grounders was a pause of fantasy, a loving remembrance of a time long ago when the springtime sun was warm and there seemed to be no limits to our energy or our possibilities.

His tireless probing into the wondrous corners of life brought forth pieces about his family that offer a warm, true definition of Shelby Strother.

In 1989, when the nation was agonizing over flag burning, Shelby wrote about an earlier time when he was tempted to burn the flag in protest. "I had the flag in my hands and I saw one more image. A man in a uniform. Rows of ribbons, captain's bars and a smile. My father. The flag in my hands was his flag. It once was draped over his coffin almost 20 years ago. Then it was carefully folded by other soldiers wearing white gloves and handed to me in a ceremony. And a man with stars on his shoulders handed me the flag that day and said on behalf of a grateful country, my father's efforts were deeply appreciated and should never be forgotten. Then he handed me that flag. And that flag is my father."

He harkened back to his own childhood, seeking a firmer footing for his own role as a father. He told a story once of his deep disappointment at his father's refusal to teach him how to throw a curve ball because his arm was too young and the muscles not fully developed. It was an experience that had exposed his father as mortal, that began the natural unraveling of "his coat of shining armor." Years later, at his dad's funeral, he learned the truth about the curve ball. "I still smile when I think of him. And his grandsons—my boys—are getting older and stronger. I think I'd like to play some catch with them."

On a recent Mother's Day, he wrote this about Lucille Strother: "Clutch player, team player, leader in the clubhouse; she played cleanup. She could pick them up and lay them down. Egos, that is. With her, everything stayed fair, in bounds, by the rules. Hands of a jockey for discipline. Hands of a mother for boo-boos and life's other skinned knees. She also made perfect corn bread. I thought she was Lou Gehrig and would be in the lineup forever. On Nov. 1,

1970, she was called up to a higher lead. Her name was Lucille. I miss her so."

Like so many other strong, young men, there was a Lou Gehrig expectation for Shelby. He exited life with the loving admiration of friends and colleagues in journalism and sports, and he left it for us to ponder the chilling reality of things.

Sometimes sorrow is more easily borne in the stories we tell. Shelby was a master storyteller and, perhaps, this collection will ease our sorrow.

Robert H. Giles
Editor and Publisher
The Detroit News

A NOTE

Shelby Strother: his whole life has been a play on words and those of us who have known him and read him have had more fun because of it. His name or sig on a newspaper story or column was the hallmark that guaranteed reading time worth investing.

Accurate, informative, interesting — to be sure. But the greatest quality: entertaining. Shelby Strother, like sport itself, is entertainment. "The toy department," is how some cynical editors refer to a newspaper's sports department. Not that games aren't important or serious business, mind you (who did play in last year's Super Bowl?). Of greater importance to me, as a reader, is what the writer had to say about the event.

Most stories told and written by Shelby Strother are the stuff of which collections are made — because they're entertaining, fun reading whether you know Muhammad Ali from Ali Baba. A Choral Symphony of sorts, but with words, not musical notes — or are they? Sweet and sour, to use another metaphor of man's pleasures, all mighty palatable to both connoisseur and fast-food eater.

Shelby Strother's wife Kim and sons Tommy and Kenny had a husband and daddy in whom they could take justifiable pride and pleasure, as can anyone who reads this collection. Great voices are preserved for posterity on records, great actors and personalities on film, great writers on paper.

I thought, as the editor of a Florida daily called TODAY, that the day might come when Shelby Strother would be the best sports writer on any newspaper in the country. The day came, but I can't give you the when and where of it. The who and what are a lot more important, anyway.

His talent wasn't limited to the games people play on fields and courts; he also was at home telling you of the political, social and economic games they play, as with the crumbling of the Berlin Wall, a recent event that WAS well-noted and WILL be long-remembered — especially by readers of The Detroit News, whose editors had the good sense to recognize the journeyman in the jock.

What else is there to say about a father, a fellow-journalist and a friend I like and admire? Write tight (he rarely did), write on time (he usually did) and write well (he always did), that's what!

And remember: Style can be taught. Soul cannot.

> Edward "Buddy" Baker
> Editor
> Hattiesburg (Miss.) American

AN EXPLANATION

"Labor of love" is one of those tired old phrases over which Shelby Strother would have cringed had it appeared in one of his stories. He had more style than that. He had more respect for the reader. He had more love for the language.

But this book is a labor of love, and no other words describe it so cleanly. Shelby took ill in the late winter of this year, 1991, and quickly was diagnosed with cancer that had settled in the liver. Where it began the doctors never did figure out. Ultimately it didn't matter, and ultimately Shelby didn't care. He knew it was terminal and while he promised the embracing world of his friends that he would "give it all my shots," he also knew that time was the only factor to be played with.

As it turned out, there wasn't much room to play. Shelby opted for chemotherapy but it didn't work, and he died March 3rd at the age of 44, just eight days after the diagnosis. No overtime.

As Shelby lay ill in the hospital, trying to decide whether and how to fight, many of us were consumed by the despair all observers of terminal illness know. It comes from the inability to do anything helpful. We couldn't take his shots for him. We couldn't pool our own healthy organs to somehow create a fresh one. We could do nothing but sit at his side and cry rivers of misery.

Out of that despair came this book. So we approached The Detroit News, where Shelby worked for the last five years of his life, and asked if a book were possible. Before the pitch could be finished, Bob Giles, editor and publisher and fan of Shelby's writing, was out of his chair and calling in Lorraine Needham, his assistant, to figure out the details.

From there, it was a sprint.

As with most sprints, things moved too quickly for details to be recorded. Each footstep is critical, but when it's over all that stands out is the finish line. But there are some acknowledgements to be made, some thanks that must be placed. First off, to Giles, Needham and assorted Detroit News editors for backing the undertaking and looking the other way when the books' compilers were busy with book-related details.

And to The Detroit News staff for typing up Shelby's old clips. Most said later they enjoyed the chance to let Shelby's words flow from their own fingertips, and a few said they learned something about writing in the process. That would have made Shelby proud.

We'd also like to thank the Detroit News library, under Pat Zacharias, for its help in sorting through Shelby's stories to find the many that lodged in our minds as noteworthy.

And we'd like to thank Kim Strother, Shelby's wife, and their two sons, Tommy and Kenny, for allowing a few of us to invade their basement during Shelby's last critical days to begin our research amid the boxes that comprised his files. Some of the articles in this book would not have appeared had we not been able to find them in Shelby's personal collection.

Finally, we'd like to thank you, the reader, for caring enough about writing and about Shelby to buy this book. The Gannett Foundation is paying the book's initial publishing costs, which means most of the proceeds from *Saddlebags* will go to a trust find to help support Shelby's boys.

The title comes from a book Shelby hoped to write about Satellite Beach, Fla., where he grew up. It was to have been called *Saddlebags* after his nickname for the area. The name also seemed fitting for this collection, with its image of a horse-backed wanderer filling his satchels with whatever he finds.

Most of the stories were selected by Shelby. The rest were

gleaned from his rather massive clipping files. The incomplete dedi-
cation was dictated by Shelby the day before he died to Mike
O'Hara, his friend and fellow sports writer at The Detroit News.

There is no real system to this book. We lumped the stories,
sometimes arbitrarily, by general category and then tried to orga-
nize them chronologically for lack of a better intrinsic order. The
stories were very much a product of their creator, who himself was
difficult to categorize.

Enough of this. The point of the book is to entertain. Let's get
on with it.

The Friends of Shelby Strother
March 21, 1991

1.

COLUMNS I

**Each Christmas Day always contains the present,
future and past for both the young and old
December 26, 1990**

It did not matter that the windchill was life-threatening. It was Christmas morning, and a bright sun stabbed the frozen land. And children were playing.

The decision over which to play with — the official World Cup soccer ball or the Turbo Football — never materialized. With all the snow, a soccer match was out of the question. So spirals of pink and black performed in the most sincere imitations of Rodney Peete and Joe Montana floated back and forth in the yard.

What a nice sight.

The Annual Second Chance is near — it's called New Year's Eve. It is that window of opportunity where the hopes and fears of all the year (not to mention the mistakes) can be erased.

But Christmas Day is a time of reinforcement and the essence of tomorrow. And children playing with toys are the finest examples of what that tomorrow looks like.

I look out the window. I've been in that yard. All young boys have. Sports become such a part of childhood. Santa is aware of all this, naturally.

1

This particular day is exquisite, I think to myself. I take personal inventory, not only of blessings and personal satisfaction, but of the presents of Christmas past. Still the kid, I suppose.

I got my first basketball when I was six. I made my first basket a year later. There was a tetherball set; I must have been eight. And a football helmet when I was ten. A Carl Furillo-model baseball mitt at eleven. There were tennis rackets and fishing poles and boxing gloves and shrimp nets and a Mickey Mantle 32-inch Little League bat and one time, even a badminton set.

Every Christmas, I'd play out my dreams and my mind would fly over the rainbow, imagination my propulsion. Of course, I would become a major-leaguer, an All-Star, an all-time great, a Hall of Famer. We all would. My vision extended well beyond the day.

My athletic ability, alas, never kept stride. It was not the worst realization I would ever make.

But I have noticed a direct correlation between Christmas gifts and sporting dreams. The dreams are for the young. So are the gifts. Usually, the two disappear in unison. The rare few who project into greatness discover they do not need imagination to make those lofty flights of fantasy. Hope is not the co-pilot. Expectation is.

It must be a wonderful view.

I was thinking about all this when another memory nudged me. My 17th Christmas I got a typewriter.

It was about the same time that I'd maneuvered my fantasy a few extra miles. I'd received a baseball scholarship to pitch at a small school in Florida. There were other opportunities, other colleges available. But none that would allow my athletic vision to continue.

I had expected a Christmas of more games in the yard. More dreams to celebrate. I got a typewriter instead.

"What am I going to do with a typewriter?" I asked.

My mother said I'd need it for college. But she also said, "Sometimes you get too old to play games. But you never get so old that you can't use your imagination."

Sometimes Christmas is taken for granted. Almost always, in fact. I think of Christmas music, and I hear bells. I turn on the radio and I hear someone named Elmo and Patsy lamenting their grandmother's head-on collision with a reindeer. I think of the meaning of Christmas, and I think of the most special birthday in the history of the world. But I turn on the TV and there are all these Claymation raisins doing Doo-Wop homages to the joys of buying machines wherein a microchip can seize command of entire generations.

Christmas is gone, 364 days to go. But children still play. They chase the wonderful image of themselves as they would like to be seen. Christmas is their favorite arena. But they settle for lesser stadia.

But remember this — the present is sometimes confused with the package it comes wrapped in. Sometimes the gift is simply the freedom to imagine. There may be no greater one.

It was a great typewriter. I still play with it.

Sports different through eyes of child

He is just a kid, hanging around a convenience store, talking about football, and things.

"I told you the Lions were no good," rails a companion.

"They've still got a winning record," the kids says, shrugging.

"Not for long."

"You'll see."

"Wanna make a bet?"

"No. I'm saving my money."

We live in a throwaway society. The generations of Me and Now, on deadline, waiting for the two-minute warning, waiting for the whales to save us for a change.

We seldom listen for the real songs of sport. We hear them even less.

Our athletic heroes are based on decimal points, prime numbers, won-loss ratios. We judge and pity and condemn any who fall short. Wagons get hitched to stars because they're there and we're here. We cannot resist sharing the gilded moments of achievement simply because the celebrity's reality embodies our dreams. But we also cannot hide our disgust when the star first flickers, when limitations are identified.

There is nothing special about mediocrity; it reminds us too much of ourselves. That's why we use up our heroes. Society boasts a jaded population.

Once in a while, you find a trespasser.

Society has tested Jason Kercher severely, even knocked the wind out of him a couple of times. But it hasn't soiled or dented him. Or changed his mind.

Jason is 12. But he knows the difference between a gift and a reward. He knows making the best of a situation involves more than simply getting a transfer ticket from one bandwagon to another.

You see, Jason Kercher loves the Detroit Lions. Even after last Sunday. He roots with his heart, not his mind. That's the best way. The heart doesn't grow calluses.

Logic tells him his favorite football team isn't very good. So does his best friend. He doesn't care.

He's saving the money he makes mowing yards and doing odd jobs around his neighborhood. He wants to take his father to a Lions game. A birthday present for his dad.

His father loves the Lions too. One might have something to do with the other. Then too, maybe this story is about something other than football.

Jason pulls out his wallet and flips through the plastic picture windows until he comes to the one of his father.

"That's him and my mom," he says, gazing at the picture, "before they got divorced."

The father lives in Pontiac. A long ways off in terms of father-son distance. But not impossible to overcome every other week and for an entire, glorious month during the summer.

His father loves the Lions and lives in Pontiac but hardly ever goes to their games, "because he usually works on Sundays.

"But they told him he could be off on his birthday."

Before he puts his wallet back into the rear pocket of his jeans, Jason shows off another plastic window. This one holds a blurred picture of a grinning Doug English, his meaty arm around a tiny fan.

"That's me and Doug English. Defensive tackle Number 78. He's my favorite, a real good guy," Jason says.

"Dad took that picture."

There is no tragedy, no heartbreak. Not any more. Society sometimes splits apart at the seams and someone spits on the sidewalk and someone else takes a wrong turn on the freeway of love. Jason Kercher keeps on smiling.

In Green Bay, the Lions threw sand on their bubbles of momentum just as a simmer was about to become a boil. The offense had its wires ripped out. The defense discovered it had a dead battery. The Lions stunk up the state of Wisconsin and twinges of embarrassment remain today. Jason Kercher keeps on smiling.

"Aw, maybe that will help me get better seats for me and my father," he says.

Jason hopes the weather stays good. Someone tells him the Lions play their home games indoors.

"No, I need good weather because I need to do at least two more yard jobs between now and November 17," he explains.

Sometimes, the world gets stale and depressing. There are these disappointments that keep on bumping into each other, idyllic fender-benders that stack up and take their toll.

Sometimes, a man has to get away, take a walk outside to get a good blast of cool, fresh air. To feel better about things.

And sometimes you can find that fresh air inside a convenience store, listening to a kid talking about football, and things.

2.

WAR AND FREEDOM

Call to war same old sad song to veterans
Jan. 16, 1991

> "I woke last night to the sound of thunder. . .
> How far off, I sat and wondered. . ."
> — Bob Seger

You pound your thigh with your fist and your lips curl into dread and then they press together and you feel all busted up inside. Again . . . how far off? Or how close? How soon? And the twinges return. The smells. The strafing memories.

Was it all in vain? Was nothing realized or learned? Did they all die for nothing?

Is that why war is poised today in some ungodly desert far from home?

Your father felt the same dull throbs. And his father. You identify it. Futility. Then a great sense of insignificance comes. It really didn't do any good. Not your part, not your father's, not his father's.

One tribe attacks another and the reasons are always the same. For the land. Or the goods. Or for simple superiority.

Pessimists tell us war is a phase, a necessary evil. Optimists contend it is a disease, entirely curable if only the cause could be isolated and identified.

And there always comes the dilemma—is it a *just* war?

Was it this way at Shiloh or Khyber Pass or Hamburger Hill or Little Big Horn or Omaha Beach or Cantigny or Monkey Mountain or Pork Chop Hill? Was there the same dull throb?

In the Cass Corridor, at the Old Miami Bar, the customers seem frantic. Like cockroaches just before an earthquake. It is as if they know something is happening before it does. Most of them are combat veterans. Some have never been able to let loose of their experience.

They know the feel of war. They know it gets embedded in the skin, under the fingernails, and cannot be washed away. The smells are still vivid. The emotions are fresh.

Joe Burke celebrated his 63rd birthday Monday. He didn't get the present he wanted. The line in the Saudi sand is still drawn.

"Only war you can win is the one that never starts," says Burke, who served in World War II and Korea. "Once it gets going, you gotta start keeping score. Nobody wins."

Behind the bar, Sam Reeves shakes his head, but not in disagreement.

"I follow what's happening in the Gulf. Are we going to war over the right to have cheap oil? Is it right or wrong—I will not know that for a long time. But all I ask, whatever you do, whatever you believe, please support the guys over there. Once we commit, please get behind our troops."

Reeves served two tours of duty in Vietnam, "almost six years in all. So I figure I have a master's degree in war. And please believe me, some of the people over there right now, right up front, are beginning freshmen. They need to know. Believe me, I know."

The owner of the Old Miami, Danny Overstreet, doesn't like to talk about his days with the 101st Airborne. Or two wounds or the 13 medals or that little confrontation known as Hamburger Hill or the time he spent in Cambodia. Ancient history, he says. Nobody's business.

But he sees what's happening. Again.

If it comes to war, he's said loud and often, "the losses are going

8

to be heavy. Thousands in the first week. We'll win. But the cost of life. . ."

"Tomorrow, or the next day, some of our children will be killed and I'm gonna be mad. And I guess that makes me an American.

"But if the president doesn't end it real quick — this country's gonna fall apart. I've seen it coming and I've prayed someone would come to his senses. But we keep sending innocents, boys and girls and children, to solve our problems. And to tell the truth, I have a familiar knot in my stomach."

Is this the voice of protest? Are these men dissidents who would rebel against the very country they once offered their lives to defend? Never. But are these the cries of experience, lamenting the utter uselessness? Are these anguished souls who wonder about a planet that in this — the 20th century — has killed on purpose more than 75 million people in the interest of war and now prepares for more?

What is a *just* war, anyway? Perception is such a problem. We forget what burn bandages look like when they slip and human skin is peeled away. We forget the sky black with smoke and the stench of sulfur and kerosene and burning flesh. We hear the term M-1 and once, for someone, that meant a rifle. Now it means a tank.

And that is progress the same way it is progress when a cannibal uses a knife and fork.

It just isn't civilization.

War gets stripped and customized and painted with disguise and suddenly all fighter pilots look like Tom Cruise, and John Wayne is leading another glorious charge over the hill and in the background, stirring music, either Sousa or Springsteen, gets everyone aroused. But that's a false face and everyone who's ever been close to a war knows it.

At the Old Miami there is a chalkboard and someone has scribbled, "Jan. 15, 1991 The Eve of Destruction."

And everyone knows the words to the old song. . .

The Eastern World it is exploding. Violence flaring. Bullets loading. You're old enough to kill but not for voting. You don't believe in war. But what's that gun you're toting? And even the Jordan River has bodies floating . . .

Want to know what real war is? It's a device called a Bouncing

9

Betty, which is a land mine designed to split you in half, starting at the groin.

War is a sucking chest wound that some brave medic has treated by placing the cellophane from a pack of cigarettes over it.

War is *Puff the Magic Dragon* and *Spooky* and Gatling guns spitting a red beam of death.

War is leeches and firing pins that jam and elephant grass that slices you up and a dust-off for some soldier whose eyes are hollow and his voice is hoarse as he screams for morphine and tries to stuff his own intestines back into the big hole in his stomach.

War is poncho liners and tree lines and vermin in the bunkers and political ambivalence everywhere and brogan boots with steel soles and heels and the big *phoom* of an artillery round. War is remote-control murder, a whisper into a radio, then a distant puff of smoke, a slight rumble and then silence.

Well, that was war, until now. Now it has escalated, been updated and become the new, improved manner of extermination. Cruise missiles. Thermal sighting devices. Atomic aircraft carriers. War is now nine seconds to get on your gas mask before the chemical and biological stuff gets you and your central nervous system goes insane.

You blink because you're now a relic. Once there were the baby boomers. Then the Vietnam Era children. Now what shall we call the new generation? Once there were doughboys and dog faces and grunts and now what?

The bodies will come home in bags again. Dress right dress. Parade rest. Folded flags—ready for burning, if you please. Dogtags and dental records and charts that account for everything, their dead, our dead. Hey Sarge, does a pregnant woman count one or two?

And the big scoreboard will determine the winner. Twilight's last gleaming will come. As will the rockets' red glare. Or are those the arc light strikes of the B-52s?

Victory without celebration? Celebration without victory? You sit and wonder. How far off? Bob Seger never knew what he was writing in those old songs.

But The Great Society keeps winning. Just not decisively enough. Not convincingly enough. Somebody always is waiting to put another quarter on the table in challenge. When will they ever learn? Or maybe, just maybe, why can't we . . . just say no?

Saddam Hussein has been called "Hitler revisited" by no less than the president of our country. And the thinking is that he leads Iraq, not Germany. At least, not yet anyway. But give a madman time and space and 15 million supporters can grow into 80 million before you know it and then there will be real hell to pay.

As if there is none today.

What did you do during the war, Daddy?

Seger said it even better in another song, *Wish I didn't know now what I didn't know then.*

Or was it Dylan when he declared, *I ain't gonna work on Maggie's farm no more.*

Or Creedence? *And I wonder, still I wonder, who'll stop the rain?*

War is human ordeal; there is no chivalry. None of them ever make sense. All of them must be supported, however.

True to American form, we shall overcome. The moral vacuum will shrink into remission eventually. Again. And we shall survive man's inhumanity to his fellow man. There will be an attrition and flowers will be strewn over another generation of military graves and orphans and widows and widowers will try to remember what a *just* war it was.

And the higher calendar that records the passage of time known as freedom will continue as if Tariq Aziz and James Baker were just a couple of strange names on the roll call of international diplomacy. And maybe Sly Stallone will make a new *Rambo* flick. And maybe they'll add a couple of new walls filled with names in Washington. And old soldiers never die, do they?

They just feel guilty all over again and these twinges come on that it really was all for nothing.

Viet War revisited, and that's terrifying
December 30, 1986

They have made another movie about Vietnam. It's called *Platoon*. But it's not for the veterans, who need no reminders. And it's not for the rest of the world, which probably still doesn't care to know what it was really like during the gnawing little police action that cost almost 60,000 Americans their lives and millions more at least a sliver of their minds.

Platoon is for the record.

It's violent and chaotic and intense, and a lot of people who go to see it wish they hadn't. In a word, it's accurate.

Art imitates life and death. Vietnam, it was just a job, not an adventure.

Ask someone who was over there to talk about it. He probably won't. You can share crusades; ordeals are a little more private.

Vietnam was the war with no healing agents. Previously, American fighting men could always use pride to cauterize their bloodless wounds. The Viet vet came home with the sucking chest wounds of guilt and shame and the mark of Cain upon him. He found out the whole horrible mess was like a dog chasing its own tail. He found out there would be no parades for him.

The movie doesn't go in for moralities. It paints no pictures of righteousness or heroism, no good guy vs. bad guy, John Wayne saves the day celluloid concoction of some Malibu Beach screenwriter's superfluous imagination. Only a snapshot of a kingdom of death with bulldozers shoving enemy corpses from the killing floor into a convenient common crater of a grave. A picture of fighting men pulled over the limit by the most basic of human responses.

Survival.

If there could be an authentic epilogue for this movie, picking up where the upsetting climax, a Cambodian fire fight that will render most people gasping for relief, left off, there would be a body-count patrol wheeling up in Jeeps to justify the carnage with an over-under number that made America the big winner.

Politicians and generals are big on numbers. So a pregnant woman counted as two killed. A patch of blood more than six inches in diameter was a kill. A confiscated rifle was a kill. Numbers. Only way to tell the winners from the losers. War—it all adds up.

But the conclusion is ours to make with this latest movie. It comes without accompanying sermon. Maybe Vietnam was something we still have trouble getting a grip on because maybe it's not far enough away yet. A comfortable gaze takes time, you know. But maybe the ones who go to this movie and see it as a sequel, a reasonable facsimile to the real thing, maybe the supporting cast, the veterans who had no doubles or stunt men to take their places during monsoon season, haven't come to grips with it yet.

There's just so much to remember, to forget.

Out in the tall elephant grass, where the smells of sulphur and diesel and burning excrement and powdered egg never really go away, there was no trust. They used to say the U.S. ruled the day, the Viet Cong the night. Whoever was there, in power at the moment, was Numba Wan, the theory of prostitution put to classic form and shape.

And as soon as you forgot that and assumed that nice old Mama-San who sold you French bread beaucoup times was on your side, suddenly that basket you picked up outside her hootch was rigged. A fresh and homemade bomb. And the next thing you know, you're lit up like a jellyfish and trying to stuff your entrails back inside your stomach, and they're on the horn trying to order a dust-off for you. Or maybe the medic is performing a stab tracheotomy to keep you alive long enough to make it back to The World.

The movie was visual and graphic and the details precise. The story line was not of war, but of people in a war. The men of Bravo Company could be any platoon or squadron, the faceless mannequins who are never young again. It could be the crew of a gunboat in the South China Sea. A flight crew from Camn Rahn Bay or Tan Son Nuht. The gang at the mess hall in Saigon. Being there, you learn to share.

The sights and sounds and smells of Vietnam were a sensory overload. The vets toted home heavy psychic baggage that is like a Claymore mine. It needs only a trip-wire to bring back to life the lessons that cannot be unlearned.

It can be the smell of cold rice in a pan or canned C-rats. Those green plastic garbage bags that look like the kind America used to stuff with the remains of fighting men. Nothing like the pop-pop-pop of fireworks at a Fourth of July party to send someone face down on the ground, hands covering his head. A Country Joe and the Fish song on the oldies station. Even the stenciled likeness of the Playboy Bunny is ruined for you. You curse Bob Hope every time he's on TV because his Christmas show was always a required formation.

And in a war zone, the only thing that should be required is survival.

You never forget. You never forget the muzzle flashes and the scorpions that would crawl into your boots if you forgot and left them uncovered. Or the twinks, the brand new arrivals in Saigon, so young and innocent that while waiting for their orders to get processed they pass the time at the service club upstairs, drinking scotch and coke. Soon never to be young again.

When you have the luxury of a bed and a barracks, survival included remembering that your mosquito netting had to hang straight before you went to bed. Get a foot caught in it, create a fold and a rat could get on the bed. And if it bit you, you got aluminum needles in your stomach for rabies. But you probably died anyway.

Ever see a rat skittering down a hall? A mousetrap stuck on its huge nose, its two-foot tail dragging and throwing dust left and right?

The sound of Spooky, the C-47 mounted with Gatling guns that can send out 6,000 rounds a minute bursting the rare quiet night with the red laser beam of gunfire. Two buddies sharing ice for their warm beer. The flight nurse giving off her bravest, practiced smile to the kid in the litter and making sure he had enough colostomy bags for the trip home. The ground crew sergeant at Travis Air Force Base in California, wearing black gloves and directing the transport plane to its landing dock. The passengers aboard come in three classes: Litter, ambulatory, caskets.

You can still see the Marines who wore necklaces with dried human ears. Or finger bones. The medics with heroin monkeys. The pilots who used to carve notches on their umbrellas for confirmed kills. You can still smell decomposed bodies hung on the concertina wire. But be careful if you try to remove it. Charley liked to booby-trap his dead, get one final use out of them. The sandbags filled with marijuana. Rifles stuck in warm sand, bayonet first, firing pins removed. The grunts used to stock up on firing pins because M-16s jammed easily in the jungle.

The villagers used to stare at you, old women holding babies with eyes already dull.

You wonder if the jungle rot ever went away. If the dengue fever, which is the illegitimate second cousin of malaria, ever returned. If the thump of mortar fire or the whistle of the 155-meter rocket will ever become deaf in your memory. Red streaking tracers, urgent voices on crackling radios and the numbing drone of helicopters. The M-16 makes a noise that sounds like balloons being shot out at a carnival. You never forget how to clear a gas mask.

They told you to make buddies but don't get too close. And it worked. You couldn't live without each other 17 years ago but back home, you were 30 miles apart and have seen each other maybe three times since. Nothing in common anymore.

You even learn to get yourself to go to Jane Fonda movies and admire Muhammad Ali. You stop short of calling the Iranian hostages heroes and Melvin Laird is another story altogether. But you let loose of some things.

You were always a few clicks from insanity.

They gave you a lot of training beforehand and even a week in the country to get used to the water, which was terrible, and the climate, which was unbearable. But they never gave you any preparation for coming home. They never let you turn back into a civilized human being again. You had to cope with Vietnam, then you had to cope with coming home.

But you made it. Maybe you were a black man, and you remember that one-ninth of America's population was black but one-sixth of Vietnam's American forces were black. And maybe you felt good about that, or maybe you remember that racism was a big problem everywhere but in the bush. And in 1968, when Dr. Martin Luther King was assassinated, hurt dissolved into hatred and little civil wars behind the lines spread like a platoon of fire ants.

And maybe you feel bad about that, just as you feel bad that the occasional headline — *Vet kills self, Ex-Vietnam soldier robs*

15

bank — brings out the blanket stereotype. They were all maniacs, killers, losers.

So you try to drown the ghosts with beer. And you drive too fast and play music too loud and seldom register to vote. And change jobs often.

You used to have bad dreams and wake up clammy and screaming about the tree line. And your wife got scared and wouldn't go to sleep until after you did. You now sleep in bursts of three hours, never soundly. You never take walks across fields. And people talk behind your back that you never seem happy.

There is a scene at the beginning of *Platoon* that shows a new arrival looking at some survivors who are going home. One of them, his eyes hollow from the horror, the ordeal, stares. The Vietnam veteran does a lot of that. Maybe he shakes his head. He is disgusted. But not at you.

He has stuffed his Bronze Star into the bottom of a drawer. Or mailed it back. Or left it at The Wall in Washington. Some wear their tokens of valor, their chests a rainbow of achievement. Folded flags in funereal triangles sit on mantles and shelves. Veterans hospitals are busier than ever.

And so is the world. Beirut, El Salvador, Nicaragua, Iraq, Iran. The range fires are everywhere. They sound incoming, and there may not be a more terrifying word. It's too close. It's like heat lightning. You get beaucoup sensations just reading the paper. Apocalypse Next, if you please.

Now they have another movie out on Vietnam. It opened in New York last week, and a lot of people got up and left in the first 15 minutes, enraged by the shocking scenario.

Where were they in 1967?

People see this movie and squirm uncomfortably for two hours. They cringe. Some cry. Some of them go home and have bad dreams.

And Vietnam veterans stare. After all, it is their turn.

"So take a good look at my face.
You'll see my smile looks out of place.
Look a little bit closer, it's easy to trace
the tracks of my tears."

16

Family rides freedom's wave into a future
Nov. 23, 1989

Once they were called pilgrims, people seeking various freedoms, a better life. They found it in a place called America.

The old man was a pilgrim of sorts, too. Only he came to America more than 300 years later and from a different direction. His Mayflower was a homemade boat, 11 feet long. His shipmates were a wife and a 3-month-old son.

They made it.

He was a teacher, a professor at the big university in Havana, Cuba. He loved to read and it bothers him still that he had to leave behind all his books except one. The Bible.

But he sensed what was happening in Cuba. He could feel the swirling change. Batista's regime was not so great. And this young revolutionary from the hills, the one called Castro, scared him. Power is an aphrodisiac and it causes strange things to happen to men whose weakness is their desperate obsession to be strong. He didn't want his new son to become a victim of someone else's greed.

So he pushed the small boat through the white soup of the shore break. It was an hour before sunrise one day in 1959. The motor had come off a lawn mower. He had rigged it, slightly increased its horsepower, made it almost waterproof. It only stalled 11 times from Cuba to Key West. The 90-mile journey took four days. It may not seem the dramatic journey of the Mayflower which braved across a quarter of the planet to escape Europe's religious and political persecution. But when a mother's breast milk has dried up and the sun is blazing and a frightened baby is screaming and the sea has become angry and rolling, the moments seem like hours. The land on the horizon sometimes appears to move backward. The teacher questioned his bold decision.

The boat stuck finally into the soft sand of Florida. The exhausted family spent the first night in an abandoned truck. They had almost $6,000 in savings. But nobody would accept their Cuban money. He used his lucky American silver dollar and their first meal was a hamburger cut in two and a quart of milk, split three ways. And they still had 17 cents.

17

The next morning the father found out something about freedom. He could feel it but could not express it. He spoke no English.

The next day he met another Cuban, who invited them to stay at his small home, "for a day or so."

That night they feasted and counted their blessings, which suddenly reappeared like majestic palm trees. The paella dish from their homeland was filled with sweet clams and plump shrimps and rich lagostinos. The pork was splendid. The rice and black beans and belichee roast and fried plantains and wonderful yucca fruit may not sound like the traditional Thanksgiving meal. But you chew on freedom in whatever form it takes. Its taste is always delicious.

The original pilgrims almost perished during their first winter. They survived by adapting to their strange new world and making friends with the locals, the native Americans. The conventional wisdom of this was not lost on the man and his family. The biggest blessings are family and friends.

They traveled north, riding on the back of a flatbed truck to a city called Miami. He would teach again, he thought. He had been a good teacher, a caring and concerned teacher and he enjoyed the launching of young minds, who took flight under his guidance. Yes, he would find work at a university once again. And teach.

But the only job he could find was cleaning toilets. His teaching credentials were useless, he was told. And he spoke no English.

And the baby was crying again.

A proud man cleaned toilets for a living. He also worked a night job, at a restaurant, busing tables. In between, two nights a week, he took classes. English classes.

"Somebody must be the best at cleaning the toilets," he would say often, his pride causing the words to sound as if they were spit out of his mouth. "I will be that man."

His son was eight when it was mutually decided his mother had to go to work as well. If they wanted a better life, they had to earn it. They told the boy it will be up to you, Leo, to help us by staying out of trouble and working hard in your own way.

The boy grew up, often alone as each step in puberty's treacherous odyssey was taken. Never neglected, always loved, but often alone.

He made straight A's in school. English was his favorite subject. He found the new life easier to fit into than his parents. But there came taunts and teases. Names that stung like the tentacles of the jellyfish. Racial slurs. But the ones that hurt most were slung not at him directly.

Leo, the janitor's son, the man who cleaned the toilets. He knew of his father's education, of his experience. He was an educator, a brilliant man.

But he cleaned toilets now and that was all everyone else saw.

Leo escaped into sports, especially baseball. He tried to transfer his anguish into line drives and diving catches. In Little League, he used to show up two hours before the game. That was OK; he was used to being alone. But he could see the field, see the old man drag the chain-link fence across the orange dirt, watch him pour the white stripes of the baselines and square out the batter's box. And he could see each play of the game before they happened.

But one day in his ninth year, he saw something at the baseball field he'd never seen. It was the old blue station wagon. His Daddy's car.

His father had never been able to come to a game before. He always had to work. Leo first noticed the car parked along the left-field line in the third inning.

In the fourth inning he came to bat.

On the first pitch, the bat flashed and the ball flew over the low wall in left-center. He'd never hit a home run before, so he really didn't know how to act as he ran around the bases.

But as he rounded first base, he heard the horn. Honking over and over, a father's joy exploding. He touched second and waved and acknowledged the ovation and wore the grin all the rest of the day.

And never hit another home run in his life.

What he did do was graduate from high school, graduate from college, get a master's degree in English and become an editor at a newspaper in South Florida.

Last year, his father lurched as the massive stroke erupted. Then seven months later, after the terrible headaches became unbearable, X-rays revealed a tumor the size of a child's fist inside his head.

The man somehow survived both ravaging assaults. He lives in a rehabilitation home, undergoes daily therapy and is visited nightly by his wife and 33-year-old son.

For a long time, he could not talk, was paralyzed on one side of his body. For a long time his face was frozen and twisted and pushed into a gaunt, helpless position. His shaved head revealed a couple of hideous scars. But this is the residue of survival. This is the good news.

And not so long ago, the eyes got shiny again. And the speech was soft and slurred. And the grip of the hands pitifully weak. But this is the evidence of progress, of recovery. And this is the better news.

And just the other day, Leo Jr., the son of the son of a brave pilgrim, made 24 saves in a soccer game. After the game, the coach of the boy's team saw the two, father and son, arm in arm, walking so close together they cast but one shadow, and he shouted, "Hey, Leo's father!"

And they both turned to hear the coach say, "You have a great kid."

That night at the rehabilitation center, the story was retold. Tears rolled into each corner of a great smile, jointly shared by two grown men. Hands squeezed and there was real strength all around. The old man nodded his head for almost a minute as he regained composure.

"Leo, do you remember the day you hit the home run?"

"Yes Daddy, you were there. It was the only one I ever hit."

"It was the only game I ever could see you play. But Leo, that night, at the restaurant," he said, and his head so noble inched upward, tilted majestically, "that night, I cleaned 102 tables."

Records were made to be broken. The great harvest that yields bountiful crops is not always measured in food. Sometimes it is the harvest of children, the world's greatest sustenance. It is the simple handoff from father to son to the future and the wonderful run to daylight. Sometimes the Thanksgiving message rolls forward and backward and the blessings pile up as high as a stack of dirty dishes. Or a child's self-esteem.

20

You see, a ship, no matter what size, can make it through the roughest seas, if the captain has a firm hand on the wheel and basic understanding of where all the rocks are. It is a Thanksgiving story of a different kind, the little tale of modern pilgrims and soccer stars, of children better equipped, better qualified and pointed in the right direction. All because a father learned all the important lessons. But of course, Grandpa always was a good teacher.

Family, friends — the greatest blessings. The promise of tomorrow, opportunity — the finest gift. Thanksgiving's boxscore is easy to keep. Just remember, freedom always bats leadoff.

Visitors play show-and-tell
2 kindergarten teachers get lesson in history
Nov. 13, 1989

BERLIN — The train from Leipzig had left at 11 the night before. Ursula Rothe and her friend Helga Rosin were on it, heading to East Berlin.

Arriving in the city Sunday, the two waited in line starting at 5 a.m. at the newly bulldozed checkpoint gate of the Berlin Wall in Potsdamer Platz.

"We will get over there and fall asleep," Ursula said, only partly in jest. The two women from East Germany, who have taught at the same kindergarten for 26 years, then laughed.

At 7:31 a.m., long streaks of the rising sun pierced the fog and at last daylight came. At 8 a.m. sharp, the line started moving.

Even back where Ursula and Helga waited, you could hear the applause.

"What is that for?" Ursula asked.

The man in front of her turned and said, "For us. We are the new heroes."

The two women shook their heads in wonder. Heroes?

"We are only going there to shop," Helga said. "We will be back on the train to Leipzig this afternoon. I do not think we are heroes."

But when the two women finally made it to the Wall, when they saw the crowd lining Bellevuestr Street, when they heard the cheers, they knew just how to act.

They smiled and waved.

Arm in arm they walked into West Berlin. Someone handed each of them a bouquet of flowers — a gift for all East Germans this weekend, courtesy of a flower company in Holland.

Police were wearing flowers in the lapels of their uniforms. Someone else handed the women packs of American chewing gum. They were serenaded by rousing songs, marching songs, soccer songs, drinking songs. A youth in a leather jacket ran up and asked if they wanted a sip from his champagne bottle. They said no.

"Do you believe this, Ursula?" Helga said, waving and smiling. "Do you believe this is happening?"

Her friend did not answer. She swallowed hard instead. The emotion, the feelings — it was suddenly too much.

The big building on Ursula's left looked familiar. The Esplanade Hotel once was the finest in all Germany. Kings and presidents stayed there. Adolf Hitler said it was his favorite. Ursula Rothe remembers when U.S. warplanes dropped their bombs and most of the Esplanade was destroyed. Just the sight of the deserted building gone to ruin made her swoon.

At that point, Berlin police started waving their arms and asked the steady procession to stop. We have a surprise, they said.

The mayor of West Berlin was there to greet them.

So was the president of West Germany.

Mayor Walter Momper smiled as one of the visitors from the East, a woman with a tiny toddler in a fancy dress with lots of petticoats, handed him her bouquet and shouted "Danke, danke, danke."

Said Momper, "Do not thank me. It was you who made this possible. With your demonstrations. With your courage. You are the heroes of the day."

Everyone then cheered and you could not tell East from West. When West German President Richard von Weizsacker started to speak, the cheers got louder. He talked, and it's likely most did not

22

hear what he said, and it did not matter anyway. Words were needless on Sunday. That latest hole in the Wall said it all.

Afterward, von Weizsacker, Momper and their security promptly climbed into a waiting Mercedes-Benz and inched through the human gridlock that had formed and stretched backward from the Wall for almost a mile.

The parade resumed. Ursula and Helga asked a stranger where the Philharmonie concert hall was. A special show was scheduled in honor of all East Germans. The Berlin Symphony Orchestra would play Beethoven and Mozart. Daniel Barenboim, one of the superstars of classical music, would conduct.

Helga remembers seeing the Berlin Symphony in 1947.

"This is unbelievable," she said.

For the younger music fans, another free concert was planned downtown, a subway or a bus ride away. English rock star Joe Cocker had volunteered. An estimated 50,000 were there when *You Are So Beautiful* brought everyone to their feet.

A few blocks away in front of the Brandenburg Gate, candles were being lit by East Germans. Down the street known as Strasse des 17 June — the day celebrated as Independence Day each year — the majestic Victory Column stood. At the base of a statue of a woman was a thick layer of candle wax. A cardboard sign renaming the street Strasse des 9 November was cradled upon her stone arms — to commemorate the day the Wall was breached.

Uwe Kreitsch and his wife Mili were back for another visit Sunday. They had spent Friday and Saturday with an aunt they had not seen for 11 years.

"We are pessimists," said the 41-year-old construction engineer. "That is why we will come over here every chance we can until the Wall gets closed back up."

Asked why, if they felt so sure that freedom would eventually be taken back from them, they don't stay on the Western side of the city, Mili Kreitsch said, "We have children. They do not live with us. We will talk to them. If they want to leave, we will leave. But our oldest son is in the army. We do not know what his requirements are."

The guards atop the Berlin Wall, dressed in drab green uniforms and with almost-smirking faces, stare but do not react to the crowds. Beneath them people hammer and chisel at the graffiti-ridden structure.

Three U.S. soldiers have a duffel bag that is filling up. In honor of the occasion, they have three bottles of wine and a portable tape player that is belching a Jim Morrison song.

When it gets to the part that screeches, "Break on through to the other side," the crowd around them sings along.

On a chain-link fence are wooden crosses with names and dates on them. These are reminders of the victims. These are the dead: Marienetta Tirkowski, 22 Nov. 1980. She was 18 when she was shot to death.

There also are fresh flowers beneath every cross. At one, in the links of the fence, a woman ties a plaid handkerchief.

"They are filled with my tears," says Natalie Densel. "My brother wanted only to come home for Christmas."

The latest — and hopefully last — cross belongs to Winfried Freudenberg. He died in March of this year when his homemade hot-air balloon went out of control and he crashed into a cluster of oak trees on the West side. His wife, who was supposed to ride with him to freedom, was arrested just before their takeoff. Friends said Sunday she is still in jail.

At the bottom of the cross is a beer bottle with pale flowers stuck in it.

"GDR flowers," says a man holding his young son on his shoulders.

"How do you know, Papa?"

"They have no color," he said. "Everything in the East is gray."

It was dark when Ursula Rothe and Helga Rosin headed back home. When they got to the gate, they turned back together for one last look at West Berlin. They will return again soon. The day was so long. They were drained. They said they felt little emotion.

"There is none left," Helga said.

Then they noticed the Wall. In contrast to the brightly colored declarations of freedom on the Western side, the Eastern side of the Wall is virgin white, with one exception.

"DIE MAUER IST WEG" — "The wall is down."

"Was that there when we came through?" Ursula asked. "I was so excited I didn't notice. Do you see that there this morning?"

24

Helga shrugged. "Which morning, Ursula?" she said. "I cannot tell when that was."

She held her flowers to her nose. They still smelled sweet. They probably always will. She says she will take them to school. Show-and-tell will be very exciting.

Has rain stopped for East Germans? Protest singer finds his song of freedom in a West Berlin pub
Nov. 17, 1989

WEST BERLIN — In the rollicking Irish Pub, a watering hole featuring live rock music nightly, the thick German accent of the lead singer makes the old John Fogerty tune sound harsher. Its message becomes more obvious and full of more, um, Creedence than usual:

Who'll stop the rain?

It is a subtle plea for peace, for the end of war, for the end of mankind's constant storms of discontent, says the American to the little man with tattooed arms and wrinkled clothes.

During the Vietnam War, American soldiers considered the song an anthem or sorts, reading vivid meaning into it.

It is a protest song, adds the American. Uwe Neumann grunts and nods. He knows about protest songs. He spent 33 months in Zeithein, an East German prison, for writing and singing one.

"It was about life in the East and how it seemed like there was not as much pleasure. The government did not like my song. I was handcuffed, my guitar was taken away. I was 18 years old."

Now, 22, Neumann celebrates in West Berlin, late in the night, early in the morning. The beer tastes better than he can ever remember, he says. The freedom tastes even better.

And the music — "I love the songs with a message the best."

Neumann has been in West Berlin since late Tuesday. He sleeps on the streets, wherever he can be warm and safe. But, he adds, "I have not been sleeping too much. Tonight, for instance, I will stay up until my money is gone. At 8:30 tomorrow night, I must be at work, at my job. Until then, I drink as much beer and listen to as much music as I can."

He looks at the band on the tiny stage, which is getting ready to throw some Little Richard, Rolling Stones—"Oondah mein Thumb"—and an oldie-goldie by Tom Jones into a curious medley that is wild and crazy and disconnected.

He blinks. And remembers his ordeal that began when someone wrote down his name as he performed on a street corner in Rummelsburg one afternoon in 1985.

In a prison overcrowded with thieves, rapists, drug addicts and at least one folk singer, Neumann struggled to adjust to life in jail. There were homosexual advances and resulting fights when he refused. He shows a scar over his right eye. A jagged piece of glass caused it.

"Actually the (homosexual) holding it caused it," he says.

Twice he tried suicide. "I drank rat poison once but not enough. I only got very sick. The other time, I had a knife but I lost my courage."

He also tried to escape. He ran away from a work detail but stopped quickly when he heard the bullhorn screech punctuated by the warning shot.

"The sound of the rifle bolts cocking is one I will remember. Also the barking of the dogs. I would be dead if I did not stop."

Shortly after that incident in 1987 he got the tattoo of a bull's-eye put on the back of his neck, between his shoulders.

"Maybe a joke, or maybe a reminder," Neumann says, reaching for his beer glass.

When you are so bored you get your body tattooed just for the fun of it, when you are so stifled artistically you start composing music by hitting the pipes of the toilets with a plastic fork in the secrecy of late-night darkness, Uwe Neumann says it is easy to understand why "I almost went insane."

And yet, when the next afternoon comes, he will go back to East Berlin.

"I hear about the jobs that are available but I do not think there is one for me. I am a convicted felon. I think if there are two people

26

who want the same job, the one who has not been to prison will get it."

He does have a job back on the other side of the Berlin Wall. He is a stone mason.

The U-Bahn train that will take him from East Berlin to Dresden is a long, uncomfortable ride, maybe 180 kilometers. But that is still in the future. That is tomorrow. Tonight is still to be enjoyed.

Another tear escapes and traces slowly down his hard face. He looks at his beer, at his cigarette. Then at his two new American friends, Erick, the Frenchman who plays bass guitar, Claudia, the West Berlin woman who introduced herself with a smile that transcends all barriers and borders and walls. All around the table, a new world. Behind him, loud music.

"I think I will get very drunk tonight," he says, wiping his eyes again.

He is free and it is his choice to return to East Germany. He laughs when he is asked if he considers himself a political criminal.

"I am a stone-cutter. I used to be a song singer when I was a child. Political criminal? Political prisoner? That was somebody else's interpretation."

There is remorse, a little guilt and a pervading sense that a wild stallion is tamer but wiser. Older now by several lifetimes he figures, Uwe Neumann has not surrendered his love of music. Nor his need for expression. He simply picks better audiences.

He hasn't written many songs since getting out of prison. He has been too busy trying to put his life back together.

And what of the song that caused such a furor once upon a time in a young man's life? Can he even remember any of the words?

"I sang it on the train coming here. I sang it loud and many times."

The rain has stopped for Uwe Neumann. Who stopped it is anybody's guess. And a song is like a life: It is whatever you interpret it to be. At least that's the way it works in a free world.

Another round for everyone is on the way. The band is taking a break but they'll be back and there will be some more music. Nobody is under anyone's thumb anymore. Except some Siamese cat of a girl. And you can find her next to the door, by the jar where Eleanor Rigby keeps her face, interpretatively speaking, of course.

27

GERMANY'S TWO SOULS
Nov. 19, 1989

Two souls, alas, reside within my breast
And each withdraws from and repels its brother.
—Johann Wolfgang von Goethe

WEST BERLIN—The Germans have a word for it—
Zerrissenheit. It means, said Edgar Baer, "a torn condition. It has
to do with the mind; it is a dilemma, because you do not know what
is right."

Baer is a policeman who every Friday patrols the sidewalk in
front of the West Berlin Jewish Community Center. He sees no
special significance in his job, even though he is aware of world
history and "every German has to search his conscience when you
talk about the Jewish people."

No, there is nothing special about his job, other than the semiau-
tomatic assault rifle he carries for his shift.

The past weeks have brought dizzying change to his homeland.
Baer still has trouble putting it all in perspective.

"Go inside the building," Baer said. "Ask them what they think
of all the things that are going on. They feel like I do. It is early. It
sounds good but it is too early to know. They say there is no fear
anymore for them. But every week on Wednesday, they call to
remind us to have the guard ready for Friday. Maybe that is how
they get rid of their fear. Ask them if ever they can relax, especially
now when there is talk of the reunification of Germany."

Baer does not stop walking. It is 36 steps one way, 36 back the
other way. He will walk this route for five hours, then get replaced.
He said he studies the history of his country as a hobby. He thinks
about it on his job. Especially on Fridays when he stands sentry
outside the Jewish center.

"I do not know if progress is so good always," Baer said.

A mile away, the great Wall, once divisive and foreboding, is
now a relic and a theme park at the same time. The celebration over
the opening of travel restrictions in East Germany is more than a
week old. The scenes are still poignant ones, as crowds gather to
watch and cheer visitors from the other side of the 10-foot barrier

28

that has divided Germany for 38 years. They gather to enjoy the loud moments and grand examples of basic freedom.

You can buy T-shirts, postcards, even Berlin Wall yo-yos. The tourists have bought up most of the hammers and chisels in stock, hoping to chip away a souvenir piece of the rock.

Eventually there will come a sobering realization. The pretty pictures of reunion force a familiar collage. Will Germany become one again?

And what is to come after that? The world has seen two World Wars spawned from One Germany. Can anyone really relax? Does anyone dare to be thrice burned?

Truly Zerrissenheit.

The Doric columns of the Brandenburg Gate, the architectural calling-card for both Berlins but located on the eastern side of the wall, glisten amid floodlights and the big arc poles of television mobile units. Each night the crowd gets larger, more rowdy, more demanding. Each night the plea to open the wall at the Brandenburg Gate comes louder and quicker. It is important, said the old woman who comes each night and yells to the stoic guards, for West Germans to have the Gate back.

"Then we can become Germany once again."

Germany once again? What is that? The glorious Rhineland, so full of cultural and industrial promise? Or the Einsatzgrupper task force of Adolf Hitler, who exterminated millions of innocent human beings? Forgive them their trespasses into doubt and suspicion but a large part of the world is not so sure it wants to see this country climb back onto its feet entirely.

Not all the skeptics are the persecuted.

No less than Margaret Thatcher, the prime minister of England, has trouble putting the big picture into focus. While she declared sincerely that the opening of the Berlin Wall was "a great day for liberty," she also whispered a touch of alarm.

If Germany is to be reunited, some have called for the removal, or at least reduction, of U.S. military forces from the country. The prime minister wiggles a wary finger of caution.

"Had America stayed in Europe after the first world war," Thatcher said recently, "I do not believe we would have had a second world war. Let us learn that lesson."

29

England and the rest of Great Britain know how hard Germany can hit. As does France, of course. Francois Mitterrand, the president of France, has not made any strong statements of concern regarding any possible re-unification of Germany. He also has not openly applauded the possibility.

President Bush has cautioned that all this talk, pro or con, is premature, adding, "It takes a prudent evolution" for such a thing to happen. Bush also said he likes the idea, though. Any smoldering fears are not necessarily valid ones.

"You can't turn back the clock," said the president last month, talking about the recent events in Germany.

The future is always unblemished, carefully packed in idealism. Pessimists have only the ammunition of the past.

But half the 60 million people from West Germany and the 16 million living in East Germany were not born until after 1948. Are they not to be trusted because of their forefathers?

Heinz Galinski makes his hand into fists as he thinks about the question. Galinski fidgets and his eyes, that seem to never blink, stare at the floor. His shirt sleeve catches on his wristwatch and he tugs it loose. But not before you spot the faint tattoo on his forearm. Blue numbers.

Galinski is a survivor of Auschwitz, the death camp and crematorium in Poland responsible for the death of millions of Jews in World War II. He also is the head of the Jewish Community Center and is its voice for West Berlin.

"Before the Wall was opened, over in East Germany, a Jewish cemetery was desecrated. Vandals," Galinski said with obvious bitterness. "We are against reunification because that means going back to 1937. Of course, we are glad people have gained their freedom in the East. By their own power. Without blood spilling."

He said he doesn't think Nazism could ever happen again: "The old system was so terrible it attracted so much attention."

"Every Jew has the right to live in Germany," he said. "But the memory should be kept alive. For safety. The responsibility belongs to the future generation. It is not guilty. But its members have the responsibility of that guilt. Old hatred usually comes out in new forms.

"When they desecrated the cemetery in East Berlin though, they

30

resorted to old, familiar forms. This was what happened in 1933. In 1938 they burned the synagogues. In 1941 the murders began. I do not think there can be another Hitler. But we must keep the memory alive to prevent it. And all Germans must accept that responsibility."

The problem is that lately, most Germans have been doing little more than celebrating. Communism all over Europe appears to be in some stage of retreat. If the Berlin Wall has not yet been completely dismantled, the power structure that existed before Mikhail Gorbachev took office in the Soviet Union certainly has.

Poland is holding free elections. Bulgaria's hard-line Communist Party leader, Todor Zhivkov, resigned after 35 years in power.

Erich Honecker, East Germany's leader when the Wall first went up, has been forced out of office. East Berlin's parliament even held its first secret election ever last week.

For two years, Gustav Husack, who took control after the "Prague Spring" liberalization movement failed in Czechoslovakia 21 years ago, has been gone, replaced by Milos Jake. Hungary is taking bows because way back in September, it threw open its boundaries to Austria. A domino effect started — all the way to the Berlin Wall — and hasn't stopped.

Now the trickle has become a flood. All along the Iron Curtain, the wobbling steps of fledgling freedom are being witnessed. In West Berlin, where welcome arms of friendship are waiting, as well as even-more-welcome Welcome Money, the lines at the bank stretch at times for half a mile. The Borse (stock market) has been going wild.

At a West Berlin train station sometime Thursday night, someone painted a curious graffito on one of the brick walls: "Nie Wieder." Never again.

It is the subtle fear of the unknown. You can get 20 GDR marks for a single Deutsch mark on the black market back East. Just don't let the secret police, the Stasi, catch you. The East German taxi driver smiles when you ask about such stuff. Then he ignores you.

Look through the wedges and cracks the ambitious hammer-wielders have created and you'll probably find an East German

31

soldier staring back. Ask them questions about how they see all this winding up and you get the same blank stare.

They are allowed to have opinions — it said so in all the newspapers — but that does not mean they will share them. Even though they are welcome to flee to the West, it does not mean they will go any farther than the bustling Kurfurstendamm shopping district to blow their riches before heading back home to the East, where it costs the average worker 850 hours of labor to buy an average-size television set.

In the West, the disenchantment already is manifesting. Teenagers said there are no jobs. How will they find work when older, more skilled workers from the East are glutting the market?

"It was bad enough when the Turks came," said Bernhard Henseldorff. "All this money should be going to West Germans."

Of course, on the third floor of the West Berlin City Hall is Die Republikaner, a right-wing group that would like to build a wall completely around all of Germany, including parts of Poland surrendered in two wars.

Franz Schonhuber, a former officer in the Waffen-SS, leads the group, which has been accused of having neo-Nazi philosophies. He denies such charges but adds the recent developments in the world "are a sign that people want to return Germany to how it once was."

Perhaps not all the fear is unknown. Or unsubstantiated.

Perhaps the two Germanys will raze the Wall, chop it into small pieces and sell it at some giant souvenir stand; thereby rescuing East Germany from its economic problems. There are all kinds of things possible.

Last week at the tiny synagogue in East Berlin, the flag of Israel was hoisted atop a pole for the first time since 1948. The 203 Jews present wept openly.

On the Tuesday and Wednesday before the Wall swung open, there were mass resignations within the East German Politburo. Egon Krenz said people were foolish to think what happened in China, when pro-democracy demonstrations broke out, would also take place in East Germany. Of course, it was the same Krenz who publicly praised the quick show of military strength in Tiananmen Square.

The Glasnost Effect appears, for now, to be one of leniency. Is there another shiny black boot still to drop? Is Germany caught innocently in the middle of a superpower game of chicken? And what's so bad about a little national assertion once in a while?

The questions pile up like requests for visitation visas. Germany has been unified only for 75 years of its existence, from the ascendancy of the Bismarck empire in 1870 to Hitler's descent in 1945. History says to be careful. So do Galinski and Schonhuber in their own special ways.

Baer gets off duty in a little while. Maybe he'll head down to the wall and meet some new people. Or maybe he'll read his history books some more.

He's just not sure what to do.

When I see the flag, I see my father
June 23, 1989

I was stressed. If it'd been the '60s, I'd be either uptight or freaked out, depending upon the condition of my karma. But these days, you only get stressed.

Pete Rose's dilemma had worn me slick. The revelations that Ben Johnson wasn't the only Olympian who relied on a pharmacist to win medals staggered me. The stench of the Oklahoma program getting laid bare for public ridicule made me gag. Why, the infractions are as high as an elephant's eye. And of course, the usual drug rehab roll call had me grasping for equilibrium.

The daily sports section is overrun with toxic waste anymore.

So I headed for the back yard, figuring I needed to unwind a little.

I figured I'd burn a couple of American flags.

You know, to relax. It'd be a protest. My Big Brothers in Washington have decided it's OK to torch Old Glory because she's nothing but a symbol. Just don't incite riots.

33

A peaceful flag-burning is like a back yard barbecue. It relieves stress.

But just as I was reaching in the closet for the folded flag, I blinked. An image.

Now I'd gone through the whole beads and bell bottoms thing and once even flashed the peace symbol to a policeman in Daytona Beach, Fla. But I never experimented with psychedelic jellybeans that melted in your mind not in your mouth. Yet I saw something.

I saw Rick Monday, clear as day. I saw Rick Monday galloping in the pastures of yesterday's outfield, running up to a couple of firebugs who were about to set a flag ablaze in the middle of a baseball game. And I stepped back. And I looked back at the flag. And I saw someone else.

This time I saw Ted Williams. Not playing baseball but flying jet planes in Korea.

Then I saw Rocky Bleier. First I saw the Pittsburgh Steeler jumping as high as he could for a pass. It was the Super Bowl and there were Dallas Cowboys all around him. But somehow he reached the pass, tipped it with one hand then cradled it and landed in the end zone, a touchdown in his arms. Then as soon as he landed, I saw Rocky Bleier again. He was lying on a stretcher and he was wearing a different kind of helmet. And he was looking down at the remains of his foot. And he was in a jungle.

My dog was at my side now, sniffing and wagging her tail. I had the flag in my hands and I saw one more image. A man in a uniform. Rows of ribbons, captain's bars and a smile.

My father.

The flag in my hands was his flag. It once was draped over his coffin almost 20 year ago. Then it was carefully folded by other soldiers wearing white gloves and handed to me in a ceremony.

And a man with stars on his shoulders handed me the flag that day and said on behalf of a grateful country, my father's efforts were deeply appreciated and should never be forgotten. Then he handed me that flag.

And that flag is my father. And it's Rocky Bleier and it's Ted Williams and it's Rick Monday.

The problem with the sports section today is that there are only great athletes living in it.

F. Scott Fitzgerald once said, "Show me a hero and I'll write you a tragedy." Alas, the great writer's long gone and while there is a frightening shortage of heroes, the tragedies keep popping up faster than Stephen King novels. Youth has been forced to search the make-believe world for its heroes. G.I. Joe and Batman and others stand sentry. Surely there must be some from the athletic world. But I wouldn't bet on it.

Forgive me my trespasses if I have misrepresented myself today as someone who douses patriotism all over himself each morning. As a survivor of the '60s and all the other wonder years that caused Father-Son talks to escalate into full-scale arguments over the rights and wrongs of the American Way, I know my hawk's wings never grew and the peace dove flew from my shoulder long ago. I just have a thing about the flag. I accepted Abbie Hoffman fashioning a flag into a pair of britches with the same grain of indifference that condoned Roy Rogers and his American-flag cowboy shorts at the movie matinees. But physically destroying an intact flag simply sends too many images on a collision course with my conscience. Too many faces. Too many heroes.

So I did not burn Old Glory in protest. Because she's just a symbol, you know.

3.

COLUMNS II

Sunshine State Serenade: Florida's sights, sounds will be missed
May 15, 1983
St. Petersburg Times

It is almost time to go, and the father and his boy walk on the pier one last time. The sun heads for its hammock. The breeze whips across their faces as they walk up the wooden ramp.

Time for a cool one.

"Draft beer and a glass of orange juice," says the man, reaching into his cutoffs for a water-logged $5 bill.

The boy, already yawning from a long day at the beach, asks, "Where does the sun go when it gets dark?"

"To Colorado."

Both laugh and sip their drinks and crinkle their noses as the taste clashes with the salty aftertaste in their mouths.

They sit on a wooden bench to watch the sun sneak away, and then they walk to the end of the pier to see if any big fish have been caught. They look as old men pull up stringers of trophies and dinner. They listen as liars tell of near-misses.

Then they walk back down the pier and let their callused feet cool on the soft, damp sand. The first hint of evening salt spray appears. There can be no better time of day or place to be than in the sand at the beach at the end of the day in Florida. The soft light massages. Bodies, worn from exercise and baked by sun, relax. The gentle glow permeates all the way to the brain, loosens the barnacles, frees the soul.

At the end of the pier, off to the left, is a vacant lot. Nothing but palmetto bushes, scrub brush, Spanish bayonet and plenty of Florida sand spurs. All around the lot, the land has been bought by people from New Jersey who wear gold chains around their necks. They plan someday to convert the entire area into a maze of steel monoliths, complete with a luxury hotel and gift shops and sushi bars that cling like sucker fish. And a smothering concrete parking lot all the way back to the highway.

Except for that patch of vacant land. It is as pesky as a no-see-um. The owner doesn't want to sell. Not for three times its value. Every time he is asked, the wrinkles and character lines of a thousand sunburns twist into a giant smile and the answer is always, "No thanks, mister."

Florida.

It's having a house with a porch. And the porch has a tin roof. The great Australian pines shed needles on the roof and the sun bleaches them rusty orange. And the little boy of three decades ago calls them Florida snow.

It's the smell of a mangrove flat at low tide.

It's the stink of the river in late summer. Foul-smelling, no doubt, but it's nature's aroma. And as long as it isn't man-made, you can deal with it.

It's pondering the needle fish, one of the beautiful creations in the water. It's also turning your head the first time you see the underside of a female horseshoe crab, surely the ugliest of God's work.

It's the music made at a marina, as the boats in dock hold a symphony, the halyards slamming in the breeze against the masts. With sea gulls shrieking back-up melodies.

It's getting up early and waiting for the fog to burn off and watching the sand pipers skitter on the shoreline. They chase the tide as it creeps backward, then retreat as the next wave crashes to shore.

Can there be any better sense of accomplishment than making your own gig, then going out and spearing a mullet on only your 20th or 30th try?

"Daddy, what's going on? You're just sitting there," says the boy, sitting on the hood of the car.

The man smiles. He has been somewhere else. He looks around. A couple holds hands and walks on the beach. They look old. But happy. Coming the other way is a man with leathery skin and a sun-bleached pony tail. He also looks old. But happy.

"See that man over there? He's a clammer. See, look at his feet. See how scarred they are. People who work with their hands you can tell it. People who dig clams and oysters for a living you can tell it, too."

The harvest of sea shells never ends. The supply builds over-night. In the morning the seekers and searchers and shellers return. Some carry plastic buckets and shovels. Others push metal detectors. A few pick up the artifacts of the deep and try to skim them over the waves.

The true Floridian learns to turn the shells over with his toes. He inspects and then, using his toes again, picks the prizes up.

There are two wonderful months in Florida, June and October. In June, the rage of summer approaches and challenges the last breezes of spring and warns of the days to come when the heat and the air are the same thing. October is when the humidity relents and the first semblance of a chilly morning appears. And you suspect a change of seasons. But you're always wrong. It is nothing but a big exhale.

Did you ever see a sting ray flap through shallow water? Like it was trying to take off and fly, right? How about going to the shrimp aquarium at the bait shop? Did you ever notice how some of the bigger, older shrimp scramble for the area of the tank where the pump is located? Do they really think you can't see them because of all the bubbles?

Drawbridges are nice. They force you to relax. You can even get out of the car and look over the side. And maybe see a sea cow.

Do fishermen still spit on their bait for luck?

"Daddy, it's dark," the boy interrupts again.

"We're eating under the pier, son. Get your flannel shirt out of the car. It's getting chilly."

The hole is already dug, the charcoal stacked and lit. The cinder blocks on each side hold the grill at just the right level. The clams and oysters begin to pop open. The feast is beginning.

Rock shrimp. How many years did fishermen toss them away as trash fish, cursing the fact they clogged their nets?

Remember the first time you tried to catch a lobster? It is even more exciting if you only use a snorkel. The pain of the memory is that you didn't know you were supposed to use gloves and your arms looked like you just lost a swordfight with a swordfish.

Smoked mullet is an art form. Except you must eat your masterpieces.

Conch chowder tastes better when you pry the mighty mollusks from their houses with your bare hands.

The man looks at the bounty of food and wonders why pirates used to scan the ocean's belly for treasures of another kind.

The sun has disappeared. Soon it will be time for the sea turtles to drag themselves to shore. With tears oozing from their sad eyes, these beasts will lay as many as 150 eggs in a night, then turn back and slowly head for their destiny, back in the beckoning sea.

The man tells his boy of that time many years ago when his father bought him his first cast net. He recounts the time of practice, learning to hold it in his mouth just right, how to drape the net over your prey. The next day, he promised his father, "I'm going to fill the freezer with filet meat."

Then the man says with a laugh that the first cast of that net had been over a school of blue fish.

"They chewed it to pieces," the man says.

The boy says, "I'm sorry."

"Me, too."

The bloat of dinner subsides. Mosquitoes begin strafing. The wind gusts. The sand stings as it slaps bare legs. The surf crashes closer. The tide is coming in. It is time to go.

The boy is asleep. The man carries him to his car, then returns for the cooler which, like him, is now empty.

Driving home, with the radio off and the windows down and the tear ducts filling, the man sings songs to himself. In the back seat, his boy suddenly cries out.

Leg cramps. Body surfing for six hours does that to young legs. And no aloe plant can make it feel better.

"It'll be OK, son. They'll go away. I had them a lot when I was your age. You just tried to do too much. Besides, you won't be coming back to the beach for a while."

The boy cries again.

A father's gift: Peace of mind
Dec. 26, 1985

On the day after Christmas, in the Year of Our Lord, 1969, the airman had powdered eggs and Jello for breakfast.

He drank the Jello. Mix it up and serve it before it begins to set and it almost tastes like Kool-Aid. Depending on how thirsty you were. It was bad; the eggs were worse. Powdered eggs were one of those showdowns that never got mentioned later whenever someone would ask what it was like in Vietnam.

This particular day, breakfast was the worst yet. A bad case of the Christmas blues had ruined the airman's appetite before the Jello and powdered eggs got a chance.

It was his first Christmas away from home. The Southeast Asian winter wonderland with the acne of bomb craters and questionable morals could not be any farther from home.

He knew when Christmas came because the bulletin board told him. A typed message declared: "Christmas will be celebrated on 25 December by order of. . ."

Oh, there were efforts and allusions. Like Christmas Eve, when the uneasy truce made things seem almost like a Silent Night. Except for the whimpers of the starving dogs out on the grassy runway. If he tried hard enough, the airman could hear the unlucky guy who drew guard duty whispering Christmas carols to himself while smoking a joint.

41

And Christmas morning, the cooks wore chef hats, instead of fatigue caps. And the line for confession was conspicuously long. And the Armed Forces Radio Network played Handel's Messiah instead of the usual fare of feel-good rock 'n' roll.

And maybe for a few minutes, the airman got that familiar toasty-warm feeling Christmas Day always provided.

Then he saw a pal, a Marine whose nerves had gotten so bad that lately he had taken to drinking himself to sleep. The Marine was feeling sorry for himself and tears tracked down his hard face. Beside him was a tape recorder, playing his two children's wonderfully butchered version of *Santa Claus Is Coming To Town.*

He hadn't written home in months.

The airman thought about saying something. Then he changed his mind. The Marine rewound the tape and started it again and his sobbing grew louder.

The ornaments and decorations that had been hung in the bunkers had been gnawed and chewed up by rats during the night. There was a small Christmas tree, but it was an aluminum one and someone had thrown up underneath it.

Mail had not come for a week.

Even the guys who didn't have hangovers felt lousy.

The depression mounted for the airman. Maybe he'd get drunk as soon as his breakfast settled, he thought.

Then the word spread that mail had arrived.

There was a package for him. Maybe some cookies. For sure, a letter, something from his kid sister or folks or girl friend, any words of support he could use to keep his contemporary world at arm's length.

It was a football.

Not just any football, but one caught in the stands by his father back in the days before those nets were hoisted in the end zone at college games. A genuine game ball from the University of Miami. It was his father's prized souvenir.

There also was a note, also from his father. His mother usually wrote. This time his father did. There was the usual small talk, but at the end, there was something about thanks for making the sacrifice.

The father was a career military man, a retired officer, a patriot,

42

the hawk who prayed nightly for the dove. Now, his country's sentiments were divided. There were people sticking flowers into gun barrels. Conscientious objectors and people who were afraid of dying and people who simply did not support what was going on. Some chose to live in Canada. The father did not understand.

Some of the Onward Christian Soldiers were challenging their conscience and questioning their purpose. The father thanked his son for spending this Christmas away from home. It means a lot, he wrote.

A football. A sacrifice for a sacrifice. The airman began realizing some things that day after Christmas and 16 years later, he still remembers a lot of them. It was a bad war and our general fears and narrow ambitions were raised to high principle. Maybe we'd get to the light at the end of the tunnel before some incoming horror lit us all up and turned us into jellyfish. The airman had thought a lot about whether the war was right or wrong. But suddenly he realized he was there in it regardless. And that counted for something.

Now he had a football.

The airman decided the thing to do with this football, this treasure of a grown man's life, was to have a game with it. Kick it and throw it and fumble it and—what the hell—just let it get all scruffy and imbedded with the funk that got under your skin and didn't go away until six months after you left the country.

The call went out. Anyone wanting to play a pickup game would meet beside the tin Quonset hut that always smelled because that was were the body bags were filled.

A nearby field was mowed. A bag of flour was used to line it. Sides were picked. Of course, there was an uneven number. Nothing ever goes completely by design in a police action.

A rumor that a kicking tee was available proved false when it was discovered rats had nibbled on it to the point it more closely resembled an ash tray.

The game started anyway and within minutes, everyone was back in his own back yard. There was no war going on. Just a bunch of kids playing football.

To the best of everyone's knowledge, the score was tied an hour later. Not that anyone really cared.

43

In the huddle, the old pump-fake play was called. Parker, a Marine who could run faster than anyone else despite the several pounds of love beads and necklaces he always wore, would take three steps, pivot, then take off. Brito, the quarterback who always bragged of the days he led his high-school team to the state finals two years in a row, promised he could fake the short pass and hit Parker as he streaked down the flour line.

The airman was a blocking back. He saw it all. Parker ran a perfect route. The defender bit on the fake and was a beaten man. Brito wound up with all his might and let loose with a mighty grunt.

The ball fluttered off to the right, bounced off a cooler and rolled down a gully into some thick undergrowth.

Brito had tried too hard. Any quarterback—Sammy Baugh, Dan Marino, Eric Hipple—can tell you that will happen when you grip the ball too tightly and try to throw harder and longer than you are able.

No search party was formed. Nobody wanted to go stomping through some area where there may or may not be some forgotten land mine. Or maybe a viper, a 30-pacer, the deadliest of snakes not walking around on two feet.

Game called on account of reality.

The football stayed there at least for the next 218 days, when the airman transferred out. For all he knows, it's still there.

Some people later criticized him for not treating the football with the same reverence his father had. He didn't care to listen. If anybody really wanted to know what he thought, he would have told them that football and that football game on the day after Christmas were the best presents he ever received.

The present was himself. Faith and hope and self-dignity and perspective and, yeah feeling. All were restored as he remembered once more what the world celebrates each Dec. 25.

He might have been only a few clicks away from being the burnt-out loser so many people became in that misbegotten country. But he found himself when he lost that football. For a day, he got to be a child again. He regressed and meandered through safer circumstances with less significant circumstances. The hopes and fears of all the year were set aside. It was glorious.

44

So many of his memories of that country are horrible ones. So many memories still strafe an overworked conscience. So many are contained in Washington, D.C., where the chiseled names on a stark granite wall include a free spirit named Parker. But the one memory that overrules all the others has to do with a football.

There always will be a danger of confusing Christmas with that day when everyone gets a bunch of nice presents. Just as people often will mistake the gift with the package it came in.

But the meaning of giving and sacrifice and Christmas, not to mention the taste of powdered eggs, will never go away for the airman who became a little more of a man by becoming a little boy again.

Young boy puts game in perspective
April 1, 1986

DALLAS—It was only hours before the coronation. The new king of college basketball—either Duke or Louisville—was eating a pregame meal. Steaks for both.

Dick Vitale was trying to avoid another case of Hoop in Mouth disease. To no avail.

A man from Kentucky has a stand set up. For $4, he'd paint your face red. If you wanted it done blue, that would be $5.

The sportswriter from Detroit needed to get away for a while. He took a walk.

On the intersection of Elm and Houston, even though it is right next to Reunion Arena, nobody was preoccupied with basketball. The Texas Book Depository made sure of that.

And the sportswriter couldn't believe the feelings of perspective turned inside out. A block away, people were talking about the importance of the Big Game. Duke and Louisville fans talked about the recruiting benefits a national championship would bring. The players silently reflected that the Big Chance had come. All those scouts, all those coaches, all those sportswriters and broad-

45

casters, would be watching. What honor and wealth was available? Just have one great game. It's so important.

And Dealey Plaza and the grassy knoll seem as far away as 1963.

Dallas is always a tough town to visit. It is an international city and practically Yuppie Heaven if you count BMWs and fern-bar mentality as the artifacts of upward mobility. But it will forever share its progress with a horrible November day when a crazy man and a rifle and an opportunity all came together.

Billy Thompson was born a week later. Johnny Dawkins was three months old at the time. They were not aware of an Age of Innocence as it crashed. And 23 years later, as they share the nation's attention span with a lingering loss from the previous generation, the basketball game flickers in importance.

That is good. The sportswriter focuses on events three days old. Of a 13-year-old boy with fantasies. And friends.

Ryan Gray has a brain tumor. It is too big and located in the wrong place for an operation. The growing, spreading, malignant hell inside his head has made walking a tough task. His back is malformed. He talks in whispers.

He doesn't have much time.

This little guy came to Dallas from Manhattan, Kan., to see his favorite basketball team win the national championship. He had become the adopted mascot of the Kansas Jayhawks this season and, if the world ran according to storybooks, Ryan would have gotten a piece of the championship nets.

Kansas lost on Saturday. And a lot of Jayhawks fans wiped away the stinging sensation of defeat by rationalizing there is always Next Year.

Ryan Gray cannot afford to look that far ahead. Doctors say everything medically possible has been done. The pain will grow.

Ryan doesn't think about the future. He is your typical 13-year-old. It is right now that matters. His team lost on Saturday, but his parents decided to stick around to see who won the big game.

"I was their lucky key chain," he says of his role with the Jayhawks. "I brought them good luck."

The blue Jayhawks cap almost slid over his ears. His voice was

46

little more than a whine. But the great flash of light was too much to take. The sportswriter turned away for a second.

The young all have their fantasies. We encourage them. A farmgirl and her dog fly away from monotony to Oz. A young president builds a Camelot with a smile. And two basketball teams chew on charbroiled feasts, trying to digest the notions of glory.

Reunion Arena rumbled with activity. Last-minute scalpers were busy. Tunnels of supporters meandered to their seats. Billy Packer was getting his makeup put on by a specialist.

The bright day was yawning to an end. Shadows start to spread. And the slow, reflective steps of those milling around the Texas Book Depository, the inevitable glances to the sixth floor, the chill of feeling suddenly smaller and more vulnerable all tame the weekend revelry into a sobering walk back to the basketball arena. What goes around, comes around. Ryan Gray says he hopes Danny Manning doesn't quit school to go to the pros.

His father carried the boy in his arms. It was late and his legs were weak and we should ask not what we can do . . .

Remembering when baseball represented the truth
May 26, 1986

Who knows where it came from? A piece of discarded newspaper at the airport. Who would even pick it up?

The Stars and Stripes, official newspaper of the armed forces. Once it was the only connection with the real world. But its pages contained more propaganda than was dropping from the sky. But baseball box scores never lie.

Hope hid behind the truth. And truth was not to be confused with reality. There was plenty of that around.

Freight planes waited on the freshly mowed runway while the body bags and caskets were loaded. The flight nurse with the clipboard and the captain's bars made little checks with her pencil. Ambulatory. Stretcher. Deceased. There was always less morphine than blankets. She shoved her bravest smile into place each day. Then, soon as possible, she got drunk.

"This kid with a colostomy in his future wanted to know if I liked baseball," she said bitterly. "These boys are something. They're out in the jungle, getting shot at and they talk about baseball."

Everyone listened, nodded and kept quiet. Rank has its privileges and she had her reasons for her nightly ritual of self-abuse. Nobody told her (it sounded too corny) baseball was one of the few things worth fighting about.

Baseball was crucial, totally American and, at the time anyway, mostly pure. The box scores in the Stars and Stripes were just as honest.

At night, the black market Jim Beam was passed among friends or anyone who had ice. Lonely soldiers, reflecting and deflecting at the same time, discussing the childhood game of their innocence.

"Seaver pitched another shutout for the Mets."

"What's wrong with the Tigers this year?"

"How about that? Brooksie Robinson made an error."

Rats skittered about the windowless barracks. The stink of the river a mile away was ripe. The rumble of distant bombs sometimes upset the bull sessions while we made sure nothing was incoming. But baseball, those box scores, kept things at arm's length.

The news wasn't exactly fresh, usually two days old by the time the paper arrived. It held the same suspense anyway. Particularly during a pennant race.

It even became a calendar of sorts. The day Johnson was bitten by the snake, the Mets beat the Dodgers. When he died the next day, the Red Sox took a doubleheader from the Indians. And when his name appeared in the Stars and Stripes under the Died Not As A Result Of Hostile Action, Baltimore got rained out.

Once, there were no papers for a week and it happened to be the last week of the baseball season. The enemy in black pajamas and sandals made from tires, carrying little plastic bags of rice and rifles made in Russia, shut off delivery. Finally, word came. The Mets won the pennant. Parker, the black man with the Brooklyn accent, was in his glory.

He was blown away a month later.

A few years ago, they opened a memorial in Washington, D.C. It's a tall chevron of black, polished granite and a lot of names that don't mean much to most people. Except as a group.

You walk along the wall, trying to forget, trying to remember. It is a solemn work of art and you hear the sobs and wails all around you. A man sits in front of a name, running his fingers along the chiseled identity of a lost friend. Somebody's mother is carrying flowers. A wife walks alone, back and forth, still lost.

You look for your friend's name. For some silly reason, you bought a pack of cigarettes. His brand. When you find his name among the thousands and thousands of the most silent minority, you try to mash the pack into the wall.

Then you see the piece of paper. A box score with a circle around the winning pitcher's name. Seaver is still mowing them down.

The war that never was declared took us into extra innings. We don't have a perfect record any more. We tied one. We had to punt.

We need to remember those who did their part. But we should never forget the things they thought were important enough to fight for. Baseball represented the truth. It was enough.

"We're going on a picnic," you say to your family. "Special day. Barbecue, watermelon, beer, the works."

Your children cheer.

"And let's not forget to take the flag."

"Why, Daddy?"

"To remember. Who do you think of when you see the flag?"

"Hulk Hogan," says the oldest.

"Rocky," shouts his brother.

"Rambo. Bruce Springsteen."

You smile. And hope all the heroes from now on will be make-believe. And you throw away that old paper. It's all old news now.

Jim Brown: Tough cover, weak soul
Aug. 28, 1986

His insidious anger has roared once again, burst into rage and violence. But his control, almost hypnotic in command over those close to him, has muffled the aftershock. There is no recoil. Another battered woman has changed her mind. Jimmy Brown is in the clear once more.

You've heard this story before. Jim Brown, former pro football great. Arrested last weekend at his home in the hills of Hollywood. Flashlights and handcuffs and fingerprints and mug shots and that little index card that has the words to every prisoner's inherent freedoms.

"You have the right to remain silent . . ."

It made the national news because of who he used to be. The first thing you noticed when they showed him being led to the police car was that he still looks like he could run with a football. Jimmy Brown, forever the galloping lion. What a man.

That was Saturday morning. Monday, the woman said she didn't want to press charges. She just wants to get back together with the man she has chosen to marry.

How many times? How much more before it's too late?

Maybe we should forget who Jim Brown used to be. Who is he now? How many times can your reputation bail you out?

If we cannot blame the lion for being a lion, then at least let us return him to the jungle where he belongs.

Jim Brown, Hall of Fame football player, unemployed actor, tragic and troubled soul, was arrested last weekend. He reportedly beat up his 22-year-old fiancee. There have been other alleged incidents, other alleged beatings, rapes and assaults. Even other fiancees, all beautiful, all the same age. The charges always seem to evaporate.

On Monday, a woman decided whatever it was that supposedly happened wasn't Jim Brown's fault. It never is Jim Brown's fault. Not afterward. Or before. Sometimes during, but never enough to develop any kind of pattern or history. Or concrete case.

Go back to the first one, the only one who ever got him trapped

50

in matrimony, 10 years' worth, and find out. You get close. Maybe you even love him. But don't blame him if he can't love back.

"It isn't that he's mean," Sue Brown said, "it's just who he is."

"Before we got married, he said there always would be other women. He asked me if I could deal with that. And I said I could. For 10 years I did. He'll hurt you, but he always tells the truth."

There's a pretty girl turning 16 every day. Jim Brown once said that in explanation of why he works so hard to keep in shape and look young. So he is 50 years old and waiting for someone else's birthday. He still looks like the greatest running back ever, from a distance. But there are gray hairs on his chest and something must be wrong on the inside.

His obsession is youth. And strength. The young and the strong. The code of the jungle; could the lion know any other way?

Sue Brown talks about the time Jim Jr. was in the hospital, sick with chronic tonsillitis. He never came to visit.

"He can't deal with weakness. Hospitals, funerals – he stays away from that. And if he ever finds a flaw in you, he presses it. He plays on you until he controls you. He isn't mean; he's scary. And if you're afraid of him, he controls you."

His rules. Brown says he wants to be able to choose those around him, declares, "I am not anyone's house nigger," and seeks out that control.

Only the pretty and young girls. Only the ones he can trust. And control.

In 1965, he was accused of sexually molesting two teen-aged girls. There was a paternity suit. Nothing was proven. In 1968, he was charged with assault and intent to commit murder by his girl friend, also 22, also beautiful. Jim Brown threw her off the balcony of his apartment, she said at first. A policeman knocked on Brown's door and promptly was thrown through a closet door. The girl changed her mind, claiming she'd actually fallen instead. Sum total of punishment for Brown: A $300 fine for obstructing justice.

In 1969, following a minor traffic accident, Brown wound up getting charged with felonious assault by the driver of the other car. The charges were thrown out of court. In 1978, Brown spent a day in jail and paid a $500 fine for beating up his golf partner. They had argued over where a ball should be placed on the green. Then Brown beat him senseless.

In 1985, a woman claimed Brown raped and assaulted her. Lack of evidence got the case thrown out of court.

The latest incident that never happened will only reinforce the anger. And sooner or later, society will realize there is but one place for a beast that knows no other way to assert dominance than with violence.

A cage.

Knight maneuvers in mental mine field
Feb. 23, 1987

Anyone who ever went through a military basic training can understand what Bob Knight is all about.

Just another boot-camp instructor, another leather-voiced stickler to detail and fundamentals, who teaches with tirades, intimidation and overbearing gruffness.

Just another guy who wants to make sure we beat the Soviets. If they ever show up.

Beat the best. Be the best. Fight through the picks. War, basketball, life. Same things, right?

But instead of KP duty and obstacle courses to go along with your three squares and a bunk, you have only a few hours of playing basketball and some scholarly pursuit for your four-year commitment to Bob Knight and Indiana basketball. And if you can make it through all the negativity and salty diatribes of this glorified boot-camp sergeant, this abrasive super-patriot, this Bob Knight, the world can sleep tight for a little while longer.

Oh yeah. That's what it's all about, isn't it? A good Knight's sleep. Lasting peace.

Bob Knight? Lasting peace? The guy who got into it with the policeman in Puerto Rico? The same guy who dumped the loudmouth LSU fan into a garbage can? The one who threw The Chair? What's so peaceful about Bob Knight?

Nothing. Bob Knight, whose Indiana team may be the best in the amateur free world right now, is a warmonger. Tell the doves to keep their distance. Stay over there with that author fellow from the Washington Post. No room for you . . . you conscientious objectors.

Militaristic themes obsess Bob Knight. He reads about ancient warriors, of Hammurabi, Patton, Woody Hayes. He could tell you Ted Williams' flying record. And every rule rendered obsolete, every line that gets erased, every concession to the Me and Now generations, is further proof of a society in decay.

Next thing you know, the cheaters will be everywhere. The Soviets will be in the shorebreak, ready to claim Amerika as just another satellite. And the first hint of the impending doom will be that someone like Jerry Tarkanian, The Shark himself, will be No. 1.

Paranoia is healthy. Peace is uneasy, as unpredictable as a half-time lead. So Bob Knight, who has forsaken that modified horse-blanket sports coat for a red sweater that constantly loses the battle to keep a burgeoning beer belly covered, fights a private war.

To keep the cheaters at arm's length, that's why. He realizes his fears are unorthodox, his methods even more so. So he keeps it all private. Only sometimes it makes it into the newspapers. His explosions don't have the long-lasting effect of Chernobyl blowing its stack. But they are more frequent.

So what if 25 of his recruits have bolted, gone AWOL or over the hill and transferred to North Carolina State and points thereabout? They left and, according to Knight, that means they weren't the kind you'd want to share a foxhole with anyway.

The man is a teacher. His style is obnoxious. His results are inarguable. He gets you through the skirmishes. His players graduate. They rarely make headlines as criminals or outlaws. They survive and go on with their lives. And there are two national championship banners that belong to Bob Knight.

Just like the guy who once taught you how to clean a rifle and how to keep a gig line straight and dress, right, dress. You learned something or else. But there were rewards for such survivals.

Play for Bob Knight and you grow up. You learn how to put up with unbearable discipline. You learn how to compete.

And that's the buzzword, more important than winning, although Knight would never admit it. The mean ol' world doesn't offer many free rides. Neither does Bob Knight. You get some of his fire and maybe it rubs off and maybe you roll up your sleeves and dig out a little place in society for yourself.

Last week, the three doormat teams of the Big Ten gave Indiana fits. Northwestern lost by a basket. Wisconsin stretched the Hoosiers through three overtimes before succumbing by a point. Minnesota fell in the final seconds on a pair of free throws.

There must have been hell to pay in practice. Iowa came to town and Knight let everyone know how disappointed he was that in all his years of coaching, only one team had ever broken 100 points against one of his teams. Iowa. A month ago.

He let the Indiana players know how poor they had been playing. And then he challenged them to compete. Help him live down his embarrassment.

And on Saturday, they put on a first-half blitzkrieg that would have made a German field commander giggle in some distant gymnasium.

It was Bob Knight's 200th victory at Indiana.

Moscow, of course, had no comment. Neither did Isiah Thomas. But across this great country of ours, a thousand chief master sergeants flexed with pride.

The system still works.

Gooden's childlike joy gone forever
April 2, 1987

Baseball is best when children play it. And the sun is a bright orange balloon and the chirping of excitement and laughter is a simple song of sport. The rest of the world — the grown-up world — isn't allowed on that magical diamond of emerald and rust.

Because something might get spoiled.

Baseball is best when the world doesn't go 100 mph, a fastball low and outside and too hot to handle.

Today, I get personal. Today, I share a little tale of many years ago; a story of warm promise and reinforcement. Today I reflect because yesterday I found out Dwight Gooden had failed a drug test.

Dwight Gooden, a 12-year-old with a smile and a Slurpee. Maybe thebest player on the best Little League team in the world. Dwight Gooden — Dr. K. — of whom the great Sandy Koufax once said, "I'd trade my yesterdays for his tomorrows."

Today it all seems a lifetime ago . . .

The Belmont Heights team had won as usual. The day was balmy and making nice promises for the city of Tampa. A typical Florida day. My former sports editor said to check out this team. Go to a game; maybe do a story on what might be the best Little League team in the country.

The score was 15-0. I remember that and I remember the pitcher. It's hard to pitch a shutout when you're 15 runs ahead. There is a tendency to let up, to cruise, get sloppy and allow a run or two. Not this kid — the score book identified him only as "Gooden" — with the big windup and a fastball that was cruel-and-unusual punishment when you consider a Little League mound is almost 15 feet closer than a regulation baseball mound.

But the discovery of yet another great athlete was not what made that day so special, so vivid 10 years later.

It was after the game that something even more impressive happened. These were Little Leaguers; most of them rode their bikes to the game. They showed up early and played catch outside the field while the old man with the stub of cigar always in his mouth lined the base paths and built the batter's box.

And afterward, after they had won, after Dwight Gooden had pitched a one-hitter and hit a home run, they all headed for a nearby convenience store.

The coach was springing for soft drinks.

Nobody waited around. Nobody hurried either. They seemed like a bunch of kids content to let the world go by at its own sweet pace.

Especially the skinny kid, Gooden.

The smile and the Slurpee were delicious. This team stationed itself across the street, hanging around the coach's station wagon, replaying every hit and out. They still wore their uniforms. Baseball was too important to let loose of just yet.

Just a bunch of kids holding onto the best of times. It was dark and time to go home. And they all knew it. Parents would worry. It started to break up and Dwight Gooden, who seemed to have such a good grip on things, shook his head.

"Sometimes I wish tomorrow never had to come," he said.

I wrote that down. I remember thinking too many children can't make time go fast enough. Gotta get older, gotta get a driver's license, get a drink, get a job, get a girl, get a family. Here was one kid, I thought, who was going to enjoy life in order, wringing each day for all it was worth. Tomorrow surely held riches and fame and even at such a tender, impressionistic age, I think he knew it. But it could wait. All of the tomorrows. There was too much fun going on at the moment to skip ahead.

But now we must skip ahead. All the way to yesterday, 10 years later. Dwight Gooden, according to the wire service reports, volunteered to take a drug test. There were too many whispers why his awesome skills had suddenly become mortal, too many rumors of dramatic mood swings recently.

We don't know if the grip loosened or the world sped up. We hope it's all wrong, a mistake. We wish the 12-year-old with the smile and the Slurpee were back across the street, talking about baseball. But that cannot be.

We can chart the maps and warn them where the rocks are. But the children must someday find their own way alone.

A Slice of British Life: From the far bus to the spiders, it was quite a Wimbledon fortnight
July 12, 1987

EDINBURGH, Scotland — Samuel Johnson, probably no relation to Vinnie, Howard or the late Lyndon, once said, "When you are tired of London, you are tired of life."

I'm not so sure. Plumb Tuckered would properly describe my mood as I departed the city limits of the town that gave the world Andy Capp and Captain Kidd. But tired of life? More like full of it.

The most valuable possession us squatters along press row owned during the fortnight of Wimbledon was, of course, the little badge on a chain we wore around our necks. It meant validation, access and a reason for people on the tubes and buses and undergrounds to stare. What's that, mate? Are ye on sale? Has Harrod's put Americans into its sale bins this year? Hee hee.

When I picked up my little badge that allowed me free and easy entry to all of the matches, the woman scanning the computer printout sheet looked up and said, "My, but you're a Biggie."

She correctly interpreted my look of confusion and quickly added, "You're a large man. Not massive or a tub, though. Just rather large. I bet you'd be great at the net in doubles."

And from that moment on, my real name didn't matter. Every day we'd pass at some time, and every time it was, "Hello, Biggie."

By a quirk of fate, I managed to procure accommodations at the one place, only area, single vicinity of England in which no other journalist was staying. A virtual outpost. My solitary travels to and from the matches each day involved a complicated series of train connections and transfers, with a double-decker bus either delivering or taking me away from the hallowed grassland. Each evening as I dragged out, fighting through the milling crowds, I would be greeted by the bobby manning Gate 5. And he would have the same sage advice.

"Far bus. You would want the far bus, sir."

Do you get the feeling it was a mundane couple of weeks? Not exactly.

The first day of the tournament, feeling positively chipper (my English studies before the trip paid handsome dividends when speaking directly to the natives), I saw a man walking about with two tarantulas on his head. Cross my heart. He was a fireman from Sweden named Lars and he was on holiday to watch his favorite tennis players and brought the eight-legged Messrs. Pets and Flo along with him.

Thusly, the concert tour of Biggie Farbus and the Spiders of Lars took stride. No drugs or nuclear weapons allowed.

In Trafalgar Square is the statued likeness of someone named King George. A bit of chiseled information beneath his feet identified him as, among other distinctions, the last king of the American colonies. As the Fourth of July (Independence Day) was nearing, I wondered if mooning the good king might be an appropriate gesture of patriotism.

Yet, I really like the English. I just sort of got off on the wrong foot. Or wrong lane.

The rental-car agency was unable to grant my wish for an automatic transmission vehicle. Joan, my travel guru, warned me I'd want an automatic. I instead got an apology and a five-speed.

Ever try to brush your teeth with your other hand? Remember the first time you ever tied your son's necktie? How do I get this thing into first gear? Had the customs people confiscated my coordination? Damn, these roads are narrow. Hey, get over on your side, buddy.

I kept the rental car long enough to incur two flat tires—caused by my running into curbs on the phantom left side, which was brought on by my absolute horror of seeing oncoming cars directly in my path—whereupon I phoned the rental agency to rescue me. One hour in the country and I was flat out of healthy tires and definitely out of the mood for driving.

Then there were the dwarfs.

Out for a walk on a sunny Saturday, I was passed by three dwarfs, their cute waddle too quick even to consider drafting upon. They did a prompt right turn into a building. I continued on my way when I encountered two more dwarfs approaching.

What's going on here? I turned once they went by and watched them turn left into the same building. I followed.

It was a tavern. Inside, 15–20 customers. All dwarfs. Except for the bartender, who was of normal height. "Am I allowed in here?"

"You got money? If you do, you're allowed. This is just the favorite place for the little folks. They're great, huh?"

I looked around. I thought I was in Santa's workshop during the office Christmas party. Little legs dangling. Little hands holding those huge heavy glass mugs all English thirst palaces use to serve beer.

When I finally left, I had met some terrific people. I also knew I was going to have a hangover, but only a little one.

My hotel sent me "complimentary bath buns" every day. It wasn't until my second week that I figured out you were supposed to eat them. I had been confused whether the bath bun was a hunk of soap or a sponge. I tried one, finally, and concluded after a couple of bites that it makes a better sponge.

The security guard in the press room was an elderly man from Poland named Stanlius. One day he overheard me asking what the British equivalent to Lipton or Tetley was. I wanted to know the most popular brand of tea in England. Stan (us Americans Anglo-size more than we Midas-ize) thought I wanted to find out the best-tasting tea. The next day he brought me a box of his favorite. A box of Polish tea. It was great, too. Gifts from new friends always are.

I really did try to get into cricket, since none of the newspapers would supply baseball scores. I couldn't even pick up Senor Harwell on the radio. But have you ever looked at a cricket scoreboard? Did you understand it? Neither did I.

How do you suppose someone goes about corking a piece of Willow?

Favorite name of the journey so far: Fatima Whitdbread. She's a champion javelin thrower. Her friends and the tabloids call her Fats.

Favorite sign: "No football coaches allowed." Hoo boy, what's Schembechler going to think about that? He'll never schedule Oxford on a home-and-home. What's that? The sign has to do with buses? And football means soccer in England? Never mind.

Great names, too, for the villages in and about London. Cock-apple. Clapham Junction. Tooting. Wonder if they sell T-shirts?

During the rainy half of Wimbledon I decided one morning,

since the rain had ceased, to head to Court One early and get a good seat in the press section. I was about to plop down when I felt a sharp twinge from the rear. A woman had stabbed me with her umbrella nee brolly. She then pointed with it to the puddle on my targeted seat.

"You might wipe it down good, sir, otherwise you'll surely suffer from the itchybum."

The taxi driver who took me home the night I finished my work after the last train had gone was a real character. He said he had a dog named McEnroe.

"Barks and whines all the time," he said.

I went to a Pizza Hut that advertised special toppings like peaches, sweet corn and Spam. Inside, I saw a Japanese family posing for pictures in front of the salad bar. The father (I guessed) clicked a shot and raised his thumb in triumph.

There was an Arab sportswriter with a portable computer that printed Arabic characters right to left. I wanted to ask him how he knew when his machine ever broke. I also wanted to ask him why, since Arabic numerals are so familiar, the Arabic alphabet is so foreign. Alas, I couldn't find the words.

When Boris Becker lost, his first words in the solemn news conference that followed were, "Nobody is dead. I just lost a tennis match."

When you think about it, that kind of attitude means you're not going to lose very many tennis matches. It does help to have the serve of Boris Becker when you make such philosophical conclusions.

Riding the trains for just two weeks changed me. There were crowds every day. Who were they? Where were they going? For the first couple of trips, I was inquisitive. I wanted to talk to them, look out the window, see the strange new world. But maybe it was the rhythmic motion of the train going over the tracks. Maybe it was the daily drone of existence. Maybe it's just that strangers don't like to talk with other strangers. Maybe the groove became a rut. I began staring, too. Not at anything. Staring through people. Watching but not seeing. Seeing things not inside the train or outside the window. Staring, just staring.

The tournament ended. I turned off the tennis like a faucet, then turned on the pipes to the real world.

Murder. The English love mystery. Agatha Christie. Jack The Ripper. *Murder, She Wrote.* But this one was not fun.

Outside of a town called Manchester is a huge, desolate moor where a body was discovered two weeks ago. It reopens an old crime and slashes apart old public wounds. Police are still digging up there. There may be more.

Sometimes it's good for a writer to kind of rub his fur in a different direction, tackle a story that isn't in the normal realm of assignment.

But up on Saddleworth Moor, watching grim people go about their grim business, watching the bleakness get more intense and the day turn grayer and night start to take over and the shadows grow tall, wide and ominous, I shivered.

I remembered Judy Garland, playing Dorothy in *The Wizard of Oz*, telling her dog Toto, "I don't think we're in Kansas anymore."

And I knew I was a long way from a tennis tournament.

Lend an ear to Olympics for Eskimos
July 14, 1987

DUNBAR, Scotland — They don't get many Eskimos in this part of Scotland. Especially one with a 12-pound lead weight hanging from his left ear.

Joshua Kunawik walks back and forth, slowly, his face a clenched fist. When he stops and removes the weight, which is attached to a leather cord, he lets the stranger from America in on his bizarre ritual of seeming self-abuse. Mind you, this is Scotland, in a small fishing village touching the North Sea.

"I'm practicing for the Olympics," he says, rubbing his ear, maybe to see if it's still there. "The Eskimo Olympics."

From July 22–25, in Fairbanks, Alaska, the 27th annual World Eskimo Indian Olympics will be held. Joshua is one of the favorites

61

in the Ear Weight competition. He's still got a way to go if he wants to set a record. Jimmy Itta, in 1976, lugged 18 pounds the astonishing distance of 1,680 feet.

"Nobody will ever beat Jimmy's record," says the 38-year-old Kunawik. "Especially Jimmy. That day, his ear almost ripped completely off his head. He's retired now."

The Olympics were started to make sure Eskimo tradition survives. Elders invented the events as a means of conditioning the young men for the freezing Arctic environment and also for the long hunts.

Ears are apparent luxuries among the Eskimos since there also is an ear-tugging event. Joshua says the tug, while similar to his specialty, "is for the real crazy people."

"A lot of people gather to watch that one," he says. "And there's always a doctor on call. You loop a leather thong around your ear and the other guy does the same. It's kind of like a tug-of-war after that. It takes great courage. It gets bloody."

The Knuckle Hop is another crowd-pleaser. Using only your fists for transportation, you see how far you can go. The record is 100 feet.

This leads into a question how this aided in either fighting off winter's rage or hunting down dinner. Joshua shrugs, "I wonder about that one too."

The Games sound like a kaleidoscope of the length and depth of the human spirit. They also sound like fun. But it's serious business to the Eskimos, stunts that have been passed down through the generations. They also rekindle the same inbred fires any Olympics do. To be the best at something, to stand in ceremony and accept the symbol of greatness, of No. 1, is a flame that burns within us all.

Think what it would mean to be the first ever to transcend the full 20 feet of the Greased Pole Walk. Nobody has ever made it all the way. One small step for man. . . .

Nalukatuk, The Blanket Toss, originally was devised to throw a hunter high into the air so he could scan the horizon for whales. Olympic rules insist a Nalukatuk performer must land upright. Considering the descent is often from the heights around 30 feet, the always-popular danger element abounds.

But Joshua is an ear weight man. He started with one-pound weights and, presumably, gallons of seal oil. Those one-pounders were the hardest. Once you build up and get to the 10-pound mark, "you're beyond pain or feelings. You're now dealing with how much the human ear can support. It's in God's hands."

Joshua Kunawik smiles. It's not for everyone. The Indians appreciate these skills. Outsiders might not.

"Like the seal-skinning contest," he says. "A woman once skinned one in 57 seconds at the Olympics. Can't you imagine that? 57 seconds. Wow.

"Then there's the whale-blubber eating contest . . . the breakfast of champions, you know."

The disregard for ears prompted another question. Are there any contests involving the nose?

"I don't think so. Why?"

"Well, it would tend to mess up romance, wouldn't it?"

"You mean, because we rub noses? Hey, we think you people are crazy for kissing on the lips. Hey, in the winter, you try that and your lips will freeze together."

You have to wish Joshua Kunawik well. He wants to be a champion. He is willing to pay that dear price. Or is it ear price?

But what's he doing in Scotland?

"I came here to relax, play a little golf," he says, smiling once more. "Got to get my mind right."

4.

UNDERDOGS

He's flirted with the hell of cocaine—now Mercury
Morris is . . . Keeping the Faith
The Denver Post
Sept. 25, 1983

HOMESTEAD, Fla.—Lunchtime in the Dade Correctional Institute. Long lines for mass-produced food; idle chatter between caged men with tattoos of snakes, dragons, playing cards and naked women.

"Hey, Mercury, goin' to the movie tonight?" asks one man.

"What is it?" says Eugene Edward Morris.

"Star Wars."

"Naw."

The man smiles and says, "If I was you, you'd better watch it 'cause by the time you get out, you're gonna need to know how to drive."

Mercury Morris. Convict. Inmate. No. 088586. Serving 20 years for cocaine trafficking, 15 of which are mandatory before any hope for parole can be granted. By the time he draws his next breath as a free man, it could be 2002.

He will be 56 years old by then. What do you do with a used-up Mercury anyway?

"Before you do 20 years, you must do 20 minutes and the days all seem the same," he says, his words coming as swiftly as his feet used to move. "I've been in prison almost a year but it doesn't seem like it. I'm spending time here and I don't like it or dislike it. But somewhere along the line the truth will be seen. It'll be just like (Don) Shula going up to the ref on the sidelines. 'Make the call, have some guts.' I believe in the system of checks and balances. I'm confident that the truth will come out eventually. Somebody will have the guts for justice to be served."

Morris sits in the visitor's lounge and chain-smokes cigarettes and talks about the future while memories punish him. The khaki-shirted guard in the background yawns in boredom.

The Dade County Correctional Institute is almost 50 miles from Miami. It is, as most prisons are, away from everywhere. The Everglades National Park is down the road. Off to the side is a migrant camp, where people are prisoners of another sort. Out beyond the bushes and palmetto and marshland are unpaved roads where smugglers often land planes loaded with cocaine and marijuana and heroin.

At one end of the prison compound is a lake. With a large, active alligator.

The prison is six years old and surrounded by 12-foot-high fences of razor wire. It is considered a medium-security prison although more than half of the 637 inmates are categorized as maximum closure prisoners.

Mercury Morris is easily the most famous.

As the one-time all-pro running back furiously rummages through the law library, sifting through volumes of legalese, looking for anything to help his upcoming appeal, he seems to be running faster than ever.

You see, Mercury Morris thinks he is somehow innocent despite the fact he readily admits that in August 1982 he served as middleman in the sale of 456 grams of cocaine to an undercover agent. He and his lawyer and a growing number of people feel the state induced him into committing a crime.

"It was a case of two wrongs making a conviction," he says.

"If I had pleaded guilty — I'd be out of here in another year. But I wasn't guilty. Not really."

He talks in bursts, almost rambling, never really sticking to the point long enough to establish it. There is a cockiness, a narcissism that tells you something about Morris' self-esteem. But there also is searing eye contact with dark, burning, clear eyes that practically plead for agreement and approval. He is articulate and moody, likeable and suspicious.

But most of all, he is mercurial.

"I wouldn't even settle for a pardon," he says. "I want justice."

When did his world crumble?

Probably when he first began playing football, he says. It just wasn't manifested until he got into pro football. And out of it.

"When you live in that tunnel syndrome, you never really get a chance to grow up," he said.

"Then all of a sudden, no one hands you the game plan anymore."

And Mercury Morris, the nonconformer, the individualist, the one who always tried to buck the system, challenge the law and outrun the angles, fumbled away his life.

The Miami Dolphins' third-round draft choice in 1969 was a halfback from West Texas State with the dynamic name of Mercury Morris. He was also — at the time — the leading rusher in college football history.

In seven seasons with the Dolphins, he ran for almost 4,000 yards. He played in three Pro Bowls. He played in three Super Bowls.

But he constantly rebelled against the regimentation and team discipline of coach Don Shula. There was always a contract squabble or a fine for missing a practice or a suspiciously lingering injury that prevented America from cradling Mercury Morris to its bosom as a full-blown hero.

In 1973, during a Monday night game with Pittsburgh, Morris floated out of the backfield to take a short pass from quarterback

Bob Griese. He caught the ball and was immediately tackled by Steeler cornerback Mel Blount.

As both crashed to the ground, Morris felt the worst pain of his life. And even though he played the next week, he knew something was wrong.

Two vertebrae were broken in his neck. And that, claims Morris, was the beginning of all this mounting hell that his life has become.

He had an operation that left a sinister six-inch scar as a souvenir. Two years later, he reinjured his neck in a car accident.

"I started getting headaches, horrible headaches that were related to my neck problems," Morris says. "Pain? You talk about migraine headaches? How about an 18-hour migraine headache? And multiply that by five years."

He admits the pain once caused him to ponder suicide.

Instead he turned to escape.

Cocaine.

Miami is a city rife with urban cancers and pocked with open sores. The Marielitos of Cuba, the Liberty City and Bucktown riots, the flood of Caribbean refugees, the rash of cutting houses of the cocaine cowboys, the ugly violence.

"You can walk 19 blocks in any direction and buy cocaine," Morris once said. "Miami is basically a good town. But there are satanic forces in Miami."

And just like that, the individualist became a pawn. The pattern has become all too familiar. Social use. Snorting small amounts. Then escalation.

For three years he drifted into the routine of the cocaine addict. He would go to the local "smokehouse" and freebase for days at a time. Then, "It was zonk time: I'd sleep for a couple of days straight.

"With freebasing, you become singular. Take one hit and you immediately want another. When you smoke purified coke—you don't eat. I lost 20 pounds. It was like a constant meditation, sliding down that skid. What was a groove at first became a rut. I would see the sun rise every morning. I can remember looking at my window for five days. And there was never any concept of the money ever running out. And every other kind of paranoia imaginable. In that disguised, euphoric state there's no relativity, no sensation of what makes sense."

In 1976 Mercury Morris lived in a nice house, owned 80 prime acres in the Florida Keys, had a $55,000 speedboat and $250,000 in the bank.

He also had a coke habit.

Like the moth that ventures too close to the flame, Morris fried himself. He soared into the sun, too close to the glare. And what is the planet closest to the sun?

Mercury, of course.

Seven years later, a period that should have been the prime of his life, everything was gone but the house and the habit.

Foreclosure proceedings on the house had begun.

His Super Bowl rings were either lost or stolen or traded for cocaine. Morris can't remember.

In 1980 his next-door neighbor, Fred Crawford, a friend who often shared his pipe with Morris, was murdered and his body stuffed into an oil drum. He welched on a cocaine debt. The man who police say killed Crawford was later killed himself.

The night before Crawford was shot to death, he begged Morris to loan him the money that would save his life. Morris refused.

"When you love drugs, you can't love anything or anybody else. Drugs become idolatry," he says.

With a wife and daughter and two sons to support, the situation festered to a head.

Albert Donaldson was Morris' gardener until he argued that Morris owed him some money. To gain revenge, Donaldson decided to become an informant for the police and set up his former boss.

Donaldson himself has a long record. He once stabbed someone with a screwdriver. He has 41 arrests for burglary. There was a marijuana charge . . . and another arrest for biting a man's ear off. Donaldson claims he attacked the man because he caught him stealing his cockatoo, a bird, Donaldson later explained, that was delivered to him "by God."

Donaldson introduced Morris to Joseph Brinson, an agent for the Florida Drug Enforcement Agency posing as a cocaine buyer.

Broke and trying to figure out how to put food on the table for his family and also desperate to continue his life with the freebase pipe, Morris was easy prey. Sure, he could get his hands on cocaine, he said.

But at least twice he tried and came up empty. Keep trying, said Brinson.

Morris claims it was the government that began the machinations of the crime. He was nothing but a common junkie. But the efforts by the state turned him into a trafficker.

He was not the supplier. He was in such miserable mental condition he would have used up his supply himself. He and a friend, Edgar Kulins, were consumed by the drug, and together they saw the chance to introduce Brinson to a dealer as a chance to score some easy money.

Vincent Cord was the supplier.

It was a honey of a plan. Donaldson was wearing a bug most of the time. Morris' phone was tapped. Almost the entire scam was on tape.

A few days before the bust, Morris was, as usual, sitting in his home, blinking, in a semi-trance, his senses veiled by cocaine. The 700 Club religious program was on television and Morris, his guilt over his pitiful plight raging to match his headaches, made a call to the program.

"Help me," he said. "I'm a former pro football player in Miami. And I'm a freebaser. Help me," he repeated.

The program contacted a church in Miami, the Sunset Chapel Assembly of God. Its pastor, The Rev. Nick Schubert, started counseling Morris. Morris claims he was trying to change "and eventually would have.

"But the state intervened."

On Aug. 16, 1982, police moved in on Morris' South Miami home and arrested Eugene Edgar Morris, 36, of 6200 SW 64th Court.

Morris had sold a pound of cocaine to Brinson, who now was identifying himself to Morris as an agent instead of a customer.

Morris took the bag of cocaine and tried to throw it into the canal behind his home.

It hit the fence.

He rushed over and picked the bag up and tossed it again.

It didn't sink. It floated to the other end of the canal, and soon was recovered.

Confiscated along with the 456 grams of cocaine were several weapons and $124,000 in cash.

The majority of the money was the "buy" money. Mercury Morris' share in the deal was to have been $1,000.

The weapons were antique and belonged to his sons. There were no shells in the house.

Morris was led to a police car. Handcuffed, he carried a Bible. Neighbors shouted encouragement and expressed shock.

The shock was only beginning.

An hour after his arrest, Southern Bell came out to his house and turned his telephone off. For non-payment.

At the courthouse, on the ninth floor, a cake was delivered, celebrating the arrest of Mercury Morris and two other men.

Morris later was offered a piece.

The trafficking charge carried a minimum mandatory sentence of 15 years. The other two pleaded guilty and the prosecution waived the mandatory sentence for both Kulins and Cord.

Each may be out of prison in less than five years.

Morris, however, refused to plea bargain. He refused to name names.

In November 1982, Judge Ellen Morphonious Gable — "Maximum Ellen" around the courthouse scene — said "Sorry, Merc," and announced a 20-year sentence.

Ronald Strauss, Morris' lawyer, couldn't believe the verdict.

"A first offender," Strauss said. "He wasn't the supplier, he was the introducer. This is the inverse of the logic. They used the big guy to get the little guy."

Only the little guy was a celebrity. A famous football player. Or at least he used to be.

In December a ceremony honoring the 1972-73 Dolphins — the only unbeaten team in NFL history — was held in the Orange Bowl. Mercury Morris was six blocks away, sitting in a cell at the Dade County Jail. The ceremony was televised. Morris' name was not mentioned. Morris wasn't watching. The TV was broken.

Morris has not been able to pay for his defense. But his lawyer doesn't look like a man who takes charity cases.

Ronald Strauss is a flamboyant man with a taste for fine suits, cowboy boots and imported Dutch cigars. His office is imposing. Located in Coconut Grove, the office has rich leather furniture, an expensive desk, a polished bar and two barber's chairs. On the wall are pictures of former clients—singer Kenny Rogers and comedian Gallagher. There also is a picture of Strauss with Ronald Reagan. On a table beside Strauss' desk is an hourglass and a bull whip.

Strauss has prepared a 45-page appeal here. Monday, Strauss expects to hear from the state attorney's office concerning the appeal.

"Mercury isn't a human being anymore. He's a symbol," Strauss says. "It's not Mercury's act, it's Mercury. Because of who he is— he's been crucified outside the gates of Rome. But if you've still got the wheels like a Chuck Muncie or George Rogers (NFL players who have admitted a cocaine problem), they take care of you. There is absolutely no reason for Mercury Morris to spend the next 15 years in prison."

If the appeal goes according to plan, it is still a year before a judgment will be made.

Morris accepts this.

He has started a Reading Anonymous program in prison. He teaches functionally illiterate prisoners to read.

"Betterment," Morris says. "Self-betterment is the key."

He talks of his faith.

"I didn't find God—God found me. It's up to you to control your own creativity, to be a man," Morris says.

Morris spent a few months in Raiford, Florida's maximum-security prison.

"This is not Raiford, by no means. Up there you get by, henceforth known as the hustle. It's tense up there. Real tense."

His first roommate was a troubled man, says Strauss. "His nickname was 'Honeybuns' and he was a sick man. But Merc didn't complain and ask for a new roommate because he didn't want anyone to think he was a privileged character. He got another roommate later, though. Believe me, nobody will mess with Merc."

His attitude is positive. He says he would never use drugs again and cites his family as the reason.

"I have my priorities in order. I want to get out and enjoy a quiet life with my family. And I'll leave here with my dignity. I refuse to bow down for my freedom and I won't drag anybody else down. But, those wheels of justice that were so fast before are now bogging down in heavy traffic."

He is asked how the drug problem can be overcome.

"I freebased my brains out because I wasn't ready to compete in society. Get people ready, enlighten people. The trick is to be aware of why the problem ever materialized. Pete Rozelle and Don Shula and everybody might think they're doing it right. But so much attention is being paid to glorifying punishment and not finding the solution to the crimes.

"Get the people. Talk to them, about their welfare, not their speed, about whether they've fallen down, not whether they've lost a step. Appreciate talent, but respect well-being."

He put out a cigarette. Time to go.

"Someday soon, I hope before the next Fourth of July, I'm gonna walk out of here and climb in Ron's (Strauss') Jaguar and everyone will clap," Morris says.

There is so much positive energy, so much optimism.

"Just being coherent again is a good reason to feel positive. Besides, I'm not going to give up. That's just not in my repertoire."

Ex-Card struggled to the end
May 20, 1984
The Denver Post

ST. LOUIS—The dog, a mutt, sniffs at the late-model Mercury that belonged to Eric Washington. The car still is parked outside the apartment complex where, on Monday afternoon, Washington put a pistol to his temple and surrendered a life that always played from the catch-up position.

Frustration and desperation give off no particular scent and the dog has no idea what has happened. But there is similarity between that skinny mutt, scavenging and searching for scraps, and the former pro football player who made the evening news the other night in St. Louis. Neither ever found what it was looking for.

The usual wave of shock and surprise that comes whenever someone commits suicide has already subsided. With Eric Washington, it was almost expected, this final station in the cycle of expected failure.

Neighbors have since walked up and looked at the door of apartment 308 at the Raintree Complex. In looks like all the others. A lot of them have sighed and wondered to what depths a man must fall before he willingly blows out his brains. They have asked among themselves how someone with a famous brother—Kermit, the pro basketball player—could be so different.

"There's no excuse for what he did but I know my brother," said Kermit via telephone from his home outside San Diego in El Cajon. "The reason he killed himself was he was afraid of what people would think. He had so much pride, and it destroyed him. He was always wanting to be something . . . It hurts me a lot, I'm almost sick . . . That man never had a good day in his life."

The neighbors have chattered about how a real-life bank robber had lived on the same floor with them and that was somehow kind of exciting. Then they have shrugged and walked away.

"Nobody ever knew him around here," says Tim Vaughn, who lives across the hall. "If you don't know someone, all you can do is say 'What a shame.' I only talked to him once. He didn't have much to say. He did seem like a pretty decent fellow. I guess he was pretty troubled, though. It's really too bad."

In an hour, several miles away, the funeral will begin. In a minute, the dog will wander over to one of the tires of the car that belonged to Eric Washington and urinate on it.

———

Last Monday, acting on a tip given to the FBI, David Ventimiglia, a detective for the St. Louis County Police Department, and an FBI agent got out of a car and looked up at the apartment window on Mollerus Drive in north St. Louis. The tipster said Eric Washington was responsible for two area bank robberies that took place in the last six months.

It was a few minutes after 4 in the afternoon. Ventimiglia saw the curtain open. A man peered out.

"There he is," Ventimiglia remembers saying. "That's Eric Washington. He's there."

It was the last time anyone saw Washington alive.

Vaughn heard the bullhorn outside his door.

"Washington, are you there? This is the police," bellowed Ventimiglia.

Seconds later, there was the muffled crack of a gunshot.

Everyone backed away. A call was made to the Tactical Operations Unit. Reinforcements arrived. Twenty officers. Sharpshooters moved into position. The apartment building was evacuated.

Vaughn remembers the moans behind the door at apartment 308.

"For about three minutes, you could hear him, groaning and moaning," Vaughn says. "Then it stopped."

For two hours, police stood vigil. Phone calls to Washington's apartment went unanswered. The bullhorn got no response. Finally, the door was knocked down and police discovered the body of Eric Washington.

A Smith & Wesson 9 mm pistol was nearby.

In the bathroom, in a sink, was several thousand dollars in cash. The money had red dye on it—the result of an explosive device that went off in the bank satchel when it was taken from the Brown Campus Banking Center, a branch of the Lewis and Clark Mercantile Bank, on May 4.

Washington apparently was trying to wash the dye off when police approached. He was a month behind in rent.

In the apartment, police also found a brown plaid suit that looks like the same kind worn by the man in the bank photo of the robbery.

There was a framed picture on a table of Eric Washington in his St. Louis Cardinals uniform. Also a picture of his ex-wife Janice, from whom he was divorced on Dec. 7, and his 9-year-old son, Eric Jr.

"We had no warrant," a police spokesman said. "We only wanted to bring him in for questioning."

———

"Say this about Eric Washington," says Ernie McMillan, a former Cardinals teammate. "He never stopped trying until right at the end. A lot of people would have given up lots earlier in life."

Kermit and Eric Washington never knew the stability of family life. Their childhood was difficult, disturbed by domestic cancers. Their parents divorced early. But not before many ugly scenes that included violence among family members.

In his book, *The Breaks of the Game*, David Halberstam wrote that Kermit and brother Eric, one year Kermit's elder, formed a bond of togetherness between themselves and put an island of distance between them and the rest of the ugliness.

"It was as if the two of them were connected to each other, against the rest of the world," Halberstam wrote.

But there still was a matter of logistics, where to stay and with whom.

The two boys were passed around like a marijuana cigarette. Uncles, aunts, grandparents.

A great grandmother provided the closest thing to a home with love in it. But she was illiterate and there was no emphasis on education.

Halberstam wrote that the two boys used to bring home report cards with failing or poor grades and tell their surrogate parent they had done well. She would make an X on the report card, and life, as it was, went on.

Growing up in the bowels of a Washington D.C. ghetto also presented its challenges. Each brother, however, was able to protect his innocence while expanding his awareness at the same time.

The message was simple: Being poor and black and warned that things would never get any better, you had to be aggressive.

Kermit Washington became a menacing basketball player for Coolidge High. Not a skilled player – but a mean one. And a very introverted, shy man.

Eric Washington played football for McKinley High. He didn't go out for sports until his senior year. Like Kermit, he was skinny and unpolished. But he had that inborn aggression. And was a punishing tackler from his defensive back position.

He also was shy and quiet.

Upon graduation in 1968, Eric Washington went to El Paso, Texas. And walked onto the football team of the University of Texas-El Paso.

He earned a scholarship his second year.

In 1971, Washington was picked by the St. Louis Cardinals in the 10th round.

The Cardinals already were loaded with good defensive backs – Larry Wilson, Roger Werlhi, Norm Thompson – but coach Don Coryell liked Washington's toughness.

"He didn't have a great deal of ability," says Coryell, now the coach of the San Diego Chargers. "But he worked his butt off and made the team. I personally liked him. He was tough. But he was also a loner."

Dan Dierdorf, a Cardinal folk hero, was on the team at the time.

"But the only thing I remember about him was his number – No. 40," Dierdorf says.

Mel Gray, a pass receiver on the Cards in 1971, remembers Washington all too well.

"He knocked my helmet off once and busted my lip," Gray said. "I told him 'nice play' and he just looked at me. He could have been a good ballplayer if he'd put his mind to it. But he was a character and a little bit wild and definitely a loner. He didn't want to be associated with the rest of the ballplayers. But he had that good size (6-feet-3, 190 pounds) and he was mean and I really thought he'd become another Mel Blount."

Two factors stopped Washington's ascent to greatness. First was a knee injury, sustained in the sixth game of his initial season, that never healed properly. Second was league legislation on pass defense. No more bump and run and mug and forearm shiver.

Washington's strong suit — his ability to knock receivers out of their routes — now was illegal.

He played nine more games before Coryell cut him. His 15-game total reads: No interceptions, no fumble recoveries and no touchdowns.

Athletes usually make three adjustments in their life. From high school to college. From college to pro. From pro to real life.

Washington had tryouts with the New York Jets and Minnesota Vikings and didn't make it either time.

But at least he had his family. He'd married the former Janice Orr in 1972. They bought a house in the suburbs, a nice racially mixed neighborhood, middle class, with frame and brick homes and lawns that are kept up.

In 1975, he went to work for the St. Louis chapter of the National Alliance of Businessmen. He worked with underprivileged youngsters, helped them find summer jobs and coaxed them into becoming full-time members of the labor force.

A year later, he quit and went to work for a carburetor company.

Two years later, he quit. And decided to go back to college.

At UTEP, he had majored in physical education but never graduated. He wanted to study something else, something more challenging.

Coryell, who once coached at San Diego State, pulled some strings and got Washington enrolled.

Washington's brother was living in El Cajon. It would be good for everyone, he figured.

Chasing a major in computer engineering, Eric Washington spent three years at San Diego State. But things weren't getting any better. Worse, his family life was starting to crumble. Eric tried to keep the family together "because he remembered what his own bad childhood was like," Kermit said. "He didn't want his son to go through the same thing."

Kermit Washington paid for his brother's tuition, rented a furnished home for him and provided a car.

In September of 1983, still without a college degree, Eric Washington returned to St. Louis. It was the last time he would see his brother. He took a job selling life insurance — the man who always had trouble expressing himself was tackling one of the professions that demands effective communication and supreme self-esteem.

Washington wasn't a good life insurance salesman.

On Dec. 7, Pearl Harbor Day, a divorce was granted Janice Orr Washington. Terms of child support were not made since Eric Washington was unemployed.

Five days later, someone resembling Eric Washington robbed the Spanish Lake Banking Center on Larimore Road.

Eric Washington had finally conceded.

The decline was tragic and swift and last Monday afternoon, all alone in the world, he killed himself. He finally was a success at something.

———

The Washington Park Cemetery does not have contracts for perpetual care. All the recent rain has given the place an unkempt, ragged, broken-down appearance.

The cemetery was opened in the '20s, before the nearby international airport was built. Before Interstate 70 sliced through the middle of the cemetery.

Weeds and dandelions are everywhere. So are headstones and markers. This is the least expensive place in St. Louis to bury someone.

This is where Eric Washington will be laid to rest.

Ted Foster and Sons Funeral Home is handling the arrangements. But someone forgot to order a vault. The ceremony is almost two hours late in starting.

Jenny Younger is unaware the ash on her cigarette is long and about to fall onto her paperwork. She's more concerned about finding a Band-Aid for the paper cut she just got.

She is the person in charge of Washington Park.

"Yes, I put the show on," she says, frowning when the ash finally plops as she licks the cut on her finger.

She looks at Washington's 3x5 card and says, "I had a little trouble with this one. We're so crowded. I actually had to create a

79

spot for Mr. Washington. It's a little closer to the edge of the road than we'd like. But it's all we have available."

Melvin Maynard dug the grave, and he too is aware that the site is only inches away from the dusty, unpaved road that serves as the entrance.

"I wouldn't want my loved one to be so close," Maynard said. "Look there — see them tractor tire tracks. When all the dirt's put back, that will be right where the edge of the man's casket will be placed."

Ted Foster shows up and immediately shoos away some wire service photographers.

"This is a private ceremony," declares Foster, who wears diamond rings on both pinky fingers and a monogrammed stick pin with more diamonds in his tie.

"Family only. This is their request, and we must honor it," Foster says.

There has been no headstone ordered.

The procession of limousines arrives. Eric Washington's father and mother have shown up. But they don't sit together.

Kermit is not there. And nobody can understand why. And if they do, they aren't talking about it. He didn't attend because he doesn't get along with some of his brother's relatives. But from a distance, Kermit poured out some of the emotion that has built ever since he heard the news.

"They buried the body of my brother and no one knows the real story. To be honest with you, my brother's problems as a human being started with life."

Janice Washington and her son sit in the front row of chairs in the open-air tent set up near the grave.

Her brother, Greg, walks to the front where the casket is set, a bouquet of red carnations atop it. There are 19 people watching. None are former Cardinal teammates.

Greg Orr pulls out two pages of typed material. It is a kind of biography of Eric Washington. After he reads it, he recites an eight-line verse of poetry.

Then he is done and everyone stands up.

Nobody has shed a tear.

The entire ceremony takes four minutes.

Orr intercepts a reporter as he is about to ask Janice Washington a question.

"We have nothing to say. Too much has already been said," Orr says angrily.

Everyone gets back into their car and the procession begins to leave. Dust flies. The whine of a jetliner taking off drones out all other noise.

"Know what I think?" asks Melvin Maynard, watching everyone leave. "I think what happened to that man was not a case of a good man turning bad. I think it was a bad man who tried to turn good and couldn't. He just gave up on himself. I also think everyone else in the world had already given up on him."

Maynard got up and headed for his tractor. "But I didn't know the man, so who's to say what happened."

The storied past of Honest John Smith
Aug. 18, 1985
Today, Cocoa Beach, Fla.

"Sir, my first name is Honest . . ."

That piece of etiquette taken care of, the old man begins telling his story.

He tells of Prohibition and running bootleg rum aboard sailboats into Sebastian Inlet, which he helped dig. Of Al Capone and the U.S. government stalking him at the same time. The obvious danger was but a spice, a condiment, for all the fun.

Lord, yes the fun. Money had little to do with it, although a case of fine whiskey could be had for $18 a case in the Bahamas and sold for $125 not too far away from the inlet.

The old man also casts off in different directions. He confesses to a sense of smallness that ominous afternoon 50 years ago, a few miles off the coast of Fort Pierce, when he realized he had a 3,000 pound Great White Shark on his fishing line.

"We had to tow it; our 26-foot boat was too small. I used a 7-foot shark for bait, about 5 miles of chain. Yes sir, that was a big fish," he says, the pride oozing like sweat from his enormous body.

They come like waves — the stories of Florida, once upon a time; stories of a man who drank of life's rich experiences and living-color adventures like it was his father's peach brandy. Stories that are never the same, always pounding, and ebbing, washing clean and muddying, ravaging the senses of anyone listening.

There is an even, muted joy in his words, a bridled enthusiasm. He is more than a historian; he is an eye witness. And he always has a salty earful to share.

But then, Honest John Smith always did know how to set a hook.

In patchquilt style, he stitches together a life commandeered by an irascible soul, a pirate, a cowboy, the free spirit who survived the rocks and sandbars and timeshares. Time has whittled his body and he is too old and feeble and fat to do much of anything but reminisce.

As the singer reminds us, some of it was magic, some of it was tragic, but he had a good life all the way.

Amen.

He recalls the last appearance of Halley's Comet, which makes the scene every 76 years. He describes oysters more than a foot long, the likes of which will never be seen again. He talks matter-of-factly about the whorehouse in the same building where he attended school, all the way through eighth grade.

Then the snake interrupts him.

It slides over calloused, gristled feet that have not worn shoes since his wife's funeral several years ago.

Neither the old man nor the snake pay any attention to the other.

"Just a rat snake," says Honest John.

"It gets the rats."

He shrugs and resumes his tale, yet another sliver of adventure, a random selection from a most remarkable, eccentric life.

Just as the old man describes the eyes of the sea bat that was 27 feet in width, the snake makes another pass.

To the outsider, it seems a stressful cohabitation. The concept of man as just another tenant seems foreign. What about all the snakes, rats, mosquitoes, all the other vermin and pests and critters that infest the fortress paradise that has been home to Honest John Smith for all his 80 years? Wouldn't he like to get rid of them?

There is a rumble and then a shudder from the old man, a silent laugh that manifests only in the form of a tremendous jiggle of flesh gone soft. A 300-pound harumph.

"Sir, I am not the one to ask about evictions. It don't matter if I like them or not. They homesteaded here; they was here first. They have a right to be here."

He is surrounded by yesterday, angry about tomorrow. Honest John Smith faces the twilight, stares it down with his one good eye. The trade winds rustle through the tall pines and off in the distance he can hear the screech of birds sensing imminent danger.

Across the creek, the squawk of a crane cuts through the serenity. Unless you're listening closely, it sounds like that bird is belching, "Aquarina, Aquarina, Aquarina."

But that's impossible.

John Smith ignores the encroachment. The world can go to hell without him. He is out from underneath it. He never quit fighting. He continues to refuse acknowledgement of progress as a necessary evil. He labored to prevent the rape of nature, to save the oysters and the dune lines and the snook. Those newfangled clam rakes. Mosquito sprays that act like chemotherapy — killing the good cells as well as the bad ones. The causeways that block the flow of water and change the salinity and bring about the salt-water intrusion. All have eaten away at the delicate balance. He is outnumbered. But mainly he is 80 years old.

Yeah, Honest John Smith held his own until he got too old to give a damn.

It is time to be content with watching the kingfisher dive for food on Mullet Creek. To know he is aiding and abetting the fragile perpetuation of a dwindling species. There are memories sweeter than his oysters. But they no longer perpetuate. Once in a while, he sees hints of life in the woods as it should be. But mostly he hears the rumble of the 20th Century, trampling around his sanctuary on the north bank of Mullet Creek near Floridana Beach.

Old Florida is vanishing. John Smith understands.

He is part of the disappearing act.

"I listen to people talk about religion. But there are so many wars with religion being the cause. I really believe it's going to be the windup of the world. We're going to blow ourselves up trying to impress this God or that God.

"My religion is knowing right from wrong. It's watching a fishhawk learn its babies how to catch something to eat. Ain't no way it can do it. But it does. That's God. He's all around here, if people will leave him alone."

For several seconds the only sounds are those of chattering squirrels. Then Honest John Smith says, "The last time that comet showed up, these people up the road who owned a hotel, burned it to collect the insurance and tried to blame it on the comet. They said it had a tail of fire that dragged so low that it caught their place on fire."

And there is another shiver of silent laughter.

And he doesn't say it, but you know John Smith wishes there would be another fire or two. And not for insurance purposes, either.

John Smith was born in the same bedroom he sleeps in today. He has never owned a television set. He once killed a black bear as it interrupted a family picnic on the beach. Hiding behind the sea oats. One bullet from a World War I Colt .45. Right between the eyes.

That's the bear's skull hanging on the wall.

The pistol? It's under the pillow on Honest John's bed.

The fish camp is run by his daughter and her husband now. The rolling tranquility of the place overwhelms at times. The man in the house doesn't get around much. But you feel his presence nonetheless.

"I got the solaroid poisoning," Honest John says.

Skin cancer. It has desecrated him.

"I don't get out in the sun anymore. My grip is bad; I can't throw a cast net no more. And ever since I had my eye put out (the result of a fall on a nail). Can't shoot with my left eye and I ain't got no right one. No more fishing or hunting; I can't hardly stand that," he says.

John Smith Jr. lives in Palm Beach now. Honest John's son,

however, will never forget a special childhood that took place in the raw wilderness. He remembers the mosquitoes.

"Dad got to where the mosquitoes didn't bother him. I used to walk up behind him and he wouldn't have a shirt on, and his back would be almost black with mosquitoes. I'd slap at them and there would be this big smear of blood all over his back. I'd ask him, "Didn't you feel them?' And he'd just shake his head.

"My dad is an amazing man."

Honest John's sense of fun, his love of shocking people, have made for some frolicking, ribald times. Never any malice. Always looking for a grin.

The old Melbourne Beach Casino is gone now. The legend of Honest John endures. . .

He walked into the bar. It was Happy Hour. Honest John raised both hands and declared, "When Honest John drinks, everyone drinks."

And the cheers bounced off the walls of the crowded room as everyone stormed the counter and started screaming orders at the bartender.

When everyone had been served at last and there was a lull, Honest John flipped a quarter on the bar and announced, "And when Honest John pays. . . everyone pays."

The story touches a nerve.

"I wasn't the most popular guy in town after that," he snickers. "I never was."

His 300-acre plantation was homesteaded by his father, Robert Tooms Smith, a farmer who fled Georgia after the Civil War.

His father showed up in Brevard County with $35 in his pocket. For a while, he worked the pineapple plantations of Melbourne. He gained the land after a long battle with another man claiming ownership.

"The deed, if I'm not mistaken, is signed by Teddy Roosevelt," Honest John explains.

"I have a lot of memories of my childhood. Like Old Man Jefferson chasing us through his banana patch. Or trading eight pounds of cabbage with Old Wag, the barber, for a haircut."

Once, when the mischief overcame his good judgment, he put a horse saddle on an untamed but captured porpoise and tried to ride it.

"About broke my damn neck."

He talks of deals and scams and treasure maps that never led anywhere.

The buddies and partners and enemies from the past have mainly passed on. Red Arnold, the retired Seabee with the terrific sense of humor, the caretaker named Mobley who once rode in the Ashley Gang. Momma Koo-Koo. Pinder, the conch from the keys, who was the best man with a harpoon who ever lived. . .

"Most of 'em's dead now," John says.

He leans back in his chair, banging against the wall of his front porch. Thousands of telephone numbers are scribbled on the wall. A huge seahorse is impaled with a single nail near an antique saw. Pieces of a man's life—not exactly displayed, not exactly treasure or trash.

Out on the spoil island, the wreckage of the World War II trainer plane halts the melody of nature and beauty. The Navy wasn't real proud of the fact a daring low-altitude, slow-moving landing technique ended up in disaster on civilian property. Particularly Honest John Smith's land.

"I believe the boy flying the plane bailed out," he says.

They talk about the trout in Mullet Creek. Monsters. They say Honest John has killed a dozen men. Murderer. The stories sometimes are devoid of wholesomeness. And filled with exaggeration.

There are some trophy trout out and about. Honest John is a masterful marksman. One has nothing to do with the other.

"I have never shot at another man. I would, though. If it was in self-defense."

And he tells of the time the motorcycle gang roared onto his property and surprised him as he slept. Give us your money, they demanded, standing over his bed.

Go to hell, he said.

They threatened to kill him.

"I told them they probably would. But I'd take at least two of them with me and I pulled out my pistol. They got the hell out of there," he says.

Barbara Arnold is Honest John's daughter. She moved back to his estate six years ago.

"It is so unique out here, so different, so fresh," she says. "I never knew how much I love this place until I moved away."

The baton has been passed.

"I don't approve of everything he has done," Barbara says. "But he has had a full life. He isn't going to change. People should leave him alone. I think that's all he wants right now."

A mullet jumps. Honest John Smith's feet twitch. There is an instinct, a calling to go grab a cast net and turn that showoff mullet into dinner. Just like during World War II, when the Hooligan's Navy—an all-volunteer vigilante patrol—made its rounds, plenty of ammo and beverage on board, in search of German U-boats off the coast of Brevard County. A reflex call to arms.

He is a protector. Last December, on his birthday, his family presented him with a flag and flagpole, to be raised at the end of the pier of his fortress paradise.

A friend played "God Bless America" on the trumpet.

John Smith stood and saluted.

And reached for a beer when everything was done.

The celebration is not in triumph over the enemy. It is in the quest itself.

"My doctor prunes me and scrapes my barnacles and tells me I'm doing all right," he says. "I coulda told him that."

And out on the water, another fish jumps. It is the cue for another story, this one about Pinder, the harpoon specialist.

"He got a sea cow once, which is the best eating you'll ever find. Better than pork. Better than sand crane, better than loggerhead turtle, better than armadillo . . ."

The jiggle overcomes him again. A perfect pull of the leg. The laugh is symmetrical, a ripple that becomes a groundswell that dies from a lack of wind near the shoreline.

A curlew flies by. It looks like a pink flamingo to the visitor. Honest John's knowledge of birds and animals is self-taught, self-experienced.

"I never ate a curlew," he says. "I will say there ain't many things though I never tried. I seen Cuba at its best, caught some big fishes.

There's been some rough riding and some narrow escapes but I always managed to have some fun each day."

The land is valuable, probably worth millions. As the sunset nears, why doesn't he sell it and become a millionaire?

"What in hell would I do with a million dollars that I can't do already?"

He smiles. The gentle side of John Smith is basking in the afternoon. His is a warmth that is eternal and on the endangered species list at the same time.

And it becomes apparent that, at least from one man's viewpoint, what the world needs most is more rat snakes.

Let the children play: Public School League offers Detroit's youth a haven from problems
Nov. 10, 1985

> "The socioeconomical situation is so low, so depressed that's it's not even as good as when I was a kid. At least people still had their dreams back then."
> —Keith Tinsley, Cooley High graduate, now a defensive back for the University of Pittsburgh.

> "These kids are going to live. They might shoot, steal, even kill, unless we teach them first. However, they're already here, and we can't send him or her back to the womb. They're going to live, all right. So why not team them how to play?"
> —Will Robinson, former coach, now the director of community relations for the Detroit Pistons.

Growing up in Detroit City. You live fast. You can die even faster. Or maybe the worst thing that ever happened to you is the extra point that hit the upright or the free throw that rolled off the rim.

The Public School League of Detroit cannot be put to any litmus

88

test. It's too vast, too different, too shifting. The good and the bad constantly butt heads. Kids with major-league arms throw bricks. Others sit the bench, happy to be a member of a team instead of a gang. The escape hatch of interscholastic sports competes with the dark tunnels of temptation. Sometimes you tumble. Sometimes you take a ride. Sometimes you get pushed.

Sometimes, the best thing that ever happened to you is that missed free throw.

The PSL is the gift offered to the youth of urban Detroit. Their participation is the return gift.

It has come to this: The arena may be the safest place to be in the Detroit Public School League. Even then, there are the intrusions
. . .

Roy Allen heard the news on the radio and immediately headed for Murray-Wright High School. He was afraid what he might find.

"A sniper opened fire today on spectators at a Public School League football game at Murray-Wright High School. Details are incomplete . . ." the radio report said.

"It was so vague, but so scary, too," Allen says.

Allen is the Director of Health, Physical Education and Safety for the Detroit public schools. His concern went beyond his profession that afternoon of Oct. 18.

"I ached inside. You hear about kids getting shot, you start hurting. When it's a football game and the kids are just there, in the way of some crazy person, it hurts even more," Allen says.

"When I got there, there were kids running. They all were scared. There were parents showing up, trying to find out if their children had been injured. They were scared, too. It was just total confusion. And all I could do was ask, "Why? Why would someone do this?'"

The game was called off with less than two minutes left in the first half. Murray-Wright, by virtue of its 8–6 lead over Northwestern when the shooting started, was declared the winner. Everybody who could, went home.

Six teen-agers were taken to Receiving Hospital; one had a fractured skull.

"I heard the noise, then I heard this hollering and then I saw this girl who was in one of my classes," says Earl Moore, Murray-Wright's football coach. "She had been shot in the leg. I ran toward her. I never thought whoever it was doing the shooting might not be finished."

Later the next week, a 17-year-old youth who didn't even attend Murray-Wright turned himself in to police. He was released once, after a witness decided she couldn't identify him after all. Then another witness came forth. The investigation continues.

"I'm still asking 'Why?' " Allen says. "People have already jumped to conclusions. Murray-Wright is already being blamed for the incident. But the worst thing is that game was interrupted. The halftime show — it was homecoming — was canceled. It was a tragedy that had nothing to do with sports. Except it ruined a football game."

———

At Redford High School, William Vaughn is the athletic director. Thursdays are usually busy days. Lots of things to do before the game that is played later in the afternoon. But this week, Vaughn has nothing to do. There is no game.

Redford High has no football team. It was disbanded with three weeks left in the season. Thirteen of the 21 players on the varsity were declared ineligible because of bad grades. Dr. Joe Greene, the Redford principal, decided against allowing inexperienced junior-varsity players to fill the vacant ranks. The season was over.

There was a dull thud in the stomachs of the eight student-athletes who were eligible. It quickly turned into anger. The anger that first erupted among the academic casualties faded into embarrassment, then apathy.

All PSL students must maintain a 2.0 grade-point average. The Michigan High School Athletic Association's current requirement works out to less than a 1.0 average. The PSL rule has been in effect for more than three years. It has never manifested itself in such dramatic form.

90

Vaughn's personal disappointment had to hide behind a stoic facade of support.

He says, "We cannot lose our sight. We cannot forget why we go to school. If we continue to use up our athletes and ignore the fact they are being put into the world unprepared, we are as guilty as any dope dealer or thief. The rules are there. They must be followed. It says you must have a 2.0 average. Some of our players did not. We only had 21 players on the team. That's because a lot of good athletes, players who could help us, were ineligible when school began. Their grades were bad dating back to June. I don't think the question is 'Why?' but 'How?' How do these kids get in such sorry academic shape?"

———

Last week, Mumford traveled to Southwestern in the season-closer. Midway through the second quarter, a Mumford player intercepted a pass and raced for a touchdown.

Nobody was there. Zero people on the Mumford side. There is no minimum grade requirement to be a spectator.

The cheerleaders danced with joy after the touchdown. But they danced alone. The security guard assigned to help with crowd control struggled to stay warm. The man taking tickets also had nothing to do.

One Mumford parent did show up for the second half. She got off work and hurried to watch her son play. On the other side of the field, two Southwestern students had wandered in and huddled together. They left at the end of the third quarter.

By virtue of its "home-field advantage," Southwestern won the game 27–16.

Mumford High is the school Eddie Murphy made famous by wearing one of the school's T-shirts in *Beverly Hills Cop*. There has not been that much to cheer about otherwise lately. Mumford won one game this year. The Mustangs did not score a point until the ninth week of the season. You could make the analogy about what kind of noise the tree makes in the empty forest, but nobody would care.

Apparently, that's the point. It brings up another forlorn question.

"When are we going to have a good team?" asks one of the cheerleaders. "When are we going to have a big crowd to watch us? It's hard to keep getting up. I mean, we're supposed to lead cheers. There isn't anybody to lead. I'm afraid they're gonna say there's no need to have cheerleaders. I don't know when it will happen, but they might say since nobody cares no more, there isn't going to be any football or cheerleaders or things for people to do after school."

She refuses to give her name.

"People might think I don't care," she says. "I do care. But when nobody else does, it's hard; it's real hard."

A teacher at a PSL school—he is not connected with sports except for an occasional assignment supervising one of the games— says the growing apathy is not because of poor performances by the teams. It touches an emotion quite different from disenchantment.

"Kids are scared to show up. So am I, to be honest. I mean, I can't spank them, but they can shoot me? You should see what goes down in high school. It's more like an animal shelter. Hey, you shake down the kids in this town who carry guns and knives to school and you could arm the Marine Corps."

The teacher also asks not to be identified.

"As bad as things are, there are some people who want to pretend things are fine. And I'd probably get in trouble for saying how I feel."

Children are being robbed of their childhood. Not all of them. But when the tentacles of society snake through the chain-linked shelter of sports, it is time to look around and identify the villains. And try to separate them from the victims. Often, they are the same person.

The PSL radiates with pride, vibrates from hard work and overflows with patience. It also shivers from an overdose of the real world. The circle of achievers seems to be shrinking. But it's an optical illusion. The outsiders simply are ganging up. The numbers in the city league aren't down. The distractions are merely up.

There are no white flags of surrender. The PSL continues despite the obstacles. Uphill, against the wind, with society's blisters and canker sores always reminding it where it is.

But not where it has to stay.

"That's the big thing," says Vaughn. "Sports can be such a good outlet, an escape tunnel from whatever hardships and temptations are out there. Me — it's my life. It can be hard to take. It can get you down to the point where you want to quit. But those kids who care — they deserve my best effort. It's not the easiest job. But it has its rewards.

Vaughn is interrupted by an urgent request for first-aid bandages. There was a fight between classes and . . .

"It also has plenty of that other stuff," Vaughn says.

"The kids are not bad by nature though," he adds. "I am informed of all incidents. None have been that severe. If you're thinking the kids are all selling dope during their lunch break, you got it wrong. If you think those kids that messed up their grades and got dropped from the team are a bunch of dummies, you're wrong there, too.

"And if you think the PSL is the worst city league, you're still wrong. Look at Chicago or some other big city. That's just how it is. Believe me when I tell you. We don't have a problem with our kids. Especially the athletes. There is an outside element. But you can control it. Things aren't that bad yet."

Vaughn paused then adds once more, "And nobody should be blaming sports for anything. Sports doesn't make those kids ineligible to play football. They did it themselves. Believe me when I tell you, for some of the kids, sports is the only thing that's going to save them. It's the only thing they have going."

If it means metal detectors and games that start when everyone's parents are still at work, and fields that have been used so much the grass is a memory, so be it. If it means uniforms that probably used to be new, and coaches' pay supplements that are a joke but maybe you can break even anyway and an administration that's as overworked and underpaid and understaffed and torn up by all the festering ugliness as anyone else, so be it. The PSL endures.

It is in its 85th year. Some of the facilities seem even older. The spirit however remains in prime condition.

Yvonne Johnson is the Supervisor of Athletics for the PSL. She's a former cheerleader, a former physical education teacher. A sports fan. A believer in teen-agers.

"You need the community. You need the parents, the adults," she says. "But if you don't have that, you go on anyway. It starts right here."

She tapped her heart.

"You do the best you can. Then you cross your fingers and your toes and hope the moon isn't full."

There are 22 schools in the PSL. Approximately 51,000 students, of whom 91.3 percent are black. No conclusions can be drawn about strengths or weaknesses in relation to the PSL's racial makeup. Forty years ago, when the black-white ratio was flip-flopped — approximately 80 percent of the student body was white — problems existed. They were overcome the same way.

"It is extremely tough now for a teen-ager to survive," says Will Robinson, who coached 27 years in the PSL. "Peer pressure is so great. There are so many distractions. But do you know what? I believe most of the same problems were around in 1945 and 1955 and 1965 and 1975. There's always going to be peer pressure. Oh, maybe it was smoking cigarettes in the bathroom that got a kid tossed off the team back then and today, it might be cocaine. But that all comes under the heading of discipline. And that's the adult responsibility.

"All of my players didn't turn out to be outstanding citizens. I let a lot of them down; I couldn't reach them and I shared in their failure. But man — you say a football team started the season with only 25 players? When I was the football coach at Pershing, we'd have to cut that many. We'd keep 50. That's the one thing I don't understand — why in Jesus' name would somebody not want to go out for the team?"

Each school in the PSL has 16 varsity and three junior-varsity sports. That is guaranteed by the Detroit School Board. A budget of approximately $10 million yearly is allocated. The time sometimes arrives when making an away trip is like the old wish sandwich (two pieces of bread and I wish we had some bologna). But, somehow things keep getting done, the games keep getting played.

94

It also doesn't take long to call roll in the front office. The administrative staff consists of Roy Allen and Yvonne Johnson.

"We're it," Allen says with a laugh.

"But hey—there are a lot of coaches working under burdens. They could use extra assistants. Some of them are lining the field themselves. It's a matter of you do it, or it doesn't get done."

For a league that has no feeder systems—there are no interscholastic sports in any Detroit middle schools or junior highs—the talent is amazing. And the oddest things keep happening. Someone who plays under all those miserable conditions, enduring all the hardships and glass-littered practice fields and bent rims and balls that are nearly round, goes on to get an education and a teaching job and a coaching position. And comes back to the Public School League. A perpetuation probably born in the heart instead of the brain.

Major-college scouts insist the well is deep and rich. The PSL remains a regular stop on scouting missions for several colleges. If you hear complaints about a lack of facilities or a lack of new uniforms, it generally does not come from within. Unless you ask.

Equipment doesn't have to be new. It only needs to be like everyone else's. It also needs to be safe.

Despite the appearances of patch-quilt facilities held together with Band-Aids, chewing gum, baling wire and faith, despite the empty seats and coaches who look at their watches too often and booster clubs that don't exist, the opening kickoff comes off every year anyway.

The athletes, the most valuable resource in the PSL, never get any older.

You are where you live. When your neighbors don't come out to cast votes for their choice of mayors, you cannot be surprised when his children choose to ignore the call to athletic glory. Some coaches coax students out of their apathy by making promises of scholarships and riches to those who do come out for the team.

"I have a real hangup with that kind of stuff," Allen says. "Making promises that might not be kept, saying things you have no control over. I have a real problem with that kind of coaching philosophy. What's wrong with 'Let's just play? Today. Have a good time, go home and come back tomorrow.' Just let the children play. Let right now be the only thing they think about. The future's going to arrive soon enough."

At most of the PSL schools, the football equipment has been stored. It, too, survived the pounding and attrition of the season. Girls' basketball is in full-court flourish. The boys' teams anxiously await the start of practice. The minor sports sometimes enjoy the blessing of relative anonymity. Other times, those teams feel ignored.

In the span of a month, a freshman from Cody High was shot in the head and died. Another child is charged with the crime. Kids in middle schools are smoking marijuana. A sophomore girl gets an abortion. Specifics and generalizations bring our attention to a level of nausea — more than you'd ever want to know about growing up in the city.

But the kittens that don't get caught up in the trees? The reserve lineman who doesn't score any touchdowns but had a 2.5 on his report card? The girl who worked on her jump shot at the park all summer and made the varsity? These are not sensational stories of numbing tragedy or unbridled glory. They are the ballast that keeps the world from floating into an orbit of chaos.

These reachable goals that lay the roadwork for solid citizenry appear mundane from a distance. Getting someone to notice those goals is like trying to get your dog to look at something on television. Tell them, order them, beg them, twist their heads in the general direction and . . . nothing.

But such tiny triumphs are like tiny seedlings. After awhile you never notice them because there are too many huge trees standing in the way. Too many prominent protruding pillars clogging up labor markets, raising families, making it within the system.

Their sons and daughters will want to play games.

The Public School League will blow up the ball and line the field. And let the children play. The dreams are still there. Just look under the umbrellas and shields.

Will Robinson is more than a coach
Nov. 10, 1985

"Hey Coach, Coach Robinson," shouted the man in the restaurant.

The smile was immediate, and the gentle warmth of two old friends running into each other radiated across the crowded room.

"Ernest Laster, how are you doing," says Will Robinson, "Coach" to thousands of youths who wandered near his proud legacy as the first black to coach high school football and basketball in the state of Michigan.

"Coach, I'm a lawyer now."

"I heard, I heard."

"Coach, you look great. You're never going to get old."

"You make me feel old. What was it? 1946? You were one of my guards on the football team at Miller High, right? The same team with Sammy Gee, right? Sammy Gee, first high school All-American in the state of Michigan. You were on the same team, isn't that right, Ernest?"

There were more smiles. Just a moment of nostalgic backpedaling and then goodbye.

Will Robinson, who twirled his coaching whistle against the backside of three decades of Detroit high school athletes, was asked about the long parade of achievers he marched toward the starting line.

"It is the greatest reward," he says, his eyes accentuating his pride. "Dr. Melvin Chapman is the No. 2 man in the entire Detroit school system. He played on my first basketball team at Miller High. Noah Brown. Big Daddy, Lord yes, Big Daddy Lipscomb. All those great athletes. I used to spend 10 minutes a day just talking to my players about how they have to be in it or get out. And then I'd tell them how to be in it. My goodness, there are some stories to tell.

"But, I can't take a lot of credit. Not really. I once went up to the Jackson State Prison, and I heard someone calling, 'Coach, Coach.' Their arms were dangling out of the bars in the doors, waving at me. Some of my players who somehow lost the way. It is a reminder for me. I couldn't reach all of them. All coaches know you can't win them all."

There are several seconds of silence as he walks on a sidewalk, ignoring the drizzle of rain.

Then the smile returns, and Coach Will Robinson says with a voice softer than a prayer, "Ernest Laster, I can't get over that. He's a lawyer now. How about that?"

Another splash of silence. Maybe Robinson is cataloguing this latest success story with the others. Filing away Ernest Laster with all the police officers and Ph.D.'s, the millionaires, the educators and other achievers in his giant flock. Perhaps a silent roll call is being taken. A Who's Who of the timid children who leaped into manhood by simply playing games with style and discipline and soul. Will Robinson did more than build winning teams. He drew up the blueprints for the game after the games.

"The money has nothing to do with coaching," Robinson says finally. "Be a banker, become a financier if you care so much about the money. If you want to be a coach, your money is love and respect. The memories become even more valuable as the years go by. And you know, the years have gone by for me and, yessir, I'm a rich man."

The Detroit Public School League existed a long time before Will Robinson moved to town. It seems, however, he gave it credibility.

In the summer of 1943, insanity filtered into the city. A riot, involving white teen-agers and black teen-agers and plenty of policemen, started on Belle Isle.

Will Robinson was teaching and coaching in Chicago at the time.

"A good job at a good school, a new school. Then I got one of these offers I couldn't refuse. The Detroit superintendent of schools appealed during this national convention for a teacher and coach who could bridge the gaps and help cool things down again. I was offered the job, and I didn't want it. But they gave me no choice."

His boss back in Chicago warned him if he turned down the Detroit offer, his Chicago job would cease to exist as well.

"So I moved to Detroit. It's the greatest thing that ever happened to me."

In the 13 years Robinson coached at Miller, his basketball teams played for the city championship 10 times.

"One game will always stick out. In 1947, the Public School League played the Catholic League in a special, special game. We played that game in Olympia Stadium, and do you know the largest crowd to ever see a basketball game in Michigan showed up? I believe it was more than 16,000 people," he says, his words carefully measured with sufficient reverence.

"We played St. Joseph's and the funny thing about that was St. Joe's was only a block away from Miller and it was the first time the two schools had ever played each other."

Robinson quickly explains how Miller was a predominantly black school, the only one out of 18 schools in the PSL.

"Matter of fact," the old coach adds, with a shake of the head, "of those other 17 schools, there was only one black player. His name was Ron Teasley. Things were very different in those days."

For instance, the team from Northern actually had two squads.

"A white one and a black one," Robinson says. "The black team practiced against the white team, and although that black squad was better, they never got to even dress out for the games."

His football teams practiced on Belle Isle, 10 miles away. The basketball team had to go to Brewster Center—where Joe Louis, the heavyweight champion, worked out. Miller had neither a football field nor a gym of regulation size.

"I used to borrow this old flatbed truck to drive my team to practice," Robinson says. "The money for gas came out of my own pocket."

What about a supplement?

"Supplement? There were none. If you coached, your pay or reward was you got out of one of your classes."

Racial tension smothered the area. A black coach with a mostly black team that won most of the time—Robinson's team once rallied from a 5-point deficit with 7 seconds remaining to win a game—brought some ugly problems.

"Tougher than you could imagine. I won't dwell on the mistakes other people made. Black people weren't allowed to get fed up back then. Being black, the name of the game, every game, all games, was survive. I'm a survivor."

For an instant, it seems a distant and long-disconnected alarm is about to go off. But, as always, the composure of the old coach remains.

"What happened, some of the bad things, are not important. What I will remember most about Miller High School are the 100 young men I placed in college on athletic scholarship."

It is no coincidence the two Project Pass scholarships the Pistons give each year are named after Will Robinson.

Miller closed its doors in 1957 and became a junior high school. Robinson headed for Cass Tech. Three years later, accompanied by similar success, he went to Pershing High.

"I stayed at Pershing 10 years, then took the head coach job at Illinois State University," Robinson says. "But my dream of being a coach at a university in the state of Michigan was never fulfilled. I came close. I steered Spencer Haywood, maybe the greatest of my players, to the University of Detroit. The understanding was that I would join him as the coach. It never happened."

Will Robinson is a survivor.

Now, he's community relations director for the Pistons. He also does some scouting for them.

"I haven't been to 10 PSL games in 10 years," says Robinson, who refuses to give his age. "I hear things are similar, yet different."

The recent rash of violence involving teen-agers from Detroit is . . . alarming, he says. But not unprecedented.

"For the longest time, the PSL didn't participate in the state basketball tournament. Then, sometime in the '50s — I don't do too well with dates or names — there was a stabbing after a game. Two teams on the West Side, I believe. I think that's when the PSL started playing its games in the afternoon. It's unfortunate. Drugs are into the picture now just when it seems bigotry is easing up a little. It's never going to be easy. These are the times where we must worry from within. Greece was destroyed from within. By immorality, Rome went the same way. France under Napoleon. All this nonsense with the drugs, the kids with guns, the robbing and raping — it tells me where the world has gone."

He chews on his words, making sure he wants to share them. Then he relents and adds, "Kids need a coach. In 1946, my teams pressed full court and people were saying I was going to kill them. Young boys can't go at that pace a full game. Now, I see girls' teams working full court presses. And I hear people talking about how dangerous that is. It's progress. Progress and good coaching."

His inventory is almost complete. The two state championships. All those faces, the victories, the games that still are talked about. This backward gaze by a man who has never stopped caring screeches to a stop as today's athlete is mentioned.

"People tell me I got out of coaching at the right time. But there's a saying in the Catholic Church, I believe, that says 'Give me a child for the first six years and you can have him the rest of his life and he will be all right.' Discipline, practice, humility, respect. These are not new words. The more things change, the more they stay the same. All you need is a teacher, a coach who will help you along the way."

The parking meter where he parked his car had expired. Will Robinson had to go. It wasn't the money or even the fine that bothered him.

"I just don't like to break the law," he says, walking faster, plunging his hand into his trouser pocket. Of course, he had the right change.

Inside the PSL: Trying to make the grade, Star at king benched by grades
Nov. 12, 1985

It isn't that Jackie Jones doesn't care about school.

He doesn't know how to care.

Nobody ever taught him.

Jones is a senior at Martin Luther King High School. He is almost 6 feet, 6 inches tall. He is considered one of the best high school basketball players in Michigan, despite having played less than two years at the interscholastic level.

He also is ineligible to play.

For the second year in a row, Jones' low grades have knocked him out of King's starting lineup. The earliest he could play would be January, if his grades improve.

It would be easy to dismiss Jackie Jones as another statistic. Write him off, toss him in the discard pile and wipe our hands of anyone who refuses to fit in.

But that would be even more tragic.

Jackie Jones is swamped by life. Listen to the silent screams for help:

"I don't like school."

"I don't have any friends."

"I don't like asking nobody for help."

"I don't like to talk."

"I never have dreams, even when I'm asleep."

Eighteen-year-old Jackie Jones hides behind a grim mask of apathy, afraid someone might find out who's really inside.

The body English is a lean, sinewy warning flare as Jones stands in his coach's office. The arms hang, the shoulders droop. Jones avoids eye contact at all times. He looks more like a criminal at his arraignment than a basketball star getting interviewed for his hometown newspaper.

Al Ward, the King coach, says most of the academic problems have been solved.

"I see him going to class, and that's a good note," Ward says. "I think Jackie realizes it's all on him. We'll monitor things a little. But the reality is that Jackie's got to get right academically. It's that last go-round."

Jones stares straight ahead as his coach talks about him.

"I'll have my grades," he says finally.

"Most likely, I'll be ready in January."

Last season, the mailman was a constant messenger, as a steady diet of questionnaires and recruiting letters arrived. Once he was allowed to play, Jones was terrific, averaging 17 points and 13 rebounds and bringing the ball up against the press. The letters came from all over.

"There haven't been too many this year," Jones adds, almost in a whisper.

He knows why.

"If you can't pass, you can't play. Same as here."

Jones tucks in his T-shirt. The large brass belt buckle with the letters "CHELL" chiseled out is revealed. Jones notices the sportswriter looking at it. He quickly pulls out his shirttail.

After some probing, he admits, "a friend gave it to me. Her name's Chellfonte."

He shrugs. The background of Jackie Jones is not a study in stability and family togetherness. His parents are separated. Apparently, the break was not a smooth one. It took a painful toll on the only child: Jackie Leroy Jones.

He stands motionless, passive. But there is a trembling of emotion building. His vulnerability is showing, like a child greeting a stranger from behind a partially open door.

He mumbles, "I stay with my auntie. Things are better now. It was bad before."

Then the door slams again. But it swings open just as quickly.

"My cousin, he's 10, he stays there too. He's an only child, just like me. I like to help him with his homework. Fact is, I probably care more about him than I do my own self."

He balls his hands into fists. It's all just beneath the surface, bubbling and boiling and about to gush forth.

"Jimmy—that's his name—makes me mad sometimes. He's starting off his life like I did. Only he's starting earlier. I think maybe if I spend time with him, he won't feel lonely."

And is Jackie Jones lonely?

"All my life."

And then he smiles. A grin of irony. A nervous concession. Jones retreats once more. He says he likes basketball but "I'd rather practice by myself."

"And I'd like to play guard.

"I'd like to go to some school that's far away. Maybe Utah.

"I'm not too close with people because I figure when you need somebody, nobody will be there."

Back to square one. So, back to the belt buckle.

"I mostly wear it all the time," he says.

"She and I take the same history class. We do our lessons together. The belt wasn't for no reason, like my birthday or Christmas. I guess she's more than a friend."

The next question actually caused him to flinch.

Does Jackie Jones ever cry?

"Used to, all the time. When we lost a game, I'd cry. Last year, when Southwestern beat us, I cried. But, not too much any more."

He and his father don't get along. His mother came to see him play a couple of games last season. He says he doesn't spend much time at his aunt's place "unless I'm with Jimmy or in my room.

"I mostly keep the door closed."

That's so painfully obvious.

Somehow, massive doses of guilt have been transferred into the defenseless soul of Jackie Jones. Psychologists probably have all kinds of theories and explanations. Meanwhile, it is the senior year and the basketball star is ineligible.

Around the PSL, opponents make jokes about Jackie Jones. They call him Jackie January. And names much uglier.

"I don't care what anyone says.

"I don't listen.

"They're probably right."

He was looking at his shoes as he talked.

A different kind of courage: Golfer Dorothy Kohl counts her blessings . . . and victories
July 6, 1989

It was the same weekend Curtis Strange was attacking the U.S. Open golf championship. TV broadcasters talked breathlessly about his bold play, his incredible spirit, his great courage as he conquered the adversity around him. This was what made him a champion, the first back-to-back winner of the Open since the great Ben Hogan.

Dorothy Kohl did not watch. She was busy that day, playing her own round at Clearbrook Country Club in the western Michigan town of Saugatuck. At stake was the First Michigan Bank Open, a two-man scramble, an amateur event that did not rate national television coverage or even an extremely large gallery.

You see, Dorothy's a handicap golfer. And in this particular tournament, her handicap was cancer.

The rain hat she wore was doubly valuable. The weather was nasty, wet and cold and uncomfortable. The hat also covered her bald head. Six months of chemotherapy has its own brand of discomfort.

"You don't need hair to play golf," she says. "The thing that I was more worried about was dropping my putter. I had very little feeling in my hands or feet. If you ever stuck your finger in an electric socket, that tingly feeling is what I was feeling almost all the time."

And then she laughs.

"But somehow I saw all 18 holes and I guess that's something of an accomplishment. Considering the circumstances."

Considering she and her partner, Sue Louis, also won the tournament, maybe Curtis Strange is not the only one capable of bold play, incredible spirit and unbelievable courage. Maybe those adjectives fit even better on Dorothy Kohl. Adversity comes in different shapes and sizes, you know. And the courage to overcome second place is not exactly the same as the kind needed to keep death at arm's length. As she has found out.

Ralph Kohl is the head scout for the Minnesota Vikings. In October, when doctors told him they were going to perform exploratory surgery on his wife of 37 years, he cringed. He knew what they were looking for. The discomfort she'd been having was mild. But she said something was wrong. And he believed her.

Three doctors worked more than three hours to remove a five-pound tumor from one of her ovaries.

"That's like carrying a six-month pregnancy around," Ralph says.

Ovarian cancer is a silent stalker. The symptoms usually don't show up until it's too late. When the doctors at the hospital in Florida (where the Kohls keep a winter home) cut into Dottie Kohl, they found a Grade III tumor, which is one step away from what is known as inoperable.

"Things looked pretty grim back then," Ralph Kohl says. "They gave her a 25 percent chance. Maybe."

And the moment is smothering. Cancer has such a well-earned reputation. Its image alone can scare you to death. It has an aura of barbed wire strapped tightly around a chest, cutting and suffocating at the same time. When a doctor quotes you such unfriendly odds as one in four, you tend to dwell on the worst possible scenarios.

"But those doctors didn't know who they were dealing with. My Dorothy . . . well, I've been in athletics all my life. Been a player, a coach, a scout. I look at the greatest athletes in the world. As a scout, I look for the ones with big hearts.

"I've never seen anyone display more courage, fight harder, have better focus for a challenge than Dorothy. She's every bit a woman but . . . she's got the heart of a lion."

Anyone who saw her that chilly day on the golf course knows that already. Golf has always been the outlet for her to let that spirit escape. Cancer, she says, took its place there for a while. But, she adds, "all in all, I think I prefer golf."

And she laughs again.

"Somebody asked me if I was going to write a book on all this. Well, I hope I don't have enough material. Maybe a little article. Maybe something in USA TODAY.

"To tell you the truth, I'm taking the summer off. I worked a lot of overtime this winter. I'm taking the summer off. I'm going to play some golf."

Dorothy Kohl has been playing golf for almost 40 years. Growing up, she discovered the great Babe Didriksen Zaharias, "who was one of the few woman sports role models available at the time," and decided she too wanted to be a pro golfer someday. Every summer her father took the family from the Chicago suburbs to Saugatuck. And she played golf.

Just like Babe?

"No, never that good. By the time I was getting grown and strong and serious about the game, I met this guy named Ralph. You know how that goes."

She remembers the great polio scares of her childhood, before Jonas Salk's precious discovery, when everyone worried about the terrible disease. She once had an aunt who died of cancer of the colon. And she was even aware when Babe Didriksen Zaharias went into a hospital, her body laced with the cancer that eventually killed the sports legend.

"But the thing I remembered was that she brought her clubs to the hospital with her. She said in a newsreel she wanted to keep her putting stroke and she planned to practice in her room. I never gave it a thought that someday I might be a cancer victim, too. When you're young, you never seem to think about sickness. Cancer? I never thought about it."

Nobody does. Dorothy said up to the day she went into the hospital for that exploratory surgery, she was thinking of every affliction in the book except cancer.

"I got my pap smear every year faithfully. But that's the thing about ovarian cancer. It doesn't show up until it's too late. The day I went into the hospital, I got the results of my latest pap smear in the mail. It was negative. And yet there was a five-pound tumor growing inside me."

Golf was out for a while. No big deal, Dorothy shrugged. She never played in the winter anyway. That is the thing about Dottie Kohl. She can always rationalize things to her advantage. She always walks on the sunny side of the street, always sees the middle of the fairway.

Nurses could not believe her soaring, radiating spirit as they wheeled her into the operating room. Dottie Kohl asked each one of them, "Are you filled with love today? I need you to do that for me. I need lots of love around me today."

She asked the anesthetist to smile. She winked at Dr. James Dawsey, one of the surgeons. To Dr. Albert Begas, an oncologist, or cancer specialist, she said, "You don't have a very pleasant job, do you?" And he smiled back, even though she couldn't see it because of his surgical mask. And Dr. Manuel Penalder shook his head in awe as she nodded and gestured to get on with it because "I've got some golf to play back home in Michigan."

In a waiting room were Ralph Kohl and daughter Jackie, sitting on a horrible shard of anxiety. Time, they figured, was on their side. The longer the better. They knew if doctors open a patient and discover the cancer is too far advanced, they simply close and say it was too late.

When three exhausted doctors finally emerged and told two exhausted people the patient was doing as well as could be expected, it was not cause for celebration, simply a chance for hope.

And chemotherapy was on deck.

Six treatments, each about 3 weeks apart. It's all a person can stand. "They take you right to death's doorstep," Ralph explains. "To hell and back. They put this poison in your body, right up to the moment it kills everything inside. It goes after everything, not just the cancer. It kills everything it touches."

Dottie Kohl laughs.

"You do a lot of vomiting," she says. "You don't act very lady-like at all."

After each treatment, there were blood transfusions, maybe a dozen in all. The first treatment is almost bearable. They get pro-gressively worse. The IVs of saline mixed with the chemo doses of Platinol and Cytoxan "are a 24-hour production number. It's tough going after a while. You spend a lot of time in bed."

All the world loves a fighter. The cards and flowers came daily, from all over. They helped, she says. So did a couple of books by a man named Dr. Bernie Siegel, who specializes in positive thinking in times of crisis.

"I was in the shower one day, washing my hair, when I discov-ered these handfuls of soapy curls. And I started crying," she days. "Ralph heard me and came in and he started crying, too. And that's when I got really mad. Cancer had no right to make my husband suffer, too. I had to focus all my energy toward healing. Nothing left for sadness. I called my chemotherapy my 'get-well treatments' and I wouldn't let any of the nurses call them anything else either. Cancer has a pretty strong reputation, but it obviously hadn't met someone like me. I don't like bullies and I just wasn't going to let it pick on me."

Sue Louis, her best friend and golfing partner, was constantly by the bedside. She had a daily postcard with some funny saying that she would trade for one of Dottie's smiles. And every time Dottie

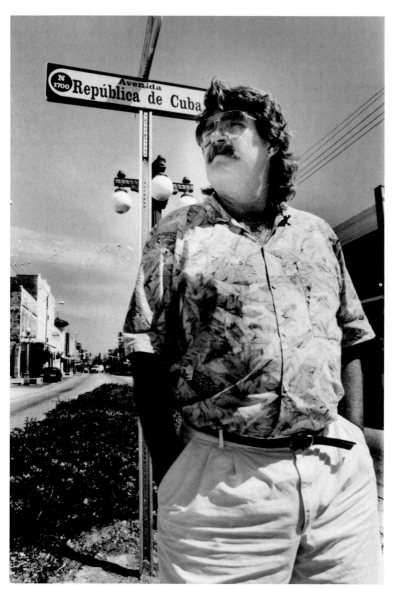

Shelby Strother in Tampa's Cuban enclave of Ybor City, a favorite spot in his native Florida. Photo by Michael S. Green, The Detroit News.

Freedom arrived in a rush for East Germany, but some of the symbols of the past came down more slowly. A soldier guards the Gate the night the Berlin Wall was breached. Photo by Steve Haines, The Detroit News.

Uwe Neumann and his tattoo of irony against the East German system that jailed him for singing a protest song. He once aborted his own prison escape at the sound of a guard's warning shot. "I would be dead if I did not stop." Photo by Steve Haines, The Detroit News.

"The Western side of the Berlin Wall is not so sinister in appearance . . . It is ridicule in the highest form—hand-painted repugnance. It is scribbled freedom and if put to music, it would be jazz." Photo by Steve Haines, The Detroit News.

In Detroit's Public School League, high school games are played before small mid-afternoon crowds. Athletes play for themselves and their futures, not momentary glory. Photo by Michael S. Green, The Detroit News.

Fans pass through metal detector before a championship football game at Martin Luther King Jr. High School. Photo by Michael S. Green. The Detroit News.

Detroit Police patrol PSL games to guard against repeats of past fan violence. Photo by Michael S. Green, The Detroit News.

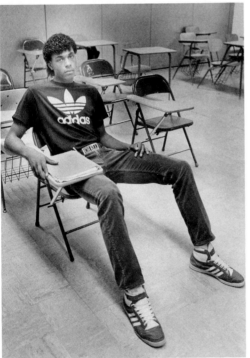

Jackie Jones, one of the nation's top high school basketball players, routinely sat out half the season because of bad grades. Photo by Michael S. Green, The Detroit News.

Will Robinson at the former Miller High School Gym in Detroit. Among the city's winningest high school coaches, Robinson finished his coaching career at Illinois State University. Supporters say his focus was always on helping young athletes, such as Spencer Haywood. Photo by Michael S. Green, The Detroit News.

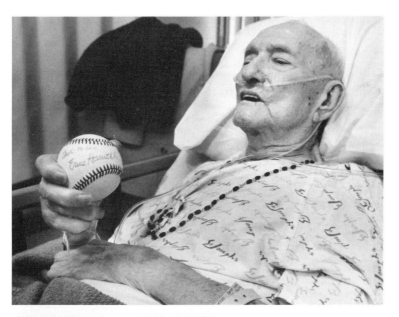

Leo Krass, a life-long Detroit Tigers' fan, with a keepsake from Tigers' Hall of Fame radio announcer Ernie Harwell. Photo by Dale G. Young, The Detroit News.

Cornbread Red, a classic hustler among Detroit's ever-changing pool halls. Photo by Kirthmon Dozier, The Detroit News.

Strother at the Brandenburg Gate, days after the border between East and West Germany was re-opened. Photo by Steve Haines, The Detroit News.

Strother among the mannequins in Ybor City. Photo by Michael S. Green, The Detroit News.

mentioned she couldn't wait to get back on the golf course, Sue Louis smiled and agreed.

"No, I wasn't pretending or hoping that might happen. Dorothy has this way of cheering people up. She's the eternal optimist. I felt her spirit. I believed what she believed."

They already had won the Michigan Bank tournament two years in a row. When the entry form arrived in the mail early this year, Sue brought it on her next visit to Dottie's bedside.

"She said if I'd take a chance and pay the entry fee, we'd give it a shot," Sue remembers.

The doctors told Dorothy something known as Second Look surgery was necessary. No, she said. Please, she begged. They explained it was crucial. They had to see if the cancer had begun growing again.

"It's not necessary; it's gone. I know it's gone. I can feel it. I know."

The doctors insisted. Dorothy Kohl said OK. See for yourself.

Their finding: Dorothy Kohl is cancer-free.

Recovering from her second major surgery in seven months, making plans for the Saugatuck tournament, expecting to get on with her life, she asked Ralph one night to take her to a movie. Something funny. A good comedy. There was this new one starring Richard Pryor and Gene Wilder she'd like to see.

"Cancer victims become experts. You know all about the disease and you know everyone who ever got it. I knew Gene Wilder was married to Gilda Radner and I knew she had the same kind of cancer I did. So during the movie, I told Ralph that Gilda must be doing lots better herself since her husband was able to be away from her long enough to make a movie. And that really cheered me up. And the very next day, there was a story in the paper about Gilda and how she was doing better and everything. And then the very next day after that, I was watching TV when they broke in and said Gilda was dead."

"And I lost it. Just started crying. You'd have thought she was my best friend. And even though I never knew her except from TV and the movies, I loved her. She had great . . . spirit."

The day Dorothy was released from the hospital, she sat in a wheelchair, waiting for paperwork to be processed. And she saw another woman, crying. She was about to get her first chemotherapy treatment.

"And she was afraid she would lose all her hair. I told her, 'Well, you better hope your hair all falls out. That means the cancer is getting killed. Honey, it's all how you look at things.' And that lady hugged me and it was just the most wonderful feeling, seeing her calm down. Just the most wonderful feeling."

Dottie's strength level was down. She had no stamina. And the first time she tried to practice her golf, she couldn't hold onto the club. Remember—it had been almost eight months.

Sue Louis remembers the phone call. We'd better cancel out, Dottie said. Find another partner. I can't even grip the club anymore. Sue said let's try again. Meet you at the course in an hour.

Said Sue, "Well, she started dropping putts on the practice green from all over. She was laughing and you could tell the tiger was back. She's a very competitive person, a real fighter."

Dottie Kohl laughs.

"When you've been married for 37 years, you know I'm a fighter."

And Ralph Kohl laughs.

"That day, watching her play that round of golf, I don't know if I've ever seen a greater display of what being an athlete is all about. If the Vikings can have that kind of spirit, we'll go undefeated and win the Super Bowl by 50 points."

The two golfers made the turn at 1 under par. They were 2 under on the back nine, 3 under for the day, entering the final two holes. Dorothy was trembling, staggering, barely able to walk.

"Tired is not the word. Exhausted is not the word," she says. "Dead is not the word, but it's closest. We bogeyed the last two holes, a tough par-3 and a very tough finishing hole. But I checked the scoreboard.

"We won anyway."

Afterward, she asked Sue to help her off with her rainwear. Then she put her hat back on and gave Ralph a big kiss and asked where they were going for dinner, for the victory celebration. Then she went to a pay phone and called her daughter with the good news.

"After dinner I went to bed and didn't move for a couple of days."

"But I didn't stop smiling either."

The old coaching cliche comes into play now. Take 'em one at a time. Dorothy Kohl says she knows her biggest opponent is no quitter either. The cancer could return.

"But I won't let it."

As for the golf, since it was the third straight year she'd won this particular tournament, what is left? What windmills are left to tilt?

"Oh, the pewter plate they give to the winners is really lovely. I've already told them I want a complete service for eight. At least a service for eight."

And the winner, the champion, the leader in anyone's clubhouse, laughs once more, adding the dead-solid perfect rejoinder.

"And I wouldn't mind a new hairdo either," she says, rubbing over the lovely stubble that is now half an inch long. And growing.

Away from Super Bowl, an ancient scourge
Jan. 25, 1990

> The leper in whom the plague is, his clothes shall be
> rent, and his head bare and he shall put a covering
> upon his upper lip and shall cry. Unclean, unclean.
> He shall dwell alone, without the camp shall his
> habitation be.
> —Leviticus XIII, 45–46

CARVILLE, La.—Far from the rattle and hum of Super Bowl revelry, the annual pageantry of the athletically unreal, the dull throb of the pathetically real roams this God-forsaken land with a grotesque grandeur. For here is where the lepers live.

The Gillis W. Long National Hansen's Disease Center stands and an eerie calm escapes like a gasp. Overlooking the twisting Mississippi River behind the levee, 67 miles outside of New Orleans, once a sugar plantation built before the Civil War, it is now the only facility of its kind in the world. There have been magnificent advances in the treatment of Hansen's disease, its victims' preferred terminology for the cruel, deforming disease commonly known as leprosy.

If detected early enough, if treated with sulfones and other antibiotics, the disease's ravaging symptoms can be arrested, and life can continue on an outpatient basis. But what of the ones who were born too soon? What of those who were not treated in time? What good does modern medicine do for 187 people who resisted and lost to the insidious twisting nature of leprosy?

"This is their home," says Julia Elwood. "They will live here forever."

Elwood is the unofficial public relations director for the center. She has worked here for 20 years. Before that she was a patient, too.

You step back. Instincts. Can't help it. She smiles. It's OK. She understands.

"You'll feel more comfortable after awhile. I'm one of the lucky ones."

Her soulful eyes burn. "They got the disease in an early stage. And I have no outward signs of the disease today."

A mile down the road a policeman sat lazily on his horse, his loaded shotgun resting across his lap, the Hunt Correctional Institute road gang working vigorously to clear the open field next to the center. At the roadside someone has spray-painted "K.K.K." onto the road sign identifying the spot as the White Castle Ferry Landing. It was here, in 1894, the first seven patients of the center—five men and two women—were delivered by order of the Louisiana State Board of Health. A coal barge carried them. A newspaper reporter in New Orleans had discovered the seven, living in squalor, their faces and hands wrapped in rags, eating out of garbage cans in dark alleys. At first it appeared the only purpose for transporting them to the rundown plantation mansion and ramshackle slave quarters was to get them out of sight. For more than a year, they were virtual prisoners, existing on food left at the gate by frightened state employees, alone with their horrible fate.

112

"It was so inhuman," Elwood says. "It took a long time for things to improve here."

She looks down a long corridor. Sister Teresa is wheeling toward her. In 1925, Maria Teresa has just joined the convent of the Sisters of Charity, a Roman Catholic order in her hometown of Quito, Ecuador. "She was 19. Eight years later she walked into a doctor's office and saw him burst into tears. The numbness in her hands — Maria, you have leprosy.

"I know that God is good," she says in Spanish. "I cried that day, too. But God gives each child what they need for salvation."

She taps one of the wheels of her wheelchair with a gnarled hand. And laughs.

"Things are better now. Much better."

She has work to do. Her English notebook, some new vocabulary words. It takes her almost a minute to make the ball-point pen fit snugly in her hand with the fingers that have drawn back and curled under.

"I try learn English," she says proudly in English. Then in Spanish, she adds, "I have time. After all, I am only 84 now."

Elwood shakes her head in admiration. A special woman, so strong, she says.

She could be talking about herself.

In June 1956, Julia sat atop a teen-age world. She had just been named head cheerleader, the first Mexican-American ever to make the squad at her high school in the Texas Rio Grande Valley. She wasn't sure which of her three boyfriends was her favorite. She was a Future Homemaker club president, a star on the basketball team, an honor student.

"I was really looking forward to my senior year."

Then one day she noticed the dull discoloration on her knee. And she became frightened. Her grandmother had tested positive for Hansen's disease two years earlier. One of the checkpoints, she'd learned, was a loss of feeling. Julia started pricking a pin into the spot on her knee. She felt nothing.

She had to leave, a doctor told her, for the good of her 11 brothers and sisters. Her shattered world would have to be rebuilt in some place called Carville, La. At a leper colony. And she'd have to leave immediately.

"A station wagon picked me up. There were two other passengers besides the driver. Two older men who also had the disease," Elwood says. "Here I was, 16; I'd never been away from my family before. I'd never been out of Texas. The trip took 12 hours. We got there at 3 in the morning.

"When I woke up, I met a woman who was in the advanced stages of the disease. Her face disfigured with lesions. She was crippled. I cried every day for two weeks."

Then one day a car that looked familiar and another one that had been borrowed from a neighbor pulled up to the guard gate and asked permission to see one of the patients.

"My whole family came. It meant so much," she says. "Some of our patients never see their family again. It is a very bad trauma when you find out you have HD, and people react differently."

Sulfone treatments, a form of chemotherapy, were developed in 1941 by one of the center's scientists, Dr. Guy Faget. Because of Julia's early detection of the disease and the effective treatments of sulfone, her condition was halted.

"I did spend my senior year of high school at a hospital. And I continued to cry myself to sleep for a long time. But I did also get better."

She also fell in love, with another patient. They married. She became a mother while still in the center. Both husband and wife tested negative 12 consecutive months, one of the requirements in those days for release. They moved west, ready to start a new life. Julia had another baby. And another, and another.

Then one day "my husband simply abandoned us."

How much devastation can one person withstand? The mother of four worked two jobs and went to college full-time. She had to get up at 4:30 in the morning to study "because that was the only time the kids were quiet" and she rarely got to sleep before midnight. But for three straight years, she never missed a class, a day of work or a meal. A college graduate now, she charged forward once more, and collected a master's degree.

Then she returned to Carville. She was forced to go there once. Now she willingly returned.

"It was the greatest challenge," she says, smiling. "It still is."

But there are so many others here, she insists. So many other furnaces of faith and spirit.

Rita Donaldson was delivered to the center, screaming, crying, kicking. It used to be called the Louisiana Leprasorium. At least in 1928, which was when Rita arrived. She has never seen any of her family since.

Now blind (a common affliction for an HD sufferers) and minus almost all her fingers and toes, Rita has retained her feisty nature through all the years of change and progress.

She says, "This place once was like a jail. We were treated like criminals. The guards outside were armed. You had no rights, none at all."

Rita and another patient married secretly, a violation of the center's regulations in those days. They ran away together, escaping through a hole in the fence. They made it as far as Port Arthur, Texas.

"My husband needed medical attention. We went to a doctor. He had us thrown in jail. We were arrested at gunpoint. We were there nine days. People came by to see the lepers. And don't ask me when that was. I don't remember. I don't want to remember."

Rita Donaldson does not want any visitors. She gave up waiting for her family. She has given explicit orders, not a request, an order, that when she dies, her family, with members as near as 20 miles away, will not be told.

The social stigma of the disease has outlasted even the disease itself. There are so many myths and so much ignorance concerning Hansen's disease. And there is no doubt the psychological pain is often as great as the physical discomfort. Of all the diseases that affect man, HD is the only one that is clearly visible when it is at work. There is no cure, and it does not kill. And that is the tragedy.

Esperanza Guevara died last year. Everyone who was able made it to her services. For there was no greater fighter. Everyone loved the gentle fire of Esperanza Guevara.

"Her face was terribly disfigured, But such a smile," Elmwood says. "She was crippled. But she forced herself to stand at times. Her hands were like mittens. She was brought here when she was 12 years old. Neighbors had turned her in to authorities. Her hands gave her away. She never went home again."

Born in Mexico, raised in Texas, Esperanza found that the only treatment available for this hideous disease was a concoction called chaulmoogra oil, a thick, vile-smelling extract from a foreign tree. To ingest it made her violently ill. She became infected by intravenous injections. She was left to fend alone against the disease.

"She told me once she would pray every day that somehow, somewhere, somebody would find out where HD comes from, where you get it, how to cure it," Elwood remembers. "She prayed that nobody else would have to suffer like she did."

But then the warm blast of a memory comes forth. A good one. Elwood tells of the countless operations Esperanza endured. And the job she finally got. She served as a translator for the doctors. She was so proud. She was even prouder just a couple of years ago when she realized she had worked long enough to collect a Social Security check. She was such a fighter, such a sweet fighter. Do you know what Esperanza means?

"Hope."

Yes, there are horror stories. Yes, there is progress. The stories inside the walls are always bittersweet. When first you see one of the older patients, there is a tendency to cringe, flinch, even look away. But the shock subsides with repetition. Yes, there is hope. More victims are being caught in time. There still is no cure and no known cause. But there is hope.

"We have not had a suicide in perhaps 15 years," Elwood declares. "That is also a sign of progress. And there are so many who can be treated as outpatients."

Pender Henderson Gosnell II lives in Baton Rouge, 20 miles up the road.

"I got leprosy in Vietnam," he says.

Now 41 and more often employed than unemployed, Gosnell's sorrowful tale allows pangs of social guilt to fly free.

In 1968, his 42-month extended tour of duty almost complete, Gosnell, an infantryman in the army, walked through a jungle and stepped on a punji stick, a bamboo stake smeared with excrement.

"That's what did it, I'm sure," he says. "A month later I got these

116

sores all over. My skin is super-sensitive, like I got the worst sunburn in the world. I couldn't stand to touch it with a washcloth.

"For 2 years I went from doctor to doctor, hospital to hospital, trying to find out what was wrong. I got real depressed. I lost weight. I started messing with drugs. I got drunk all the time.

"I was in this bar in Ashville, N.C., when the police come in and grabbed me. They drove right by the jail house, and I asked where are they taking me. They say they have orders to take me straight to the VA hospital. I go under quarantine. No visitors. I was really scared."

The next day he is taken to a waiting room and told to wait. Gosnell picks up a magazine "and you won't believe this, but it's about Cuba and how Castro had all the lepers lined up and shot when he took over the country."

Then a door opened and he was asked to come in the doctor's office. He saw his mother and father they were crying.

"The doc says, 'Son, you have leprosy,' and I faint deadaway."

He said he was afraid he'd be put to sea on a raft, to drift forever, or else stuck on some island with other victims.

"I saw that movie Ben-Hur with the leper caves and everything. Then I went to Carville. I was only there four months as a resident. But back home they had a write up in the paper on me. My friends wouldn't come near me. My girl broke things off. Even some of my family . . . Hey, I've seen horror in people's faces just when they see me."

And there is nothing outwardly wrong with Gosnell. Except he has trouble holding onto a job. Co-workers find out he's "one of them lepers," and they demand he leave.

"If it wasn't for my veterans disability payments, I couldn't live," he says.

It will rain soon, a sudden storm, a torrent. Jose hates the rain. Any HD sufferer does.

"Please do not use my last name," he says.

A lot of victims of the disease take aliases to protect their families. Many of them wind up being buried in graves under assumed names. Jose is different.

He was a prize fighter in Cuba. He won his first 13 matches. He lost No. 14 and could not figure it. Even more curious was that he

could not feel the punches as they hit his face. He lost his next fight
and felt no pain. He swam the next day in a mountain stream that is
usually almost icy cold. He felt nothing.

"I was told I had the disease," he says.

Fifteen years later he and a couple of friends pushed a tree log
into the ocean waters and for two days floated around the coast of
Cuba. To the Guantanamo Naval Station. And he said he was a
leper and he needed help.

He came to America with one possession. A picture of his wife.
They had two sons and a daughter.

"You cannot use my last name. They can never know where I
am. Never."

The anguish builds, then explodes. Tears track down a hard
face. Hands that once were the tools of a dream curl obediently.

He is asked if he feels sorry for himself, cheated. Does he ever
ask, "Why me, God?"

And his answer is more tears.

Maria Teresa is back. She hears his sobbing, and the motor of
her wheelchair is a soft purr. She puts an equally crooked hand on
Jose's shoulder and says, "God's will. God's will."

And Jose nods.

It is raining even harder.

All-Star Rodman beats his past
Feb. 10, 1990

MIAMI — Does it register with everyone what has happened?
Worm warfare has overcome the NBA to the point Dennis Rodman
is an honest-to-goodness All-Star. And you know what that means.
Real defense is going to be played today at the 40th All-Star game.

La Revolucion she may be here.

Dennis Rodman is asked what it all means to this 28-year-old
manchild who dares to bring a scoring average of 8.9 points and
actual defensive intensity to the greatest playground game there is.

118

"It means maybe I can sit next to Larry Bird."

Oops. Is the mouth moving too fast for the brain again? Is Rodman about to open another, umm, can of worms? Is the Worm attacking the Bird once again?

"Oh no, I'd just like to get to know him a little bit," Rodman says. Then he grabs a microphone from the several stuck in his direction and says with Nixon-like emphasis. "He's really a great player, you know."

And his smile is matched by everyone around him. This is *Hollywood Squares*, right? And that was his joke answer, naturally. And now the real answer?

"What does it mean? Let's see now. It means that my game is appreciated. Defense is the name of the game today anyway, especially for someone like me, who couldn't score 20 points if I was locked in a gym all alone."

And this smile is more sarcastic than joyous. In your face, Al Bianchi. Earlier in the week, the Knicks assistant coach lamented that Charles Oakley was not named to the team and Rodman was, suggested the All-Star Game would be tainted by the presence of someone who earned his pay doing such insidious things as playing defense and rebounding and pumping his damn fist like some country yahoo from Oklahoma or somewhere. Hence the remark about Rodman's scoring ability.

"Aw Bianchi's . . . something else. I could outscore him blindfolded. Anywhere except at the foul line."

And everyone rumbles. Oh yeah. Rodman also can't shoot free throws. Remember a couple of years ago when he bricked 15 in a row? Hired him a shot doctor, thought about getting hypnotized. Maybe even slip quarters in his ears like the old days in college. Now Pistons assistant coach Brendan Malone has taken over the job of shooting guru. And Malone insisted there's nothing wrong with Rodman's shooting form. It's excellent, in fact.

"But I rush everything. Everything I do in life, I go too fast. I'm hyper, ultra-hyper. Must have been all those Sugar Crisps when I was little. I'd eat about four bowls a day. I guess the sugar got clogged in my system. Anyway, that's why I have trouble shooting. Coach Malone tells me be quick but don't rush. Keep my eye on the target, leg lift and follow through. When I'm not excited I can

119

shoot OK. But when a game is going on, well, you've seen me. You know how I play."

And Rodman rolls his eyes and giggles. Maybe it's a defense mechanism; maybe he pokes fun at himself so he can beat everyone to the punch. Maybe he doesn't want anyone to know that any critics who can't believe Rodman has joined the skywalkers and mad bomber and ultra-glide scientists in roundball's midseason carnival have nothing on him.

"I can't believe it either," he says. But he's here and you can bet he'll be the first one in the Miami Arena today. You can bet he spent a large chunk of Saturday night squirming his toes under the bedsheets, blinking hard to make his eyes stay shut. His Pistons teammates swear Rodman never sleeps. On road trips, nobody wants to room with him.

And why he loves the game so much is simple, he says.

"For a long time I didn't know how I was going to make it in life. For a while I was afraid I'd be in jail or just plain dead. I was nothing but a bum. And now I'm an NBA All-Star."

And the pride puffs his cheeks full. What's the question again? What does it mean to be here with the All Stars?

"I think it means that hard work can make a miracle. And also that it's never too late to be somebody."

Yeah Worm. Show 'em what kind of man you've become. Tell it like it is. Wad up the old labels people put on you. Nothing fits anymore, just like that two-year period when your glands and hormones went berserk and you sprouted from 5-foot-9 to 6-8 and God seems to post your bond and spring you from your former lifetime. Every few years, and all of a sudden, life seems to get better for Rodman. But you Worm, remember: Take it as it comes. Let it go at its own sweet pace.

All the hate mail you got following your rookie year in the NBA when you made that unfortunate remark about Bird being over-rated because he was white really hurt. You'd already become a rival to Bill Laimbeer and Rick Mahorn for the favorite villain with your exuberant and outlandish ways of celebrating a Pistons basket, particularly your own, at enemy gymnasiums. You quickly became a hot dog nobody outside of Michigan could relish.

But nobody understood Dennis Rodman. Nobody ever has, not

completely. His is not the usual pedigree. He got cut from his high school team in Dallas when he was a junior. Too small, he likes to tell people. Remember 5-9. But Spud Webb had gone to the same high school. OK, Rodman smiles, you got me.

"I was a klutz, couldn't even make a layup."

His senior year, he sat the bench until midseason, when he quit. His two sisters were the basketball stars in the family. Debra was an All-America at Louisiana Tech. Kim was an All-America at Stephen F. Austin.

"But they were both over 6 feet tall. I was 5-9 and a klutz."

Debra and Kim will be in the stands today, watching little brother Dennis. So will Mom and a favorite auntie. And what about Dad?

"He left us when I was 3. He lives in the Philippines now. Owns a restaurant there, I think. We don't talk much. The All-Star game will be on TV in the Philippines. And I'll get a letter from him saying how proud he is of me and that we ought to get together soon."

"But we probably won't. I don't know. It's tough for me to think of him as my father. I mean, I don't remember him at all. It's just tough for me."

Tough is what life was before those spurts of good fortune. After high school, he got a job at the airport in Dallas. Janitor. Start at the bottom, he figured, and stay there. His sisters got all the breaks and the height. He got a push broom.

What is it they say? You must touch bottom before you can start going up? One night, sometime after midnight, Rodman discovered a new use for his broom. He could stick it through the railings of the airport gift shop and hook these fancy watches, worth as much as $50 each. Rodman copped 15 watches and gave every one of them to friends. Terribly shy and introverted and uncomfortable around people then, he realized he had "about 13 watches left. So I gave the others to would-be friends. I mean, who wouldn't be friends with someone who just gave you a new watch?"

He smiles, maybe gasps at the distance that has been covered since then and shakes his head.

"I was a real mess. No confidence. No goals. The best thing that ever happened to me was getting arrested. Of course, I didn't know that at the time."

He sat in a jail cell for 18 hours, scared, ashamed and disgusted.

"I could see I was going straight to hell."

But a deal was cut. Rodman recovered every one of the watches. And the charges were dropped.

"I decided then I wasn't ever gonna go back behind bars. I knew I already got my lucky break."

He took a job cleaning used cars. And then he started growing. And he walked to the playground and tried basketball again. This time it was a little easier.

He enrolled at Cook County Junior College in Gainesville, Tex. And 14 games later, he was declared academically ineligible.

"I blew it again. I went back to Dallas and starting hanging with a bad crowd. My mother would give me money to go find a job and I'd spend it at the video arcade.

"Then my mother kicked me out of the house."

Rock bottom again. Luck, however, started to find Rodman about then. It arrived in the form of Jack Hedden, coach of Southeast Oklahoma State, an NAIA school. He remembered watching Rodman play pickup games and wondered whatever had happened to the skinny kid with the weird ears and the tremendous knack for rebounding. Rodman was ready this time.

He played like a star and hustled like a walk-on. And the distant gaze and point to nobody in particular in the stands. The fist that punched the sky like Sugar Ray riddles the speed bag became a trademark. But so did the work ethic. And the love for playing defense.

He'd rather not talk about it but there were times when he'd watch the NBA on TV and declare, "I could guard that guy" or "That guy ain't nothing. I could shut him down."

Well, yes, Larry Bird was among the stoppables. So was every other superstar in the league. Dennis Rodman's self-esteem had grown along with him.

His story is too much like a soap opera for one person. He had to have help, a little buddy. One day in the Southeast Oklahoma gym, Rodman met a 13-year-old boy named Bryne Rich. They immediately became friends, this rebounding wild man on the rebound and this young teen-ager, also on the rebound.

Bryne had been drifting aimlessly for years. In 1982, his best friend had been accidentally killed when Rich's shotgun fired as he closed the barrel. Maybe Rodman recognized the hurt behind the dull eyes. Maybe he sensed the lost feeling and frustration and unavoidable guilt.

Bryne Rich's mother had told her distraught son three weeks earlier that she was going to pray to God that a new friend or a little brother would come into their life. Maybe that was what was needed for Bryne to snap out of his prolonged grief and sense of guilt.

"Then Bryne brought Worm home."

Blacks are rare in Bokchito, Okla., where the Riches live. The entire population is only 600 or so and people just don't know black people personally. Mrs. Rich flinched when she saw her son's new friend, all 6-foot-8 of him. He's black and older, a grown man, she thought correctly. Yes he can stay for dinner, she said.

"I felt like I was auditioning for a role in a movie. I was trying out for the part of The Friend. It was a strange dinner," Rodman said.

Then Bryne asked if his new friend Dennis could spend the night. Afraid to upset their son, his parents said OK. For the first time since the shotgun accident, Bryne Rich did not have nightmares. Rodman slept on the floor beside Bryne's bed.

"I really believe both saved the other's life," Pat Rich says today.

Dennis Rodman never left the Rich house until the Detroit Pistons drafted him in the second round of the 1986 draft. And pressure? Forget foul-line pressure. When you're in a barn, helping some laboring cow give new birth, you find out all about real pressure.

The story is a nice one, one that is color-blind. And when he found out he was going to get a chance to play in the NBA, he went for a drive in the old car the Riches had given him and he fixed up, complete with flashing lights. That night, on the country roads of southeastern Oklahoma, there were seven UFO sightings reported.

The police dispatcher said not to worry — that's just Worm letting off some steam. He's going to the NBA, you know.

It is a great story of perseverance, of hard work paying off. So where is his little friend, Bryne Rich? Why isn't he here to watch Dennis Rodman play in the All-Star game?

"He can't make it. See he's starting at point guard for Tarleton State, it's a small school in Texas. He's doing real good too. I'm real proud of him."

5.

COLUMNS III

Tears? Nah, says the Martina Machine

NEW YORK — "OK guys, wheel her in," says the man in the white lab coat, yawning.

In an underground laboratory, several miles from the tennis complex of the U.S. Open, a parade of bored men with portable generators and futuristic tool kits is trying to look busy. Cooldown at Flushing Meadows.

Team Navratilova's pit crew is prepping, performing more meager maintenance on The Greatest Woman Tennis Player. Tighten the bolts on the circuitry of reflexes. Apply another glaze of wax over the cold, depthless eyes. A squirt of oil for the industrial-strength-intensity turbines. Small stuff. Preventive stuff. Monotonous stuff.

The crack team of nutritionists, physiotherapists, cheerleaders, outright shrinks, robot experts, itinerant philosophers and one guy in a ducktail whose name is "Mr. Goodwrench" gather around the operating table. Post-op. Strictly routine.

"Blood acceleration. Check. Caloric regimentation. Check. System flushing. Check."

Suddenly, an alarm sounds. A screech that pierces the stale, boring air of the warehouse.

A scientist hurriedly scans the electrodes sticking to the temples of Mighty Martina and reaches for his checklist. There has never been a problem before.

A man wearing a coal miner's helmet shouts, "There it is! The malfunction has been isolated."

Steamy strobe lights focus. Infrared devices click into position. Sure enough—a trickle of foreign matter traces down the side of Martina's stately, stoic face.

"Get a smear. I need a slide," bellows one man.

Another man, this one wearing a pointed hat with astrological signs on it, holds up a magnifying glass and announces, "It's moisture. Definitely wet."

Heads nod.

A cotton swab is placed delicately upon Martina's face. A petri dish balances on her chin. On her forehead, an electron microscope is ready and waiting. The only sound is the pounding of each second on the overhead clock.

A door swings open. A man with a stenciled mustache and a pronounced lip says triumphantly, "Vee haff established identification."

The doctors chant, "Good God, man, tell us."

"Eet is generic perspiration. Common sweat."

There is a huddle and several seconds of mumbling. Then the heads nod once more.

"It must be from her match today. Not so automatic."

Then more whispering.

"How could it be? She is not programed for stress. Not until Saturday, when she plays Chrissie in the finals. Look at the charts. Biofeedback simply does not lie."

Nobody notices the door as it opens again. A little girl carrying a teddy bear with one eye missing walks over to a wall and pulls a lever. A trap door opens and everyone disappears except the little girl and Martina.

The girl walks to the still-sleeping Martina. With a corner of her frilly dress, the girl dabs at the second appearance of the mysterious substance. Martina's eyes open.

"Hi, Martina. I came to rescue you. Those mean people treat you like a machine."

126

Martina reaches for her plug and looks for an outlet. She wants to stand up.

"Wait, listen to me Martina. They found something on you. It wasn't on any of their microfilm. They did all of these experiments."

Martina asks, "What was it?"

"They said it was persp-something. But they're wrong; I know what it really was. You were crying, Martina. That was a tear. I know tears. I cried all night when Stinky Bear's eye popped out. Martina—you were crying."

The Greatest Woman Tennis Player snarls, "Silly kid. Crying? Why would I cry. I'm the best. I win millions of dollars."

The girl pleads, "But Martina, it's all right to be human. Those tears are signals. There's still some little girl in you. She's trapped in there because all the high-tech and software is piled on top of her. Those tears are the only way of letting people know she's still alive. Please Martina, take a break. Play with me. Let's play baby dolls or something."

Just then, two security guards grab the girl and drag her away. She screams.

"Quiet you little brat!" Martina yells. "I must have my pre-scribed rest."

Then a thought rushes at Mighty Martina and she fliches.

"When the hell is a baby doll, anyway?"

And the little girl and the doll were never heard from again.

Walk, drive, buy why jog?
Sea and sky, invisible urges set runners in motion
Oct. 18, 1987

Cruising on an unusually balmy Friday, punching buttons on her car radio, trying to decide between Merle Haggard, Tap Dancing Bats and Paul Harvey. Something outside catches my eye.

127

There he is, shamelessly expelling carbon dioxide on the side of the road. Topless, stomach muscles that look like hideous speed bumps. Not a love handle anywhere. Wearing little nylon shorts with slits there actually by design.

A runner.

You can recognize a show-off by his solitary chin. Total absence of jowls, no thighs slapping together. His feet never touch ground. The air around him refuses to resist. There's some kind of apparent euphoria going on.

I can't help it. I must know. I pull over, and yell, "Hey man, why do you run?"

The streamlined show-off never stops, just eases by my car, glancing to notice the snug fit between my tummy and the steering wheel. He says with a smirk, "Why don't you?"

I am ready to let him have it with my horn. One long blast, maybe a hand gesture, too. Where's a mud puddle when you really need one? Us mouth-breathers have rights, too. Such insolence demands a good swift kick in the skinny butt.

But I instead remember the story of the lemmings. Those merry little fatalists who ritualistically wobble down to the sea and take the plunge. Thornton Wilder once wrote of intercepting one of these lemmings and demanding to know why it chose to fulfill the watery death wish.

To which the lemming replied, "And I've never understood why you humans don't."

So I meekly pull my car back up beside the runner. He says he's getting in one last workout before the Free Press marathon. That last word—marathon. Twenty-six miles, 385 yards. People actually run that far without someone chasing them. Do you realize how far that is? I get tired just driving that far.

I always used to think this running thing was the conspired invention of podiatrists and shoe salesmen. I used to think jogging (the designer synonym for running) was something you did if you weren't coordinated enough to play real sports. Could I have been wrong?

Twenty-six miles and change. If my math is correct (a dangerous assumption most of the time), that means about 55,000 strides. Talk about your agony of de feets. . . .

Of course, assuming you have both legs, you get to divide that number by two. This does not translate well. How many home-run trots is that? Has Walter Payton run that far yet? I need reference points.

The question remains. Why run all that way, all at once? There seems to be a common denominator of an answer. Philosophy. Runners talking about running often sound like Rod McKuen talking about clouds or kittens. In goes the good karma, out goes the bad air.

I have heard the story of the woman who was asked about her husband's recent obsession with running. "How does he reconcile his religious beliefs with the fact a lot of races are held on Sunday?"

"Oh, he's not a Methodist anymore; he's a runner."

A national magazine ran a one-question survey of "100 serious runners" not long ago. "If you had to abstain from one, would it be running or sex?"

Seventy-four said they would give up sex.

I'm confused. Does running cause celibacy? Is a 5-K race a suitable means of birth control?

My perspective was further muddied recently. I was in a super-market, buying a six-pack, doughnuts and other daily staples. Waiting in the checkout line, I thumbed through one of those weekly tabloids — *Woman's Head Falls Off While She's Asleep, Is Your Pet A Space Alien?* — and stopped at an item describing an obviously angry flock of crows that mercilessly pecked a jogger to death. Perhaps a classic case of Hitchcockian revenge.

What's so healthy about that?

Almost home now, I wave good-bye to my running buddy. He asks me if I'm going to the marathon. I shrug. He says, if I can find it in a book, I should look up what Roger Bannister, first man to break the four-minute mile, had to say about running.

Bannister, who also was a doctor, was an eloquent writer as well.

"I can remember quite vividly a time when as a child, I ran barefoot along damp, firm sand by the seashore. The air there had a special quality, as if it had a life of its own. The sound of breakers on the shore shut out all others. And I was startled and almost frightened by the tremendous excitement a few steps could create. It was an intense moment of discovery of a source of power and beauty that one previously hardly dreamt existed . . . the sense, or perhaps a subtle combination of all the others."

If that doesn't make the clouds puff up like the cheeks of angels and the kittens flail tiny paws of innocence, what does?

Throwback unites fantasy with reality
March 30, 1988

LAKELAND, Fla. — I froze. Leaning against a fence down the right-field line, watching batting practice, suddenly came the challenge. Man vs. Line Drive.

The ball dripped and took one hop — a bad one. It clanked off my shin. The flare of soreness was immediately overcome by a desperation to retrieve the ball before it stopped rolling. I assumed the classic fielding position, that is if there's anything classic about limping bare-handed.

The ball bounced up against the chain fence and ricocheted back, striking me about the chest and then the shoulder before it collapsed once more to the ground, in apparent exhaustion.

If you can't beat 'em, outlive 'em.

The ball was dormant and still as I cautiously reached down and strangled it with my grip. Then my anger and embarrassment subsided. When you are near a baseball, the urge is irresistible. You pick it up and you look at it for just a moment. It feels right. Who designed a baseball, who decided it would be the size it is, made out of what it is? And who put those precious little red stitches in it?

He did it right. A baseball goes into your hand and there's never the slightest doubt what you're supposed to do with it. No matter what involvement you've had with the game, be it a T-ball dropout or someone who held onto a dream of the big leagues until it was frayed and torn and stuffing was coming out of the sides, you know that when you pick up a baseball, any second now, you're going to throw it.

And how long has it been since you really let loose? A real throw, a glorious, over-the-rainbow peg, all the way back. How long? Who cares? You can almost hear the voice on the radio: . . . and here comes the throw home."

The clown-like sequence along the fence is forgotten. So is the fact you're in a Hawaiian shirt, not a double-knit uniform. Those are flip-flops, not cleats. You're just a civilian, a normal person, someone from the other side of the fence who's trespassed and gotten caught. But also someone who's gotten this little window to open and for just a twinkling of the mind's eye, he's part of the game. In the playground of imagination, there's now a runner rounding first and the ump is squatting down, ready to make the call.

Then you stop your windup and look at the ball once more. The runner disappears, the ump walks away, the radio is turned off.

You'd learned the game 30 years ago. Learned it on a sand field with palm fronds for bases and no hitting to right because that's where the sticker burrs were. And today there's a condo on the field and who are you trying to fool? This ball's too new, the dreams too old.

The ball doesn't shine like the kind you get out of the box at the sporting goods store. And because you're a sportswriter and you've gotten this two-week privilege pass to cover spring training (and even get paid for it), you know why. The day before, you'd spotted the coffee can and asked what was in it. And the clubhouse guy had simply said, "Mud."

Rubbing mud, the stuff umpires slap on new baseballs to make them "playable." Because you asked around, you now know that Lena Blackburne's Baseball Rubbing Mud comes in 1-pound cans and that's enough to rub down about 8,000 baseballs. It is special mud that comes from a creek off the Delaware River and undergoes "secret processing to remove the impurities," which sounds like a good way to say it's different from regular mud because they couldn't charge money if it wasn't.

The ball now was good for only batting practice, sullied by use and age. And a terrible feeling came over me. Out there, it's only for the players. Throw this ball with special mud and you get unmasked. What if it's a wimpy, feeble throw? What if you bean Billy Bean? What if everyone laughs because you've been sullied by use and age?

There comes a time. Fend off the demons of doubt. Dare to be a ballplayer. Be Clemente, be Kaline. Throw the damn thing. And the ball sails, a frozen rope, if you please. Then it pops into someone's distant mitt. And the ump is shooting his thumb back and the runner is dead meat on the base paths.

The tiny window slams shut. It was just a pause of fantasy on a balmy spring day. Just one throw; a throwback. But as you can see, it was important enough for a lucky man to write home about.

No holds barred in the game of love
Sept. 1, 1988

The Emmys were on; Mike Tyson and Robin Givens were about to present the award for some category. It was silly.

Boxing champions do not belong in tuxedoes. Mike Tyson looked painfully uncomfortable. I used to think people in tuxedoes looked uncomfortable because they wore rented tuxedoes, and that meant at least 53 high school seniors had already worn the tuxedo to the prom, gotten sick all over the outside of the tux and there's no telling what happened on the inside. But surely Mike Tyson, the undisputed heavyweight champion of the world, *owned* his own tuxedo.

Surely his wife, the head of the class, picked one out for him. There doesn't seem to be much doubt who wears the pants, tuxedo or otherwise, in that family.

Wayne Gretzky married actress Janet Jones, which, upon first glance, seems to prove the Great One is nobody's fool. But before the wedding presents were all opened, and the blender and toaster ovens put in motion, the pride of Canada was whisked off to California, to become, of all things, a Los Angeles King. He did it for his wife's career, for the truckload of endorsements that could be theirs, for his own as yet unborn career in show business. He did it for love.

Meanwhile, the Big Canadian maple leaf was lowered to half-staff and the whole country cried 99 tears.

Not so far from L.A., in a trendy little community called Malibu, Gretzky might find the shape of things to come. It is called John McEnroe. Once the greatest tennis player on this planet, McEnroe met a movie star named Tatum O'Neal. Tatum and the Tantrum were moonstruck, married and became Mom and Pop. Tennis no longer seemed so important. McEnroe now is located somewhere in the middle of the tennis pack, just another California dude.

Prediction: Gretzky will no longer be the Great One but, umm, the Snarly One. Or maybe the Absolutely Gorgeous One. Or Gretz Babe.

There are exceptions. Football quarterback Bob Waterfield and actress Jane Russell married and neither career suffered. And could there be any greater example of glamour epitomized than the spectacularly holy union of the great Joe DiMaggio, the most classy ballplayer who ever lived, and Marilyn Monroe?

That is, until they divorced several years later.

Maybe it has something to do with ego; maybe the harsh spotlight of celebrity is not wide enough for a couple to snuggle comfortably beneath its glare. Narcissism has big muscles and strange appetites.

But then you look at nice examples like Ray Knight and Nancy Lopez, two athletes who found each other. Each is famous, wealthy, and, from a distance, happy. The late pro wrestler George Zaharias and Babe Didricksen, maybe the greatest woman athlete of all time, were perfect examples of Till Death Do Them Part. And from first impressions, Chris Evert seems genuinely happy being Mrs. Andy Hill. And vice-versa.

Tennis champion Jimmy Connors married a Playboy bunny and he has never been the same, although advancing age seems more at fault in his case. Connors, however, does seem to smile more these days. And Sean Penn is only an amateur fighter; therefore, his marriage to Madonna is disqualified from our little debate. And please, no pictures.

The most perfect poster children for the *Cause D'Celebre* of prohibiting the exchanging of nuptial vows between athletes and show business figures can be found in New York. While someone else might suggest one bimbo deserves another and Mark Gastineau and Brigitte Nielsen are a match made in Wine Cooler Heaven, I, however, feel a responsibility to protect the addled and unsound.

Gastineau, who has demonstrated his confused nature in the past by dancing at football games and fighting at discos, and Nielsen, whose previous experience with athletes was being married to somebody who portrayed them, decided to prove once and for all to the agnostic world their eternal devotion. They had each other's name tattooed onto each other's rear end. No greater love, eh?

I suppose in the event of divorce, community property should be properly marked and identified but I'm not sure the dispersal procedure would be an easy one in this case. A fool and his autograph are not so easily parted. The alleged impending marriage should be right off the silver screen: *Rocky*.

Hey Wayne Gretzky, isn't Mark Gastineau's jersey number 99?

Mike Tyson and Robin Givens may stay married for the next 100 years, and I truly hope they do. It certainly beats the alternative. Ask Wade Boggs.

"Did you ever think about becoming a movie star or a singer or getting into show business?" I asked my wife.

"Not," she answered, "since I played the part of seaweed in a dance recital and sang *Shrimp Boats Are A-Coming* back in kindergarten. I wore a green tutu."

I smiled. She smiled. Since the most athletic thing I do anymore is bounce on one leg trying to pull off a wet bathing suit, or carry children upstairs to bed after they fall asleep on the couch, heaving and gasping and ready to join them when I finally reach the top, I figured we were safe.

"Besides, I promised my father I'd never get a tattoo.

"How about if we initial each other's big toe with Magic Markers?" she asked with eyelashes flickering like hummingbird wings.

"Only if you put on that green tutu."

True love hath no out-of-bounds.

Sailor's heroic deed shows Olympic spirit alive, well
Sept. 26, 1988

SEOUL, South Korea—The American classics had a lousy weekend. Carl Lewis, Edwin Moses, Mary Decker Slaney, Chris Evert, Mary T. Meagher.

Seouled Out.

The fall from athletic grace was handled better by some than others. Lewis and Moses, track stars and practicing capitalists, could not bring themselves to acknowledge their conquerors in the 100 meters and 400 hurdles, respectively.

After finishing 10th in the 3,000-meter run, Mary Decker Slaney had her usual pile of excuses and alibis—some valid, others almost as imaginary as the ghost of Zola Budd, who always will be hounding Mary, Mary, so contrary, if only in her dreams.

Evert, the tennis legend whose presence in Olympic competition is awkward and I can give you eight million reasons why—one for every nonamateur dollar she's won—looked at a stat sheet. It said she had made 62 unforced errors in losing to an unranked Italian. Evert shrugged and said, "I couldn't get fired up; I had a bad day."

Then she said something about the unbearable struggle to deal with taxi cabs and cafeteria-style food and headed for the nearest limousine. I wonder if she ever compared those horrible taxi cabs with subways or buses. Or hitchhiking. I wonder if cafeteria food is so terrible to the Bangladesh athletes.

Mary T. Meagher, who won three gold medals in 1984 and who still owns two world records, settled for a bronze medal and a seventh-place finish in Seoul. But she made her exit with a soft grace, explaining that she knew, by looking at the rest of the world's times, "that I've been caught. It's time to take off my swim suit and put something else on."

So where have all the heroes gone? It could be Florence Griffith Joyner whose joyous smile that last 20 meters of her Olympic-record sprint makes a nice exclamation point for what spirit is. But alas,—by the time her news conference came around, Flo had composed herself to the point of smugness, indifference and a lingering thought that she was more interested in her designer fingernails than anything else.

135

So you want a hero? I have a nomination. Lawrence Lemieux of Canada.

Yeah. Here's the scene: Lemieux is a sailor. He was competing in the 470 men's Finn competition Sunday. The seas of Suyong Bay grew choppy, then rough, then precarious. Lemieux was having a good sail anyway. He was in position for a silver medal, running a strong second at the beginning of the second windward leg of the race.

Then he saw the man in the water.

Joseph Chan of Singapore had been swept off his boat. He had hit the water wrong; his back was hurt. He was wearing a weight jacket that sailors use in racing.

He was drowning.

"Do you need help?" Lemieux yelled as he sailed by Chan, who was shouting, floundering in the heavy waves, flapping one arm.

Chan cannot speak English. Lemieux went by the man in the water, then made a decision. He turned his sailboat around, helped Chan aboard, took off Chan's weight jacket and called for help. Then he resumed his race. And finished 21st.

"The first rule of sailing is to help people in distress," Lemieux said later.

"There really wasn't any decision to make. The man was desperate. He was hurt and exhausted."

Peter Holmberg of the Virgin Islands was in a boat trailing Lemieux's. He said, "'What the Canadian did was commendable. His nose is pointed in the correct direction, all right. It was a bloody good statement of safety."

Unless you are Dennis Conner, sailing has no lucrative hooks. It is fun and the value is intrinsic. At the Olympics, there are rewards less abstract, namely medals. Then there is common sense.

Hooray for Lawrence Lemieux, who made his mark.

Hooray also for a certain attitude. Kadima Tshibalababa of Zaire is a 26-year-old heavyweight boxer who lost his first bout last Thursday, his Olympic dream ending flat on his back and a referee counting him out in the second round.

The Zaire athlete wept uncontrollably, saying he was embarrassed and humiliated. Korean officials and translators tried to console him. But Tshibalababa could not stop crying. Finally, one Korean said, "Maybe you can win another medal."

Soon, the big heavyweight with the glass jaw will compete in the Korean Folk Singing contest. He has learned the words, actually had to memorize the sounds since he doesn't speak Korean, to a song called, *My Heart Goes To You*.

Said Park Ih-Jong, an organizer of the contest, "The man is very sincere and he has a good voice. The judges will like him for trying so hard.

"I think maybe he will win third place."

You have to love it.

All a bewildered boy can do is cry
Jan. 17, 1989

MIAMI — The policeman ducked behind his plexiglass riot shield. An empty bottle crashed behind him. Less than 20 feet way, a shirtless child, a little boy was crying. Maybe 5 years old.

"Get out of here. Get out of here," the policeman screamed.

A rock skidded along the ground. Then a brick. The little boy cried louder.

From the bridge on Third Street, you could see what the policeman was trying to do. He wanted to get to the little boy to protect him. But the boy saw the shiny helmet with the dark visor, the shield, the holster that has a gun in it and maybe he was afraid of what he saw. He backed up as the policeman moved closer. And he moved more and more into the open.

You could see it all from the bridge because of the light from the burning van. It was probably 50 feet away from the little boy. Except for the occasional gunfire and the pleas of the policeman to the crying child, there was silence in Overtown.

The place was ablaze. At Twentieth Terrace a junkyard was set on fire. You could smell the burning tires. For just a moment, there was a temptation to get closer to it and get the story.

Over the bridge and down the hill and just one block away was the warehouse, flames flickering above its roof. Halfway there, you hear the voices. Coming from the darkness, coming from nowhere. Just voices.

"Don't go there man. Don't be going near that building."

The voices made you think twice. Keep at arms' length from trouble. That's when you saw the CBS cameraman go down. It looked like a rock got him in the head. Than came the robbers. Really, just kids. Teen-age looters. Their heist: a TV minicam and recorder.

Then they were gone. Back into the night.

And so were you, back to your car, back to safety. Headed away from Overtown.

What caused this flash of anger? The radio said someone has been shot. It said a policeman exchanged gunfire. A motorcycle crashed into another car. There was a body.

When more police showed up and the sirens screamed and cut through the night and things got louder, more congested, more tense and the gunfire kept popping, trouble was on the streets. Fifty deep in some places. There was a fire truck and it couldn't get close enough to put out a fire. Its windshield was smashed. Its driver had ducked under the wheel.

That little boy isn't the only one afraid of police. But so far, the crying child doesn't express his fear with violence.

He just cries.

Where are his parents? What was he doing on such a mean street at such an unlikely hour?

You don't know. You're not in Overtown anymore. The radio screeches details until after midnight. There is an important public safety message: Five elementary schools will be closed Tuesday. Please keep your children at home.

It was after midnight now. Somewhere behind you, a policeman is still trying to convince a little boy that he's not a bad man. And that's not easy. Not in Overtown on Monday night, six days before Super Bowl XXIII and one hour after the holiday commemorating the birthday of Dr. Martin Luther King Jr.

Miami violence: Resentment boils over onto Overtown streets
Jan. 18, 1989

MIAMI — The talk was of police, death and troubles that might get worse before they get better.

Gunshots have ripped the silence on the streets of Overtown minutes earlier on this hot Tuesday afternoon. Outside an apartment building, a large crowd milled around. The night before, a policeman shot a 24-year-old man on a motorcycle and he died on the spot.

Tuesday, shortly after it was announced his passenger also had died, the anger grew.

One teen-ager, his eyes filled with anger, ran several steps toward a rental car stopped at the corner of Third Avenue and 16th Terrace.

He spat on the windshield and screamed at the driver to stay out of his neighborhood.

"I'll burn that car, shoot you dead. Don't be coming to Overtown tonight, you hear me? You hear me?"

Overtown is a two-square-mile area just north of downtown Miami. It has a population of about 10,000, most of them blacks. It is home for Edgar Mason, a bricklayer who called in sick Tuesday. He stood in front of the Brotherhood Coin Laundry, sipping on a beer wrapped in a tiny brown bag.

"I ain't sick," he explained. "I'm just tired of paying taxes that pay for murderers to murder people.

"How many times do the police set to kill somebody and get away with it? That boy last night was being chased for speeding. You don't shoot somebody in the head for speeding.

"We don't trust police. Nobody, no white people. That's why so many people throw rocks and bottles."

It's 1:30 in the afternoon when more shots ring out. Six police cars speed by, lights flashing. Several of the cars have shotgun barrels sticking out of the windows.

Across the street from a junkyard that burned all night, the stench of burned rubber from the piles of old tires is strong. In an open field beside an apartment building, three children play on a mattress someone tossed out. Two woman run out, grab them and take them inside to safety.

Two blocks away, at the abandoned Lyric Theater, a woman is cooking on a small hibachi at the entrance. She has no home. A policeman tells her she has to leave. She picks up the hibachi, balancing her meal and the burning coals, and walks 30 feet. Turning the corner, she stoops and sets down her meal. Home is where the hearth is.

There are probably 5,000 people on any given night sleeping outside. Homeless.

The area merchants say business is terrible. The Just-Rite barbershop never opened for business. At the Two Butchers Market, a woman at the cash register says there have been no customers in more than an hour.

"Something's happening," she says. "Something bad."

Two men wearing holsters with pistols walk around the rubble at Georgia Meats, a discount meat distributor. Their building was looted during Monday night's violence. They're waiting for the insurance man. Sixto Mendez, the owner of the gutted building, says there is probably close to $100,000 worth of missing inventory.

Francis Blanchard stands in front of a TV camera and says he wants the truth to be known. His brother, Allen, was the passenger on the motorcycle. His brother's death, Blanchard says in a thick West Indies accent, "will be a waste if the truth cannot be known. I do not feel this violence is helping anything. I do not think it will being my brother back to life."

A rock crashes off the wall behind him. Ten feet away is the hand-printed graffiti, "Satan's Playhouse."

Many thought it would calm down Tuesday. But by late afternoon, shotgun-toting police had to forbid anyone rom entering Overtown.

Ficus trees with hanging Spanish moss throw long shadows, providing a deceiving tranquility. The Phillis Wheatley Elementary School is quiet, its doors never opened.

At the Mount Zion Baptist Church, one of five churches on the street where trouble flared out of control Monday night, a little girl in tiny curlers is dancing for the TV crew. It's the Ickey Shuffle. She smiles and it is a relief from the scary scenes. But then her mother scolds her and tells her to get away from the TV camera. And the mother spits at the newsmen.

There was supposed to be a professional basketball game at the Miami Arena, a block away. It is canceled. Still planned is Sunday's Super Bowl game at Joe Robbie Stadium in north Dade County, far from the inner city location of the arena.

They are still angry in Overtown. Things are getting more tense, more dangerous.

There are crowds and they are loud. The squeal of sirens, more police arriving. In front of Lucky Sam's Pool Palace, someone has stuffed a burning rag into a bottle. In a few seconds, he throws it at a parked car. It bounces 10 feet short.

The policemen move an orange-and-white barricade and give the warning, "Stay away."

Nobody talks about football.

Overtown: It's just the 'eye of the hurricane'
Jan. 19, 1989

MIAMI — Sergeant Henry Weatherspoon's eyes darted left and right. The Miami policeman would not forget why he was in Overtown. He heard about the cop who got shot the night before and his bulletproof vest saved his life. He would not be fooled by the lethargic calm that fell over the area early Wednesday.

"Eye of the hurricane, if you ask me," Weatherspoon says. "This thing ain't done. Everyone's just resting, getting a second wind. I wish I had a bazooka. I'd shoot this thing right in the eye. It's a hurricane and this is just the calm part, the eye. I don't think we're done with trouble yet."

He looked up 20th Street. He could see the crowd gathering. A couple of people throwing rocks.

"Don't they ever get tired?"

141

The whine of sirens sounds once more. Fifteen police vans roar down the street, lights flashing. Inside are special troops. Riot-control specialists.

"Welcome to Strike Force Hotel everybody," Weatherspoon says.

The special task force of supercops is part of the Alpha Field Force of the Miami Police Department. The message is explicit: It is time to get tough.

Major Arnold Gibbs leads Strike Force Hotel. He says there were reports of gunshots.

"We're pulling regular police out. They're just targets. Any civilians who do not live in the area will be removed. Anyone committing a crime will be arrested."

But there is a problem. The night before, about 300 people were arrested. Area jails are already overcrowded. According to Roy Lang, a public relations spokesman for the police department, "Because of the crowding situation, these people could be back on the streets in a day."

Eight miles north in Liberty City, the residue of anger still smoldered. The abandoned church that was set afire late Tuesday night still has wisps of smoke coming from its rubble. The convenience store where Andrew Heegan always buys his cigarettes was closed, a big plank of plywood nailed over the hole that used to be a window.

"I don't know what this proves. Anybody can throw a brick. What the hell good does it do?" Heegan said Wednesday afternoon.

Liberty City used to be considered part of the dream. It was going to be the suburbs, the new, improved black community, the wave of the future. Thousands of Overtown residents moved to Liberty City in the '70's. They rode on the buoyancy of hope.

Hope got burned down. The dream was scorched.

"It's an economic thing," said Rita Lyndes. "If everyone here had a paycheck, a regular job, some reason to feel good about tomorrow, I believe there would be no trouble. But there never were enough jobs and now that all the Latins are coming in, there are even less jobs. I even think there's favoritism going on. Black people aren't getting the breaks."

The 34-year-old woman, unemployed since 1986, said, "Most of the time it's not anger, it's frustration. The other night though, when that white policeman shot the black man down in Overtown, that was bad. People feel the police got nothing better to do but shoot people."

In an emergency meeting of the city commission Wednesday, where an independent review panel was announced, a couple of private citizens' impassioned pleas rang out.

Bill Hardemon stood before Commissioner Miller Dawkins and said in a voice laced with emotion, "I live in Overtown. The police are shooting us like we are black birds. But . . . we are human beings. It is dangerous to be a black man living in South Florida. And I hope you notice this. I pray you do something about it."

The man wiped away a tear.

Florida Gov. Bob Martinez announced a plan Wednesday that could draft a 500-member National Guard troop force within two hours. He added he hoped it did not come to that.

Vera Cash said it probably will. She and her husband Charles have owned the Two Butchers Supermarket in Overtown for 17 years. She says the store has been broken into only once in that time.

"But the kids the other night told us we were next," she said. "They'll come looting. It isn't the residents. It's outsiders. We're a black business in a black neighborhood. You would think we'd be safe. But they told me the other night that we were next."

The shooting stops. No injuries are reported. No fires. No looting. The restless crowds dissipate. The only real signs of activity are bustling TV news crews. And those police vans, slowly patrolling the area.

"Forest fire travels on the wind," Weatherspoon said. "Violence uses tension. You feel it here. Not as bad as yesterday. But it's still here."

The pro basketball game the other night was called off. The car that the referees drove was pelted with rocks, bricks and bottles. Less than 30 feet from one of the entrances to the Miami Arena are some railroad tracks. This is the unofficial city limits of Overtown. You don't need the greatest arm in the world to be able to throw a rock far enough to hit someone. And if you have a gun. . .

143

The Chicago Bulls are supposed to play the Miami Heat tonight in an NBA game at the stadium. That means Michael Jordan, perhaps the draw in professional sports. The game has been sold out for months. It will be the only appearance by Jordan and his team in Miami this season.

Across the tracks, the crowd of kids, mostly teen-age boys, gathered around to answer a few questions.

"I ain't got no money to see no basketball game," says Larrue, who says he's 16.

The taller, older fellow next to him says he hopes the rest of the city "gets as broke as I am. Super Bowl don't really mean much around here. Ask that dead man on the motorcycle what he think about the Super Bowl. I hope everybody gets broke. We start out even — my chances are better. I figure I got the edge. I been down lot longer than they. I got experience on them."

6.

VICTORIES, DEFEATS AND OTHER ASSORTED TALES

For Richard, the road back is paved in tests of patience
June 7, 1982
The New York Times

SARASOTA, Fla. — The windy aftermath of Hurricane Alberto buffeted the Ed Smith Sports Complex, home of the Sarasota Rookie League. It was an hour before the Friday afternoon practice, and J. R. Richard, once the dominating pitcher in baseball, sat in the rickety bleachers behind home plate.

The breeze seemed to rake the scowl from his face. The tension of coping with where he is and where he used to be and where he is going subsided for a while. Richard, the only right-hander in National League history to strike out more than 300 batters in a season, relaxed and stretched his 6-foot-8-inch, 250-pound frame over four rows of seats.

"Things are falling into place, I guess," he said, eyes closed, hands clasped behind his head. "I'm here and I'm all by myself. But I don't have to worry about places to go and things to do. I have patience."

He sighed, sat back up and, looking across the minor-league ballpark that's so far away from where he normally is during the first week of June, he added, "and that's more than anyone else has for me about now."

The enormous man with the huge hands and broad shoulders and tiny teeth and gigantic smile and glorious memories and no athletic future to speak of is in the midst of a comeback from the stroke that threatened his life in the summer of 1980. Few people expect him to make it. Maybe not even Richard does.

Two years ago at this time, he was overpowering the National League with his 100-mph fastball and 90-mph slider. He had just signed a contract estimated to be worth $800,000 a season. There seemed to be no ceiling to James Rodney Richard's greatness.

On July 30, 1980, that ceiling collapsed. While working out in the Astrodome, Richard suffered a blockage of the subclavian, innominate and carotid arteries. A stroke at age 30.

"I should have died right then," Richard said, remembering that afternoon. "Anyone else would have been dead."

Age, of course, was on his side. It seemed he was so young, too young, to have a stroke.

Richard survived the stroke and the emergency operation that followed. Then, after a long recuperative period, he announced he would report to spring training for the 1981 season.

Nine months after being rushed into intensive care and almost dying, Richard was back on the field for the Astros in Cocoa, Fla. Houston's spring training base.

It was a sad sight watching the giant of a man fumbling with a glove like a little leaguer. Observers turned their heads when Richard couldn't follow ground balls hit toward him. They cringed the first time a line drive went whistling by Richard's head and he never even reacted to it.

"I had to learn to do things all over again," Richard said. He also said he had some special help:

"Last year I had this blind spot, this big black dot where if the ball went there, I couldn't see it. The doctor told me it would never go away.

"But it did go away," Richard said, almost yelling. "It was another of God's miracles."

Richard sat out the 1981 season. He worked out in Houston and there were stories he would be reactivated. It never happened.

So when the Astros reported to camp this spring, it was almost taken for granted that Richard would be competing for his old spot as the stopper on one of the game's stronger pitching staffs.

That's the problem with modern miracles. People are too impatient waiting for the miracle to be complete. The recovery wasn't enough. They wanted to know when he'd be back to the J. R. of old.

"Man, where I was before—it took me 30 years to get there. How am I going to be my old self in a matter of months? You can't take a step, then all of a sudden, know how to jump. If you don't know where you're going, how can you start?" Richard said in March, after facing batters for the first time in almost two years.

Richard wasn't impressive. A sore back and some tendinitis in his arm set him back. He reported to spring training overweight, too. His manager, Bill Virdon, said in late March: "Right now, I don't see how J. R. can help us in the big leagues.

"But he has made progress. And where there's progress, there's hope. I've been asked for two springs now how J. R. looks. I really don't know. I've never had to witness the rehabilitation process of someone who's gone through a stroke. So I might think he doesn't look so good and he might be making the most remarkable recovery in medical history. I can only judge his recovery from a major league player's perspective. And right now, he's just not there yet."

Al Rosen, president and general manager of the Astros, said, "I don't think you need to be a Phi Beta Kappa to figure out J.R. isn't going to make our major-league staff."

It was suggested that Richard report to a minor-league team instead of going on the injured reserve list, where he spent the previous season. He balked at first, then said he would.

"I'll go to the minors if I get the chance to pitch there. I'm improving every day. My rhythm's still off and that affects my control. I need to pitch. I may be the minor league player of the year," he said.

"It's for sure I'll be the highest-paid minor leaguer in history," he added.

That was at the end of March. Now it is some two months later. The decision to send Richard back beyond square one, beyond the lowest minor league, hit hard at his pride. Most of the players in the Sarasota rookie league are still in their teens. Richard is 32. He probably earns more than the rest of the league combined.

———

The refreshing confidence of the spring has vanished. Winter seems to have struck already. The frustration of trying to do something he knows he used to do better has taxed his outlook.

"I'm feeling better in a lot of ways, better than in a long time," he said the other day. "But I'm also bitter in a lot of ways. What has happened could have been prevented. It should have been prevented. My entire life was shattered. Physically, I'm just not the same. And I miss my family. I've been having troubles at home."

Richard has filed a lawsuit involving his stroke and what he and his lawyers contend was negligence and incompetence by doctors and team officials before, during and after the tragedy. Richard admits that suit still preoccupies him.

"The suit is going fine as far as I know," he said. "But how do you arrive at a figure?" His lawyers and his agent, Tom Reich, have set the figure at $25 million. "Somebody else on the other side says much less. But man, you're talking about my life. Me. How do you put dollar signs on someone's life? The money I could have made, the accomplishments I could have done, the things my family and I went through. To me, not even $100 million is enough."

An Astros' spokesman said that the team is making no comments about the lawsuit.

Richard folded his arms. Shaking his head, he continued: "It's not too bad here. Like an extension of spring training. I've improved a great deal too. I'm getting the breaking ball over. I know I can pitch in the major leagues again.

"But I don't know if I'm hungry enough to dedicate myself again. I don't think I'm hungry anymore. I'n not totally back and I know it. But I don't know. There's so much bitterness inside. . .

Richard then added, "I'm like everybody else. I want the best I can get. And I want what I deserve."

The strange thing about Richard's performance in Sarasota, especially since he questions whether he's still hungry enough to pitch, is that he has looked very strong. So says Jose Tartabull, the 44-year-old manager of the Astros' farm team.

"He's doing tremendous. If you saw him in spring training and now, you'd think he was two different pitchers," Tartabull said. "The only problem is his motion and he still has a little problem with reactions. But physically, he's healthy. He has a great arm."

A major-league arm?

"From what I've seen," Tartabull said, "it wouldn't be impossible. Sometimes he's wild high. But that can be worked out. It's his motion. He still has that nasty slider and he's been getting it over good. His fastball has been timed in the 90s. We send a report every day to the big club."

A few weeks ago on Mother's Day Richard took off for Houston. He missed his family. Rumors spread that Richard had gone AWOL, that he had suffered a mental breakdown, that he had retired.

"No, no, that wasn't it at all," Tartabull insisted. "He came to me and said, " 'Jose, I gotta go home.' He said he let the big club know, too. As far as I know, that's all there was to it. He came back a few days later. Nobody thought anything about it."

There is a problem now, though, says the manager. "J.R. is too good for this league; he's ready for Double A or Triple A right now. If his control gets a little better, he could go back to the big club."

James Rodney Richard looked out at the field once more, perhaps seeing it from a different vantage point than before. He took a deep breath and said: "If this suit goes through like I expect it to, then I don't know. Maybe I won't want to play anymore. I don't really know right now. I'm too bitter to give a straight answer."

He has pitched six times since coming to Sarasota, the longest a five-inning stint. He works out in a gym on his afternoons off, sparring with a couple of boxer friends, jumping rope, hitting the speed bag, doing as many hand-to-eye, reflex-improving, reaction-sharpening exercises as he can. The condominium he rents from Dave Parker, the Pittsburgh Pirate outfielder, "is real nice, but kinda lonely, too." His wife and five children are supposed to arrive here this week.

Easing out of the bleachers and walking slowly toward the clubhouse, Richard said, "I'm still ready to pitch in a World Series. I'm the same old J.R. in a lot of ways. But things are also different, know what I mean?"

As he walked past the fence down the first-base line, a teammate, an infielder out of high school less than a year, yelled to Richard, "How's it going, Mr. Superstar?"

Richard, the fallen giant who now believes in miracles because he feels he is one, at least a part of one, said with a smile, "You talking to me?"

A Hometown Mourns Joe Delaney: Haughton, La., Only Had One Hero and He Died a Hero's Death
July 3, 1983
The Denver Post

HAUGHTON, La. — The Pentecostal Church is selling fireworks by the side of the road. For its building fund, explains the boy behind the plywood counter. Business, he says, is lousy.

"Joe Delaney's funeral is all that people are thinking about right now. I think they forget that Monday's also the Fourth of July," he says.

Joe Delaney, running back for the Kansas City Chiefs and the most important citizen of this tiny Louisiana town, died Wednesday afternoon in Monroe. Some children got in trouble in a pond near a city park and Joe Delaney tried to help them. He and two of the children drowned. Now the 1,200 or so people of Haughton are getting their suits and best dresses dry-cleaned for a funeral.

"Hope we get some breeze," sighed Bobby Ray McHalffey. "That gym will really be steaming if we don't get some kind of a breeze."

McHalffey was Delaney's high school football coach. Since he heard the news, he admits he hasn't gotten much work done. "I still got a pit in my stomach as round as a washtub," he says. "I still can't accept it. Man, he came out for football in ninth grade as a 130-pound defensive end. But he had that special something, you know? There wasn't a bad bone in his body. I came home and my wife told me Joe was dead and I said, 'Aw, you've got to be kidding.' He's like one of my family."

Bobby Ray McHalffey then shook his head and said, "The way he died was the way he was. He'd do anything for somebody else."

There is one traffic light in Haughton. It always blinks yellow on one side, red on the other. It's the only thing in Haughton that would make you slow down. There is one post office, one library, one fire station. There are three churches. And one high school and no swimming pool.

Railroad tracks knife through the town, dividing it. Blacks on one side, whites on the other. It's always been that way. People sit on front porches and fan flies and progress away. They mow their yards on Saturday. Kids walk barefoot on the tracks and head for the fishing holes. And most of the roads leading out of Haughton are dead ends.

Haughton used to have a celebrity. But he is dead. And so, it seems, is Haughton. Once more.

Five in the afternoon. Beer thirsty. Happy hour at the unmarked tavern with the neon Budweiser sign in the window. Men with dirty necks and sore muscles sip from long-necked bottles and peel the labels and talk about the death of Joe Delaney.

A man with a front tooth missing declares that the post office should lower the flag out front to half-staff.

"Joe was damn fine people," he says. "Hell, the flag would be lowered if it was some politician who died. Joe Delaney did a whole hell of a lot more for us than any politician ever did. It would be a good way to show our respect, I think."

The woman behind the bar shakes her head. Rosa disagrees.

"He was just a football player and you got to be more famous than that to get the flag lowered. I'm just as sick as everyone else that he's dead and I sure hope his wife and little girls get along OK. But he was just a football player and you know that's another thing. I can't believe that a football player didn't know how to swim."

While everyone thinks about that, Merle Haggard sings on the jukebox. Rosa admits to the stranger that her real name is Rosemary. She gets more tips as Rosa "because I guess it sounds sexier."

The door opens and someone named Eddie walks in. Rosa immediately begins pouring a draught. Eddie says he heard on the radio that the funeral had been switched from the Galilee Baptist Church to the gymnasium. Everyone nods.

"That makes good sense," Eddie says after taking a big swallow of beer. "It's too hot for that little church. This way, everyone can get in, too."

A few blocks away—from one city limit to the other—other men sit on a table under the shade of a big tree in front of the Boom Town Grocery. They too drink beer and reminisce about Joe Delaney.

"He always had time for anyone," said the man in the green tank top and his hair in plaits. "He was the best this town ever seen. I was a sophomore when he was a senior at Haughton. He was the best. Man, I can't believe he's dead."

The others move their feet and shift nervously. They don't know what to say. It's all been said before.

In a month, training camp for the Chiefs will open. Joe Delaney was looking for something to do, some way to kill some time last Wednesday when he decided to take several neighborhood kids to Chennault Park in Monroe. A TV station was letting everyone in free. Delaney and the kids piled into his car and began the 80-mile trip to Monroe.

He was playing catch when he heard the screams. Tyrone Dickens yelled for help. He was safe but his friends, Harry Holland Jr. and Lancer Perkins, had gone under water and not come up. They had gone into the water and didn't know how deep it was. Dickens felt the mucky bottom and noticed the quick drop off from knee-deep to over his head. He reached for a branch of a tree. It broke. He reached for another and this time was able to pull himself to safety. But his friends were floundering under water and he yelled for help.

Joe Delaney heard the cries and did what was natural. The father of three either forgot or ignored that he was a poor swimmer. Without thinking. Like a running back. You react, you don't think. You follow your instincts. Like a running back.

It was 2:25 in the afternoon. Ten minutes later, sirens pierce the laziness of the day. Officer Charles Brown arrives first. Then assistant police chief E.M. Smith. Another call is made and Marvin Dearman, another department member and also an expert scuba diver, rushes to the park. A huge crowd gathers and ambulances pull up and men with grim faces unload a lot of space-age equipment. CPR begins. But an hour later, at St. Francis Medical Center, a spokeswoman says curtly that Harry Holland Jr., age 11, is dead. So is Joe Alton Delaney, age 24. Twelve hours later, Lancer Perkins, age 11, dies.

The CBS Evening News carries the story. In between the story on dioxin and the one on President Reagan's knowledge of Jimmy Carter's briefing papers. It is the nature of the world that someone must die to make the prime-time telecasts. If Joe Delaney could have jumped in that pond and pulled those children to safety, it would have been none of Dan Rather's business. And the three major networks would not be asking directions to Haughton High Gym. And there would be a lot of fireworks on the country's 207th birthday.

———

Marvin Dearman estimates the depth of the pond at 20 feet. He points out that the muddy bottom could create a sucking effect and could easily pull down an inexperienced swimmer.

A day after the tragedy, signs are posted everywhere: No Swimming.

On one, someone has scribbled, "Too late."

The day after Joe Delaney and two 11-year-old boys died, Chennault Park is open. A crowd stands around the two acres of water that swallowed up the only man in Haughton ever to be asked for his autograph on anything except a check. People look at the still water and try to recreate how it must have been. They look around at Critter Creek, the amusement park with the water slide and the kiddie rides and the cyclone fence.

Lawyers are arguing behind closed doors about the jurisdiction of the pond where the three people died. Who is responsible for the property and any legal actions that may follow? To hear both sides the amusement park owners and the city — nobody is.

John Alston, director of community affairs, tells reporters the pond is off-limits to swimmers. The pond was created, he said, after dirt was excavated for the park's big water slide. People aren't supposed to swim there, he repeats.

Now people listen. A lot of people stand on the banks. But nobody goes in.

"It's not a swimming hole," Alston says again. "They had some ducks and geese in there. It was used to add some aesthetics to the park."

Today it is a bad memory, aesthetically or otherwise.

———

Joe Delaney's home fits right in with the neighborhood. It is newer than the others, but it fits. Wood frame structure, a screen door that slams. He had the house built around the corner from where he grew up. A TV crew waits outside, its sinewy cables crisscrossing the yard, live mini-cam reports waiting to happen. Inside, it is quiet.

The rooms of Joe Delaney's home are small and noise travels well. A clock with four footballs on it ticks off each minute of a depressing day and it sounds like a time bomb.

Pictures fill the paneled walls. Most prominent are a 1982 team picture of the Kansas City Chiefs and a portrait of Joe Delaney and his three daughters.

Carolyn Delaney, the new widow, walks into the living room and walks out. She says nothing. She doesn't let herself hear anything. People from the funeral home were there earlier. The Rev. R.B. Jones, who will deliver the eulogy, also dropped by. Carolyn Delaney, who used to hear her husband talk about the pressures of being a football player, the pressure of the big game, the pressure of the playoffs, has learned about real pressure. About the pressure of facing the morning without her man. About the pressure of being the mother of three and nothing to look forward to but a funeral.

She has nothing to say. To anyone. Not anymore.

"Would someone like some iced tea?" asks Eunice Delaney Kennon, Joe's mother.

She doesn't cry. Her family wails with grief but she remains strangely calm.

"We can't undo what God has done," she says. "We have to accept what is given to us. I understand. Understanding is the best thing."

Someone asks if her son could swim.

"He said he could. But I never saw him swim. He was just a good boy and I don't believe he would lie to me."

She sits down and the woman who raised her eight children mainly by herself smiles and says, "I'll never forget the times we would sit on the porch and just talk. We'd just talk and relax. . ."

She closes her eyes and takes a deep breath. For a moment she is able to undo all the tragedy. But only in her mind.

Joe Ann Brazeale is Joe Delaney's twin sister. She tells the visitor that she and her brother were so close "that we felt the same feelings and thought the same thoughts. When I used to watch him play and he'd get cramps in his legs, I'd get the cramps, too. On Wednesday, I was home and all of a sudden I got these terrible pains in my chest. I felt my heart was hurting. I knew something wasn't right. I said, "Something's wrong with Joe.' Something bad had happened and I knew it 'cause I'm his twin sister. A few minutes later, the phone rang."

She fans herself with a newspaper as she pauses. The clock pounds the expulsion of each second throughout the house. Then Joe Delaney's twin sister adds, "When I close my eyes, I still see him."

Flowers arrive every few minutes. The area between Monroe and Shreveport is football country. A lot of good football players grew up there. James Harris, the first black quarterback in pro football. Sammy White, the Vikings wide receiver. Charley Smith, the wideout who played on the Eagles' Super Bowl team. Billy Joe DuPree, the Cowboys tight end. Eddie Robinson, the Grambling coach. Terry Bradshaw. Football country. One who does not send flowers of condolence is Larry Gordon, the Dolphins linebacker who was born in Monroe. He died last week of a heart illness.

"We have to try to understand," whispers Eunice Delaney Kennon, her heart aching but her eyes dry and clear and strong.

The reaction to Delaney's death was predictably similar all over the country. Shock. Hurt. Personal loss. Glowing remembrance of a special man.

Sen. Foster Campbell of Bossier City and a former teacher of Delaney at Haughton High, interrupted the Louisiana Legislature with the news. There was a moment of silence.

David Dumars, a defensive back for the Denver Gold, played against Delaney in college. Dumars was watching TV when he learned of Delaney's death.

"What he did and how he died," said Dumars, "that's the way he lived. That's the kind of attitude he had. He liked to help people. I'll always remember the first time I played against him. On the first play, he broke one for 85 yards. He was never one for boasting. He just went out and played. I'm thinking about him a lot. I can't go to the funeral. But I would if I could."

Marv Levy, his former coach on the Chiefs, said, "What does one say when a friend and member of the family is suddenly taken from this earth?"

A.L. Williams, his college coach, said, "Always trying to help someone, that's Joe. He'd do it again if he could. It cost him his life. But he'd try to help those kids again if he could."

Harold Harlan, the Haughton High School principal, said, "Only his ability changed — not his personality. He was the same person all the time."

156

The weather report on the country music station said it was 90 degrees. It seems hotter, says the lady selling cut flowers and eggs from her front porch. The man who cuts the meats at Pee Wee Anderson's corner store says it will get worse before it gets better. In small towns the talk about weather usually dominates the conversations. But now the talk is of Joe Delaney's funeral and then the weather.

"I wouldn't be surprised if the whole town showed up," said McHalffey. "That's how popular Joe was. Everyone loved him like their own son."

Heroes live; victims die. Joe Delaney lives. Haughton is preoccupied with its loss. Neither Rosa nor the Pentecostal Church is making much money these days. And on both sides of the tracks a genuine hero is missing.

"Sure hope we get a breeze soon," says McHalffey. "It's too damn hot for a funeral."

From Heisman to Counterfeiter
Billy Cannon's Star-Crossed Life Takes a Turn Toward Prison
July 17, 1983
The Denver Post

BATON ROUGE, La. — The child within the man has faded. Billy Cannon, once the town's most important citizen and the acknowledged southland idol of college football, sits in a Southern courtroom, ready to plea bargain.

Everybody's All-America now is a paunchy, middle-aged orthodontist hopeful of exchanging information for freedom.

Dr. Billy Abb Cannon, says the federal government put together an elaborate counterfeiting scheme.

157

It is Friday and Cannon usually gets together with friends for a breakfast during which they put their cowboy boots up on the table, smoke long cigars and shoot whatever breeze there might be. Instead, he sits in a chair and waits for his ignoble destiny.

He shows no emotion, just stares ahead, seeing something neither inside nor outside the room. A few feet away, the government men who have said Cannon conspired to print and pass $6 million in phony $100 bills stand with folded arms. Cannon's attorney and the assistant state's attorney in charge of the prosecution lean back on their heels and jingle the change in their pockets and whisper something about how glad they are the air conditioning finally got fixed.

A door opens. U.S. District Judge Frank Polozola walks into the room.

"All rise. Hoo-yea, hoo-yea. This court is now in session . . ."

Whatever it was that pulled Cannon off the top of his world has something to do with not looking at something that's standing right in front of you. It has to do with a person's being bigger than life and believing he's even bigger.

It is too difficult to understand, too hard to figure out why someone with a six-figure income in a town that adores and reveres him, would become a counterfeiter. Nobody understands, but everybody talks about it. And the only thing anyone really understands is that Cannon was back on the evening news the night before.

A woman with meaty arms sits in the second row of the courtroom. She pushes a bra strap inside her sleeveless white blouse and lets out a sigh that is part fatigue and part frustration. "I'm so disapointed at Billy, but if I could, I'd go up there and hug his neck. He looks like he doesn't have a friend in the world."

Indictments against Cannon and five other men now are public record. And if he had not agreed to help the government by supplying information, Cannon would have been staring at a possible 30-year prison sentence. As it is, the winner of the Heisman Trophy at Louisiana State University in 1959 could still receive five years in a federal prison.

"The court will accept the guilty plea," Judge Polozola says. A former LSU baseball player, the judge shows no emotion as he explains to Cannon that his willingness to cooperate means that other charges will be waived, but that no deals or promises involving his sentence have been made.

On the first row of the courtroom, Harvey Cannon, brother of the defendant, and Billy Cannon Jr., his son, squirm nervously. In a few minutes, the judge dismisses Cannon. Buck Kleinpeter, long-time attorney and friend of Billy Cannon, leads him through a side door. Free on recognizance bond, Cannon waits in the basement of the federal building until his son and brother join him. Then they quickly walk to Kleinpeter's white Continental, saying nothing, acknowledging none of the questions from a mob of reporters, and are gone.

The house at 1640 Sherwood Forest Boulevard is across the street from the country club. A real estate agent said these are older homes that sell for six figures. Cannon's home is a ranch-style structure on an acre of land. It has four bedrooms.

His pickup is parked outside. The house curtains haven't been opened for more than a week. By going to the street behind Cannon's, to Bellemeade Street, and walking through a backyard, a person can get a good look at the place where Cannon lives.

That backyard is part of the home of John P. Stiglets, 51. He is the man accused of making negatives and plates and then printing the $6 million in phony $100 bills. Stiglets, former LSU boxer, lives at 1749 Bellemeade, the house right behind Cannon's.

Where everybody else figures in the scam, or how they came to be a part of it, isn't known. The prosecution indicates that the situation is fraught with implications. Crimes beyond the crimes. The lurid hint of illegal gold smuggling. Drugs. Public figures. Elected officials.

All that has been mentioned, but not explained. All that ugliness most likely will surface in coming months.

Ray Smith used to own the Hawk's Nest bar. He used to lease the property from Cannon. The bar is adjacent to Cannon's office on

Lobdell Avenue, where children come to get their teeth straightened and adults still ask the doctor for his autograph.

"There's shysters everywhere," Smith said. "Billy just bought himself a bad deal. Maybe he got blinded by his own light. But no way will I ever say he was a bad man. To me, he was a straight-shooter, a nice man, a hell of a landlord, and he had a way with kids that was unbelievable. I'll say this—I would like to take my children no matter where he goes to jail and let him take care of their teeth. That's the way I feel about Billy Cannon."

Smith owned the Hawk's Nest until 6 p.m. July 8, when he and his wife walked into the back door at Cannon's office and undid the lease.

Cannon had just returned. He had been out, with Charles Whitfield and Timothy Melancon, at a vacant lot he owns. Federal agents were watching. They saw Cannon dig up an ice cooler and hand it over to the two men. The cooler was filled with the bogus bills.

And the world hasn't been the same for Billy Cannon since.

Strangers and outsiders have to understand something about this area. The people who get elected to office aren't always the most honest. And the constituents have seen their favorites wind up in jail at a rate that would alarm many other people.

In the 1950's, a big building boom occurred in Louisiana, followed by many unions, followed by labor problems in the 1960's. Colorful characters were everywhere. Especially behind bars. A sheriff was even re-elected while he was serving time.

This was the environment in which Cannon grew up. Born in Philadelphia, Miss.—ironically the same hometown as the University of Oklahoma's Marcus Dupree, this year's No. 1 Heisman candidate—Cannon and his family moved to Baton Rouge when he was three years old. It was a growing city, and anybody who wanted to work had a job. If one were a kid—well, he could stay busy, too.

Cannon developed into the country's premier high school football player at Istroma High. As halfback for the Istroma Indians, Cannon scored 39 touchdowns his senior year. He was already considered a world-class sprinter. He won state championships in the 100 and the shotput, a rare double on any level. But he also has a tempestuous side.

During the summer after his senior year, Cannon and some friends were hanging out on Third Street. A car stopped and honked. Cannon was pushed toward the car by his friends. It was a familiar scene. Everybody knew what was going on. Ellis Brown, who was Cannon's principal at Istrouma, explained, "It was some (homosexual), a professor at LSU, I think. Well, Billy got in the car and when the guy made a play for Billy, he let him have it. Beat him up a little, you know. It wasn't that big of a deal. It happened a lot.

"There's always been (homosexuals) in Baton Rouge. Well, this fellow gave Billy a bottle of whiskey and dropped him off, and a little while later the police came by and saw these kids with a bottle and stopped. And then when the D.A. found out Billy had assaulted this (homosexual), he took him in and booked him. Well, it really wasn't that big of a deal at all. It came to be that he got a suspended sentence, and some probation, that's all."

But some have said that's how Cannon, recruited by more than 100 colleges, came to choose LSU. He had no other choice, some say. The judge who heard the case — Judge Collie Huguet, now deceased — stipulated that Cannon be confined to the parish of Baton Rouge and not leave it for longer than 48 hours at one time for the next four years.

Others have said that wasn't how it happened at all. They have said Cannon decided to go to LSU, where his one-legged father worked as a custodian, because there he could run track as well as play football. The other places, like Oklahoma and Houston, wanted him to concentrate only on football.

But Montet, now retired but at the time sports editor of the Baton Rouge Morning Advocate, said he's heard all the stories, even one that suggests LSU tried to get Cannon in trouble on purpose so it could have him for four years. He said, however, that most of that is nonsense.

"Oh, there was that incident with the (homosexual) all right. But that was back when (homosexuals) were still in the closet," Montet said. "That guy didn't press charges. He was afraid to do something like that. Billy was like a lot of other kids. Not wild. Just a little restless. You have to understand how it was. Anyway, I don't believe LSU tried to tamper with his life. He went to LSU because that's where he wanted to go. I believe that."

A few days after the incident, Cannon stood up and told the congregation at Istrouma Baptist Church that he was sorry.

"That was in 1955, and you could already see what a leader he was," Brown, the principal, said. "There are a lot of sad hearts around town lately concerning him. But he was an All-America in every way until this latest thing. He was a leader, a fine student and probably the most-wanted athlete in the United States at one time."

At LSU, the legend of Billy Cannon grew. The final reference point is Oct. 31, 1959 — Halloween night. The fog was rolling in off the Mississippi River. Tiger Stadium was overflowing. LSU, the defending national champions, had won 18 games in a row. The Tigers' No. 1 ranking was due to a swarming defense nicknamed the "Chinese Bandits" that had 68,000 lucky ticketholders chanting its name.

And the ranking was due also to Cannon, the left halfback in the split-T attack who personified every coach's dream.

The game was with Mississippi, LSU's biggest rival. The Rebels also were unbeaten. They were ranked No. 3. It was at the very least that week's game of the century.

With 10 minutes left, Ole Miss led 3–0. It had been a game of high emotion and brutal blocking and tackling. The crowd reeled from spent emotion and anticipation. Rebels Coach Johnny Vaught ordered his team into punt formation on third down. The thinking was that his team might be able to force a fumble deep in Tiger territory. Jake Gibbs' line-drive punt traveled 47 yards and looked as if it might bounce and stop inside the LSU 10-yard line.

LSU coach Paul Dietzel had a cardinal rule that all punts inside the 15 not be fielded. But Cannon watched the ball bounce towards him and, gathering it in on his 11, took off.

He broke six tackles. At the 50-yard line, Cannon ran so close to

162

the Ole Miss sideline that Vaught could have reached out and touched him. He ran 89 yards, and scored a touchdown. Never was Cannon's aura so bright.

Mississippi stormed back and drove 67 yards, racing the clock until 18 seconds were left to play. The Rebels lined up for a play that, in their dreams, would bring them victory and make people forget Cannon's punt return. Reserve quarterback Doug Elmore tried to slant off tackle. LSU defenders slammed him back. The first one to hit him was Cannon, the Tigers' defensive halfback.

The night shivered from the cheers.

A few weeks later, Cannon accepted the Heisman Trophy from Vice President Richard Nixon.

But Camelot began to crumble. After the Tigers were soundly thumped in a rematch with Ole Miss in the Sugar Bowl, Cannon stood under the goal posts and signed a contract with the Houston Oilers of the infant American Football League. It surprised some people. But Oilers owner Bud Adams revealed a side of Cannon that wasn't well known. For all his abilities, Cannon could also hear money talk.

Then the problems began. The Los Angeles Rams, who had selected Cannon in the draft, announced they had a contract signed by Cannon. Secretly, they had flown Cannon into Philadelphia, where a deal was made. The Rams hid him in a downtown hotel under the name Peter Gunn. That contract superceded the one of the Oilers because this one was signed in November. There was Cannon's name on one side. And on the other was the name of the Rams' general manger: Pete Rozelle. It was the first swash of the serpent's tongue. A court battle ensued. Cannon belonged to the Oilers, a judge declared.

Cannon ran a football in a straight line. He used little deception. It was strength and speed. More physics than poetry. He was the foreshadowing of what Herschel Walker is today.

His second year in pro football, Cannon led the league in rushing.

A back injury convinced him that football wasn't forever. He started dental school in the off-season. Baton Rouge beamed at what an outstanding citizen its favorite son had become.

After 10 years of pro ball—the final seven with the Oakland Raiders—Cannon retired and became an orthodontist in Baton Rouge.

Cannon always had been familiar and friendly with local politicians. He had worked for the Teamsters during summers of his college career. He became interested in the way things worked in government. An endorsement by Dr. Billy Cannon was sought after by politicians.

Some of his political friends and labor leaders got in trouble. And some people in Baton Rouge wondered why Cannon bothered with it all. Why couldn't he be satisfied with the psychic income of his town's adoration and the cushy and financially beneficial lifestyle he had made for himself and his family?

Meanwhile, LSU's football program was slipping. That's another thing one must understand about Baton Rouge: although it is a prosperous town with a population of more than 200,000, football still dictates what to do on a Saturday night. And although Charlie McClendon still was taking the LSU Tigers to a bowl game almost every year, fans saw no indication that a national championship was imminent. A sniping campaign began. Some have said Cannon was behind it. Of course, the people who have said this don't want to be identified. To say something against Cannon used to be a sacrilege.

"Like spitting on the flag," said one former LSU athlete. "Billy felt he was above the law for a long time. He felt he was the good ol' boy who was the wheeler-dealer, and he thought money and life was like a Monopoly game. But you can't use my name 'cause I still gotta live around here."

So McClendon was let go. About the same time—about four years ago—Cannon's son was raising eyebrows at Broadmoor High. In the image of his father, Billy Jr. was an outstanding football player and a top-notch baseball player as well.

————

A shortstop who could run and hit with power, Billy Jr. was leaning toward a professional baseball career as his senior year approached. His father allegedly discussed his son's future with George Steinbrenner, owner of the New York Yankees. Steinbrenner agreed that Cannon's son was a fine prospect. Cannon told him he'd like a package that, when added up, came to about $350,000. Steinbrenner said that if Billy Jr. was still available when the Yankees' turn to pick came in the annual baseball draft, he would be taken by New York. Cannon fired off telegrams to the other major league teams, asking them not to draft his son. He warned them that if they did select his son, he would play college football instead. Several teams told Commissioner Bowie Kuhn about all this. Kuhn voided the Yankees' selection of Billy Jr. He also accused the Yankees of tampering. Meanwhile Billy Jr. announced he would play football somewhere.

Everyone in Baton Rouge assumed "somewhere" meant LSU. But a few weeks later, an announcement was made that Billy Jr. had chosen Texas A&M. Cannon Sr. admitted that he had advised his son. But he added that the only reason his son was leaving the state was because Texas A&M had a superior baseball program.

The outrage wasn't as much as Cannon felt it was, said Brown, now retired from the school system but still a friend of Cannon. "There were some people who said things like his jersey ought to be un-retired. But not many at all. People understood that he was just doing what any other father would do for his son."

Billy Jr., a prospect in both baseball and football, was arrested in 1981, after a fight in which he and a student from another school fell through a window at a fast-food restaurant. The son of LSU's only Heisman Trophy winner wasn't disciplined. He did miss the next week's game because of 14 stitches in his shoulder.

Earlier this year, Billy Sr. was asked to appear before the grand jury to give testimony about the Teamsters Union, of which he used to be an officer of a local affiliate. Also, earlier this year, the National Football Foundation announced that Billy Sr. had been nominated for induction into the College Football Hall of Fame. The ceremony was set for December.

But then his greatness butted heads with shame. On the silver anniversary of that glorious national championship team, Cannon has been accused of counterfeiting.

———

It apparently began in April 1981, April Fool's Day. Stiglets, who had been to prison before for counterfeiting, received $15,000 from Cannon to buy equipment to make counterfeit money. In Lake Charles, La., Stiglets made the first delivery, $1 million. Six months later, he handed over $5 million.

A few months after that, a phony bill turned up in Knoxville, Tenn. The U.S. Secret Service began an investigation. Last December, at a shopping mall in Baton Rouge, security guards caught a Houston couple trying to pass two bills that had the same serial numbers. In addition to a supply of the phony money, authorities also received a name.

Dr. Billy Cannon.

A Pensacola oilman, agents learned, had agreed to buy more than $2 million of the counterfeit money from Cannon. Timothy Melancon, the oilman, was supposed to get some of the bills from Cannon for a sale he had arranged.

What Melancon didn't know was that he had struck up a deal with an undercover agent. The agreement was $5 for every fake $100 bill. For $1.2 million of bogus bills, Cannon would receive $240,000. And that's what Cannon was doing that Friday afternoon, digging up something on his vacant lot, shortly before he signed a change-of-tenant lease with Ray Smith.

According to Dennis Shaw, a secret service agent who worked on the case, as much as $87,700 was passed. Rand Miller, assistant state U.S. attorney, told The Dallas Morning News, "If a real bill is a 10, then the standard counterfeit bill is a 3 or 4. These bills are a 7 or an 8."

U.S. Attorney Stanford Bardwell Jr. said Friday that Cannon

has yet to receive the first penny of profit from his scheme. A deliberate man with a straight spin and a starched personality, Bardwell said carefully, "As a prosecutor, I'm very proud of the collective work done by the various agencies. Personally, I'm disappointed in Dr. Cannon and have an obvious concern for his family."

"The dogs bark but the caravan moves on," John F. Kennedy said.

Former LSU Coach McClendon is in Hawaii and has not issued a statement.

Neither has Paul Dietzel, Cannon's coach at LSU, now operator of a ski lodge in North Carolina.

Jerry Stovall, who took over the left halfback position for LSU when Cannon graduated, is now the LSU football coach. He hasn't issued a statement.

Paul Manasseh, sports information director for LSU, pointed out that the university really hasn't had much involvement with Cannon for several years. Manasseh said LSU is no more involved in Cannon's affairs "than Pittsburgh is in Tony Dorsett's. And if you'll check the local papers, it is not a sports story here. It is a news side story."

As might be expected, neither Cannon nor anyone in his family has made any statements. Calls to their unlisted phone number are politely answered, then abruptly hung up. Attorney Kleinpeter has no comment.

G.A. "Goober" Morse, who usually is in the group that gathers for breakfast with Cannon, has been out of town. Ex-principal Brown is disgusted that a good man has made such a mistake. J.C. Politz, a retired radio announcer and the man who described Billy Cannon's Halloween Night run to glory almost 25 years ago, says that "Billy Cannon must be given the chance to repent, to come back and be the hero to the kids that he's always been.

"Whatever he was, whatever he thought he was, is our fault. We made him bigger than life. And if you ask me, we are all guilty of whatever crimes Billy Cannon commits."

The shock remains. The resigned sorrow prevails. And, in a world of Frogman Henry and Huey Long memories, big rollers who get together at TGIF are playing liar's poker with an extra special eye these days. And people who stare out of screen porches at strangers, eat fruit with pocketknives and talk about this year's LSU team compared with those wonderful days of yesteryear really don't understand what's happening.

The fog came earlier than normal this season, it seems.

The appointment to the Hall of Fame has been put on hold. Cannon sold his practice earlier in the week. A board of dentistry will decide soon whether his right to practice should be lifted. His sentence eventually will be given out, and chances are good that he will go to prison.

"But he's not a bad boy," Ellis Brown said again. "He was an All-America in every way. He was a hometown hero until this and I don't think people should forget about that."

NASA's challenge: Space program takes road back from disaster
Jan. 28. 1987

CAPE CANAVERAL, Fla. — Nature usually lives in harmony with technology in the woods that connect the Merritt Island National Wildlife Preserve and the Kennedy Space Center. These days, though, technology has gone into seclusion. It is what they call downtime for America's space program. No launch today.

One year after Missions Control said "Liftoff!" for the last time, the Challenger disaster still sends out shivers. Two thousand space workers have been given pink slips. The National Aeronautics and Space Administration has undergone a major shake-up; careers are finished. An entire community, the Space Coast, has become disheveled, traumatized, thrown into confusion. At a time when interest rates are favorable, real estate has stumbled. Rents are being lowered. Unemployment is rising.

But John Tanner, a bounty hunter for the National Aeronautics and Space Administration, is working overtime.

"I might kill gators, or wild pigs, snakes, any kind of critter that could screw up things for the space boys," says Tanner.

In his pickup truck are two dogs — pit bull terriers — hunting dogs trained to flush out the growing amount of prey wandering toward the relative quiet of the space center.

"It sure gets busy out here," he says. "I wish to hell they'd hurry up and get that shuttle back in the air."

His eyes are slits as he stares off in the direction of Pad 39-B. It was there, 28 days into 1986, that a quarter century of fantastic success left the ground and exploded following 73 fateful seconds of flight, and grim trails of smoke in a cloudless sky ripped away a precious badge of credibility.

Seven astronauts were killed a year ago, and the blahs of complacency caused by NASA's constant success immediately turned into the blues of depression.

Those fateful words, "Go at throttle up," the last transmission from the Challenger crew, the last words uttered by flight commander Francis "Dick" Scobee, serve not as a cry to trample the horizon, but an epitaph.

"They need to get their act cranked up again," Tanner says. "It's like riding a horse. They need to get on back in the saddle."

It is not so simple. At the nearby NASA press center, evangelistic spokesmen speak idyllically of recovery. The program is not terminal. It shall return. But the overriding sense of betrayal sends tentacles of suspicion in all directions.

The aftermath of investigation, the hint of possible negligence, of bungled management, of poor judgment, has turned the space audience into a mob of skeptics.

"We made the impossible look easy for a long time," says Jim Ball, a NASA public relations officer who also is a city councilman in nearby Titusville. "Then very talented, very skilled people were suddenly stopped by total failure. It was a terrible accident; our loss will never be forgotten. Morale has suffered. There is a huge sense of letdown. But we're on the way back. You can feel the optimism. In the fall we had a performance countdown for Atlantis (the newest shuttle orbiter) on Pad B. All the players were back in their roles, working at their jobs. It was a great lift for morale.

Things have perked up since then. You can feel the confidence in the air again."

But on Tuesdays and Thursdays, you can still see the tragic reminders. At the nearby obsolete silos that used to house Minuteman and Atlas missiles, huge cranes reverently and delicately lower the tons of debris that once was STS-51L, the Challenger, into a futuristic crypt not far from the scene of what turned out to be as much a crime as an accident.

Public trust has had the wind knocked out of it. It is like catching your spouse with someone else. Despite your basic beliefs, it is hard to have faith.

"That's why we need to get another bird up," Ball says. "The public wants to believe in the shuttle. We get thousands of letters suggesting as much. Now we've just got to go ahead and do it."

Only not at the risk of compromising safety for the sake of a schedule. There is a target date of Feb. 18, 1988. Already the rumors fly. The whispers say there is no way the new and improved shuttle will launch.

There's too much work to do.

This month, the modified O-ring, that quarter-inch synthetic rubber fleck, Exhibit A in the Challenger accident, failed its latest test.

Also this month, the two millionth visitor during the past fateful year took the guided tour of the space center—an all-time record. It is the only business booming in the area.

The woman with the badge stating simply, "My name is Diana," explains that when the buses wheel by Pad 39-B, creeping to a stop so picture-takers can focus their cameras and get a shot of the place Challenger took off from, a lot of people cry.

"There is something about the pad that lets out a lot of leftover feelings," she says. "I think it's good though. I don't think we should ever forget how precious life is or how risky spaceflight is."

In Houston, the astronauts for the next shuttle flight hold a news conference. They joke about the hesitant response they received when friends and family found out they would be the next to attempt space flight for the United States.

The trust just isn't there.

———————

"Get it back up, get everyone back working, producing. Right now it's like everyone is waiting at the bus station," says Shawn Folding, who was laid off from her aerospace-related job after Christmas.

"There's a real bad mood out on the Cape now," she says. "Even the companies that have nothing to do with the shuttle are kind of going through the motions. Any kind of progress will help. That's why that Trident launch was so important."

The Cape rumbled with familiar activity earlier this month when a Trident II missile, the superweapon that attracted anti-nuclear protesters like ants on a piece of dropped cake, was poised for a launch. It was supposed to be a secret launch, but a local television broadcaster leaked the scheduled launch time. Protesters were everywhere an hour before sunrise.

But a launch was in progress, and the lesions of scar tissue were being ripped away.

The missile lifted off two hours late, but then streaked into perfection, a plume of smoke that turned into a speck before disappearing. A flawless launch.

An uneventful success.

"This has happened before," says Anita Moore, of the Job Placement Program at nearby Brevard County Community College. "When Apollo shut down, there were a lot of layoffs. The area became depressed economically. Well-educated men and women with families found themselves pumping gas to hold onto their homes. Foreclosures were everywhere. We're determined not to let that happen again. Maybe their jobs won't pay as well, but maybe we can make it through this tough time."

Ed Trusser, who lives in Titusville, has a couple of engineering degrees from Georgia Institute of Technology. He also has a bitterness he can't hide.

"I went in for this counseling where they're supposed to help me find a job until the Cape gets back on its feet," Trusser says. "And they told me stuff like air fares are low and the cost of gas is down too. And the terrorist scare is making a lot of people stay in America for their vacations and that would help tourism. And that would mean more jobs around here. But I'm a scientist; I don't want to sit in a hut and sell shark teeth."

Lockheed Aircraft Corp., the primary shuttle contractor, is the largest casualty. Grumman Aircraft lost a lot of workers too. But spokesmen insist there will be recalls. Stick it out and their old jobs will be available once more.

Lynn Smith worked in technical services for Grumman until May. Then he was laid off for the fourth time in 14 years. He decided enough was enough.

He is now a registered stockbroker.

This is called survival, according to a labor market analyst in the area who will throw figures at you nonstop, say a few things about the economy being more diversified than ever before and proclaim the problem is not as severe as feared.

But you wonder. Why are auto rentals way down? Why are the area nightspots suffering so much? Beauty salons report business is terrible.

Waiting.

At Cape Canaveral, the temperatures dipped into the 40s recently. People could not help but talk about the weather.

It was 36 degrees at 11:38 a.m. on Jan. 28, 1986. Seventeen degrees colder than the previous low for a shuttle launch.

A few miles inland, Regis Taylor shakes his head.

"Terrible, you know, just terrible," he says. "I blame it on the weather."

He is talking not of space, but of his modest orange grove. When Challenger exploded, Taylor was already feeling sad.

"The cold burned me out. Killed the whole crop. Busted me good. Maybe I'll recover, maybe I won't. It was sure terrible when that rocket blew up, but it was a bad day before it ever began for me. Night before, if I remember right, it got down to 23. I knew then there was trouble on the way."

Col. Edward O'Connor Jr. was in charge of recovery operations after the hopes and dreams of a proud program were scattered along the Atlantic Ocean. He also was instrumental in getting the debris lowered into the silos at the Cape.

"It is essential to remove the reminders so we can get on with erasing the question mark," O'Connor says.

The colonel looks up in reflex to the rumble in the sky. It's an airplane and it tugs a banner.

"Rosie O'Brady's Goodtime Saloon."

O'Connor smiles.

"Life does go on, I guess," he says. "The Challenger is gone; the challenge remains."

———

A year has passed. Countless trees of memorial are taking root. Most of the economic bad news has been issued. Now there is hope, even expectation, something good is on the way. In Idaho, Barbara Morgan, the runner-up to Christa McAuliffe to become the first teacher in space, has reaffirmed her wish to travel space.

NASA will get a second chance.

Children in the area, boys and girls who were marched outside or left to open windows to watch the launch that never made it, have probably recovered from any trauma. Suzanne Sohel, a family counselor, says any unresolved grief among the young has been allowed to ebb away.

"There were some who needed special help because they were confused," Sohel says. "They knew their father worked at the Cape. They saw the explosion. They thought their father had been killed. Some others, terrible as it sounds, saw the accident as little more than something they've seen in a "Star Wars' movie. They were encouraged to talk about it, share their feelings. I think they've put it behind them."

At McNair Elementary, formerly known as Pineda, the anniversary of the accident is something nobody wants to ignore. Ron McNair, one of the seven Challenger astronauts, had taken a special interest in the school, which is near the Cape. He was supposed to speak there two months after his flight. After the disaster, the school's name was changed in his memory.

"We will draw some pictures and talk some," says Irene Thomas, a second-grade teacher. "Children bounce back so much better."

Adults carry grudges.

"Everything NASA perceived itself to be got thrown into the wastebasket," says Melinda Gipson, an editor at Space Business Week magazine.

A 256-page presidential commission report told of a serious flaw in the decision-making process. Most of those decision makers have been replaced. Only three of the 97-member astronaut corps dropped out.

The lingering images of salvage ships hoisting wreckage with an American flag on the side persist. An intact astronaut's helmet sported on a desk aboard a Coast Guard ship. It was the story that would not go away for so long. The space program needs to get rid of that image before John Tanner runs out of ammunition.

Has the healing begun?

"Yes, most definitely," says Col. O'Conner.

"We're on our way back," says Ball. "Maybe the hiring freeze will be lifted soon."

There was an exhale when the Trident II blazed into flight. It held no symbolism, no guarantee. But it was activity. The mourning period is over. It's time to get going again. But first, make sure all the snakes, not just the ones John Tanner seeks out, are gone.

———

If there was a time when morale touched bottom, it had to be a few months after the accident. The word passed, and the road leading to the shuttle landing strip was lined with aerospace workers. It was a bright spring day, once again cloudless. You could hear the overhead sea gulls screech. People barely said anything.

When the procession of seven black hearses arrived, it got even quieter. Some of the space workers dropped to their knees in prayer. One by one, the hearses passed, heading for the runway.

A parked Air Force C-141 transport plane was open. There was a full color guard in formation. Seven flag-draped coffins were reverently loaded aboard.

Destination: Dover Air Force Base in Delaware. The dead heroes were headed for their final disposition.

The plane readied for takeoff. It taxied down the long runway, 15,000 feet long, long enough for a shuttle to return from space safely and took off. It headed north for a few seconds and then made a sweeping circle to the right. It was directly over Pad B when it turned again, this time headed west.

It is an old Air Force tradition, dating back to even before the U.S. Army Air Corps days that if a fellow pilot didn't make it back from a mission he was never referred to as killed or dead.

"My friends went west," was how it was put.

———

"There can be no thought of finishing, for "aiming at the stars' both literally and figuratively is a problem to occupy generations, so that no matter how much progress one makes, there is always the thrill of just beginning."

—Dr. Robert Goddard, generally considered the father of modern rocketry, in a 1932 letter to author H.G. Wells.

Chasing Shadows
Hagler's haunting image lures Leonard into light
March 1, 1987

HILTON HEAD, S.C. — On the hard sand, the image of that shaved skull will sometimes appear. And Ray Leonard will flinch as he runs along the beach.

Hagler.

Even the ghosts sometimes haunt each other.

175

For so many years, Marvelous Marvin Hagler felt the eerie presence of Sugar Ray Leonard. Teasing him from the other side. Hagler was always next. Always waiting his time, desperate for his chance at the riches and glory that always came relatively easy for his flashy pretty-boy counterpart. Only one solution—get in the same ring. For years Hagler fumed privately, staring at the man who had all the money, all the respect. Always waiting to fight Sugar Ray Leonard.

And it did not happen. A detached retina in Leonard's left eye prompted a hasty, glitzy retirement in 1982. Sugar Ray Leonard, then 26, in a tuxedo and holding a microphone, looked at Hagler and said of their once-anticipated dream fight, "It'll never happen."

Reckless words.

In 1971 Sean Connery, the distinguished British actor, declared he was through with James Bond movies. Never again, Connery vowed. Several years later, Connery, back in the 007 saddle again, starred in the aptly titled *Never Say Never Again.*

Ray Leonard laughs at the story, then adds, "A good lesson for us all."

Then he is asked about another James Bond movie, one even more personally symbolic.

For Your Eyes Only.

Leonard never hesitates. "I didn't see that one."

After his retirement, he made an aborted comeback attempt in 1984 in Worcester, Mass. Hagler sat ringside. And listened to a second retirement speech. "I can't go on humiliating myself," Leonard said.

Eventually, big paychecks, respect and recognition came Hagler's way. Hagler convinced himself he did not need his sweet ally, after all.

But now the porch light has become the moth. And the spirit world has been turned inside out.

As an HBO commentator, Leonard was ringside for Hagler's recent domination of the boxing world. Retirement was uncomfortable, even unbearable. Each fight made Leonard squirm more and more. Suddenly, he knew.

So Ray Leonard, a 30-year-old multimillionaire, runs on the

hard sand of the South Carolina beach, chasing not an exorcist but the demon himself. He sees the image again and again. Hagler. Four miles each morning, just as the sun is yawning and stretching over the Atlantic. Always in the company of his magnificent obsession. Hagler.

———

One fight, that's all. Two men somehow sharing the same umbilical cord. At last, they shall hear the sirens; their shadows can make each other shiver once more, this time together. In the Nevada desert, on April 6 at Caesars Palace in Las Vegas, they will fight. It is the only way it could end.

Leonard has become consumed by Hagler. He has seen the steam rise from the shaved skull between rounds as the chill of the evening collides with the heat of passion. He has seen the Mephisophelian scowl; all the rage and fury radiate and fuel the defenses against the constant parade of challengers. He has seen the blood of Marvelous Marvin Hagler trickle all over that ominous head. And he has seen that smug smile of triumph, the one that changed sides without ever being contested.

A prizefighter is measured by the greatness of his opponent. Leonard himself had been blessed with the likes of Tommy Hearns and Roberto Duran. Ali had Frazier, Dempsey had Tunney. But Hagler and Leonard? Leonard says he must find out. And Marvin Hagler must also know. They must see each other from the same shadow.

"Marvin is my mountain," Leonard says. "Because he's there. That's why. Nobody else. I don't want a comeback, only a fight. It was inevitable."

Ray Charles Leonard, named, ironically enough, after a blind man, walks on the beach on a gray day in February, his four-mile run concluded. The ghost is walking backward and he can see it ahead of him. Smiling. Still taunting. Still gloating.

Leonard is now the outsider. He only enters the ring when they introduce the former champions. And Leonard flinches once more;

177

he shakes his head as if to chase away the apparition. He has to find out.

"People think I'm crazy, don't they?" he says. "But they've never been in that ring, never pulled on gloves, tight, over the knuckles. They never heard the cheers or felt the feeling. And they've never sat and stared at someone else and wondered, "Can I beat him?' I can't spend the rest of my life wondering."

Leonard has fought exactly nine rounds in four years. He is jumping two weight classes. And of course, he is putting his famous retinas in jeopardy against one of the more savage fighters of this star-sprinkled era.

"Look, I have a note from my doctor and even my wife says it's OK," Leonard says, flashing his dazzling smile. "And by the time we get in the ring, it will be more than a year since Marvin's fought himself. And by then, well, how old does he claim to be? Thirty-two? Whatever. He's got some things to overcome, too. This isn't some fantasy trip.

"I really think I can beat him."

Confidence is essential. Leonard's is, as always, unbridled. Not only that, it's contagious. People see him and remember. He looks the same, a little bigger in the chest and arms. He talks the same. Always the charmer. And they want to believe the timekeeper can be cheated, that an athletic life can have a bookmark put into it and, years later, be picked up and resumed. Some even put their money where their heart is. The early 4–1 betting odds favoring Hagler have shriveled. Now it is 2–1. The fight is sold out. Ticket sales for closed-circuit have been brisk. More and more people are becoming convinced the Sugar Man can defeat the Marvelous One.

"That's got to make Marvin a little edgy, too," Leonard says.

The makeshift training room at the Inter-Continental Hotel already rumbles with activity. And confusion. Pounding the heavy bag is a bald-headed man in a left-handed stance.

"Is that . . . Hagler?" asks the older man in the argyle sweater.

"Naw, just a sparring partner," his friend says, squinting to make sure. "Yeah, that's a sparring partner."

Dwayne Cooper pounds the bag and people lean over the velvet ropes to take pictures. He calls himself "The Barbarian." The shaved head was his own idea.

"I thought Ray could use some inspiration," Cooper says. "Seeing a bald head across the ring might help."

Janks Morton and Dave Jacobs are huddled, talking about the day's workout. Eight rounds of sparring. Cooper and two other sparring partners. All are ambidextrous. Like Hagler.

Morton and Jacobs are two of Leonard's trainers. The other, Angelo Dundee, is in Miami. He won't join the entourage until two weeks before the fight. But every day the three talk by phone, planning strategy.

Leonard is waving as he climbs through the ring ropes. Yes, it's all about eyes, but not his. Public eyes. Fickle eyes. Star-crossed eyes. He is like an animal on the highway, frozen by oncoming headlights. This is the void that could not be filled with all the millions he earned and held onto. This is the rush of excruciating drama that smothers all fighters whenever they climb through the ropes.

Leonard shadow-boxes several minutes, still exquisite in motion, hands and feet so swift, the combinations a blur. A sweat broken, his legs springy, his muscles loose, Leonard nods and stands in a corner as the headgear is strapped on. It has been so long since he went into the ring without the headgear.

What will it be like?

"Not like last time," Leonard says. "No apprehension or hesitation this time."

Cooper is a natural middleweight, very physical and clever, if brutish at inside fighting. He tries to manhandle Leonard. But the footwork of the former welterweight king is amazing. Hagler is a master at cutting off the ring on opponents; Leonard is just as adroit at escaping such traps. Cooper has been instructed to try to work Leonard into a corner. Leonard dances away each time.

Suddenly, Leonard ducks into that familiar crouch, almost beck-

179

oning his opponent to come closer, his face stuck out, his hands low. Cooper closes in and Leonard flashes a right jab off his nose.

Sugar has switched to lefty. Another jab and another and the red gloves are blurs and the feet dance and dart and shift and then a big left hand smacks Cooper's chin. The galvanized crowd cheers.

Is it a hint of upcoming strategy? Will Leonard counter the lefty-righty prowess of Hagler with some ambidextrous trickery of his own? A sneak preview of fight night? Or is it more head games, more synthetic news intended to filter across the country to Hagler's California training camp? Like the incandescent rumors — Sugar's got a broken hand, a blood disease, a problem with gaining back weight lost from the flu, etc. — is this going to mess with Hagler's concentration?

"One thing is sure," Morton says. "Hagler's got to worry what Ray's doing. He's got to be ready for everything because Ray's always been so versatile. And when you're thinking more about what the other guy is doing than what you are, you're going to lose."

Another bully, bigger than Leonard, stronger. Oscar Pena. Also slower, less mobile. Leonard rains combinations that, despite the oversized gloves and the headgear, stagger Pena. The constant motion, the quick moves, in and out, left to right, mesmerize like a snake's dance.

Pena's punches are easily slipped. Leonard has always had the great ability to make an opponent miss. And there are more cheers. And then another sparring partner. And another strategy unleashed. A little different, a little the same. Always the movement, once more the stunning brilliance of combinations, crisp and very much on target.

"Ladies and gentlemen," says Ollie Dunlop, holding a microphone, "Sugar Ray Leonard."

The overflow crowd is thrilled. Leonard towels off and hits a speed bag for several minutes, then heads to the heavy bags. Morton grabs the bag and leans and shoves it toward his fighter. And Leonard responds with those flashes of fist. And Morton screams that he needs two minutes. Two minutes, Sugar Ray.

And Leonard's boyish face erupts into rage. The smooth mocha face scrunches into a sneer. And a hundred Instamatics flash in syncopated frenzy, turning the scene into an old-time, flickering, black-and-white moment. A fighter swivels his shoulders, his hips dug forward, the uncharacteristic grunts attesting to the barbarity of the ballet. His fists punctuate every emotion.

"Yeah, Sugar Ray, yeah!" shouts someone from the crowd.

Whoops and whistles and clapping hands take over. And the two minutes are spent with one man showing off his will. And 200 people pivoting in unison and accompaniment to each assault.

Ollie Dunlop repeats, "Sugar Ray Leonard, ladies and gentlemen. Sugar Ray Leonard."

And Leonard stops and that smile blinds. And he waves, out of breath, gloriously back in harness, his body basking in the pool of public eyes once more.

"Now Mr. Leonard is going to work out with the jump rope," says Dunlop, who used to run the rec center in Maryland that a 12-year-old Ray Leonard once walked into on a friend's double dare.

The huge cassette player, bouncing with rock music until then, is suddenly silent. And Leonard, facing a portable full-length mirror, whirls the rope from side to side, skipping slowly, building the tempo. Then the scratchy sound of the rope on the floor becomes a percussion instrument and the dance begins, at first slow and simple. The rope obediently twirls over head and under foot, all motion muted and thrifty.

And then the music begins.

"Sweet Georgia Brown." Leonard has the rope humming. It gets more intense with each chord. Faster, faster the rope seems to screech as it whips through the air. Leonard's feet flutter, his arms vibrate. Then he is jumping higher, the rope passing twice under him before he lands. It is a hiss. The sweat flies everywhere. He smiles as the crescendo approaches. Now he is higher. Then higher still. The rope is invisible, his hands and legs blurs. People are on their feet, cheering someone jumping rope.

181

Sugar Ray Leonard drops the rope just as the song ends. And drinks from the standing ovation that is his.

But it is more than this. More than beating up on hired hands. More than putting on shows in front of tourists and retirees at a beachside resort hotel. Charisma becomes devalued once the bell rings. Once Marvelous Marvin Hagler begins measuring you, closing in on you with that famous head tilted, his jaw stabbed into his chest and eyes that look like the popped-up high-beams on a Corvette glaring at you, you'd better be ready for something other than a game of jump rope.

"Let's face it, Marvin has the better resume," Leonard says later. "It's more current and up to date. And he's bigger and stronger, and I doubt if I can knock him out. But he can be beat. I've seen how."

The first hint was when Hagler fought Duran, winning an unglamorous 15-round decision. In the ring, Duran spotted Leonard and shouted, "Sugar, you knock him out easy. You fight him, you knock him out."

Leonard already was thinking. He saw some things during the fight that. . .

"I had to wait until I got the video of the fight to check," Leonard says. "Roberto did some moves, some little things that really bothered Marvin. Things I can do better. Since then, I bet I've seen that one video 100 times."

Even in Hagler's three-round destruction of Hearns, Leonard spotted some things that made him think Hagler was more vulnerable than marvelous.

"And all that scar tissue over each of his eyes," Leonard said recently. "A smart fighter could nip and peck and really do a number."

Then, when Hagler knocked out John Mugabi in the 11th round last April, Janks Morton spotted Leonard standing up and wringing his hands.

"That's when I knew he wanted to fight again," Morton says. "I could see it in his actions. He never could hide his feelings from me. I've known him so long."

In 1973, in Boston, 16-year-old Ray Leonard fought for a national AAU boxing championship. During the day, a battler named Leon Spinks lost, Howard Davis won and Ray Leonard, not yet sweet, lost. Later, dejected and holding sore ribs, Leonard returned to watch some of the other championship bouts. In one, a scrappy kid from Brockton, the same town that gave the world Rocky Marciano, won the 165-pound championship.

His name was Marvin Hagler.

Soon, they meet again. In the same shadow, in the same glare.

The mood in the room is electric. Carnival. Leonard nods to Dunlop. If everyone is quiet and orderly and forms a straight line, "Sugar Ray will be glad to pose for your pictures with you," Dunlop says.

Men hold small babies for him to touch and hug and smile at. Women get bold and ask for kisses. Fat people suck in their stomachs to stand next to the once and maybe future champion.

"Oh no, no championship," Leonard says, smiling. "Just this one fight. One time."

A pause and another dazzle of smile and, "This time, everyone believe me."

Standing up, pulling on a Gucci sweat suit, walking out of the room, slowing down just long enough to look in the portable, full-length mirror one last time, Sugar Ray Leonard heads for the door. Walking fast, heading for his suite, he suddenly turns and walks to the speed bag, hanging still, its surface smooth and oblong as a shaven skull.

One punch, a right hand, rocks the bag and the sound is sweet.

Heiress apparent: Graf family charts plan for tennis success
June 30, 1987

WIMBLEDON, England — Peter Graf remembers the pained, pathetic voice on the telephone.

"Papa, it is snowing and I am freezing. I have no coat or boots."

Long distance from Chicago. Steffi Graf calling home. Bruehl, West Germany. Collect.

"I tell her to go buy a coat," says the father of the next queen of women's tennis. "She is almost crying because she says she looked. But the one she liked cost $230. I say "Steffi you have millions. Go spend your money. Get yourself a coat."

Peter Graf laughs hard and shakes his head. "My Steffi. She is still such a child. She sees nothing of the real world. Only the tennis. That is her world. It has been her world, I think, all her life."

The competitors' tea room at Wimbledon is almost empty. Peter Graf has slipped in for coffee. In a few minutes he must man his spot in the stands at Court No. 1. He must be there when his daughter plays her second-round match. It is her destiny, he says, to become a champion. And it is his to take her there.

"I must protect Steffi," says the 48-year-old Graf. "That has become my life. I don't push her; I protect her. I am not popular . . . it is the price I pay."

His 18-year-old daughter, the No. 2 seed at Wimbledon, the winner of 42 straight matches, the latest and most serious threat to Martina Navratilova's six-year reign as the best woman tennis player in the world, walks onto the court just moments after her father has taken his seat. They don't say anything, or even gesture. But she knows her father is there. And he knows she knows.

Her warm-ups are brusque, almost impatient. And it is only a minute or so before everyone notices why the world anticipates, even expects a changing of the guard. Steffi Graf simply hits the hell out of a tennis ball.

First, foremost at least for now, there is the forehand. Hers is the singular most dominant weapon in women's tennis.

Such power comes from two sources: A looping backswing that almost resembles a hockey slap shot. It was a similar loop and forward transfer of weight that gave a young Bjorn Borg the put-away shot he lacked when he first came into world-class tennis. Steffi Graf showed up with it.

Exceptional timing generates racket-head speed that once would have been considered unfeminine. Steffi Graf has been pounding a manly forehand like this for . . .

"Three years, 10 months," Peter Graf says. He laughs again.

"That is not how long she plays tennis. It is how old she was when she started."

On the court, the young girl smashes balls with a relentless consistency. Hard shots that skid on the grass. Winners. Peter Graf likes what he sees, even if he never lets on.

"She is incredible. All she wants is the tennis. When she was that little girl, not yet 4, she used to beg me to let her hit the balls. And the first time she picked up the racket, she held the head up. Always, the racket head was up."

This is the tennis instructor's favorite warning. Peter Graf says he has never had to tell his daughter to hold the racket up.

Graf runs a tennis instruction camp. He also used to sell cars and insurance, until Steffi's flaring success "demanded" he retire and devote all his time to her career.

"They say I push her. They think I manipulate Steffi. But this is what she wants."

Graf tells of the days when his tiny daughter would "plead with me to let her hit the ball. She would beg and I would always let her have her way."

Another lesson in the tennis instructor's prayer book is to understand the importance of always getting the ball back over the net. Concede nothing.

Graf set up a string between two chairs in his house. The imaginary net. He sawed off part of the handle on an old racket so his tiny daughter could grip it right. And she started hitting.

"We broke a few lights. But she would not quit," Graf says. "We used to play games and have contests. If she could hit it back 10 straight times, I would give her a bread stick. If she could hit it 25 straight, we would have ice cream and strawberries."

185

Then an odd smile, a cold hissing grin slices the face of Peter Graf.

"But most of the time, on the 25th ball, I would hit it hard so she could not return it.

"Because you can't have ice cream all of the time."

Steffi Graf advanced to Wimbledon's third round with a 6-0, 6-0 demolition of Tine Shuer-Larsen. Such power. That forehand. Such impatience. The match lasted 40 minutes.

When the merciful final point is delivered, Peter Graf stands and applauds. His daughter, who never smiled during the mismatch, walks off the court, pausing only to tilt her racket in her father's direction. Just a little nudge. An acknowledgement. And yes—the racket's still turned up.

"Every day on grass," Steffi Graf says, "I get better. I feel better. But I need to work harder. I must play more on grass."

She seems at first an unhappy victor. Unsmiling, monosyllabic in expression, singular in thought. Joyless. Daddy's little girl. Steffi Graf seems to have all the child-like qualities of an Ivan Dragos. Her father appears to be the quintessential Little League father.

And someone asks her the inevitable. Does she think her father has too much control and influence over her? The question, while not the most original and certainly not a new one to her, nevertheless brings a startled look to her blank countenance.

"He is my father. How can a father have too much control over his daughter? He is also my coach. I think the only problem is my coach and father sometimes forget who is which."

And the numbers won't go away. They are so numbing they knock you off your feet. Eighteen.

And then, three years, 10 months.

And then the killer—Steffi Graf has been consumed for 14 years. Already.

When she plays, there are the special hints that regardless of the amount and intensity of parental guidance that has taken place in her tennis, she belongs where she is, which is on the threshold. Sometimes Graf actually charges a serve by her opponent. Anything to get maximum power into her forehand. And she will dare opponents to hit to her strength, sometimes standing in the backhand corner. Waiting.

186

There has been no neglect of her backhand either. She hits it three ways — slice, flat drive and an occasional topspin. Her quickness is stunning and efficient. She's not a poser, in that a player who maintains her follow-through after a swing. It is hit and then the legs slam into gear and hit again.

Chris Evert says Graf "has always played like she was in a hurry. She's got all the shots though. And someday she'll win all of the tournaments."

Adds Navratilova, "Steffi may make me want to get over the hill sooner than I expected. She is very tough and has a great attitude."

The thought of a timetable infuriates Peter Graf. His stare is icy arrogant. His words sizzle.

"We are in no hurry. She will be a champion — I have seen that since she was five. But we are not in a hurry. She will not win Wimbledon maybe this year because she doesn't have experience on grass. But you see her play — why is there a hurry when she plays like she does?"

Steffi Graf says she always wanted to play tennis. Her father's stories are true. She never got tired. He did.

And when she is asked about the childhood never lived or experienced or enjoyed, she simply shakes her head in disagreement. And then she is asked if she ever just wanted to stay home — not go to the courts and play with her dolls. She looks 100 years old as she says, "There never were any dolls."

Three years, 10 months.

Today, back home in the Rhine Valley small town of Bruehl (pop. 15,000), a mountain of mail arrives each day. The telephone must be kept off the hook whenever she plays a big tournament. The world clamors for Steffi Graf.

A millionaire admirer sent her a Porsche as a present last year. It was intercepted by Daddy Dearest.

"Can you believe it? A car like that?" her father scoffs. "Steffi does not even have a driver's license. These kind of admirers she doesn't need."

Steffi says the car was a gift with no strings attached, "only a big ribbon. The man was not crazy. He was a criminal lawyer."

Her father erupts. "The man was an idiot. This is why I am so important. Did you know someone also tried to kill my daughter last year? At a hotel, they sent her poison marmalade. I want to protect my daughter, and people think I am bad for this."

The joyless demeanor on the court is a mask, he insists. Off court, Steffi "is very normal. And I remember an under-8 tournament when she broke down crying. The referee made a bad call and she started crying. She told me the ball was a meter outside."

There is a concerned look on Peter Graf's face as he says, "I think that is the last time I see her cry. I mean real tears. At the U.S. Open (a loss) that was not real. At the French (a win) that was not real. No crying, no smiling. That is not such a bad way to be when you play tennis."

And that reminds Graf of a story. A psychiatrist once told him a child should cry if it is necessary. It is normal.

"So I told her if she needs to cry, cry. And she says, "Papa, I don't need to.'"

Another time, Richard Schonborn, chief coach of the German Tennis Federation, asked Steffi to smile more and she said, " 'Either I play tennis, or I smile.' Not both. I can understand that. She can. Why not everybody else?"

Occasionally there have been some invasions through the chain-linked discipline. Phil Collins albums. Cooking her favorite apple cakes at home. Walks in the forest with her two dogs, a boxer and a German shepherd.

But no boyfriends. Not yet.

"I think someday there will be many," Steffi Graf says, sounding like she is talking about inventories of winter coats. Right now, they seem too expensive.

Her father says the boy in his daughter's life already has been selected. He will even let her make the choice.

He says, "Oh yes, she knows even what color hair he will have. But there is no time now. She wants the tennis so much. She could not share herself with another person."

Present company excluded.

"Yes, I hope he will play tennis too," Steffi says. "But he must understand what my life is all about."

She looks around. Her father is outside, waiting. There is no censorship. Nobody to tell her don't talk, don't say that, don't think that. Steffi Graf even smiles slightly as she says, "I have my tennis as I want it. And it is the perfect life at the moment."

And the blond hair and blue eyes and radiant face of the prodigy flatten out even more. Steffi Graf has put herself into another room without moving. But her face betrays her. And there is a delicate moment when she looks delicate, as fragile as porcelain. Followed immediately by a complete recovery and a steely countenance that is as cold as porcelain. A porcelain baby doll advanced to the fourth round of Wimbledon Saturday, beating Laura Gildemeister of Peru 6-2, 6-1.

Nobody cried. Nobody smiled. Maybe because nobody taught anybody how.

Discovery of body in moor revives 20-year-old nightmare of children's murders by Ian Brady and Myra Hindley
July 27, 1987

MANCHESTER, England — The bedsheets billow and flap on the clothesline. In front of the small house, two children on tricycles, playing. In back, their mother, bending to grab a damp pillowcase, clothespins in her mouth.

Then the whine of gears. A car approaching, downshifting.

The mother stands stiff, ears perked, a deer sensing danger. A mother concerned, her umbilical rolled into a lasso. The car passes. She hears her children, still playing. Just a subtle, little fear. But on the horizon, beyond her clothesline, a menacing reminder.

Saddleworth Moor.

No fear is too subtle, too little.

The bleakness of the moor gets softened by summer. Its tall rocks flatten in the sunshine and the wind is but a breeze. The usual uncomfortable stillness is distorted into a misleading peacefulness. It is a mistake. For these are the killing fields.

Almost a quarter of a century ago, Ian Brady and Myra Hindley murdered children for no other apparent reason than amusement. How many? Nobody's sure. But two weeks ago, the soft murky peat of Saddleworth Moor shared one of its secrets. And yielded another body.

William Topping is superintendent of the Manchester Constabulary. Also the father of two daughters. Lately, the moor has been his mistress. Since November, he and a special eight-man task force have boarded a mini-bus daily, armed with shovels and peat cutters, ridden to Saddleworth and dug for bodies. When winter's biting winds howled defiantly in December and blew everyone off the desolate summit (1,400 feet above sea level,) Topping attacked with words, trying once more to shovel inside the two people who know where the bodies are. And why.

In late March, Topping and his crew returned, suddenly armed with the breakthrough reinforcement of Myra Hindley's personal direction. She has finally pointed on a map and told where she and her lover buried dead children in the early 60's.

On June 30, 1987, around 4:30 in the afternoon, Topping's walkie-talkie squawked.

"I think we've got something."

Topping immediately set down the ordnance map and the aerial photographs he was studying and put on surgical gloves. It took six hours to remove the body, found three feet under the ground and 150 yards off the road. With the meticulous caution of an archeological expedition, Topping's crew removed a body. Then came the shocker.

Due to an airtight seal provided by the slick peat, the body was almost perfectly preserved. It is almost as if a cruel bookmark has been put into the twisted tale of Ian Brady and Myra Hindley. Dr. Geoffrey Garritt and three other pathologists at Oldham Mortuary examined the body to determine probable cause of death. Its identity was almost a foregone conclusion. A few days later, almost in anti-climax because the remains were so readily identifiable, it was announced that Pauline Read, missing 24 years, had been found. Up on Saddleworth Moor.

For Topping, the emotions cancelled out each other. Relief and gloom. There really are more dead children up there. The comfort in knowing grieving families at last can bury their dead children is balanced by a sobering truth.

There really are more dead children up there.

There is no cause for celebration. These are the hollow victories in a policeman's job.

"Other than the comfort one family will gain, the knowledge that their dead child can be given a decent burial at last, I don't feel good about anything. It's all still so pathetic," said Topping.

The sight of a veteran police officer on all fours, scrabbling in icy muck with his bare hands a week before Christmas, is also pathetic. And how pathetic is it when a mother stands at bus stops for months, looking at every face, waiting for a vanished daughter to come home? Or another mother, banging on strangers' doors, asking, pleading, begging, "Have you seen my son?"

The crimes of Ian Brady and Myra Hindley have not allowed healing agents. The wounds have never been cauterized. With the discovery of a body also comes the excavation of horrible memories. Memories of a sensational trial that strangled a national attention span like none other in modern British history. Details so grisly the all-male jury still refuses to talk about them. Of a witness for the prosecution so disturbed by his personal involvement that nightmares persist relentlessly. The list of victims also must include the grieving relatives, torn apart both physically and mentally. William Topping's dogged pursuit of justice and peace of mind for a few families demands the rest of the world endure the ugly story all over again . . .

☐ Twenty-four years ago today, on July 12, 1963, Pauline Read went to her first teen dance, at a youth center 600 yards from home. She never made it there.

Sixteen years old.

☐ On the day after John F. Kennedy was assassinated, John Kilbride sneaked down to a nearby market to carry bags and packages and earn a few shillings of spending money. November 23, 1963 was a cold Saturday in Manchester and TV and radio reports were dominated with stories on the U.S. President's death. Late that night, another story was breaking. A little boy was missing.

John Kilbride, age 12.

☐ On the day after Christmas 1964, Lesley-Ann Downey went

191

to a neighborhood carnival with a group of friends. In the middle of the afternoon, she vanished.

Lesley-Ann Downey was 10.

☐ On June 12, 1964, Keith Bennett and his mother stood at a street corner, saying goodbye. She walked that far with him from their house because she worried about the busy traffic. Her son was going to his grandmother's house. Two hundred yards from where she hugged him and told him to call later. Two hundred yards.

Keith Bennett, also 12.

Edward Evans was 17. The world knows what happened to him.

On October 7, 1965, based on a tip from an eyewitness, police discovered the mutilated body of Evans, wrapped in a blanket in a house at 16 Wardell Brook Avenue in the Hattersley suburb of Manchester. The coroner later determined there were 14 gashes in the victims' head. All delivered by an axe.

Evans' body was found in the bedroom of Brady and Hindley, who were having tea when the police came knocking. Hindley's grandmother, the owner of the house, was still asleep in her bedroom. Next to the one where the body was found.

"Even as a hardened copper," said Bob Talbot, one of the officers who went to the house that day, "you have to rub your eyes once in a while."

A breathless call from a hillside telephone callbox before dawn broke the case.

David Smith was Myra Hindley's brother-in-law, the 20-year-old husband of her sister. He was invited to the house on Wardell Brook Avenue, he later testified, because he thought Ian Brady wanted to drink wine and show him more pornographic books on sexual torture and humiliation. It was a routine they'd established over the preceding months. But when he arrived, he walked into a room where Brady was raising an axe over someone's head.

Smith witnessed the whole ordeal. Then he was asked to help clean up. And finally he was offered his wine. When he was allowed to leave, he ran home, woke his wife and made her go with him to the emergency callbox on the hill near their house.

Dial 999. Report a murder. Please come. Fast.

The news spread around the city and several detectives, frustrated in their efforts to locate certain missing children, asked to speak to the suspects. Maybe there was a link.

A search warrant was issued. A sketching pad confiscated. Some strange doodling. Ian Brady's writing. Names of movie stars. Drawings. Names of nonexistent people. And one name that conspicuously jumped off the page.

John Kilbride.

Brady and Hindley blankly denied any knowledge of any murders except the body that had been found in their bedroom. Ask Ian, Myra answered with a shrug to every question. Ian said he had never heard of John Kilbride. He didn't know why he'd written the name on a sketch pad.

"Is he someone famous?" Brady asked, smiling.

On October 16, nine days after Edward Evans was hacked to death, a heavy rain on Saddleworth Moor uncovered a shallow grave. Lesley-Ann Downey. On October 20, Brady and Hindley were charged with murder. Two hours later, the body of John Kilbride was discovered. Again, Saddleworth Moor.

Brady and Hindley maintained their silence. Sheer coincidence, they said.

Five police forces were sharing the same round-the-clock obsession now. The Royal Air Force contributed fly-over photography. Sniffer dogs were all over the moor. What about Pauline Read, the police grilled the suspects. Nothing. Keith Bennett? Nothing. Why did you kill children?

Nothing.

A trial date was set. The Crown vs. Ian Brady and Myra Hindley. A special glass case was built: It was bulletproof. Dozens of death threats had been received. Hundreds of letters urging swift justice, even swifter execution of "those two sick, perverted monsters," as one note writer put it.

Police continued to search for proof linking the two with the other murdered children. Finer combing of the house produced the most shocking evidence of all.

Rummaging through a desk in the parlor, Deputy Chief Inspector Jack Tyrrell felt something strange in the white prayer book that belonged to Myra Hindley. In the binding, a lump. A claim ticket for left luggage, claim number 7843, Manchester Train Station.

In a locker at the train station were two suitcases filled with odd items. A wig, a book on the Marquis de Sade. Nine Polaroid snapshots. And several small reels of tape recordings.

The snapshots were of a little girl, a man's scarf gagging her mouth, aside from shoes and socks, naked. In nine forced poses, Lesley-Ann Downey.

Then the tape; 17 unbearable minutes. Footsteps and silence and then harsh, obscene commands, both masculine and feminine. And tiny sobs and shrill screams and pitiful wails of horror building to a hideous crescendo. And then as if accompaniment was needed, a Christmas carol in the background. *The Little Drummer Boy*. Then more sobs. Then footsteps, leaving. Then the flapping sound of the end of the reel of tape.

The voices were identified. Ian Brady. Myra Hindley. Lesley-Ann Downey.

The tape evoked waves of revulsion in the courtroom. Police officers wept. Barristers blanched. The judge demanded everyone regain composure. One couple never lost theirs, they'd heard the tape before.

Public sentiment was out of control, fueled by bitter frustration. For in November 1965, Parliament had abolished the death penalty. No matter what crimes Ian and Myra had committed, no matter how many children they had slaughtered, the worst punishment they could receive was life imprisonment. Public consensus: Not nearly enough.

On May 6, 1966, the jury deliberated two hours and 19 minutes and declared Ian Brady and Myra Hindley guilty on all counts.

That night, someone threw rocks through all the windows at 16 Wardell Brook Avenue.

Brady and Hindley both requested and received maximum solitary confinement. They did so because child murderers are no more popular inside prison than outside. They began writing each other weekly love letters, suggestive, graphic, pornographic. This kept up for several years until Hindley started accepting visits from a Methodist minister.

She told him she'd like to talk about God and her chances of getting into heaven.

When this piece of news reached Brady, he refused to accept any more letters from her.

Hindley has appealed for parole several times, claiming she physically committed no murders. Her only crime, she has said often, "was falling in love with Ian Brady."

In 1980, after hearing about a TV program that featured a panel discussion of possible parole for people convicted of violent crimes, Ian Brady mailed a letter to a London newspaper that said in part, "Myra should never be granted parole. Such an idea is ludicrous. Believe me. I know . . . "

Meanwhile, the lingering agony for the parents of Pauline Read and Keith Bennett persisted. Joan Read started having problems shortly after her daughter didn't come home one night and the world stopped making sense. Today, she is a patient in a mental hospital on Manchester's north side. Most likely she will never be released. Her husband Amos has decided not to tell his wife their daughter's body was found last month.

The parents of John Kilbride divorced. So did Lesley-Ann Downey's.

Since remarried, Ann Downey West says she suffered a miscarriage five months after her daughter disappeared. She adds, "I've had two heart attacks since then as well."

She now works as a waitress. She admits she has written letters in the last year to both people convicted of killing her daughter. And once a month, without fail for the past 20 years, she delivers flowers to a small grave at a cemetery in South Manchester.

Winifred Johnson, Keith Bennett's mother, is a canteen worker in a hospital. Lately she has been involved in a letter writing crusade to Ian Brady.

Explains Mrs. Johnson, "I asked him to please help in the search. I heard Hindley wrote him, asking the same thing. And his reaction (Brady refused to open the envelope) re-opened a black hole of despair for me all over again. I want to put Keith properly to rest and place flowers on his grave.

"Wherever he is now, is not a grave."

Myra Hindley, inmate number 964055 at Cookham Prison for

Women, has made two trips to Saddleworth lately. In December and again in March. She freely admits remorse, but continues to deny guilt. She will be 45 in 11 days. She says she has given up hope of ever being free. The public, she says, would never allow it.

"Neither would Ian."

Ian Brady walked the Saddleworth Moor once again on July 3. He relented to the pressure that Topping, Mrs. Johnson and his once-beloved Myra had been applying. For 11 hours, he walked, handcuffed to two policemen, surrounded by two others, talking to Topping about things that are nobody else's business. Not just yet. Wrap-around sunglasses and a fake camel hair coat made Brady look like he'd stepped out of the past, a Teddy Boy from Carnaby Street. His first taste of freedom in 8,034 days brought out a curious phenomenon. The moor and Ian Brady thrive on each other. A bright sunny day suddenly turned into a blustery afternoon, with swollen skies and biting wind. Ian Brady walked briskly for five hours, stopping only to point at rocks and trees and a creek.

Said one policeman, Leyland Trissen, "I thought the guy would be really feeble. He hasn't been outside for more than 20 years. But the no good bastard actually seemed to get strength from that place. He was stronger at the end of the day than when he began. He's an evil one, he is."

Brady was herded into a car and delivered back to room No. 4 at the Park Lane Hospital for the Criminally Insane, where he was transferred two years ago. Brady's sullen look is dull, his cold, gray eyes glazed over with medication. Patient number 490. Ian Brady, 49 years old. For years he complained of "strange voices in my head. I have trouble keeping the curtains pulled closed on my past. It flies open more and more. It is disturbing."

Four years ago, Myra Hindley was caught trying to escape from prison. Irene Hayes, Hindley's lesbian lover and the prison guard in charge of her wing at the prison who helped in the escape attempt, was given a five-year sentence. She committed suicide a month later, hanging herself in a boiler room.

Last year, Ian Brady himself tried to commit suicide by stabbing himself in the neck with a pair of scissors.

William Topping says, "We will keep looking and we will keep digging.

196

"I hope the day never comes when murder has a time limit. Meanwhile, we should consider the victims. Not just the murdered children. But all the victims."

David Smith, the eyewitness who most likely prevented Edward Evans from becoming another grave on Saddleworth, says he has been beaten up "at least 50 times" simply for being involved with Ian Brady and Myra Hindley during one of their nightmarish evenings of murder."

"Somebody always wants to call me names, push on me, taunt me," Smith told reporters recently. "Then they beat hell out of me. Gangs of them. I've been lucky to be alive several times. But can you imagine what people would do to Ian and Myra if ever they set foot in public?"

William Topping has another chilling thought.

"If David Smith didn't call the police that morning, we can only shudder and imagine how many more shallow graves we might be searching for today."

Smith, divorced and 39 years old and unemployed more often than not for the last 20 years, once served three years in prison himself. He stabbed a man. Three years, a terrible part of his life. But not the worst. Smith tells of a dream, constant and recurring. In the dream, he is riding the elevator to his apartment. It stops at another floor and the door opens.

"And it's Ian there. And he's got his axe."

On the moor, the mood is still gentle. The smell of newly mowed grass sweetens the air. Two days ago, a newborn lamb walked on shaky legs. Life goes on. It has been a long time and time is supposed to eventually close over any wound. But old sins cast long shadows. The sheep herders carry good-luck stones in their pockets, handed down by their ancestors. For a thousand years before Ian Brady and Myra Hindley were ever born, the stories have been told of evil and murder and a place where "the devil's children rule the night."

That baby sheep will be led to slaughter soon.

It was announced earlier this week the body of Pauline Read was wrapped in a blue coat that once belonged to Myra Hindley. And on top of the coat, on top of the body of a child, thrown there before the rain-sodden peat of the moor was dumped back into the grave, was an empty potato chip bag.

Apparently, someone had been eating while digging graves up on Saddleworth Moor.

Isiah vs. Magic: Later this summer we can be friends again
June 7, 1988

LOS ANGELES — The far bedroom near the pool of his Bel Air mansion, the place Magic Johnson calls "the Isiah Thomas Suite," is empty.

"He's not staying here this time," Earvin Johnson says. And the absence of a smile is conspicuous.

Back across the country, in a luxurious pocket of suburbia outside Detroit, the basketball is a metronome for the stillness of a Sunday morning, a droning messenger from the heart of Saturday night. Isiah Thomas dribbles in the solitude of the court outside his West Bloomfield home, dealing with the unavoidable hyperactivity. How many times have he and his friend, the Magic Man, gathered there, shooting it up together, giggling, kids frolicking in a grown-up world? The one-on-one games, H-O-R-S-E for money, the therapy, the escape? All the time the bouncing basketball punctuated a sizzling friendship. Magic and Isiah. How many times has the basketball court been an excuse to let free tiny secrets? How many private dreams have been in-bounded, and shared?

Isiah Thomas chased down his rebounds alone last weekend. If basketball was the common denominator at first, when originally it was their mystical love for the game that allowed them to discover everything else the uncommon athletes had in common, it also is what has suddenly driven them into delicious isolation.

"It's been a fantasy of ours for years, playing each other for all the marbles," Magic said last weekend, after the Los Angeles Lakers had claimed their spot in the Finals. "Now, it's reality. Head to head. The marbles, the chips. The money."

For years they talked about this most special rendezvous. Now, both grow silent. No talk.

Magic and Isiah. The NBA Championship Series. At last, the sacred union, the wonderful divorce. At last, the opportunity to force a glorious exile and put aside a mutual love. Also, for Thomas, at last the chance to come down out of the stands and not be a spectator to the world title, but a contender.

"I've seen every championship series since I've been in the league," Thomas says in slow, measured words.

"I wanted to learn what it took to be a champion. I observed."

Almost every year, Magic Johnson performed for his friend in the grand climax of the NBA season. The Lakers made it into the championship series five times in Isiah's first six years, and each time, Isiah Thomas squirmed and yearned and the envy oozed freely from his pounding heart.

Observing.

"Earvin is my friend, one of the best people in the world. And we have been there for each other a lot. But he's not going to tell me the secret of how to be the champion. It's a secret he and Larry Bird have shared. And neither of them ain't going to tell how it's done."

Especially now, when his good friend, the magician, tells the western half of the sporting world that, "Later this summer we can talk, we can be friends again. Right now I got to try to kick Isiah's butt. Take no prisoners. Socializing comes later. I got to slam him if he's going to the hoop. Same thing the other way."

Isiah Thomas licks at his smile. It's not one of those blinding grins he can let loose. But a door just slightly ajar that quickly slams closed. Yes, they will back away and draw the battle lines and the joust will be fierce and focused and devoid of kindred spirit. And yes, neither will invade the other's lane and expect friendly and uncontested entrance. But the cold-turkey atmosphere is only a further silent nudge of the solemn respect they hold for the game and one another. The game is so important, the thrilling need to compete takes such priority that unplugging their friendship is the noblest salute of all. When buddies rattle their sabres, the searing focus of competition burns holes on the basketball hardwood. And

199

the abrupt silence is the perfect rejoinder of all those dream sessions over the years.

"I'm playing for the championship," Magic Johnson says, big round black eyes burning with sincerity. Still no smile.

"Isiah understands."

In that bedroom in Bel Air where his friend has stayed so many times that he even has filled one of the closets with personal clothes hangers, Magic Johnson has had new sheets and pillowcases put on the bed. In a few weeks he says he'll invite Isiah Thomas to spend some time with him.

"If we win," he adds. And then the big smile floods everywhere. He laughs and everyone knows his little joke, his little pretense that a friendship might actually be determined by the won-loss column, has been exposed as a playful fraud.

And then the smile disappears. Because while the championship series is in progress, nothing is a joking matter. And nobody on the Detroit Pistons, trespassers to his Magic Kingdom, is a friend.

The way it has to be.

"He is playing for his fifth championship ring," Thomas counters. "Five world championships. . ."

His attention span flickers. And something causes him to flinch. Like some dark shadow that suddenly appears in front of you. Thomas stops himself.

He shakes his head and says, "I'm playing for peace of mind."

So many critics have misinterpreted his envy for jealousy. His magnificent obsession to be the best has never been accompanied by the accomplishment. And there are many who claim this complicated, almost cosmic star, has wandered—from driven to out of control.

He does not answer the question of how hard it has been to protect his sensitivity to failure, a word which to him will always be defined as not being the best. He concedes there have been several unfortunate instances where his frustration has crackled dangerously like an exposed electrical wire. But when reality cannot match up with dream, there is always a backlash of disappointment.

"For seven years, I've been infested with a disease," Thomas says. "It's eaten at me daily. I don't like sitting in the stands, observing, watching Earvin and Larry play for the championship. Hell yes, I want to be out there too. It's more than obsession, just like basketball's more than my job. It's a disease and I'm more driven as a result. But I'm also more appreciative of the game. And now I have the opportunity to. . ."

And he stops himself once more. Christmas is coming for Isiah Thomas. Santa Claus arrives tonight in The Fabulous Forum. And the hopes and dreams of all the years get unwrapped at last.

Magic Johnson snarls. Isiah Thomas erupts. It will not be the Magic and Isiah Show, they chorus. What do you think this is an All-Star game? One of their summer-camp exhibition games? You think these two amigos are going to go out and try to flash and trash the NBA Finals? Smile and joke and make faces at each other during foul shots?

"It's for the world championship," Isiah barks.

"Sometimes you let the people in the stands feed off you, Magic says, "and other times you get all charged up by them and you hope everybody has a good time. But this is money time. This is the game. It's the reason you play. To get to this. It's for the world championship."

Every kid-on-the-playground's dream, tugging on the same golden umbilical. As usual, the roads traveled are varied, meandered, gone from dirt to super-highway to yellow-brick.

Lansing is, of course, where the Magic began. And beneath the giant smokestacks of the nearby General Motors plant is the modest town that easily could have inspired a Rockwell painting. Not far from Middle Street is the Quality Dairy where Earvin Johnson used to dish out ice cream cones for $2.30 an hour. He came to work dribbling a basketball. Went home the same way.

The smell of new paint being applied to Oldsmobiles and the shrill cheers of children playing softball and basketball at the big park are aromas and sounds that haunt Magic Johnson, invade his thoughts even through the rumble of his oversized Jacuzzi as he encounters an hour or so of life in the slow lane.

"I was already happy even before I had money," he says. "And when you hear kids playing at the playground, throwing up hoops and somebody yelling, 'Just like Magic, just like Magic,' man, how much is that worth?"

Not so long ago, he says, "I was the one screaming 'Just like

Bing.' Hey man, I'm Earl the Pearl. I'm Wilt. Playing the game, oops, finger roll. Oops there's a steal. Hey I'm Clyde. Clyde Frazier. Yeah. ."

Making All-City Lansing was the first dream. Everett High winning state well that was another. The national championship at Michigan State, winning the NBA title as a rookie.

"Lucky, lucky me."

Then the head twists. Another look-back memory. This one closes the eyes. Reggie Chastine. Best buddies in high school.

"Think about being the best," Chastine used to always tell Johnson. Reggie Chastine was 5-foot-3, not really a great athlete like his friend. But he had what Magic Johnson calls "the spirit of winning."

"He wouldn't think about anything else," Johnson recalls, "and he believed in me to the point I started thinking the same way."

Only the summer before their second year, Reggie Chastine was killed by a drunk driver who ran a stop sign.

Sometimes it's best not to dream. Sometimes you need to keep your eyes open.

"I love Lansing; I love Michigan. There are places I can go eat lunch and nobody bothers me. I don't have to be Magic because I'm still just Earvin."

While all this idyllic meandering was running its almost Nutra-Sweet course, there were different rites of passage taking place around the other end of the Great Lakes.

K-Town on Chicago's west side copped an attitude a long time ago. When Dr. Martin Luther King Jr. was assassinated, the place burned with anger and helpless frustration. Isiah Thomas was 6 years old.

Ever see a kid in elementary school lying on the ground, bleeding to death? Ever been robbed at gunpoint? Ever shared a bed with a brother who was addicted to heroin?

There was a playground there too. Tough place. The games were somehow more real. One time, when the gangs were putting pressure on him to join, Isiah Thomas' mother threatened the chieftains to stay away from her son. And they did. It's always a matter of who's the baddest. Who's weak and who's strong?

"One time we went to Maywood, which is where Doc Rivers

(Atlanta Hawks' guard) lived," Isiah says. "We played ball (pick-up games) and the games were really competitive. And Doc might tell you his team beat our team four out of five times or whatever. But the time we beat them well, you're just not supposed to beat somebody at their court. And after we won, everybody started throwing rocks at us. I mean big rocks, too."

And he shakes his head. He grew up without a father; he'd bolted long ago. Isiah got a scholarship to a Catholic private school in the suburbs and that meant for the longest time, two buses and a train and leaving for school long before the morning's ever bummed a light. And while he tried to keep all his transfer tickets in order, and the buses lurched and rumbled through mean streets, the time was passed with basketball fantasies.

"The Big O and Da Bing, Pete Maravich, Rick Barry," Thomas says. "But the best basketball player I ever saw, the one I wanted to be my biggest hero, was my brother Lord Henry.

"He didn't ever make it big."

Thomas smiles at the memory of the state championship, especially relishing the fact it came over his buddy since grade school, Mark Aguirre. He nods satisfaction about the national championship he guided Indiana to in his sophomore year of college. That time last year when he surprised his Mom on Mother's Day and had her walk down the graduation line to pick up his college diploma, finally fulfilling the guarantee contract he had to sign before he left Indiana for the NBA—that was great, too. But he also gets jolted by reaty, the painful reminder that living, not basketball, is a matter of life and death.

Last year his father died. Only recently before, they had become close. Only recently before had Isiah Thomas forgiven and embraced the man who brought him into this chaotic world.

"A piece of me died too," Isiah says. "I've used the basketball as an escape at times. But it took me a while to want to go back out on the court."

Sometimes the ball gets deflated. But it always gets pumped back up. Last year when Mary Johnson, Earvin Johnson's stepsister, passed away, surrendering to the cancer on her 33rd birthday, he trembled softly on the telephone to his mother. "I don't know what to do, Mama."

The Lakers had a game with Dallas the next day.

"Should I come home and be with you and Daddy?"

And Christine Johnson, who worked in a junior high school cafeteria for most of her adult life, said, "Play your game. It's going to be on TV. It'll give your father something good to think about."

A few days later, the most famous citizen of Lansing, Michigan, was back in town. His best suit had been pressed nicely by the local cleaners. There was a funeral to go to.

That night he talked on the phone for an hour. To his friend, the Detroit Piston.

Sometimes they call and the next thing you know know, one's on a plane headed to the other's home. Or maybe they call up Aguirre and rendezvous in Central Park in New York. And ride in a horse-driven carriage all day. Or sometimes, like 1984, when the Lakers were beaten in the seventh game by Boston at the Garden, they gather in a hotel room and stay up all night, "Just talking."

Johnson has said, Isiah Thomas "is one of my cushions. He knows when I'm hurting. I know when he is. We're there for each other. Like friends are."

Only just not this week.

Each has an impact on the face, pace and grace of pro basketball. Each has matinee appeal, packs the house, draws the spotlight. But only one knows what it is like to be the best.

Isiah Thomas offers that he knows what it takes.

"It's the biggest step ever," he says. "You're not talking about being the best high school team in a particular state or the best college team one particular year. It's the world championship. The Lakers, like the Celtics, don't beat you with athletic ability. It's their will. They have championship determination. Take a breath — Bam, it's over. That's why controlling my emotions is so important. I wanted to know what it took. It's not making mistakes. Not getting distracted. Right now, I'm just floating, I'm so happy. But I have to put everything away. We have to be versatile to win. For me to go out and just try to run it up and down, fast as I can, fast as I'd like, means ignoring three important parts of our team, Bill Laimbeer, Adrian Dantley and Rick Mahorn. This can't be the Isiah and Magic show. I can't have friends right now. I don't know. I honestly don't know what it's going to be like. I don't know how it's going to be playing against Earvin even though we've played against each other a lot in the past. It's the world championship. I do know this—I'll do whatever I can, I'll go as deep inside myself, reach all the way and squeeze my heart, do whatever I need for us to win the game."

The quest for peace of mind. The drive for Five. Friends in imposed silence.

A final question for Isiah Thomas. Would it mean as much if it were not Magic Johnson and the Los Angeles Lakers on the other side?

"The Lakers are the defending champs. If they weren't here, it would just be two challengers."

A question for Magic Johnson. Since they talked on the phone last Friday, before the Pistons eliminated the Boston Celtics and the usual good-luck small talk and giggling reminders that the long-awaited dream match was but one victory away for each of them, does he have any last parting words for his friend?

"I hope all my shots go in and all his rim out," Johnson says.

The long scar on Isiah Thomas' thumb is ominous. As are the blue pads that protect the brittle knees of Magic Johnson. Nothing goes on forever. Some things take forever in arriving. Appreciate them while they are here. Enjoy their special competition even if they cannot. Not yet anyway.

Isiah Thomas says, "I don't know if we'll get together after the final game. Usually when we play in regular season, we go to a movie or out to dinner afterward.

"But this time, one of us is going to be busy, celebrating with his team, the world champions."

Hustlin' in Detroit: Shootin' serious pool can be a way of life
July 24, 1988

"When The Rack closed, for a lot of the players, the big boys like Cornbread Red and Salami, Chicago Bugs, it was like getting laid off from the Ford plant. The big money went away, just moved on. You can still find a game; there's still a lot of money out there. But you gotta work it hard, take it in little chunks, moving all over town. Nope, it ain't like when The Rack was goin' good."

And then he is up from the bench, walking away, pushing open the big glass doors of the pool center, heading somewhere else. The sprinkle of rain on the hot street brings a hiss to the afternoon. Just a face in a pool room. Nondescript, jeans and T-shirt. Maybe 30, maybe 40. Who knows?

"Hey man, what's your name?"

Never even breaking stride, not bothering to turn around, the man says, "Just call me The Kid. I don't want no heat. Don't make me known. I play pool for money. I can't be known."

The one who got away, got away fast. It had been several minutes of conversation, talking about pool hustlers, wondering where they hang out, how to meet one. And he was there all along.

It is a semi-secret society, a subculture within Detroit. That green felt island of high seriousness. Because you never know who's your buddy and who's a fan and who's the IRS, they stay within themselves, a bunch of faceless mannequins, average citizens, folks you'd never suspect play pool for money. Lots of money. Nobodies, strangers sitting on a bench. Waiting for the sucker.

Known? Are you kidding? Grady Matthews is one of the champions, one of the legends. Drop that name in any pool joint in the country—they'll know Grady Matthews. See the movie? See *The Color of Money*? Grady was in it. He's so known, he's famous. Famous as a movie star. Can't fool anybody anymore. All those years of disguises, all those years looking like some rube who just walked out of the library. Lot of suckers got reeled in, rook 'em for a lot of money. But when money is involved, everyone gets sharp;

206

they want a spot, a handicap. Gimme the seven plus the nine plus the break, Professor.

Hard to keep fooling everyone, making them think you're somebody else. Even the suckers. After a while, Grady could shave his head and he couldn't fool you. He's a champion, a legend. He's known.

But because there's one born every minute and not everybody saw the movie and besides, suckers are going to give up their money anyway, to somebody, somehow, Grady isn't ready just yet to give up the subtle art of being lucky. If you want a game, call Grady. Right now he's in North Carolina. But if you want to play some pool, and the money's good, he'll be wherever you are. First thing in the morning.

But if you want to play a legend and don't really feel like waiting, just give 'ole Corn a call. He's right here in Detroit. Cornbread Red. He's cut a few heads in his time. Been playing Minnesota Fats for 40 years; Fats hasn't won since Cornbread was 17 years old. Willie Mosconi? Steve Mizerak? Ask them about Cornbread Red? Hear about the time he ran 14 straight racks of 9-Ball? Or the night at The Rack, he set up one shot on the table, one shot, for $100,000?

Of course he made it.

Yeah, you let him get that poor-mouth stuff going through your head, telling you all about how old he is, how sick he's been. Yeah, let Cornbread Red tell you how tough times have been since Gil Elias closed down The Rack and moved to Florida. Listen to that Kentucky drawl slide down smoother than good bourbon and next thing you know, you're actually giving him a spot, playing him for cash money, falling into the sucker pocket of Cornbread Red.

"Don't nobody come looking for me," says the 57-year-old man with the slicked-back hair that was once as red as an apple.

It's a shock of white now with streaks of yesterday still hanging in there. The bypass surgery went well two years ago. He's dropped about 30 pounds, given up the cigarettes and chewing tobacco. It's been a good while since he took a drink. And those pills he used to pop to stay up and make it through the big games that sometimes took two or three days to finish, are so far in the back of his memory bank he's forgotten exactly when it was he quit.

"Getting old," he says.

Then he stabs you with a stare. Blue eyes that are glinty slits suddenly make you for what you are. Which is not a player. No need for the hustle. No need to deny anything.

"I broke ever' player you can name, all of 'em. I made a lot but I spent a lot. I been called No-Bread Red before too. Pool players don't live too far into the the future, don't live by the month or week or even the day. You live by the game."

His arms are folded. On one is a tattoo of a skull and crossed bones. The other has a heart with "Mother" etched in the middle. On his inside forearm, the naked woman will do the Hootchy-Koo if he flexes and rolls his muscle. He reaches up, inside his shirt, and fingers the gold chain and the ornament on the end.

"It's called a Chai," he says. "It's a Jewish symbol for life. Friend give it to me after I got throat cancer. For luck. I got 30 of them radiation treatments shot up under my chin and everything went away, including I don't have to shave under there no more. Now I got this quadruple thing on my heart out of the way. Things is goin' good, I guess. But I'm wonderin' if my Chai ain't getting a little wore out. Maybe I need a new one, huh?"

And the eyes soften and smile cracks his face and the sides of his mustache curl up and the rakish spirit of the hustler is flushed by a quiet laugh.

Ken Goldenburg, manager of the Cushion and Cue at Thunderbowl in Allen Park, says, "There aren't many like Cornbread. I mean, he'll tell you about his life. He'll talk about some of his big money matches. A lot of the others, the really good players, they don't have anything to say. Some of them have their reasons and it has nothing to do with modesty. They've had big nights, too. But they won't talk about them. And then there are a lot of players in this city who'll tell you stories left and right, about how they broke this guy for $10,000 or somebody for $50,000. And be lying all the time.

"But believe me, the true stories about pool in Detroit will blow your mind. If they ever could have set up a camera inside The Rack, recorded some of the stuff that went on in there, wow—that would be the movie."

The Rack. For three decades, the hottest spot, the pool hustlers' retreat, sanctuary, paradise. Today, there are approximately 15 places in Detroit you can find a game any day of the week. On weekends there are another dozen. It's trial and error stuff. Some owners will tell you that stuff doesn't go on at their place. They don't allow it, it's illegal. But it's there. You just have to know when and where.

Used to be The Rack hogged all the action. Used to be you'd cruise over to Oak Park, down Coolidge, off on Capitol. Right across the street from The Stanley Steamer. Capitol Billiards was the real name, but it was always, simply, The Rack. A private club; nobody got in unless you knew somebody. And everybody had a nickname. What you were and who you were in the real world didn't matter. Inside The Rack, the game was pool. And the game within the game was making money. And all the colorful characters who talked loudly and carried a big stick, the roguish crew of eclectics who made the atmosphere inside The Rack equal parts of nicotine and earthy capitalism, understood this. Money earned never feels as good as money won.

Like when Pittsburgh John nicked Jew Paul at The Rack that one night back in the mid-'70s for $285,000. Cash money. The guys who were there say you should have been there. Played one-pocket for about 25 hours. Pittsburgh got paid off all in tens and twenties, money was coming out of every pocket. It was stuffed in his shirt, down his pants, under his arms. He looked like the Pillsbury Doughboy.

Another night, this trick shooter, George Middledish, made a spot shot with his mouth. Put the nine on the spot, put the cue ball in his mouth, and from behind the break line, sank the nine by spitting the cue ball at it. At The Rack, they'd bet on anything. Any kind of pool; banks, one-pocket, you name it. And any kind of bet.

Once a man named Al Sherman said he could, within four tries, make a cigarette stick in the wooden ceiling of The Rack. Second try, just throwing it up there underhanded, it somehow stuck. Al won $1,000. Know what else? When The Rack closed down a couple years ago, that cigarette was still up there on the ceiling. Lasted even longer than Al Sherman, who passed away six years ago.

"I'll never forget the night someone called me," says Bernette

Burge, "and told me I'd better come quick. Cornbread was playing for big money blindfolded. When I got there, I saw that he wasn't really blindfolded, he was just lining up his shot, then looking away before he shot. That was the bet. I asked him if he knew what he was doing, because it was back when he was still drinking, and he said, "Baby, I'm about $13,000 up, so leave me alone.' "

Bernette Burge is Shortbread, wife of Cornbread Red, whose real name is Billy Joe Burge. She says, "Life at The Rack was always exciting. There were plenty of interesting people. Some of them were crazier than others."

And some of them were more tragic than others. Pittsburgh John, for instance, had been sleeping on a bench somewhere the day before he struck it rich. A backer, known in the pool room vernacular as a stakehorse, found Pittsburgh John—"He always wore the same pair of brown pants with all these geometry designs"—and told him he'd put up a few hundred and let's see what happens. And things just took off from there. The hours passed and hundreds turned into thousands, then hundreds of thousands.

"Next day, after he went to sleep, the binge began," says Incredible Walker. "He bought a Cadillac. Maybe he bought two. He went crazy, just threw money around like it was sand. It wasn't a year, I bet, before he was flat. Back sleeping on that bench. Pittsburgh John never had no discipline."

So where is he? How do you get in touch with him, ask him some of the stories, get him to talk about playing pool for money?

Incredible shrugs. The guy next to him simply walks away. Don't ask about another man's business in the pool room. None of your business. Finally someone says, "He's back in the penitentiary."

Seems that Pittsburgh John, who loved to let it rip, take it to the limit, double or nothing, play with his life as though he were tossing some of those fuzzy Styrofoam dice down some grungy garbage can, was led into terrible temptation by his obsessive, compulsive nature. He developed a taste for jamming spikes filled with cooked heroin—mixed jive is its street name—into his veins. And there were times when his arm got hungry and there were no suckers around to break or champions to borrow from, he took to finding things before they got lost. Stealing. Breaking and entering. All so

210

he could rob from himself. And every time he'd get out of jail, that hunger would return.

"I saw him two weeks ago," says the young blond with the pool stick in one hand and a beeper in the other. "We went to dinner. But I heard he slipped up again."

The word out is he broke his probation. He failed a drug test. He's back in, someplace in Minnesota.

Scott Rubin is 21; he's been hustling pool for 10 years. He's not a legend, not a champion, but if the game is right, "I'll beat anybody's (butt)."

"I hate the game. But I love to gamble. God, I love it."

Rubin used to live in the apartments that were right behind the Rack.

"I used to make $50 washing somebody's big Caddy. Yeah, $50. Hey, what's $50 when you're inside playing for zillions? That's where my education began. I'm smart. I got a good con. I play mind games better than most. And I'm always looking for a game. Twenty-four hours a day, 365 days a year. You want my beeper number? Call me if you wanna play pool?"

The lip curls, that sneer looks familiar. But Sean Penn is older than 21. John McEnroe plays tennis, not pool. Scott Rubin, wise beyond his years, says hustling pool is a flame and he's the moth.

"I can't resist it. No way."

The next day, in a different hall with different players, the game is one-pocket. Rubin's off to Ann Arbor. The Kid is back, watching. One-pocket; pick the pocket where you're going to sink your shots. All the others are off limits. The man with the cowboy boots, baseball cap, beeper and one thumb, lines up a shot. One-pocket is a thinking man's game. Like chess. The lean, the bridge of the hand, the stick goes back, then forward, several times. Then the stroke and the clack of contact and the touch is softer than a mother's kiss. The ball drops into the pocket.

"Me and him," says The Kid, watching the action, "once went to New York. Little place on Bailey Street and we lost. We had to hock our sticks and a leather jacket and a watch just to drive back home. But we raised up enough money to go back. Me and him. We broke that pool hall, won a big pile too. Our pockets had mumps

211

when we got back. I'll never forget his car. Blue Thunderbird, white top, white interior."

The Kid is good, a player with style and a barracuda attention frame. Maybe the next heir, now that the others are getting on in years. Maybe. The Kid is also different. Cornbread never finished seventh grade. The Kid attended Wayne State. Some of the others talk about the game as instincts, guts and ego and playing those head games with the suckers. The Kid talks in terms not nearly so concrete.

"If I can concentrate just on the game, I can beat it," says The Kid.

Kahlil Gibran is one of his heroes, read all of his stuff. He's even written some of his own. Mostly poetry. There's this philosophy he put together on the perfect pool player, pretty heady stuff about humility and cosmic grace, a 12-point plan. But it's private. Like his real name. Like his picture that nobody is allowed to take. Sorry man — not for public consumption.

Shooting pool, The Kid does say, staring at something that might not even be inside the room, "is like a concentrated beam of light. Draw a thin line from your mind to the center of the pocket. Draw another line from the cue ball and stretch it into infinity. Where they intersect is the shot. And only there. Nothing, nobody else, matters."

The pool hall at the end of the universe is actually anywhere you can find the right game. The sucker is anyone who'll play and still let you have an edge. And the bet is whatever. Not whatever you can afford, because a lot of car titles have changed hands, a lot of rent money has been handed over not to the landlord but to the shark who just ran out the table.

"Jewelry, cars, even some mortgage titles. Yeah, houses. I seen 'em all put up," says Cornbread. "One time I won a truckload of honey."

"Money."

"No, honey. Jars of the stuff. The guy I beat didn't have the money."

A good hustler, most everyone agrees, won't totally break a sucker. Take it all, win every cent, then loan it back. Give him a little something. It's called a walking stick.

212

"One time, I got beat out for about $11,000-$12,000 and this guy, The Bulldog, says "Here, Cornbread, take this thousand. And I was all hot still about losing and I said I didn't want any of his damn money. Then when I got coolt off, I got to thinking what in hell had I done, turning down $1,000? I went over and asked if I could still have that walking stick?"

The laugh causes the squint lines of a thousand sleepless nights at The Rack to resurface. Cornbread Red says The Bulldog was the perfect example of how important it is to make good games.

"I been knowin' him for a long time and I ain't never hardly ever beat him. And he can't shoot a lick. Not now, not ever. It ain't the big thing to shoot a good stick. The Bulldog proves that ever' time he makes a game."

Down at Willy T's on Fenkell Avenue, the big buzz door opens and a stranger walks in.

The big man with the big smiles says, "There's not gambling allowed in here. It's illegal and you have to deal with me. I'm the manager. My father owns this place."

Curtis Alford is a big man — "If you want to be real nice, say I weigh, oh, 301 pounds" and he says hustling pool, the real thing, the big games for the big money, died when The Rack died.

"There's lots of players who come in here. Legends like Taxi Dan. Gingerbread. Shake and Bake — he's my godfather. A guy named Shane will play you. Yeah, Shane's now. Myself, I think I've got an up and coming stick. I play banks."

Alford, who says a lot of people call him Fenkell Fats but that he prefers The Muffin Man, adds that the ones who play pool for money "and I ain't saying I never played for, you know, lunch money or something like that" will always find a way. Someplace.

"It's all in their blood. Your heart gets a-thumping. There's money on the line. It's a performance and we all like to perform. You get that aura. When you play, win or lose, you feel like you've been in combat.

One table away, Panama Red, who seems locked in a late-'60s time warp, judging from his Carnaby Street hat and lime green bell-bottoms, claims to have made 44 banks in a row "one night in 1977 at the El Dorado Club on Grand River. It's closed down now."

Someone nudges The Muffin Man and asks if that could possibly be true. Forty-four banks? In a row?

"Play the man. Find out for yourself."

Ronnie Daya smiles. The guy they call Shane is his cousin and "we've been playing for 20 years. I play banks, too."

In his spare time, Daya is lead singer for a rhythm-and-blues group called The Ghetto Connection, "but playing pool is how I'd like to make my living. Pool is art; I'm an artist. I heard all about Cornbread, Taxi Danny. Chicago Bugs, the best there is. Miami, the best with one hand. I've seen Shake and Bake blow them racks of 9-Ball. Chico the Banker, Ice Man, Cecil the Serpent, certified killer from California. I know about Old Man Frog. Tony Black, the best combination shooter there is. Detroit Whitey, English Bill, a guy called Saturday Night. Shermon Cochrane, the ultimate go-off artist. I seen them, I played with some of them. I'm ready to take their place."

Muffin Man agrees.

Told that Cornbread might want to hear from them, they laugh and say, "Not yet. Not no legends like him yet. But soon. Maybe."

Taxi Dan might be coming in, Muffin Man says. You know, he still drives that cab out at Metro Airport. Shake and Bake's kind of laying low since his wife died. Shane—he's here and there and everywhere.

Lots of nothing lately, though. Cornbread says he remembers when hustlers were easy to spot because "they'd all be wearing them $500 alligator shoes.

"I was goin' around in coveralls then, trying to get people to think I was a farmer, askin' what 'one-pocket' pool was. Things is all different now. I seen guys dress up in Texaco uniforms, hunters' clothes with the big rubber wader boots. There's even one guy who tries dressing up as a woman, trying to hustle women players."

There's a warehouse there now. Where The Rack used to be. Every once in a while, you'll see a car pull up and someone will get out and stand there, showing someone else where the big games were. Where The Rack used to be.

"They used to pitch pennies for $100 outside," Red says. "It was a great joint. Lot of memories. One time I'm playing Pittsburgh John and we've been goin' at it for while. And I get this call. It's a kid named Jockey and he's downtown and he wants me to be his best man and witness at his wedding. So I pay this other boy $50 to take 'ol John across the street to the steam room. I drive 90 mph to get there; it takes about two minutes to get the boy married. By the time I get back, John's got all lazy by that steam room. His eyes are glazed and he's so limber he can't even tell one pocket from the other. Man, I proceeded to break him so bad at the table, it was like robbery.

"It reminded me of some of my games with 'ole Fats. Damn, those were good times."

Just business? His eyes say otherwise
Feb. 16, 1989

LOS ANGELES—"I need a cab. Gotta go to the airport."

And Adrian Dantley's eyes looked past the bellman at the hotel in Marina del Rey. The soulful eyes of Adrian Dantley, the 10th leading scorer in pro basketball history, always seemed to be searching elsewhere. They never offered a clue to the great furnace beneath the veneer. The eyes of a doll. The eyes of a shark. Nobody ever really knew.

"I have something to say," Dantley mumbled almost in a whisper when asked to comment on his trade Wednesday to Dallas for Mark Aguirre. "But not right now. Please. I can't talk right now."

And the eyes betray him. For just an instant they turn to glass, slick with emotion. Inside, a long-disconnected burglar alarm is clanging. But then he blinks and sees that something so far away. And he is OK once again.

"Just a business," he says softly, still looking for the taxi cab that will take him away from the Detroit Pistons for good.

It was almost midnight the night before that Dantley finally left the Forum. As usual, he had taken his time, gone through his standard meticulous cool-down after a game. After midnight. It was just about then that Pistons general manager Jack McCloskey was telling the Dallas Mavericks it's a deal. Dantley for Mark Aguirre. Finalize the deal in the morning. Make it official.

"Yeah, I knew," Dantley said. "But nobody ever told me. You kidding? Why would they tell me? I've been expecting this for a while. But when it finally happened, I was still shocked. Jack called me this morning and told me he was coming to my room to talk. I knew then what had happened."

He'd slept well. He always does, he says. In the locker room after the dramatic 111–103 victory over the Lakers, Dantley had told Harry Hutt, a Pistons' official, how much he'd appreciated working with him. Hutt asked what that meant. And those eyes stared somewhere over the rainbow as he said simply, "I know I'm gone."

The game is a business. You go to sleep nestled in the euphoria of a great win over the defending champion. You wake up to the chaos. Traded.

Does that mean someone wants you or someone else wants to get rid of you? It means both. It's all a matter of how you look at the world. Adrian Dantley stopped looking at basketball as a game a long time ago. He stopped feeling secure about the same time. When you get traded three times before your 22nd birthday, you grow calluses on your heart.

"That's why I rent homes," he said. "I still got one in Utah I'm stuck with. Play in the NBA, you can't put down roots. You can but you better be ready to get disappointed."

The talk with McCloskey lasted just a few minutes. McCloskey thanked him for being such a great player. He wished him luck. He said he hoped Dantley understood why the deal was made.

Dantley only nodded. McCloskey later said it was simply a matter of "perpetuating what we already have. Mark Aguirre is four years younger than Adrian Dantley. Adrian's been very productive for us, he's a truly great player. But so is Mark Aguirre and he's four years younger."

Pistons players explained later that Dantley's style of play was not perfectly conducive with the Pistons. Aguirre's, however, will fit right in.

Adrian Dantley sneered and his lip curled up and disgust escaped.

"No matter what anyone says, this ain't got nothing to do with basketball."

There is a private demon within Adrian Dantley today. It has been there awhile. He cannot help but feel that Isiah Thomas played an instrumental part in the trade. Aguirre is one of Thomas' best friends and Dantley has said several times he is convinced Thomas was trying to make the trade happen on the basis of friendship.

But Dantley is wrong. It is a business, not a fraternity. Who can remember when Magic Johnson was drawing criticism because he allegedly was trying to orchestrate a trade with Dallas that would unite him and Aguirre a couple of seasons back? The deal never happened. Johnson never tried to engineer any such deal. Same as Isiah. No matter that someone is friends with someone else, the bottom line is that bottom line.

"Mark is a better player," Isiah Thomas said with words carefully measured. "People keep forgetting that Mark is a great basketball player. He was the top player taken in the entire draft once. Yes, he is my friend. But the reason he is becoming a Piston is that he is a great player who can help us win a championship. I really believe the trade was made solely on the basis of talent. Mark is simply a better player."

And Isiah Thomas took a deep breath. This is hard work. He wants to be a diplomat, say the right thing, not hurt anyone. But a trade is something that shreds the comfort of routine. It affects so many people other than the leading characters.

Vinnie Johnson said he was shocked when he heard A.D. was gone. Then he said he shrugged because he knows the feeling. He knows what it is like to wake up not knowing where you work.

"It happens to me about every year," Johnson said. "A.D. is a great guy. We'll miss him. He's a class guy. But he's been traded before. He knows how it is. We all should be aware of how it is."

Isiah had something else he wanted to say. Make sure people know, he said, "that Adrian Dantley was a true Piston. Very loyal to us, the team. He worked hard and we all appreciate that. Mark Aguirre has a tough job now. There are some big shoes to fill. Adrian's gone."

There was a practice soon. A bus for the Pistons to catch. No

217

time for melancholy. There's another game coming. Sacramento tonight. Golden State on Saturday. Denver on Monday. Trainer Mike Abdenour scurried through the lobby, making sure everyone knew when the bus left for practice. Abdenour had crossed through 11 of the 12 names on the list.

The other guy was already outside. Waiting for a cab. He wasn't going to practice. He was headed for the airport.

Dantley said he still wanted a championship ring. Like Isiah and Vinnie and the others, he has had just about everything else. But he wants a championship ring. And now he must chase it in the name of the Dallas Mavericks.

"I wanted the ring. Last year, we came real close," Dantley said. His eyes were closed, his mouth shut tight. And his head shook slowly back and forth.

And then the spell dissipated. He craned his neck. Where's that damn cab?

A flight attendant on the Pistons' private plane shouted, "We'll miss you, Adrian. Real bad."

"Yeah. Me too," he said, barely turning. Then in a lower voice he muttered, "Miss that plane, too. It's hard leaving. But I'll do it. That's just how it is."

Darryl Dawkins came outside. A handshake, some private words. Two large men, coping. Others had come by his room, quietly, quickly. No fanfare or violins. Just last goodbyes to The Teacher.

He approached the game like a heart surgeon might get ready for a bypass surgery. He was well-read, knew all the latest techniques, got his rest the night before and executed flawlessly. As a player, nobody had a greater work ethic. His footwork was the best in the league. He was tough, the ultimate pro.

United Independent Cab No. 195 wheeled up to the hotel. Adrian Dantley nodded, handed his luggage to the driver, tugged his black overcoat over the bright red sweater and ducked into the back seat. The driver clicked the gear shift into drive and the car pulled away. Adrian Dantley looked straight ahead, seeing something. Seeing nothing. Nobody ever knew. As he left, he turned just for a second, looking over his left shoulder. And waved.

Hail, Michigan
What a finish! What a feeling! U-M wins an overtime thriller
April 4, 1989

What does someone see when he stands there, alone, naked but for the millions of eyes on him? What does it look like from the standpoint of 15 feet away and the entire college basketball season loaded upon your shoulders? Is it dark? Bright? Does the mind build a tunnel to that orange rim? Does the human spirit grow blinders that make everything else dissolve, out of sight, out of mind?

So many questions. But only one answer. Really only one way to express yourself.

Swish. What'd you say, Rumeal? Say it again. Say it even louder this time.

Swish.

Hail to the Victors.

Two free throws with three seconds left in overtime. Michigan beats Seton Hall by one point, 80-79. Three seconds left and alone at the line, where privacy is impossible. The rumbling sound of a powerful beating heart. Wolfen in nature. Body by Fisher. Twelve men — nobody is young ever again by this time all piled into one muscled form.

"I wanted it to be me," Robinson said later. "I wanted the ball and the shot. In the past in games like this I passed the ball to someone else and tried to hide. But tonight I wanted it."

Got it, too. Then made the statement that explains the times of a lifetime. Swish. Swish. Blue Heaven. The Wild Blue Yonder. Blue skies, nothing but blue skies. These are the times of a lifetime.

The last picture show: Robinson's fist thrust high, a pulsating answer to the questions. Offered in body English. Bold print. Underlined in red. Self-addressed. Lick the stamp, mail it into history. The envelope, please. Your NCAA national champion for 1988–89 is Michigan.

A gremlin guard named John Morton constantly poured salt on an ever-widening gash Tuesday night. There easily could have been a hideous scar instead of a shiny trophy for a souvenir of this team's message to the world of college basketball. The three-point dagger Morton jammed into the heart of the Michigan Wolverines in overtime could easily have finished off a beast with a normal heart. But remember, there were 12 hearts inside.

As it turned out, Seton Hall never scored again. And that has something to do with answering a dilemma. A chorus. Barbershop harmony. Words are cheap anyway. Words are ugly, not vivid enough. Songs should be sung today. Play it loud.

Rumeal Robinson balanced on the crystal pyramid there at the riveting end. But any geometry teacher will tell you about the foundation below and all around. He was at the sharpest point. But Michigan had all the angles covered.

Heroes, enough of them to force the spotlight to spread wide. Windows of opportunity that flew open and someone always there to slam it, secure it or jump through it. Whatever it took. Instrumental music. Neon marquees shout the news this morning. Headlines usually reserved for wars and presidential deaths run across the tops of pages. Believe it. It's gospel. Just the facts. A mute's response that is too loud to bear. Lyrics by Michigan. Body by Fisher. Free throws by Rumeal Robinson.

The game kept being pried loose from fingers not able to grip it for long stretches. A (Seton) Hall afire threatened to steal away back to New Jersey with the victory near the end of regulation. Morton put a torch to a Michigan lead that had been built since the first half.

Michigan then turned to its most reliable fire extinguisher.

Buckets of Rice. Glen Rice, firefighter.

It never rained but poured for either team the rest of the way. Maybe a better game has been played most everyone who witnessed Monday night's masterpiece was too out of breath to do any research.

Three seconds on the clock and it was time. Time to win. What'd you say? It was 'Meal Time? Say grace.

The first half was a guided tour of the Wolverines' enormous restoration project that has been going on since Bo Schembechler decided three weeks ago he would not allow Bill Frieder to commit athletic bigamy.

As Seton Hall discovered, the new improved Michigan team features a versatility seldom seen on the older models.

Robinson surrendered his point-guard status at times, preferring to play as if he were one of the big trees in the paint. He pounded the boards, posted up, slapped rival shots away. And oh yeah, he was the same ol' Rumeal a lot, too.

As if NBA scouts needed any more input, Rice also showed a different side. His rebounding was almost as accountable for the Wolverines' lead at halftime as his scoring.

The brief threat of scoring by Loy Vaught and Mark Hughes was enough to keep the Pirates bordering on honesty. And on those occasions Seton Hall double-dared Michigan by double-teaming one of its matinee men, the result was usually two points.

Terry Mills was ragged, guilty of trying too hard, but his blocked shot was a bugle that signaled the cavalry charge in the last minutes. Sean Higgins flailed his own terrible swift sword as well. Twelve hearts. Body by Fisher. Free throws for dessert. 'Meal Time.

The first half was good, the second half better. The overtime ran away from description. Can you say it any simpler? Michigan is the champion.

But in spite of all these evidences of potential finally being realized and put into motion, the five-point halftime lead was hardly enough for Michigan fans to begin gloating. Seton Hall's grit has been industrial strength throughout the playoffs and Fisher would make no resume entry before its time.

So the Blue Crew cranked it up to that extra notch everyone talks so much about in times of challenge. The athleticism of the Wolverines, once so raw and undisciplined, struck manly poses all around the Kingdome. Defensively, the droning noises of 100 practice sessions could be heard. Sneakers squeaking. Grunts of communication alerted of obstacles; there was recognition and reaction and help was always sliding over. Learned response to the times of a lifetime. The challenges from within.

The noise at the other end of the court was more familiar. We've heard Rice's 3-point shot click through the nets. We've even detected the slight jarring noise Robinson makes when he soars above those aforementioned trees for a dunk, although baseline reverse stuffs in a national championship game are not the most normal sounds you might expect a 6-foot-1 person to make.

At any rate the lead exploded, lapped itself, even reached as many as 12 points. And wolfen nostrils flared at the strong scent of Pirate blood.

However, the buzzards were quickly shooed away. Seton Hall responded and divided the lead in half with play not so lovely but just as functional. At the eight-minute mark Michigan led by six. A minute later, it was down to two points.

These are the times of a lifetime. The precious moments. Now or never. Put up or take home the second-place ornaments. Every game ever played within the walls of imagination has chunks devoted to just these moments. Players squeeze them, palm them, bounce them around. It is why they play the games in the first place.

So when Rice slid around the deployment of screens and received a pass at the top of the key, his team's two-point lead feeling scrawny and emaciated as it whistled in the heavy wind of Pirates' momentum, it was like it has been all through this dance of downtown dreams.

Now, Glen. Now.

Rice buried it.

Then he buried it again with a minute left.

When Sean Higgins stared moments later at that ominous orange rim and offered his version of two made free throws and two open windows latched shut, it looked like the Wolverines might be home free. But Morton dialed long-distance again. Two fierce hearts, beating madly. Michigan and Seton Hall. A silent feast.

It could have ended at the buzzer of regulation. Rice was back in the dream, back in the position to launch the rainbows that come out after such springtime showers of tempest and drama. But it rimmed off. The overtime ensued. Five more minutes would be needed.

And the answer man, Rumeal Robinson, the wonderful mime whose pantomime at the foul line, wordless response to the crushing but strangely comfortable pressure all around him, showed how strong a heart running on all 12 cylinders can work. He had the final say. He punctuated it with a fist and a smile.

In so many words, *Hail to the Victors* and the times of a lifetime they shared with the world.

Joe Fan: Detroit's No. 1 sports enthusiast: Joe Diroff's mission, which he happily chooses to accept, is to spend his retirement in a whooping, sign-waving, cheerleading frenzy.
Dec. 10, 1989

> Them that don't know him won't like him
> And them that do sometimes won't know how to take
>   him
> He ain't wrong, he's just different
> But his pride won't let him do things
> to make you think he's right.
> —Waylon Jennings and Willie Nelson

Why do they laugh? Don't they understand what this is all about? Why do they throw peanuts and rotten fruit? Can't they see past the ends of their noses?

Joe Diroff reaches for the plastic banana. The Lions need a spark. Rodney's hurt; Barry just can't get it going against that stacked New Orleans defense. Come people, they need our help. Get with it. Get up—c'mon people . . . LET'S GO BANANAS!!

And Joe Diroff, who knows what everyone else doesn't, who got it directly from The Coach Upstairs, kicks his right leg out, then the left. The banana is held high. C'mon everyone, get with it. If we don't make some noise, we'll lose. And we'll have no one to blame but ourselves.

The Silverdome is alive. The Brow is at work. He doesn't hear the groans. He doesn't even feel the occasional projectile thrown at him. No, there's no stopping Joe Diroff. When he gets the legs going and the voice is feeling all right and he senses the least bit of attention being paid him, when someone actually starts cheering and making some noise and maybe stomping his feet or clapping or whistling, when the people in the stands start caring a little, making some real noise for a change and getting behind the home team, well, there's just no way they can lose.

Then there is the roar. Bob Gagliano's pass is perfect. Richard Johnson cradles it to his chest. Joe Diroff turns his head. What's happening? He sees Johnson speeding down the sideline on the other side of the field. And he takes off, running also, his banana a knight's lance, the sword of Excalibur flashing. That way, go Brow, go, go, go.

He makes it down an entire row, the people who were standing to watch the Lions receiver suddenly rearing back as The Brow blazes to glory. He doesn't collide with anyone and, for a change, his upper dentures stay in place too. Touchdown!

He flips the banana in the air and then circles under it. He drops it, but hey—the Lions scored. They're ahead. They're going to win. Come on, Eddie, extra point. Everyone make some noise. Let's get pumped up, be die-hard, come on, you bunch of bananas.

The Lions win. The feeling puffs through his body as he heads for the exit. The signs must have worked; the players must have seen them and gotten psyched. The cardboard signs with the cut-out letters that look like a kidnapper's ransom note are smeared with the corn-pone wisdom of the author, The Brow. But they hit home. Can't anyone understand that? It's not for himself that he gets out there, a 67-year-old man with a heart condition he doesn't want anyone to know about and an eyebrow that defies description, a retired math teacher who just happens to believe the support in the stands—the people caring enough to go bananas or get pumped up or do the ol' strawberry shortcake, gooseberry pie cheer—is just about the most important mission a civilian can undergo. No, it's for the team. It's for Detroit itself. The Brow? He's just a foot soldier in the sky.

And he has it on good authority that he's right.

God told him to be The Brow.

"I retired from teaching in 1980," Diroff says. "I had the idea that a rocking chair and slippers and once in a while a fishing trip or a game of golf was what was left for me. For two years I did just that and every day I felt a little sicker, a little tireder, a little older. I prayed to God and asked Him to please let me know what He had planned for me the rest of my life on Earth."

He says the distinctive eyebrow was not an overnight creation, "it just kind of grew on me," and it too offered him a hint that his life was star-crossed in a blessed/cursed way. It starts around the temple area on each side, rises into a crest, like some giant hirsute wave off the north shore of Oahu, and seems in danger of collapsing over his eyes and face. But it never does. A younger man might have twisted it into dreadlocks or at least moussed it into some hepcat monolith to Elvis. Joe Diroff decided, however, to make peace with it — he leaves it alone and vice versa. Suffice it to say, however, that Leonid Brezhnev, Wally Moon, Michael Dukakis and any other known eyebrow owner could wander into its underbrush and never be heard from again.

Diroff struggled with the aimless feeling for weeks and weeks. After arming generations of children with arithmetic skills, he suddenly felt helpless and useless.

"Then one night I went to Cobo Hall for a playoff game between the Pistons and the Celtics. Well, I've always been a cheerleader, all the way back to high school at Holy Redeemer. And I was in the stands with my bicycle pump. You get, LET'S GET PUMPED, and it was in the second quarter when this Pistons official, I won't tell you his name, asked me if I'd like to get out on the court at halftime and do some cheers."

Would a wolf like to work the night shift at the pork chop factory? Diroff said sure, of course, he'd be glad to get out there. See, he believes in cheerleading. You better have spirit, no matter if you're an all-boys Catholic school team or the big, bad champ-een of all the professional sports world. Athletic ears are one and the same.

And something strange happened that night in downtown Detroit. He had gone through the whole repertoire. The people at Cobo Hall didn't know quite what to make of Joe Diroff, this elderly man in the fishing hat, jumping around, screaming these singsong cheers of another era. Joe himself didn't really feel much of anything, either. Time was still, stopped in its tracks as he asked the staring people, "Are we gonna win this — Yes . . . Yes . . ."

Then he felt everything in his right shirt pocket fly free. The little plastic holder, his ball-point pens, his pencils, stamps, a couple of coins, a few slips of paper. Littered all over the court.

Oh no. Diroff got down on all fours, scooted around to retrieve his belongings, stuffed everything back into his pocket. And the giggles in the stands started. Then they got louder. He was a Chihuahua on a fast break. Where's the banana when you need it?

Those two big legs looked like Kent Benson's. Sure enough. The Brow looked up and waved. The crowd loved it. It screamed so loudly you couldn't separate the yells of disgust from the ones of support. Hiya Zeke. Lam, my man. Uh-oh green shorts, Celtics.

Maybe if he lifted his leg — oh that would raise the roof. What if he nipped at the shoelaces, got Kevin McHale's untied or put a knot in Robert Parish's. His mind was racing. He was free at last, a stallion in a pasture. A million scenarios came at him and he couldn't get out of the way of any. The noise, and laughter mixed with the cheers — it was the most wonderful thing he'd ever felt.

"Then there was a strange pair of legs. Long pants. Then another pair. Security guards. The long legs of the law.

"They pulled me to my feet. Then when I tried to tell them I was invited to be out there, they wouldn't listen. And I resisted a little because I was right and they were wrong. And they got tough and threw me clear out of Cobo Arena."

His pants were ripped. His knees skinned. He was back on all fours, his hat beside him, his glasses in front of him. And he was crying.

The tears rolled into his big smile as he tilted his head upward, eyes closed and shouted, "Thank you, God, thank you, God. Now I know. Now I know."

That was more than seven years ago and he's still gaining momentum. He never misses a Red Wings game at Joe Louis. Or a Pistons game out at The Palace. Or the Lions. He made 78 of 81 Tigers games last season. Then there was the Detroit Drive, perfect attendance. And U-D. Then there are the send-offs at the airport whenever a team is embarking on a road trip. Or the welcome home. They get tired and when they land at the airport, it's usually after everyone else has gone home. Somebody's got to be there to cheer. That's the thing. Be there for them. Get pumped up. What's good for the team is good for the city and what's good for the city is good for the people. And it's people that can make it happen. If only they'd show up. If only they'd sleep on their couch so as not to wake up anyone else in the family, set their alarm for 2 or 3 in the morning, whatever time is needed to get up and grab a couple of signs and hop in the Dodge and make it on out to the airport. Like The Brow does.

Most of the time he's alone, in the shadows. Empty gates, moving ramps that have been turned off, the screaming silence of an empty airport. Maybe an occasional janitor but usually, just The Brow and his magnificent obsession.

"No, I don't condone it," says Bernadette, her Irish dander in usual place. "I hate it. It's an addiction just like any of those others that other people have. While he's off doing whatever you want to call it, what do you think is happening back here? We have nine children. No, I don't understand it, I don't understand it at all."

Early this year, Bernadette Diroff underwent quadruple bypass heart surgery. She came through it like a valiant. Like everyone who knows her knew she would. She came through major surgery with such relative ease that the jokes started while she was still recovering. Gee, wasn't it considerate of Bernadette to have her surgery on a night the Pistons and Lions were off and the Wings were on the road?

Bernadette bristles. She says, "Well, I will say this — he was there by my side all the way. The whole family was. They came from all over. We're a close family. Don't ever forget that no matter what Joe does and what anyone thinks about him. We're a very close family."

And the bride of 42 years shakes her head. That time she wanted a nice family portrait, the six sons all nice in their suits and sport coats, the three daughters smiling and so pretty in their fancy dresses. And the girl from Minnesota who fell for the sailor boy from Michigan. It would have been such a nice portrait she says, shaking here head again, if only Joe hadn't kept punching his arm into the air and yelling "Pump up" every time the camera clicked.

"Joe is a hopeless sports fan," Bernadette Diroff says. "He's a very obsessed man. I don't understand him at all anymore."

Joe takes off his hat and reaches down with his tie — The Tie that

227

doesn't belong to him and he feels so badly about it that he wears The Tie every day of the year—and uses the tip to dab at his ample forehead in mock despair.

"Nobody understands me," he says, and the blue eyes twinkle. And the eyebrow has no comment.

"People ask me if I ever get embarrassed or ashamed. Yes I do. When a visiting team comes into one of our arenas and makes more noise, I feel like a total fool, a total failure."

He's not ashamed to tell anyone he was born in Toledo; he just doesn't immediately offer that to strangers. He's from Detroit. He's a Detroit man. He would rather tell you about every time he went out for a sports team when he was growing up.

"I got cut. I wasn't any good."

Oh, there was this time he stuck on the Holy Redeemer baseball team and manned the far end of the bench, "a scrub was all I was," and was thrilled to be there. But every other time, every other sport, he was cut.

"So I became a cheerleader. It was like I was part of the team, still. And I got great seats."

When he graduated, he did what everyone else did during those days. He enlisted in the service. U.S. Navy. Stationed aboard a minesweeper, an escort ship in the Pacific theater, he suddenly got a wild hair in addition to those atop his forehead and decided he wanted to be an officer.

The war ended while he was in St. Paul, Minn. One night he and a buddy went to a bridge party. The problem was Joe didn't know how to play bridge. He spotted this girl, who also was sitting out the games. There was some music playing. He asked her if she'd like to dance.

"The jitterbug was my specialty. Once on the West Coast I got asked to leave a dance hall for jitterbugging with two girls at the same time. So anyway, here I am in some bridge party, tables all over the place, and people playing cards and I'm jitterbugging in the aisles with some girl named Bernadette."

She shakes her head. All her life, growing up in Minnesota, she figured, "I'd wind up marrying some blond-haired blue-eyed man. I wound up with Joe."

"Did I tell you I fainted at the altar?" Diroff says, smiling. "It was too late; I already said I do."

Bernadette, The Brow's biggest enemy and her husband's biggest fan, says she married a good man, a caring man with a good heart who doesn't cheat or lie or do anything terribly wrong.

"Except his sports."

In the early going, he really had to scramble to get into games. Rick Mahorn of the Pistons would leave him complimentary tickets. For Tigers games, first it was Dan Petry, then Frank Tanana. The Red Wings loved him and any player on the team was willing to get him in the door. The Lions front office immediately recognized the sincerity and began the trend of simply leaving tickets at the box office, a practice soon followed by the Red Wings and Pistons.

"The Brow is a good man," says Jacques Demers, standing in the airport, watching Diroff set up his Red Wings lawn chair with the yarned red crest in the middle.

"He cares about the right things. And our players like him. He's a little eccentric, I think. But he's harmless. There are some super-fans out there that I consider dangerous. The Brow—he's just a good guy."

Unsuccessful in his attempt to recruit well-wishers to join him in saying goodbye to the Red Wings as they take to the road, Diroff approaches each player, wishes him luck and health and shows them his latest sign, "The seat of Wingsdom."

Someone asks about the tie. Diroff shakes his head.

"It belongs to someone else now. I sold it before the fourth game of the '84 World Series. It's my Bless You Boys tie, the one that helped the Tigers win it all. A man from San Diego saw it and thought the little angels were really padres. I said it wasn't for sale. But I was looking to buy a ticket to the game and he said he'd sell me one in exchange for the tie. I asked if it would be OK if I wore it for the game. He said just as long as I found him after the game and turned it over then.

"I never found him."

Reneging on a deal between two honorable men is not Joe Diroff's style. He called San Diego newspapers and took classified ads ("I have your tie"). He called radio and TV stations asking if it

229

were possible to put out an all-points bulletin. It has all failed to date. He still has the tie and a sense of guilt.

"But I know I'll run into that man someday. That's why I wear the tie every day. I don't want him to think bad of me."

Other than his family and his sports, Diroff also has his religion. He lives across the street from the church he and his family attended for almost 40 years. Only it used to be called St. Monica and it used to be a Catholic church.

"It was one of the ones that got closed down," Diroff says. "I filed suit against the archdiocese. I lost."

Today it is a Baptist church, The Second Corinthian, bought for a lot of money. When the first service was held there a few months ago, Diroff stared. Mayor Coleman Young was there. He struggled with the symbolism. Then because it's his nature, he decided to become a fan.

"I made a sign for them and stuck it on the tree in my front yard. And I went outside and did a cheer for the Baptists, the strawberry shortcake cheer. I had to let bygones be bygones."

You get out of something what you put into it. The wheel comes 'round. Good things happen to good people. Like that time the Red Wings invited him to ride on the team plane.

"I had to go to the bathroom and I got up and headed down the aisle and Stevie Yzerman got up and put quite a check on me. And I didn't know what I'd done wrong."

Yzerman smiled and said on behalf of everything he'd done for the hockey team, for always being there for them, the players had taken up a little collection. And he handed The Brow a roll of bills, more than $400.

Diroff started crying. But there's no time for individual emotions. He asked if it'd be all right to do a little cheer "to express my gratitude."

It was 40,000 feet in the air. It was late at night somewhere over North America. Grown men, rich men, famous men, sat mesmerized as The Brow went bananas once again.

"Then they gave me three cheers, hip, hip, hooray and everything.

"And people ask me why I do what I do."

The Pistons handed him an envelope filled with money in a

ceremony last season. He used it to fly to Los Angeles and root for them in the Finals. He says he did a good job of counteracting the Lakers Girls even if he did get kicked out of Game 3 before it ever started.

Kirk Gibson once hugged him and said, "Thanks, Brow, for everything. You're a true fan," and, well, what can you say after that? Especially when you're on a Mission from God.

And don't think he's forgotten where he came from. The stranger who handed him a $100 bill and told him to fill his car with gas doesn't know the ol' Dodge. Even if she's 13 years old (car years) she doesn't drink that much. There may be holes in the floorboard but the gas tank's intact.

So he gave the rest of the money to his church, the new one he had to find when the old one got sold right out from under him. Who needs money, anyway?

But where's his help? Who will inherit the bananas and the pump and the obligation? There is no one to take the handoff.

"You'd think out of 4 million people in this area, there'd be a few more like me, wouldn't you?"

God's work is not done. Sure, he'd like to be home, jitterbugging with Bernadette to The Muskrat Ramble. He'd like to take it easy. But he can't. He is needed. In his basement, where the signs are assembled, there's a baseball propped on a Dixie cup, the foul ball he once chased down at Tiger Stadium.

"That's something not many people get. A real baseball from the major leagues. I once went out for the football team. I was a defensive tackle and the first play they ran right over me. Flattened me. I know how special it is to be an athlete. But I know they can't do it alone either. I never won a game in my life. But maybe I helped not lose a few here and there. People think I'm crazy, but I already know it and it's not so bad. People leave you alone."

He looks at his watch. What time is it? What day is it? Are the Pistons coming home today or tomorrow? He's got this new cheer and wants to try it out. Actually, he tried it once before. But maybe the world is ready for it by now.

"It's all in Morse code," The Brow says. "I scream, Gimme a dit-dah-dah-dit! See that's P. Then, gimme a dit-dit. That's I. You spell out Pistons in Morse code. What do you think?"

231

Sleep tight, Detroit. Your teams are safe. And also relax—there's only one Brow.

"I'm going to visit Probie (Bob Probert) soon. He's in jail somewhere in Minnesota. I'll make him a special sign and do a whole set of cheers. I once visited Denny McLain in jail and he seemed to appreciate me. I am not a man who makes judgments. I won't cast any first stones. Everyone needs someone to care. And cheer."

The banana is in his pocket. He pulls it out and holds it high, a silent salute. Then he shouts and his teeth fly out of his mouth and he drops the banana but catches the upper plate.

"That happened once on the floor and I was so embarrassed. A man came up and handed me something. I couldn't believe anyone would give me money for that stunt. It was a dentist's business card. He wanted to help."

He reaches for the cardboard tie, the one that fits over The Tie and stays there with the help of paper clips. He's got to go. He's got work to do. The ol' Dodge is waiting. He walks to it, opens the door, turns around and gives his home a three cheers and one GET PUMPED UP for good measure.

Life is rich.

Preacher Bound for Glory?
Foreman, at fortysomething, marking new image
Jan. 14, 1990

ATLANTIC CITY, N.J.—Can something that appears so insulting become somehow intriguing, even appetizing? Will the sporting world stomach George Foreman? Has the notorious fat man, the lard of the ring, somehow bitten off more than he can chew? And when does a man's dream become too old to fly anymore?

The very large man with the large voice bellows the daily message. The Rev. Foreman is speaking. His congregation is a group of newsmen.

"Oh yes. See, if I throw the left hook and miss, and I try to land the right cross and that doesn't work, either," Foreman says, using his huge fists as visual aids, "then I just bellybust them."

His ample midsection thrusts forward abruptly. There is no laughter around.

"See, I've picked up a new punch."

And the fight with Gerry Cooney on Monday night at the Atlantic City Convention Center becomes increasingly palatable. With each helping of the new George Foreman, with each wonderful session of soul-baring with the once menacing and surly former heavyweight champion, there is this surge of belief. Yea and verily, the flock grows. Faith in Foreman abounds.

An hour earlier, he had adorned the gear of his art. The red gloves pulled over taped hands. Someone had to cut the sleeves of his T-shirt to free the arms; those incredible biceps need room. It is hard to mug someone in a phone booth. Foreman himself had rubbed a glob of Vaseline across his face, from the top of his shaved skull to the bottom of his chin, singular once more instead of the several chins he has sported on several occasions. And the protective mask that covers everything but his mouth and his eyes and produces a heavy-breathing version of a fistic Darth Vader.

And in a twinkling, something happens. The pages of the calendar seem to flip backward. Foreman plods about the ring like a mastodon or some prehistoric churl. But that's the point — it seems like everyone has gone back in time.

In the background, Sam Cooke soulfully suggests, from his seat inside the cassette recorder to come on and let the good times roll. The old music, the old singers, Jackie Wilson, Otis Redding, all the oldie-goldies, send shivers of innocence everywhere. They make you feel so young. Foreman waves a gloved paw and the first sparring partner climbs inside. There are four of them, all different styles and sizes and weights. There is a welterweight named Roscoe, peppering combinations at Foreman, harmless in clout but purposeful in that those nuisance blows force Foreman to react to the onslaught.

Then there is a 7-foot sparing partner "Mike the Giant, we call him," Foreman says later and this is an entirely different kind of challenge, requiring entirely different reactions. Then a slender fighter with a swift and accurate left hook "our Cooney clone" and still more work, still more variety from a man whose legend is forged almost entirely from his ability to distribute pain rather than avoid it. The last sparring partner is stopped as he steps through the ropes. No more. George says he is done for the day.

Foreman is slow. He was always slow, though. He is huge. He was always that also. And Lord he can punch.

He holds up his right hand later, after the Vaseline is wiped away, after the sweat has dried.

"I can still get your attention if I hit you. I don't surprise you anymore. You just can't teach a lion to be a rhinoceros. And if I hit you and you still can stand up, well, then you surprise me."

It's that simple. The life of George Foreman has never been so simple. Or so serene. Or so pure.

He pats his belly. Yes he believes in training rules. Proper rest. Daily discipline. You must watch what you eat, he says.

"Or else you might drop some on the floor. Seriously, I eat whatever I feel like."

How about vegetables, someone asked.

"Oh, yeah, lots of vegetables, sprinkled with meat. And vitamins too. My vitamins are made by some company called Häagen-Dazs."

How much do you weigh, George? Everyone leaned forward. None of your business, he says. Everyone rocks back. Then he relents.

"Maybe 250 pounds, maybe 260. Back when I made my comeback, I tried to put my old boxing trunks on and they didn't fit. I'd say I was about 315 pounds. So I got me one of those state-of-the-art scales, one of those fancy things that talk to you. And I went to work real hard. Ran every day, went in the gym every day. For a whole month. I'm excited now; I was gonna wait until I knew I'd lost a lot of that weight before I got on those scales. Finally I stepped on and that thing said "301 pounds.' Man, I stepped off and said, "You lying!'"

He licks at his smile and adds, "I got rid of those scales. Ain't nobody gonna humiliate George Foreman."

The critics say this is all so silly, that someone 41 years old (other sources claim he's 42) is whistling by the graveyard if he thinks he can suddenly end a 1977 retirement a decade later and seriously contend for the world championship he held once upon a time.

But 18 of 19 tombstones have been knocked over in the process. And the other one, a unanimous decision victory, was perhaps not an impressive display of ferocious punching power but you have to admit, it did prove that Foreman, a dinosaur from the life and times of Ali, Frazier and Norton, can still go the distance.

Joe Hand is a boxing promoter and closed-circuit distributor in Philadelphia. He says it is easy to see why people still have this lingering curiosity about Foreman.

"What if someone came up and asked you if you'd like to see some pictures of Elizabeth Taylor with no clothes on," Hand asks.

"Well the first reaction might be, "Aw, she's fat and old now.' But then you start thinking. And pretty soon you're curious. And next thing you know you're asking how much."

Foreman laughs when told of the comparison. Old and fat? Yes, he is The Chosen One. Now and ever shall be.

"I think the mandatory retirement age for a fighter should be 65 years," he says and the mischief is everywhere. He points over to his trainer, Archie Moore.

"The mongoose there might have another year of eligibility left. You must understand age is a state of mind. Archie Moore had a 38-3-2 record after the age of 42. He knocked out 25 men after the age of 42. Don't tell me about being too old. And of course, you ought not to try to tell Archie anything he don't want to hear, either.

"There was a time when I was looking at death before I was looking at puberty. My idea of security was a long prison sentence or a residence down at the graveyard. And everyone knows you don't get any older than dead."

He does not like looking back. There have been so many startling developments, so many crossroads, so many evolutions. Foreman has three sons — all of them named George Foreman Jr. That's OK, he says, "There used to be a bunch of George Foremans walking around, all in the same body."

Growing up in Houston's Fifth Ward, a tough place to get a grasp on life, Foreman was confused. He says his idea of a hero was "someone who had a scar on his face. Or someone who'd been

235

to prison. I was robbing, mugging, beatin' up on people, the enforcer in my street gang."

He was 15, hiding under a house from police. He thought maybe there would be dogs chasing him. They'd climb under the house and bite him if they smelled him. He rubbed mud all over himself.

"I was in the slime, under there with the rats and snakes, covered with mud, trying to hide from dogs. And I realized I really was what everyone said I was — a loser."

He joined the Job Corps. He tried fitting in with society. And he had a thing for flags. At his camp, because his was the biggest and strongest, he was given the responsibility of digging a hole and erecting a flagpole. And hoisting the American flag.

"I always loved the flag. People always remember my little flag at the '68 Olympics. But my patriot period really started when I was in the Job Corps, when I built that flagpole and raised that flag."

The storms built up once more. He could not handle the glare of fame. He could not think of anything to do with outrageous fortune except spend it. He was heavyweight champion of the world in 1973. He bought every Cadillac from every store window he passed. He felt invincible, indestructable.

"Then I went to Africa. Muhammad Ali destroyed me. I couldn't believe I could be beaten. Then I couldn't handle it when it happened."

There were explosions inside his head. More confusion. He had a dozen alibis for his loss to Ali. He changed management. He got a new trainer — a man named Gil Clancy, who will be in the opposite corner Monday night.

He fought seven more fights. He won the first six. Then in 1977, in Puerto Rico, on a sweltering evening, Foreman lost a 12-round decision to Jimmy Young.

"I was angry, dazed, confused again. I walked to the dressing room and I heard a voice tell me, 'You might as well be dead.' I lied down on a table and my head started rolling back and fourth. I felt blood trickling down from my head. I thought I had a crown of thorns on. I started babbling passages from the Bible, things I didn't even know. My skin was rubber. I felt myself floating. I saw Jesus. He kissed me on the lips. I said 'I don't wanna die. I'll give you all my money.' And he said, 'I don't want money, I want you.'"

Strother interviews former basketball star Curtis Jones on the Jones family's front porch. It was one of Strother's last profiles. Photo by Michael S. Green, The Detroit News.

Rumeal Robinson signaling victory for the University of Michigan after
making a game-winning free throw in the 1989 NCAA Finals against
Seton Hall. Photo by Michael S. Green, The Detroit News.

Joe "The Brow" Diroff, Detroit's Super fan, at a Red Wings hockey game. "Go bananas!" Photo by Diane Weiss, The Detroit News.

"The Brow" preparing one of his homemade signs. Photo by Diane Weiss, The Detroit News.

Curtis Jones, a long way from the 1960s when fans cheered him on on the basketball court. With his mother and caretaker, Henrietta Jones, in Detroit. Photo by Michael S. Green, The Detroit News.

Jones and one of his oldest friends, Lolita Wyanna, at a neighborhood gathering spot. Photo by Michael S. Green, The Detroit News.

"My best friend," Jones says of his shadow. "Sometimes my only friend. I know I'll never walk alone. I got that shadow. It's stuck with me for life." Photo by Michael S. Green, The Detroit News.

Jones heads home after a pickup game at an alley basketball court. Photo by Michael S. Green, The Detroit News.

Spencer Haywood: "Cocaine takes away everything. It is Satan at his ungodliest, and, believe me, working on that plantation back in Mississippi wasn't near the slavery you have when you're hooked on drugs. Believe me—I know." Photo by Donna Terek, The Detroit News.

Haywood, former NBA star, joins in a practice game at his alma mater, Detroit's Pershing High School. Photo by Donna Terek, The Detroit News.

Shelby and Kim Strother. Photo by Steve Haines, The Detroit News.

The Strothers' sons, Kenny, then 7 (left) and Tommy, then 11, in Cocoa Beach, Fla. Photo by Kim Strother.

Shelby Strother, 1946–1991. Photo by Donna Terek, The Detroit News.

Clancy says he will never forget the moment. Foreman slid off the table and screamed, "Jesus is within me."

And Foreman kissed Gil Clancy on the lips that night in Puerto Rico 13 years ago. A month earlier, a gangly kid from New York had made his professional debut. His name—Gerry Cooney. He recorded a first-round knockout.

Doctors later said Foreman may have been hallucinating because of extreme heat prostration. Foreman shakes his head.

"No, it was a miracle."

For eight years, he was a preacher, first in the streets, then in his own tiny Texas church. He said he never balled a fist in all that time. Then one day he woke up and declared, "I'm gonna fight again. I'm gonna be champion again."

Financial problems are no religious experience. The youth center he started ("to keep other George Foremans out of trouble") was swimming in red ink. He did not want to surrender it or his lifestyle.

"I put on the gloves."

But nobody took him seriously until lately. Now his daily work-outs are studies in blind faith. He doesn't look as good as he sounds. But those arms, those building fortresses of power and destruction can persuade the most agnostic to concede there is always a puncher's prayer.

Foreman sometimes looks like someone whose wife gave him a membership in the heavyweight division for Christmas. His punches lack snap. They are shoved. He looks easily hittable. And there is no denying that he is at least 41 years old. That is irreparable. It is not 1968 anymore. Or 1978. Or 1988. The critics say Foreman is slick in the same way bacon grease is slick. He is a con man, some claim. He will tell you whatever you want. He will make you believe whatever he wants. The fight with Cooney is cauli-flower earmarked. It is a race.

Right?

The mission is to fight for the championship. Right now that means Mike Tyson. First Cooney. Then Tyson. Foreman says keep the faith. And either get out of the way or get into the ring with him.

237

"Muhammad Ali used to call me Frankenstein. Well I've changed. I'm more like Godzilla these days."

Others have tried comebacks. Larry Holmes, Joe Frazier. Pitiful failures in each instance. It is because they were not willing to start back at the bottom. Foreman did. Now he is near the top.

"Archie tells me I'm just a growing boy still. If I can get rid of some of this baby fat. . .

He thumps his stomach and a laugh comes loose.

"It's empty. Gotta load up. Look everyone, 40 is not a death sentence. Neither is being round. I have the heart of an Olympian. They tested it back in Texas. I like myself. And the sky is not the limit. I've learned what all is out there. When you can smell death, when you are in the saddest tunnel, the darkest place, when you're afraid God thinks you're better off dead, you make the best of everything afterward. I'm bound for glory, you all better climb on board."

Punches leave powerful impression.
Jan. 16, 1990

ATLANTIC CITY—When he sees them wobbling like that, gasping and frantic, trying to get their legs underneath again, trying to make the brain unscramble and command forth coordination, equilibrium, consciousness, George Foreman says it feels strangely bittersweet.

"Sometimes they look like foals just being born—starting a brand new life," Foreman says softly.

"Only when you're dealing with horses, you pray they stand up. When it's another fighter, you hope he stays down."

Foreman saw Gerry Cooney falling on the canvas in the second round Monday night. He knew.

"Yeah, I knew he'd get up, even though he shouldn't have," Foreman says. "See he's got courage. He's a fighter."

Cooney had just been hammered with six heavy punches, all

destructive. His eyes were glazed, his confidence drained. He looked over to his corner. Gil Clancy was screaming, "Hold on, clench, stay out of the way."

Foreman stood at the other end of the ring watching referee Joe Cortez. Cortez rubbed off Cooney's gloves, asked once again if he was OK, and then allowed the fight to resume.

And it was this look — a snarl of disdain and dismay on the huge face of George Foreman — that could have alerted everyone to what was about to happen.

"I don't like to end 'em like that," Foreman would say later. "I like the ref to come to the rescue. But when it was time to fight some more, I couldn't take any chances."

Cooney staggered forward, hands up but limp. And came a ferocious left-handed uppercut. It clanked off the bottom of Cooney's lantern jaw.

Then came the right hand, the signature of George Foreman through four decades of boxing. It is one of the stiffer right hands in fistic history. There are 61 men who can vouch for its authenticity.

Including Gentleman Gerry Cooney, at 1:57 of the second round Monday night.

"You can't let me hit you that many times in a row," Foreman says.

Today everyone listens. Foreman's wonderful crusade to return to the heavyweight throne room has been elevated from lounge act to matinee billing in the main showroom. He got $1.2 million to jettison Gerry Cooney into upright position and semi-coherence. After all, they shoot horses, don't they?

Meanwhile the price of Big George will soon go up. Even higher than the $5 million offer sheet Foreman handed back to promoter Don King with a Thanks But No Thanks.

"It'll be like Rip Van Winkle, the old man who came out of a deep sleep and whipped Mike Tyson," Foreman says. "It would be a spectacular event. And the same thing happened to Gerry Cooney, my best friend and a true brother, will happen to Mike Tyson." Suddenly he did not look so old.

Someone asks Foreman what is the difference now and then?

239

How is the new George Foreman different from the one who ruled the world 17 years ago?

"I was a lot slower back then."

And the mischief crackles off the walls.

He is self-effacing, the butt of his own jokes. He says he likes to beat people to the punch line. The critics will claim he beat up a statue, that there is no honor in hammering a man already asleep on his feet. But the fact remains George Foreman rained bombs with incredible accuracy and increasing devastation upon a heavy-weight fighter who had won 28 of 30 fights before Monday night. And it is unlikely any man could have withstood such carnage and remained perpendicular to the canvas.

Including Mike Tyson?

Most definitely. There is no questioning the raw power Foreman forges with his fists. He can tenderize a side of beef. He could topple a bull with such combinations of left hooks, uppercuts and clubbing right hands.

He is slow and despite Archie Moore's installation of his trade-mark wrap-around defense, extremely hittable. But when you can punch like George Foreman, you always have a chance.

It was a great finishing job. Regardless of the opponent. Gil Clancy, Cooney's manager, said with a small smile, "Fight fans are going to have to take this man seriously."

There is a new shadow on the horizon. It's really an old one. But not a really old one. And it's also kind of a round one. But it's also kind of a scary one.

It got a whole lot scarier Monday night.

The old man finds peace in the sea
July 1, 1990

TALAMONE, Italy — In the small tavern, the old man's voice bounces heavy as he tells stories of the sea. Paolo is a fisherman now for 48 years; since he was 14. The younger fisherman already know most of his stories. But they listen anyway. The one about the Scali Elephante, the giant shark he hooked in the Adriatic Sea, pleases Paolo.

Hey Paolo — remember when you brought home 400 spigola, the best-tasting fish in the Mediterranean, all in one day?

"Yes, one day. But 21 hours in the boat is one long day," He says.

Chairs screech on the cold concrete floor as the fisherman inch closer to the old fisherman of Talamone. He usually drops by once a day. Then someone realizes it is Wednesday, and that means tomorrow Paolo will chase the polpi. The Octopus. Every Thursday, Paolo Di Angelo takes his boat La Daniela, along the cliffs, where the water always stays dark. It is his favorite day of the week. For some reason, the octopus is his favorite challenge.

"Hey Paolo, how many polpi will you catch tomorrow?"

"All of them."

Everyone laughs. And the crowded face, small eyes and a Roman nose and tiny mouth all on the top of each other, relents. The white mustache looks like a cowcatcher from an ancient locomotive. The smile pushes it aside and crooked teeth seem to bend to let the laugh escape. Someone reaches over and pats the wide-open spaces of his head, where hair used to be. Now, there are only creases and gullies plus a couple of scars he'll be glad to tell you all about. His skin is an old leathery saddle, polished and worn and comfortable.

You hardly notice the half-moon arc of scar tissue on the left side of his head.

He stands up, the barrel chest pushing the T-shirt farther than his belly. The vermicelli-thin legs seem hardly able to balance such a trophy, and yes — the left knee swells to the size of a gourd every once in a while and he must go get the fluid siphoned from it. There is a good story somewhere there, too. "I will see you soon," he says. And there is alarm, then a collective groan. "Paolo, it is only 5 o'clock." He doesn't look at his watch. He doesn't stop. It is time to sleep. The octopus knows. You can fool the fish. But the octopus knows who is ready for the day. It can smell the drunk man. It can sneak away from the sleepy one.

When he was a boy, 6 maybe, his father taught him how to catch

241

the tiny polpi. A rock tied to a cord, then wrapped in a white cloth or something that reflects light. You drop the rock into the water and wrap the cord around your hand. "To this day, I do not know if the polpi loves or hates the color. Only that it cannot resist attacking it," he says. He remembers yanking with all his might, pulling the hideous sea monster from its depths. And then he remembers the finality. He had to bite the octopus just near the eye, sink his teeth into the brain. "Today the children have learned that if you turn the polpi upside down, it will drown in its own ink," he says. "But that seems too much like play," he adds. If you want to go out in La Daniela with Paolo, you must be ready for a long day. To spend a day away from his regular fishing, it must be worth the while. He will need to bring many octopi. "We will leave at 3." He is a fisherman, the best in all of Talamone. And he makes a nice living, the only one who does. The others see the glamor of the big fish. They just for the adventure. And they seek the freedom. But the commitment. . .

Who else but Paolo brings in a full bin of fish, then works for six more hours, mending the hand nets he uses? Who else but Paolo would walk over to the young fisherman who slipped on his boat and broke his leg and discretely slip some money into his shirt pocket? Only Paolo drove his boat to the big demonstration in Porto Santo Stefano two months ago to protest against the big boats and their drag nets that are raping and pillaging the sea bottom like the worst pirates of eternity.

Down at the docks, his stories are bigger than life. And some of them may not always be harbored in truth. Sometimes you must filet away that which really happened from the bones of contention. This 62-year-old tells stories so outrageous that nobody believes them. Nobody will ever deny that Paolo knows how to set a hook.

But is he for real?

Women used to find him irresistible, says the bartender, a man named Tony.

"There are at least five women in Talamone who say they have his baby." There is another woman in Fanteblanda who says she has a daughter from Paolo. In Ortebello, there are at least three women who claim Paolo fathered them a child.

Tony says his father was good friends with Paolo. And if his father ever heard anyone say anything behind Paolo's back, "he'd go after him with a stick."

"My father loved Paolo until the day he died, three years ago," Tony says. "No, I think some of the young ones are jealous. Paolo is a real man."

At the boat slip, he is waiting, wearing a plain white T-shirt, black bikini bathing suit and yellow rubber boots. He'd tell you about the time he caught his trousers once on a cleat and fell onto the deck hard, on his side, breaking five ribs. He then tumbled into the water, and it was the coldest day of the year of 1963. And somehow he pulled himself back aboard. And somehow he made it home, shivering and fraught with pain. And somehow after fooling with the controls of the gas stove, delirious with pain and worried about hypothermia, he somehow managed to catch his face on fire as the flames burst out at him.

He'd tell you the story but he doesn't have time, you see. But anyway, that's why he only has one eyebrow.

Talamone is a fishing village and nothing more. During the winter, maybe 200 people live there. In the summer, 10 times that many. It is nestled is a curl of shoreline at the southern tip of the Ucellinas Mountains. The water is unbelievably clear, and it is a sailor's delight once you get out past the rocky reefs. This is due to the protection the mountains offer.

"Only wind from the southwest can be trouble," Paolo explains, as he aims his 25-foot boat toward something only he can see. For it is totally dark at 3 a.m.

"You learn to look at the sky. But in Talamone, you have help."

It is why the Etruscans once built an entire city here, for the protection and the view. It is why the Spanish fortress was erected thousands of years later almost on the same spot. The fortress still stands, and every time Paolo looks at it, he remembers another childhood memory.

"The children used to think it was that fort the Germans were afraid of," he says, eyes still staring at the night. "We used to think that was why the warplanes came and dropped the bombs."

Talamone was hit hard by the Nazis, who in turn suffered terri-

243

ble losses on the Tyrrhenian Sea. The fact that nobody stayed a child in such times is obvious. Nobody was ever young again.

His father was a fisherman. But not a very good one, Paolo says. Just as he wasn't a very good father, either. There was never any time for bonding, for games a father and son play. No teaching. The boat was always late coming back. There was always an excuse. The sea was rough. The wind was blowing the wrong way.

"I think maybe my father spent a lot of time in the bar when we thought he was at sea. He was in the bar when the bombs hit. My mother was walking to the bar to get him. She carried him home a lot of nights. But that night nobody came home."

His father was killed. His mother spent a month in the hospital with wounds. And Paolo Di Angelo became a fisherman not long afterward.

"They must have thought we were fortified and that is why we became a target. But the fort was hundreds of years old. It is an archeological exhibit, and they bombed Talamone because of it."

The harsh grunt of diesel motor is the only sound for the next several minutes. It has 132 horsepower, Paolo had said earlier. Capable of 14 knots. And the tank holds 100 gallons; La Daniela can go a long way without stopping.

Streaks of sunlight appeared as the old fisherman expertly made his way along the rocky coast. Stay close to the cliffs, he'd said, and you avoid the fango—the muddy bottom. Your best friend when you are at sea is your eyes. Mud becomes an enemy. He'd shown everyone in the bar the fingertip that had been sewn back onto his hand 15 years ago. A sea snake had gotten him. He simply did not see it.

To be an individual commercial fisherman in Italy is not easy. For one thing, you must do your work alone. Or else you are considered a corporation and must possess a very expensive fishing license. So when Paolo goes fishing, he goes alone. And he sets the nets and put out another two dozen baited hooks and lives out his passions in solitude.

Not so when he goes after the octopus. That is such a bizarre job, figure the marine authorities, that if you want company, fine. But do not come back to Talamone with anything but octopi.

"No more than 10 years ago, this place was filled with big fish,"

244

he says, stopping the motor. "Shrimp all over the place. Wonderful fish. But the drag nets, the big boats have killed all the eggs and the little fishes. It is terrible."

Now there are only octopi in the area. He checks to make sure the spear guns are ready. He looks also for the rifle. And then he grabs the small nets.

"Throw them and if we are lucky, we will not have to get wet," he says.

In a couple of minutes, he grunts and hoists a dripping wad of net aboard.

"Polpi."

Two of them flop on the deck. They are neither the small fries of Paolo's youth nor anything delivered from the vaults of Jules Verne's imagination.

"Maybe 20 kilos," Paolo says, reaching down to pick one up.

The octopus is not the loveliest of creatures. Its huge head is really its body. The eight tentacles are unnerving to the novice fisherman. For they move with a pace all their own, almost a paradox; too slow and too quick for comfortable reference points.

It only looks slimy. There is a gentle heat to its texture at least on board a boat and in full range of the torrid Tuscan summer mornings.

It is still not appealing. The tentacles undulate and those suction nodules—the ones that were able to rip a man's flesh off in the chambers of childhood fantasy— are grotesque-feeling. This anatomically acurate octopus, built to scale, can make you shiver and blanch. But it hardly seems life-threatening. To the contrary, it has a pathetic nature,unable to move very quickly, owning no weaponry other than the disgusting ink secretion.

But even the old fisherman dislikes the clamp of one of the tentacles on his forearm. He lurches at it with his free hand.

"There is nothing like that feeling," he says. "I think of the vampire sucking at my blood until my heart explodes. I cannot stand that feeling."

The market price is about $3 a pound (about 4,000 lire), and that is not enough to make a living. But without fail, once a week, he come to chase the octopus.

"Maybe I am like the polpi," he says. "I don't know if I hate it or love it. But I do it."

Is there a story behind the scar on his face? Was there some giant octopus?

"I will tell you later."

The nets will do all the work, he explains later. It is tiresome, throwing them and retrieving them. But they are all you need.

"Unless you get too near the ridges and reefs."

He does not really enjoy the water as he once did. He used to revel in the blue-green exhilaration. He'd lick at the white foam and pretend it was ice cream. He loved putting on his diving mask and going underwater and seeing what new wonders were down there waiting.

"Then one time I was under, getting nets free. A polpi like you have never seen came behind me. It was the size of a small man, but it had the strength of a large one. And it was smart. I had a spear gun and I was trying to get it up to the eye.

"But the polpi butted me into my own net. I panicked. I was sure I would not get free and I would lose my air. Remember I had no tanks. I got free somehow and rushed to the surface and scraped my head on the side of my boat. I was bleeding badly. I got on board and lied there for an hour, crying.

"It is the only time I have ever been afraid at sea. I have caught a 19-foot shark. I have killed with my rifle an eel as long as a horse. That day I was afraid."

The octopus does not get as big as the one Paolo described. Not around here. Was it one of those exaggerations the fellows at the dock were talking about? Or might there be an eight-footed Big Foot lurking down there?

"That is what the rifle is for. And why I prefer someone to come with me when I fish for polpi. I am not proud of the story. It shows I have a coward inside me."

The day becomes a chore. More spots are tried, more nets are thrown and hoisted. The bin starts to fill up with octopi. The door is pungent after a while.

"Do they taste good," he is asked.

"I don't eat them."

Does the burger flipper at McDonald's eat Big Macs?

No, he has seen the polpi alive, felt it resist and fight for life. And he has done the same. He understands the helpless feeling. It is not a matter of a hunter eating his game. And it is not a regression back into childhood, that as every octopus is taken aboard, Paolo Di Angelo bites hard onto the spot near the eyes.

"It is a better way to die, I think," he says.

The day is almost done. It is 8 o'clock in the evening. But the sun will be out for two more hours. Time for a swim in a blue grotto near a small island. Paolo floats on his back, squinting at the sun. There are two dozen octopi on board. Almost 300 pounds. A good day. He climbs aboard and pulls out a bottle of mineral water.

"The sea is a whore," he says, his drink rolling down his chin. "She will treat you good, but you must always pay."

"I have never married. Fisherman are bad husbands. No time for responsibility. My friends are slowly dying. One of them — Signor Giuseppe Prociti — is quite a man. During the war he drove a tug-boat. There are 75 ships that sank out there between Elba Island and the Sardinian Sea. Giuseppe recovered the bodies and brought them back to land. He is a sad man because he says he will die alone. He spent all his money on girls but not the right kind. And now he is sad. Giuseppe helped build the lighthouse on Archipelago Toscano, which saved thousands and thousands of lives. And he is sad. And he is right. When you share yourself with only the sea, you will die alone."

In a minute, he will start the boat. Go back home, go to the bar and tell some stories. There are no great adventures to report — only once did he have to go in the water to unhook a net. The rifle was not fired. Everyone on Talamone who wants to eat polpi tomorrow night will be able. And it will be fresh.

"What the hell," the old fisherman says with a laugh. "It is not paradise. But it is almost."

An American Tragedy
Sept. 2, 1990

There are five seconds to play. Always. Curtis Jones pushes the rewind button in his head and it returns to that point in time where he is forever stuck. He ignores the butterfly weaving around him. Everyone on the abandoned wood bench in the empty lot with the big shade trees looks up just for an instant. It is the end of another summer. Some of the fellows are having a cold one. So yeah OK, Curtis, tell us about it one more time. And everyone raises his paper bag to have another sip.

"Four seconds," Jones shouts, holding an imaginary basketball in front of him, shifting his right foot forward, then sideways, "I throw my move. My man falls down, I look at the referee. No foul, no call. Three seconds, two seconds. . ."

Jones' glazed eyes see all the way to the moment that is now 23 years old. He leans forward and pushes his bony right arm up and follows through, long fragile-looking fingers raking at the sky. And he blinks. The shot went in the basket that glorious day in 1967 when a playground legend became king of the city. It has gone in a million times since. Time and space are helpless. Always, five seconds to play. Hit the rewind. Blink.

It was probably the last time Curtis Jones sat on top of the world. It started rolling over on him not so long afterward. And he couldn't stand it. It has to do with seeing something in front of you that makes you flinch. You stop and gasp and discover you're seeing yourself. It's you wandering around the neighborhood, helpless to your own sluggish momentum and you can't stand it.

So you turn around and go back to where it's safe.

"I was gonna be the best there ever was, you hear me? I should have been a millionaire. Ain't nobody could dribble like me, pass like me. You hear what I'm saying? I'm God. I'm the Lord. I could have put $15 million in the bank. I made that shot, they carried me off on their shoulders. I could hear them yelling, 'Curtis Jones, you the best ever.' You hear me?

And everyone nods and has another sip. Jones' tongue splashes out of his mouth, his fingers twitch, his eyes roll. And he reaches for his own bottle of beer. He is breathing hard, excited, nervous.

And the eyes—liquid jelly floating in their own stagnancy—have no focus.

In a minute he'll jump back up and there will be five seconds to play once more. All he has to do is blink.

"Curt, you been taking your medicine? Taking the pills you're supposed to?" asks the shirtless heavy-set man with the roll of skin that hangs down over his belt at least a foot. "You're talking so fast Curt. Slow down. Relax, man."

And Curtis Jones, an American tragedy, closes his eyes. He can't relax. Can't sleep. Can't let loose of that moment. Something became disconnected in his mind a long time ago. He retreated inside himself, ran all the way back to when it was OK to be Curtis Jones. Before everyone knew about his illiteracy and second-grade reading aptitude and 73 IQ, before he was herded off to a foregin land called Idaho, to some junior college five miles from where the neo-Nazi Aryan Nation religious group was founded about the same time. Before he stepped outside himself and saw what was happening to Curtis Jones. Before he jumped back inside and pulled a nervous breakdown in over him. He lives in his own tunnel now, permanently disabled in the eyes of society, permanently disfigured in his own mind's eye, permanently persecuted in his permanently medicated mind.

Sometimes his mother will get a call to come get him; Mrs. Jones, someone saw your son on the other side of town and he was in an alley, eating mashed potatoes out of a garbage can. Or he might wander into his old high school, the scene of his long-gone glory, not to mention the scene of the crime, stagger through the hall looking for his picture on the Northwestern High Wall of Fame. He'll wear his faded and stretched-out letterman's sweater, carring a bunch of his old trophies, the rusted and dented artifacts of his faded glory, and scream in those corridors. The echo is loud and pathetic. He'll wail about who he used to be, what he was supposed to be. That's him up there. Yo, world—does anyone remember Curtis Jones?

Only in his mind, inside the cloudy tunnel where a barrage of daily medicines govern his moods and try to fend off the fear that's always so near, he still is that person. Still that smooth innocent smiling face up on the wall. And sometimes he makes so much racket the the security guard must be called. Once upon a time, he was carried on the shoulders of fans. Now he gets shoved out the door by beefy sentries, raving at his own shadow. One of the Colts of Northwestern High, maybe the greatest assist man ever to step on its court, could use an assist. What happened to teamwork? They shoot horses, don't they?

A human being either slipped through the cracks of the system or was pushed. The disgrace and the grandeur cast off eerie lights. Guilt is a like greed — everywhere. But the system is faceless. It was a crime of grand collaboration and mass complicity. But only one person has been punished.

Wayne County Probate Court records reveal that Curtis Jones, 41, illiterate and unemployed, living on his deceased father's Social Security benefits, has been committed to the Northville Regional Psychiatric Center eight times since 1970. The diagnosis: acute schizophrenia. He is considered an outpatient now. Doctors say as long as he takes his Prolixin, Cogentin and heavy-duty B-1 vitamin pills, he doesn't have to be in the hospital.

But he cannot keep the rage from escaping.

"I got too close to my dream and my soul could not bear it," Jones says. "But someone let me get too close, you hear me? I can't read. I can't write. Never could. I knew it would catch up to me. I always had an inferior complex. Man, when you can't read nothing, you can't feel no other way. But I can play ball like a bitch. Still the greatest dribbler of all time. You hear me? Ever see anyone dribble a ball behind his back, 'tween his legs, using just one finger? I invented Larry Bird's shot and he took it from me. Magic's shot — that's mine, too. My passes were stole by Pistol Pete. Isiah took my moves. Earl the Pearl. Damn, ask Jimmy Walker, Dave Bing what I did to them down at the Y. I was in the eleventh grade and I was taking 'em all. I was the Father, the Son, the Holy Spirit. You hear me? I took the shot that won the city championship for us. Aw man, you see it? Was you there? Aw, man, there was five seconds left to play. . .

And he stops himself this time.

"They say I'm crazy," he says, almost whispering. And he blinks. Pain? What pain? Spencer Haywood remembers Jones' shot all too well. It beat him and his Pershing High teammates Feb. 21, 1967.

Northwestern won the game, the first prep game in Michigan history to be televised, 63-61 on Jones' 19-foot jump shot with two seconds left to play and claimed the Public School League championship. It was the slender junior guard's only field goal of the game.

"Curtis was so far ahead of his time," says Haywood, a former NBA star who has had his own share of personal demons to overcome. "He was Mr. Wizard on the court. A fantastic playmaker. Everything you see the pros do today, Curtis Jones was doing when he was in 10th grade. At one time, there was no doubt in anyone's mind that he was going to make the NBA and was going to make a lot of money. No doubt whatsoever. That day, that game — I'll never forget it. There were about 20 seconds left to play and Curt got the ball and just dribbled the clock down and everyone in the gym — man, the state of Michigan stood still for this game — just knew he was going to score the winning basket. Just like he did. It's a shame what's happened to him. A tragedy. But before he got sick, he was the greatest little man on the court there ever was."

Haywood is a recovering addict who regularly attends meetings to help cope with his problem. He also is a major partner in a real-estate development company and president of another company that trains and places computer technicians into the labor force. He shudders when he thinks about the two different paths he and his old rival have traveled.

"I was just like Curtis at one time," Haywood says. "I couldn't read or write in 10th grade. I had no self-esteem anywhere except that court. Just like Curtis. But I got great help from great people. I got through it. I also went off to a junior college that seemed like Nowheresville, right on the Colorado and New Mexico border. Curt went to Idaho. But I didn't go to my school alone. I had a friend, a teammate from high school, in fact my best friend, go with me. It was tough and definitely a hard place for a black man from the city to try to adjust to college life. But I made it. Curtis didn't.

"And I don't know who's to blame except maybe all of us. Curtis' failure is America's failure."

Haywood says the last time he saw Jones "was last year when I was giving an anti-drug talk at a school on the east side of Detroit.

251

From a distance I saw him as I was walking into the gym. But inside the gymnasium—it was filled with kids—I looked and I couldn't find him. I was going to introduce him to the crowd. Then when it was over, I walked out the door and there he was.

"He'd come all that way to ask if he could borrow some money."

Sometimes the lightning crackles inside Jones' head. He feels rumbles and he gets dizzy and, "I'm scared my head's gonna explode. I know something's wrong with me. I just don't know whose fault it is."

One night several years ago, he became convinced a taxi driver was actually an agent of the Ku Klux Klan. It's the reason, said Jones to the police, he had to steal the taxi when the driver parked and went inside a party store.

Said the police report filed on the incident. "Subject also claimed to be God."

———

Henrietta Jones injects herself daily with insulin to control and regulate the diabetes that shoots through her system. There are pills that help keep the blood pressure down. She takes other medicines for the congenital arthritis that forced her to retire from her job with Chrysler 18 years ago. One of her sons was killed in a barroom fight two blocks from home in 1978. Another son, she says, "has let the street get hold of him. He's messed up with that drug. He's got problems, bad problems."

But Curtis, her baby boy, brings her the most pain.

"He just can't stop feeling his dreams were failed," says the 67-year-old woman, her voice soft as a prayer. "He's not evil; there's so much good inside him. Really there is. But he's so confused what all's happened. We knew he shouldn't go off to college; he was special, went to the special school for years. But he saw something he had to chase after. He tried and there was just too much pressure. That ability to play ball was God's gift to him, I'm sure. It was compensation.

"I see him cry sometimes, two hours without stopping. He says 'Mama, I'm no good. I'm no good.' I worry so much, I pray every night for the strength. I'm afraid he's going to kill himself. He just can't let loose and go on with his life. He gets nervous and he can't sleep . . . just walking around, talking to himself, talking about how his life got stolen from him.

"When he can't sleep, I can't sleep. And when he gets that way, I know pretty soon he's gonna have to go back in the hospital at Northville."

She takes off her glasses to wipe at her eyes. "It hurts me so much to have to go downtown and fill out the court order. It hurts so bad to have to write 'My son is mentally ill.' I do it because I love him."

A mother sobs for several seconds, shaking her head. The umbilical cord is so frayed and worn. It is a lifeline about to snap, not from apathy, but overuse. She stands up regularly and asks the people in the congregation at Holy Cross Baptist to pray for her son. She is not ashamed, her son is sick and a mother's instincts are to do whatever she can. When she gets calls that Curtis is in trouble, he just got beat up, he's drunk and can't find his way home, she always goes to help him. Get him home.

Rev. James Porter, pastor at Holy Cross Baptist, warned her years ago it would take special prayers, special strength, to pull Curtis through the storms that pass behind his eyes.

"I just want my son to know peace in himself," Henrietta Jones says, swallowing hard. The corned beef on the stove needs turning. She lifts herself up from her chair and walks to the kitchen.

Curtis stays down in the basement, she says. His room — he calls it "my private closet" — is seven by 10 feet and consists of a small bed, an ashtray and a single-bulb light that hangs from the low ceiling.

"He's safe there though," says his mother.

Up the street from the little house on McGraw Street, five blocks from Northwestern High, back at the lot with the sparse grass and thick weeds, Jones licks once again at his thirst. People see him and brand him. Just another drunk. But the beer is only a substitute. When you live in the in-between world, between the gaps where even a streak of light gets bent and twisted and flowers seem evil

253

and hairbrushes can walk, unable to cope with anything except yesterday, which happened an entire lifetime ago, your thirst is for redemption. Jones wants redemption. He pleads for it. The shame of society he wraps around himself like some blanket or flap of cardboard he finds in an alley on a cold night when he can't find his way back to his mother's house, is so uncomfortable. He hates the feeling, coarse as burlap; he hates how it irritates him. So he douses it with the beer. It washes away the feeling. Pain? What pain?

He asks constantly if we hear him. Do we? Do we hear Jones' searing anguish? The streets are full of these soft moans. Everyone has a sad story to tell. Jones' is just more complicated than most. Will anyone take the time to hear the story? Redemption's not here just yet.

So he hides behind a sad facade. Jones holds out his palm. Want to see him hold a lit match in his hand? He'll do it for a beer. One time he offered to let someone shoot him in the hand. A gang member laughed.

"He had a gun and I didn't have no money. I told him he could shoot a hole through my hand if he bought me a case of beer. Man, I don't feel that kind of pain. I can hold fire for long as you want me to. Watch this."

He reaches into his pants pockets, squirms and feels around. Then curses.

"Ain't this a crying shame. I got $156 million owed me and I ain't got a damn match to my name. Ain't got a damn dime. Greatest player who ever lived and I ain't got the fire to burn my hand off."

And he sticks a forefinger to the side of his head and squeezes an imaginary trigger and mouths the word, "Boom."

Then he reaches for his paper bag and another cigarette.

"Smoking cigarettes since I was 7. Smoking made me ambidextrous," he says, laughing as he swallows hard.

There was a time when Jones was considered the finest high school point guard in the United States. Letters from colleges all over the country arrived daily. Scouts were stopping at the service stations on Grand Boulevard regularly, asking for directions to Northwestern High, where the great Curtis Jones played. They called him Mr. Wizard. The Magician.

"Before there was Isiah Thomas, there was Curtis Jones," says Will Robinson, now a chief scout for the Detroit Pistons. "Passer, playmaker, leader, shooter. He was the whole package. But he never should have tried to go to college the way he did. He was doomed to failure. He had no learning skills developed. Somebody should have cared about the person inside the basketball player. The kid is always more important than the final score. I used to tell my players there is a life after the game is over. You must be ready for it."

Robinson was coaching Pershing High that day in 1967. With any kind of luck, Jones could have been playing for Robinson.

"I tried to get him to come to Pershing. He had an aunt or something he could have stayed with. This is all hindsight but I think I could have helped him. Spencer was in the same boat, you know. When you have a deficiency or a disability, it isn't the end of the world. When I used to teach at Miller High, I had a student named Walter Jenkins who also was special ed. But you can reach him today at Northern High. And it's Dr. Jenkins. From special ed to a Ph.D. That's what can happen. But you have to evaluate each one as they come. I think Curtis got special treatment that he shouldn't have. He got pushed up through the system. All that's doing is prolonging the eventual failure. Most kids, that happens and all they do is flunk out of school. Curtis had a nervous breakdown."

Robinson hasn't seen Jones for years but, "I hear he's still living in the past. That's not good. That one game may have been the crowning glory of the PSL. I've heard people say it was the best game they ever saw. Jones scored the last basket. That was how he played. He'd spend the whole game setting everyone up—he was a very clever, very tricky passer—then he'd take the shot that decided the game. But I also remember something else about that season. We came back and beat Northwestern in the state playoffs. Pershing won the state championship that year."

255

Robinson then adds, "See what I mean? You gotta let loose of the past."

James Jones was a welder who worked for Chrysler up until the day he started coughing blood into his handkerchief regularly. The lung cancer spread quickly. His youngest son, Curtis, brought all his Little League and rec league trophies to the hospital so his father could have them around him. Then one day he was told, "Daddy died last night."

Curtis was 12 and the loss was devastating. For years his father and mother had tried to work with him about school, reading books to him, trying to teach him how to make his letters. But when his father died, "I took it hard. And I didn't care 'bout much at all for a long time."

One day his mother came home from work and saw clothes from the line strewn all over the floor. Curtis was in the bathroom, sitting on the floor, playing a basketball game in his head, using clothespins as players. There was Wilt Chamberlain and Oscar Robertson and all the stars of the NBA playing a game on the tile. The clothespin with the ball—that was Curtis Jones.

"Basketball was his only interest. You couldn't force a book in his hand. You couldn't take a basketball out of it," his mother says.

On 16th Street, behind a house, through the back yard and into the dirt-road alley is a basketball hoop someone nailed to a pole. Curtis wants to show off. He bounces the basketball that has part of the cover missing on the lumpy road, once, twice, three times. Like a puppy it responds, obeys as he pats it gently, forcefully.

"Bet I make it from here," he says, letting loose with a leaning jumper. Airball. "Come on, bet me somebody."

The next shot clanks off the back rim.

Then he starts in his relentless replay of that one brief shining moment. Five seconds to play. The ball swishes through the dangling net.

"You lose."

And his laugh is a cackle. And for a moment, the glory returns, soaking him, washing away everything else. A small boy walks up, watching. Jones hits four shots in a row. Then he starts dribbling.

"Marques Haynes dreams about handling the ball like this.

256

Curly Neal needs five fingers to do what I do with one," he says, putting the ball around his back, twirling around, dropping to a knee.

"Whooee man," the boy chirps, smiling. "You good. You should be in the NBA, huh? You the next Magic Johnson."

And Jones says, "Man, I was the first Magic Johnson."

Jones and his mother claim Fred Snowden, Northwestern's coach back then, promised a college scholarship to his star guard. Snowden later became an assistant at the University of Michigan, then the University of Arizona before entering private business.

Jones assumed he would follow his coach to U-M. But his high school transcripts were atrocious. His scores on the college entrance exams were even worse. He ranked in the bottom one percentile. Translated, it meant every student in the country theoretically could read better than Curtis Jones.

Jones claims a deal was struck between him, his former coach and Michigan. Go play for North Idaho Junior College for two years, get your grades up to an acceptable level, then come to Ann Arbor and have two years of eligibility left.

It was 1968 and a troubled, confused, scared teen-ager from the streets of Detroit left for the wild west of Coeur d'Alene, Idaho.

"From all black to all white," Jones says. "There was maybe six blacks in the whole town, maybe the whole state. There was racial tension. I dated a cheerleader, a white girl. I got in some trouble. One time someone slipped some LSD in my drink at a party. I was messed up. Things got tougher and tougher. I tried. I tried hard. School—nobody cared what I did there. When I had a test, I'd sit there a few minutes, then go to the bathroom. Someone would be there with a test, already filled in for me. I was making C's and I still couldn't read a word."

Then one day he missed a class when there was a test. And he had to take a makeup test. And there was nobody waiting in the bathroom with the answers. He asked a girl first to fill in the answers for him. She refused. Then he asked her to read him the questions.

She laughed.

"I couldn't stand it. The word went around like fire. Everyone laughed at me. They called me names. I did more LSD. My girl-

257

friend back home was pregnant with someone else's baby. Friends of mine from Detroit who went to Vietnam and won medals were getting shot and killed. There was riots going on. There was so much blood in the street, so many needles sticking in arms, murderers and killers. I couldn't adjust to Idaho; then I couldn't adjust back to Detroit.

"Since 1970, it seems like I have a friend a year die violently. I think maybe they have it better than me. Their suffering's over."

Shortly after returning to Idaho from summer vacation following his freshman year, the sparks and blank spots began appearing. The short circuits manifested at first in anger and rage, then bizarre behavior, episodes of confrontation with school officials, campus arrests, ordered psychiatric evaluations.

"Then . . . I don't remember what came then," Jones says.

On Feb. 17, 1970, Dr. Joseph Grismer, a psychiatrist in Idaho, performed a mental evaluation on Jones and suggested immediate help and treatment. On March 23, back home in Detroit, Jones was committed to Northville for the first time.

"I was tied down. I had roaches in my hair, bugs in my mouth," Jones says.

His mother says she's not aware of that ever happening. Sometimes, she adds, "Curtis thinks things he saw when he was in the hospital happened to him, too. He hates the hospital."

On the sidewalk in front of the Jones' home, Curtis talks in rambling flurries, raving about cruelty that is everywhere. Then he looks down and points.

"My best friend," he says, looking at his shadow. "Sometimes my only friend. I know I'll never walk alone. I got that shadow. It's stuck with me for life."

Another cackle of laughter. The mind is racing. He says he really is God. He talks about taking "limbs from the octopus and I gave them to the fish. It's reincarnation."

Then he talks in gibberish, unintelligible. Then another big grin.

"Basically, in the tree of life, my plum fell off and rotted."

Jones and his mother walked into an office almost a decade ago and told their story to an attorney, Jerome Quinn. There have been several lawsuits filed on behalf of Jones. A multimillion-dollar suit

258

against the Detroit Board of Education claimed Jones was pushed into college prematurely and ill-equipped and therefore, was exploited, causing his mental breakdown and subsequent problems.

"I took it to the Michigan Supreme Court but that's where it is," Quinn said. "The Court refused to hear it. That doesn't mean you're right or wrong. It means the Supreme Court refuses to hear it. And that's where it is right now — going nowhere."

Quinn hesitates then adds, "I'm really amazed. I thought Curtis would get his day in court. I literally worked on that case 10 years. It was a good case. And it's a very tragic story."

Roy Allen is Director of Health and Physical Education for Detroit public schools. In 1967 he was a teacher and cross-country coach at Northwestern High.

"He may be the greatest talent I ever witnessed. He had unbelievable skill levels, incredible presence and vision. And he probably was the most popular kid in the school. I used to work the gate at the games and usually didn't get to watch until the second half. We turned away crowds. They wanted to see Curtis Jones play. Being truthful, Northwestern was only a little above average, talent-wise. Curtis Jones carried those teams to championships with his unique talents. If you could have seen some of the things he could do. Things that today would amaze you. But back then, well, nobody ever played the game like he did."

Allen says education should be the dominant part of the scholar-athlete's high school experience. He grunts when asked about what happened to Jones. There was no 2.0 minimum grade requirement back then. Bills that required special-education students to be mainstreamed into the general population at schools were still in the future. Tutorial programs had not been developed. There was no Proposition 48 or any of the safeguards that have been instituted to maintain academic standards for college qualification.

"Curtis never should have been sent off to Idaho. He should have been put in an environment where he could become a total person, a functional, literate person. It should have happened in high school and didn't. Then the insult got compounded. He is an American tragedy. I'm not throwing stones at anybody but he is a true and tragic example, the most tragic I'm aware of."

259

Two years ago, Jones tried to get a job with the parks and recreation department. He couldn't pass the required test. Last year, he tried to find work as a janitor. He couldn't pass that test, either. He says he's getting tired. And he's crying more and more.

"There are some hot streets in the neighborhood. Smoke that crack, buy it, sell it. Me, I obey John Law most of the time. Smoke some reefer once in a while is all. Drink my beer. But I'm tired, you hear me. There are contracts out on my life and I know that. My teeth got knocked out by a gang. I been shot at. A man with an Uzi came in a bar and opened up on everyone. There was a body in the trunk of a car two streets away. This is a hot area and not everyone is my friend. Not everyone knows how great I was. I'm tired. Been walking in a circle for 20 years. Got nothing but time. A big circle. That street to that street to that street. Just me and my friend. The shadow."

———

Perry Watson remembers the personal duels, the games within the games they enjoyed in high school. Watson played for Southwestern. Today he is the school's head basketball coach.

"I took pride in my defense. But Curt made anyone take his game up an extra notch. I remember one game he backed me all the way down court, dribbling the ball entirely behind his back. He never brought it in front of him. Nobody could get it from him. He was an amazing player. Truly the best I ever saw. What you see Earvin Johnson do today, Curt did 25 years ago. Only he was 6-foot and Earvin's 6-9. He should have gone right from the 10th grade into the NBA. That's how good Curtis Jones was."

Before his time. How ironic is that? Two months after he suffered his breakdown, Haywood signed a contract with Denver of the American Basketball Association, claiming hardship. It was the first time a player who had started his college career was signed before his college graduating class arrived.

"If I coulda just held my head together two more months," Jones says.

Lolita Wyanna walks up and hugs him. Friends since he was 8 and she was 6, they laugh easily around each other. They stare at each other the way old friends do.

"She used to read me my horoscope, tell me what was in store for me," Jones says, smiling. Lolita laughs and pokes him in the arm.

"I couldn't even read what was in my stars. I'm a Virgo. Damn, baby, why didn't you tell me what was going to be? Why didn't you keep me home?"

Lolita's smile fades. While Jones erupts into another version of The Shot, she sits patiently beside him, patting his leg occasionally.

"I cry still about him," she says. "You see, I know who Curt Jones is supposed to be. I know who he was. I know the whole story from the beginning. He is a victim of modern slavery. He was sold out just like they used to do. And I still cry about what happened to him."

Jones sits up and back down, then back up. Nervous. It's a big circle all right.

"Maybe five years ago, it was almost dark, it was raining, almost snowing," he says. "I was up on the interstate, dribbling my ball, faking out the cars as they came. I realized where I was and got scared trying to get off the street. I was walking back and I saw one of my trophies. It done got run over."

Jones blinks. Contact is lost. The tape begins again.

"John Wooden was looking for me. I got letters. The ABA wants me, too. And the NBA. Ask anybody. They all know me. Muhammad Ali one time gave me $50. I told him we both were the greatest of all time. Ask Ali. Ask Stevie Wonder, I used to ride him around on my bicycle. I used to be somebody great, you hear me? You can ask anybody about that."

'Tis still baseball season All-time Tigers fan: Christmas cheer visits ailing Leo Krass, 93.
Dec. 24, 1990

In the wind the candle flickers, fighting against the darkness, burning still. It's simple: you play until the final out.

Leo Krass has a look that is between places. There is fear, confusion. And there is pain. But he rolls his head and the eyelids arch to free a vacant stare. The smile slices through the gloom. A deep breath comes and Leo Krass reaches for the rosary beads around his neck.

Heads droop. Grandchildren rub their eyes. This isn't one of his good days, someone says. He comes and goes. Yesterday, he was great, telling stories, singing, laughing, making everyone else laugh. Tigers games in the '30s, old pitchers who were barely in the league long enough to wash their socks, a home run Lou Whitaker once hit. Leo Krass is a Tigers fan, they say, the all-time Tigers fan.

But he's not doing so well today. Outside the sky is a gray marshmallow, swollen and heavy. During the night a bad wind and a cruel wind came. And then so did the snow. They tried to cheer him up when they arrived. It's going to be a White Christmas. But he just stared at them with that look. Between places.

"He's 93 years old. They had to take his leg in October, you know," says Carolyn, one of his daughters.

"Gangrene."

Then the other day, there was some internal bleeding and he had to come back to the hospital. Everyone's worried.

John Jr. and Joe sit in the conference room, hands clasped together, afraid to talk. Paula, who just got married to a Marine, Lance Cpl. Rick Ware, three weeks before he shipped out to Saudi Arabia, paces around. Her man's not going to be home for Christmas and her grandfather's laid up in the hospital. And it's Christmas. It seems so unfair.

"It was. . . the same day Ernie Harwell was dumped," says Marian, another daughter, remembering this latest trip to the hospital.

"He loves that man. I really don't know that he's ever consciously missed a Tigers game on the radio since Ernie came to Detroit. You see my father's also been almost totally blind for a long time. Ernie's been his eyes.

"And now Ernie's going to be gone. It's very depressing to us all. But especially to Dad."

John Jr. nudges Joe. Remember how Grandpa taught us to keep score off the radio broadcasts? And at last, smiles come.

The room on the third floor of St. Joseph's Mercy Hospital is crowded. The family comes every day, sometimes only a handful, other times a couple dozen. Whoever can make it.

Leo looks to his left. There's a tiny Christmas tree on the table next to his bed. And a picture of his beloved Minnie, his wife of 50 years who passed away early in 1968.

And a portable radio.

Marian's husband, Roger Persyn, laughs at a favorite memory. A wedding day in 1984. Ralph, one of Leo's grandsons, was at the altar.

"Leo kept sneaking this tiny transistor radio to his ear to see how the Tigers were doing. He said Ralph had a lot of nerve getting married during the World Series."

Lord, has there ever been a man who loved baseball more than Leo Krass? When he was a kid growing up in Detroit, he'd walk a mile every day to the bridge to Belle Isle. Where the sandlot games were. And when he couldn't find enough kids to have a real game, he'd head into the alleys in the back of his house on J Street.

"We'd make our own balls most of the time," he'd tell his eight children over the years. And then he'd tell their children the same wonderful tales. Save his pennies and buy cord and wind it, around and around, make it tight. Make it into a ball. Then tape it with white adhesive. It wouldn't go very far when you hit it. But in an alley, where neighbors' windows were unavoidable temptations, you could really got a hold of someone's fadeaway or knuckle curve and never have to worry about breaking anything.

"Sometimes we'd stand outside Bennett Park and wait for Tigers to hit foul balls," Leo used to declare. "In those days you could get into the games free if you presented the foul ball. But I always kept them. So we could play ball."

263

Bennett Park? Tigers? Yeah, that was before it was called Navin Field, which was before it was Briggs Stadium, which was before it was Tiger Stadium. Leo Krass has outlived three stadium addresses and if you believe the rumors, is about to watch a fourth one cross over the bar.

"All my doctors have died, too, except these new ones," he says, his head trying to tilt up.

That's nothing. Leo Krass has been around long enough to see 17 U.S. presidents come into office. He's got a high school diploma awarded him in The Year of our Lord 1913.

"I met Ty Cobb when I was 13 years old; 1910, I think it was," he says, eyes closed now. "He taught me how to drag-bunt."

Across the street from Bennett Park, on the roof of garage buildings, there used to be something called the cat stands. Cost a nickel to come up there. Later the prices jumped to a quarter. Any way, a perfect view of the ballgame was there. And in the lean times, somewhere between pennies and actual dollars, so was Leo Krass.

He tells everyone that one time when he was actually in the ballpark, "George Mullin pitched a no-hitter. Hell of a screwball pitcher, Mullin. And I was there."

After high school, he took a job with the railroad, the Michigan Central. In 1917 he married Minnie. Then an opportunity with the Chrysler Motor Car Co. came. The dream was always of baseball; he played semipro and city leagues, an outfielder with good speed and fair arm and "Ty Cobb's tenacity but not his batting eye."

The '34 Series was great. Charlie Gehringer and Mickey Cochrane and Hank Greenberg. Remember it, Dad?

The names are magical. Heinie Manush. Harry Heilmann. Germany Schaefer. Dizzy Trout. Virgil Trucks. Sometimes, they roll out of his mouth as if he were reciting the batting order for last year's team. Sometimes he can't remember his children's names.

Sometimes he gets stuck in a painful moment in time. His first son's first communion. Leo Jr. was in the street, playing with his new roller skates. The driver of the car never saw him.

"He was 12 when he died. It was 1930," Leo says.

Jack Fredal, Carolyn's husband, says, "He's an amazing man. But he's 93 years old. We have to remember that. He wears his emotions on his sleeve. He always has. But sometimes he gets confused about things."

For 41 years Leo Krass worked for Chrysler, worked himself up to General Export Traffic Manager, which meant simply he was in charge of all overseas shipping for the corporation and then suddenly started to fall apart.

One day he woke up and could not see. The blood vessels behind his eyes had burst. His arteries had hardened.

"Somehow he drove to church. He couldn't see a thing. Somehow he made it to his church," Fredal says.

Baseball is his love. But his Catholicism is his grand consumption. The family loves to tell stories of Grandpa Leo, on vacation at their old cottage in Ontario, his old buddies waiting around the house while Leo went to mass. Never missed one. Not even when he'd travel abroad for Chrysler. In Switzerland, France, Italy, Belgium, it didn't matter. He'd find a Catholic Church.

They talk in front of him as though he wasn't there. Child is father to the man. And it is as if they were spelling out things so small children can't understand. But there is no condescending. Instead they tell stories that might embarrass him. But they tell them with such love and admiration that he comes out not only the star of the show but part of the audience as well.

"When he went into surgery to have his leg amputated," Roger, his son-in-law, ways, "he was really excited. Cecil Fielder had just hit his 50th home run. That really pleased him. He'd seen two Tigers — Greenberg was the other — hit 50 home runs." And when he came out of surgery, say the children, "he was singing. What was the song? *Dear Old Girl*. He's always singing; we all are. We're a singing family."

Carrie looks at Sharon. The two giggle. First song either of them learned — *Ein Prosit*. An old German drinking song. Grandpa taught it to them.

In the hall of the hospital, Christmas carols arrive almost on cue. Ron Pavelek, who works at the same elementary school where Carolyn teaches, strums a guitar. His mother Leona, is there, along with her family. Just a little gesture of love, something they like to do at Christmas time. When they sing *Silent Night*, Leo Krass sits up and starts singing. In German.

265

Then comes the voice, the one so familiar. The Christmas surprise for Leo Krass.

"Is there a Tigers fan here? I'm looking for Leo."

Ernie Harwell walks into the room. Please don't write about me, he says. And no pictures. Please.

The talk is small, personal stuff, baseball stuff. Chatter? Yeah. Baseball chatter. Just a few minutes. Long enough for a room to explode with joy, to let a river of tears slide into permanent smiles, the salty taste a wonderful savor as sweet as any Christmas candy.

And then, of course, one more song.

"Take me out to the ballgame. . ."

The room sobs, hugs, feels better. Maybe for just a moment. Harwell hands Leo a shiny new baseball and says, "I'll see you at the ballpark, Leo. Come see me."

The excitement is good for him. His eyes are slits. They scan to see the man who owns the voice of baseball. He cannot see him or anyone else, of course. But he turns to his left. Where the radio is. Where his eyes live.

"That Ernie Harwell is a hell of a sweet guy, isn't he?" Leo Krass says. Christmas Eve, 1990. A candle in the wind. Like a Tiger, burning bright.

Leo Krass nods his noble head up and down. And his fingers squeeze the precious ball the way ol' George Mullin used to do it. And the smile is gentle because you know the pitch was a beauty. On the outside corner.

Ernie called it before the umpire.

7.

COLUMNS IV

Florida fish story has Ruthian dimensions
Mar. 15, 1989

ARIPEKA SPRINGS, Fla. — The big aquarium, where the live shrimp are kept, makes a rumbling noise. Draught beer's 65 cents a glass. The pickled-eggs jar needs refilling. Only one left, floating conspicuously in the red, murky fluid. But it's cool inside and the stories are lusty, poignant, as often unbelievable as not. This little tavern near Uncle Pearl's Fish Camp usually brings only fishermen to whet their appetites and wet their thirsts.

Usually the talk is only of the big ones and where they are biting. Or of where they used to bite and how much bigger they used to be before the encroachment of the 20th century. But today there are tales of baseball, of long home runs that traveled great distances. Today, at the little bar in the Florida fishing villages near Hunters Lake, they talk about Babe Ruth.

And the little man with the neatly trimmed mustache (Boston Blackie style) reaches into the Windbreaker and pulls out the baseball.

"See here, this is the one he gave me," Luis Armando Calle says proudly. "See here what it says?"

The ball is yellowed, lopsided from sitting on the same shelf for almost 61 years. Its seams are no longer red. They have turned black from old age. And the writing on the ball has faded. But it is still legible.

"To Looie, a great kid."

And it was signed, "Your pal, Babe Ruth."

Calle does not let the ball leave his grasp. He walks from bar stool to bar stool, holding the ball at eye level for everyone to see.

"I was Babe Ruth's fishing guide," says Calle, his back straight, his lips pressed tightly together pulled into a slight smile.

It's true, the bartender says. There used to be a picture of the two of them. Kept it right here behind the bar on this mirror. But someone stole it.

Luis Armando Calle is 75 years old, a retired carpenter, a life-long fisherman. He says he knows the way a bass thinks. He says he still can take someone where nobody else goes. Where the big ones get lazy in the warm sun of the springtime.

"I took Babe Ruth there many times."

He was 13 when he met the great ballplayer. And even though the Cuban-born teen-ager had not been in America long (two years) in 1928, he knew the lakes and streams of Pasco County. And he knew of Babe Ruth, the king of baseball.

"He said he wanted privacy more than he wanted fish. He said he wanted to relax first and fish second," Calle says. "And that is why sometimes the lines never got wet."

Calle remembers Ruth as a friendly man, burly and robust and loud and never without a smile. Language was no problem. Not with Babe Ruth's universal communication system.

"I spoke a little English and he spoke no Spanish. But we got along very easy. No problem."

There was no trophy bass taken on their fishing trips, Calle says. Ruth was not patient enough to catch the big ones, the smart ones. If nothing hit his first cast, "he was ready to start the boat and move somewhere else."

"He liked big bottles of beer, too," Calle says. "We would go way back into the bushes and the mosquitoes would be very bad. But he would pour beer on his face and chest and laugh and say, 'Now they will leave me alone.' But they never did. He would yell at the bugs and I would tell him he was scaring the fish. And he would laugh and pour more beer on himself."

Sometimes, Calle adds, "he would just want to go into the woods at night. He said he liked the sounds that came out at night. The owls, the wildcats, the snakes. So we would get a lantern and go out. One time there was an armadillo and I don't think he'd ever seen one of those before. But I told him to just stand still. I cut off the lantern. The armadillo is very nearsighted and very stupid, too. It forgot we were moving and maybe thought we were trees. It started looking for bugs to eat. Then Babe, he suddenly lit three matches all at once and yelled at the armadillo. And it ran away very fast. Babe, he really laughed hard. He told that story all the time back at his fish camp."

Oh yes, the Babe Ruth Fish Camp. It's still standing, although it hardly looks regal enough or even large enough to hold such a famous personality. It is across the way from Uncle Pearl's and looks just slightly larger than an outhouse. It was actually a small hotel and someone put up the sign as a joke.

"He played cards there, big poker games that lasted all night," Calle says. "I used to stand guard for them. To watch for the reporters and photographers. Sometimes, other baseball players came. One time I met the boxer Jack Dempsey. They played cards and drank their beer and told funny stories. Every once in a while, Babe would come check on me. He'd ask me to flex my muscle and he'd squeeze it and whistle. And he always handed me a $5 bill and told me, 'I feel safe with you.' "

Calle's eyes are soft. His thoughts are somewhere else and for several seconds the only sound is the aquarium rumbling gently, bubbles coming to the surface and live shrimp scurrying about beneath. Calle then says, "I will always remember Babe Ruth. He was the best."

Calle feels the baseball through his coat pocket, squeezes it and smiles. Someone walks in, looking to buy a dozen shrimp. Not all life will go on. Back at the bar, there is an argument over how far one of the Bambino's home runs actually went — the choices are 587 feet, 606 feet, 612 feet — and who was the pitcher. The ballgame's on the radio and that lonely pickled egg is still for sale. The 75-year-old man won't stay long. He wants to get his precious souvenir home as soon as he can. He pulls out the ball once more.

"See here, he misspelled my name. But that's OK. Everyone knows I was Babe Ruth's fishing guide anyway."

And he stuffs the ball back into his pocket and heads for the door. Somehow, he looks taller.

Young bloke acts out hustle on cue
July 9, 1989

MANCHESTER, England — You've been to the Red Eagle before. Most everyone has. The ceiling is the color nicotine would be if you could see it in its original form. The walls are plastered with rock-concert posters, past and future. The floor, if you push the litter of cigarette butts away, is pure concrete.

"Damn, aye can't sink a bloody thing tonight," yells the young Turk with the long and outrageous haircut. His pool cue hits one of the overhead lights. Accidentally.

Quiet. Genius at work.

Mick "Better call me Mr. X if you're really gonna write it up in the paper" just botched a straight-on shot and probably lost the game of eight-ball he and a stranger were playing. Sure enough, the stranger, a student from Leeds, sank the easy shot and won two pounds, which we foreigners recognize as more than three of Uncle Sam's dollars.

Mick reaches for his glass, spills his pint of bitters for the second time in the last hour. He reaches into his pocket and pulls out some coins and a roll of bills falls on the floor. Accidentally. The student, who doesn't like Mick because "he's got no business playing money pool when he's obviously (drunk)," suggests raising the stakes.

"Ow bout 20 a pop, mate?" the student asks. Somewhere, an invisible cash register rings. Mick shrugs and says, "Let's have a try. Maybe it'll help me luck."

The bait was dangled (in this case, dropped). The fish bit. Two hours later, closing time. Mr. X. walks out to catch a bus home. He's got 80 pounds of the other fellow's money. He even lost the last game they played.

"That guy will play me again. He still thinks he's better than me. That's because we played all night and he must have won two-thirds of the time. But hustling pool ain't about winning. It's about money."

This Fast Edwardian then took a bus two blocks, whereupon he got off and climbed into his shiny, white Volvo. "It doesn't look too good if you drive away in a nice car."

He looks worried. He doesn't worry about his victims. They've been set up so well, they couldn't figure out his scam. But, he explains, "it's the ones who caught your act somewhere else who saw you do the same dumb stuff and somehow still walked away with everyone's money. Them's the blokes who can be trouble. You gotta be careful because to hustle, you need your hands, feet and eyes to all work. I heard stories, bad stories, of hustlers who took it too far."

Mick says there are plenty of hustlers in Manchester, a town in a bad mood ever since the textile industry flattened out several years ago and almost 20 percent of the population started hanging out with Old Man Unemployment.

"You gotta meet Charley. He's the best hustler ever. Because he's retired now. I can take you where he likes to sit."

Charley is 47, fat, with a constantly red nose that derives its color from sources having nothing to do with sunshine.

"I likes the whiskey these days. All those years of watering up the bottle so the sucker could think I was (drunk). I never knew I'd have a genuine fierce thirst for it," he says, watching, from the corner of his eye, a game of nine-ball.

Hustling pool isn't a permanent job, Charley says. "I got out because you always hold your cards so close to your chest. You carry your life in your pockets and you find yourself living a lie. Really, it's a dead end."

Don't tell Mick. He's got almost $1,000 in his pocket. And he's setting up his next game.

In another tavern now. Arrows and Quills. Nicer—no posters. Mick's never been in the place before. He needs to check out the tables. How fast? How much sponge in the rails? The cushions? Is there any real money?

Mick's hair is slicked back. He's wearing nonprescription sunglasses. He's trying to look nerdish, nondescript, a part of the background. At one of the tables, two men are playing for money. A pound a game.

Stereo speakers rumble as Echo and the Bunnymen serenade the joint. A haze of cigarette smoke, the sound of pool balls clashing, laughter. Someone's on the make in the back of the room. A wheezing cough is at the bar. Someone just told another dirty joke. The life of the pool hustler is not about glamor.

It's about money.

"I may be back," Mick says, slipping out the door, heading for the bus stop. One last question. How old are you, Mick?

"Eighteen," he says, maybe lying, maybe not.

Gathers' death puzzles, but he competed to end
March 6, 1990

You spin the ball on your finger and try to keep it going, spinning around on the slender tip of undivided attention and hard work. It takes practice, discipline, a certain tedious skill. But mainly it's a delicate balance. And it is called life.

And the ball eventually falls. And that is called death.

But when the ball drops so soon, too soon, after only 23 years, there is the dull throb of confusion. There is unbearable grief, even from a great distance. And anger rakes over it all.

Hank Gathers' heart exploded Sunday night, and the world stopped making sense as something delicate became something jagged and mangled and finally rolled to a stop on a cold hardwood floor in California. Today, the gloom hangs like wet laundry.

But first there is the confusion to push out of the way. Why him? God, why take someone so precious and majestic? How could someone with as much vitality, as much spirit, as much — God, this

272

is such a cruel irony—heart as Hank Gathers lies today in a coroner's office?

Sometimes the ball bounces uncontrollably, off-balance, wobbling like a football with too much air in it. We'd heard about Gathers' suspected arrhythmia, which is an irregular heartbeat that can be fatal. But we also heard about the clean bill of health doctors gave him early this year. We remembered that Terry Cummings, an NBA All-Star, has lived with a similar problem for years. Medication has allowed him to play night after night, his life as routine as anyone's in pro basketball can be. Why not Hank Gathers?

In February, he scored 44 points in a single game. We rejoiced. Hank the Bank was back for good. Or so we thought. He would soon climb onto the marquee of some NBA team. Within the year. Or so we thought.

There are questions today not even an autopsy can answer. Cause of death is one thing. Why is another. We appeal to a higher authority. Why Hank Gathers? Why so young? Why so soon?

But he is dead, and you never get any older than that.

When another college basketball star, Len Bias, died of a heart attack a few years ago, we felt the same spiraling confusion. Until we found out massive and lethal doses of cocaine coursed through his veins. That seemed so awful, so tragic and senseless. But it also served as a cauterizing agent. In January 1988, when Pistol Pete Maravich died of a heart attack (also while playing basketball) we shrieked again with sorrow and lament. Pistol Pete was gone at age 40. So young, we said. We were told there was a congenital problem, something he had all his life. But at least we had his career to relish and use as a crying towel. We rationalized that it wasn't like he never got a chance. It wasn't like he was 23 years old or something.

With Hank Gathers' death, there is no balm or salve, no healing agent. Everything was ahead for Hank Gathers, tucked into tomorrow, a bloom still to open. It is like when Lions receiver Chuck Hughes collapsed on the field and died of heart failure. There were so many heroics, highlights, vicarious thrills snuffed out along with the lifeless individual.

And it is a selfish sensation. We hurt because we feel sorry for

. . . ourselves? We suffer because we feel cheated. We wanted more of Hank Gathers, of Chuck Hughes and Pete Maravich and Len Bias, than we were allowed. And our sorrow is misguided, and our confusion is clouded with guilt.

And now comes the anger. What can we do to stop this from happening again? How can we avoid our unavoidable sorrow?

First maybe we should take a step back and look again. Get our bearings. Last month, in Colorado, an amateur boxer named Sean Lee collapsed while jogging. He was getting ready for a big tournament, the national championships. He died of heart failure. He was 18.

What is the age limit, anyway? When are you too young to be struck down? Can you outlive the curse of being mortal? Does it matter whether it is an All-American athlete from California like Hank Gathers or a Detroit police officer like 40-year-old Sherdard Brison? Brison's life ended officially Monday when the plug was pulled on the support systems that were artificially sustaining him. Is the piercing pain any less? Is the loss any greater when it's not a sports superstar? Ask Officer Brison's family. Ask any survivors in any death in any family.

We asked why and there are no good answers. Never. But do you know what we have? There are games still to play. Keep competing until you hear the whistle. Chase whatever is within the heart. Play, work, live as hard as you can.

And cherish each fragile moment, the delicate balance of the spinning ball. While it is still in the air.

8.

PROFILES

He's long gone, but the mystique remains over . . .
Sonny
June 12, 1983
The Denver Post

LAS VEGAS — The caretaker pointed to a corner of the small cemetery and said, "His grave's over there, right by that Arborvitae bush. Not many people come to see his grave. Usually only other boxers. It's like people have forgotten all about Sonny Liston."

Charles "Sonny" Liston
1932–1970
"A Man"

The marker is rusting. Weeds surround it. A lousy Requiem for a heavyweight. Sonny Liston, once upon a time the most feared of boxers and the lonely outlaw of the sport, has neighbors now. Katherine M. Cassidy, "Loving Mother of Denise, Shirley, Ronda," is to his right. Beyond his nondescript grave is another, this one with plastic flowers atop it. Mary Chamberlain "God's Most Beautiful Angel" is buried there.

Even in death, he is out of place.

"He used to be a hell of a fighter, huh?" the caretaker asked,

275

flicking the ash from his cigarette, then wiping sweat from his eyebrow.

"Now he's just like everyone else, though. When you're planted out here, you're no better or worse than anyone else. And it's for damn sure nobody cares anymore."

But there are so many rumors, so many stories that contradict. True to the code of the mean streets he found no matter where he lived, Sonny Liston never told whatever it was we thought he knew. He never offered his viewpoint of the controversies that tailed him. He sat on his stool and silently didn't answer the bell. He slumped on the canvas, groaning from a punch nobody saw. He collapsed and died and nobody knows if heroin sucker-punched him or if his great heart simply surrendered and stopped trying.

Nobody even asks.

Thirteen years have allowed a lot of curiosities to subside. The mystique is as thick as ever. What happened to the man who escaped from the bowels of ghetto life and punched his way to the top of the boxing world?

The people who might know don't want to talk. The people who think they know talk in different directions. The one who does know died of heart failure alone on the golf course on the last day of the year of our Lord, 1970.

Paradise Gardens Cemetery is baking. The sun scowls just like Liston used to do at the start of a fight. The temperature went over 100 an hour before the afternoon matinees at the big hotels began. Before Don Rickles and Suzanne Somers and Mac Davis went on. The city that never goes to sleep braces for the rage of summer.

Sonny Liston seems out of place in the serenity of lush grass and oleander fences.

"Ever since I was born, I've been fighting for my life," he once said.

The cotton fields of Arkansas were a tough place to begin work. Especially when you are 8 years old, like Liston was. Food was as scarce as love. His father regularly beat each of his 14 children and Sonny Liston's back was dotted with permanent welts, reminders of his childhood. Dr. Mark Herman, the coroner who examined his body, noticed the welts before he saw the needle tracks.

"The only thing my old man ever gave me was a beating," Liston used to tell his friends.

"Things that he did," said Angelo Dundee, the trainer of Muhammed Ali, "well, considering his background, you can't blame the guy. I'm one of the people who liked Sonny Liston. But I can only say what I saw in the ring. I didn't live with the guy."

Dundee paused and said, "As a fighter, though, he was a monster. If Muhammad hadn't come along when he did, the world would remember Sonny Liston a lot better as one of the great fighters of all time. But Superman ran into someone who could beat him. It's the fate all fighters face. There's somebody out there who can beat you. Sooner or later."

Sonny Liston fought 54 fights. He knocked out 39. He lost an eight-rounder early in his career to someone named Marty Marshall. Liston fought the last six rounds with a broken jaw. He was heavyweight champion of the world for 17 months, demolishing Floyd Patterson twice with first-round knockouts. He in turn was knocked out twice by Cassius Clay, although neither was in the classical mode.

"Nothing ever came easy for him," Angelo Dundee said. "A lot of his people, his handler and trainers, are dead. They're all members of the underground now. They're down there, playing pinochle with Sonny."

Ray Schoeninger runs Meade's 66 on the corner of Fourth and Meade in Denver. He is a brawny man with huge arms and big hands and a physique gone soft. He used to spar with Sonny Liston.

Liston moved to Denver in the early '60s, saying he liked the mountains. In the beginning he also enjoyed the city.

"I'd rather be a lamp post in Denver than mayor of Philadelphia," he told reporters.

"He was as big around in the shoulders as that soda machine over there," Schoeninger said. "I've never seen a person as strong as him. Very heavy-fisted. He shattered my teeth. He knocked my shoulder out of place. Hey, I lost three teeth when he hit me with a jab wearing 20-ounce gloves. He knocked me on my ass from a foot away. It just wasn't worth the $15 a round I was getting paid. Too much punishment."

Schoeninger smiled and you could see where his teeth used to be. Then he added, "But he was an all-right guy. He was ignorant and he was uneducated but he was a good guy. He was suspicious of grown-ups but he loved kids. He liked Denver but the cops hassled him all the time. Denver was a cowtown back then and Sonny got treated pretty crappy, if you ask me."

Newspaper stories regularly reported Liston's brushes with the law. Schoeninger estimates he was stopped by police "100 times."

"One time, Sonny got stopped every day for about 10 straight days. Sonny used to drive this big, fancy Cadillac and the cops would just wait for him to get on the road. Then they'd pull him over. Just to see his driver's license, stuff like that. Just to hassle him. I started picking him up in my old Chevrolet and things got better."

Schoeninger nodded to himself and said, "The cops were always bugging him."

His hands were each 14 inches around. Too big to fit into a baseball glove. He had to catch with his bare hands. Too big for police handcuffs. They had to use rope to tie him up.

"I taught him how to write an autograph," Schoeninger said. "All he ever knew was chipping rocks and fighting. But he wasn't no dummy. He learned fast. He just never had the chance before."

The Denver Police Department has no record of Liston being arrested. Ever. Spokesmen smile and say they know he was arrested but "apparently, his lawyer petitioned to have his rap sheet purged. If you have been arrested and found not guilty, you can get this done. If you have been arrested and the charges have been dropped, you can get this done. Apparently, this is what happened because we have no index card on him."

St. Louis certainly does. Liston went to prison for armed robbery. He stuck up a restaurant. The pattern had been obvious since childhood. He stole to stay alive, then progressed/regressed to stealing for the sake of luxury. He used to joke that he "found things before they got lost." But the collision course with prison wasn't such a laughing matter.

He was about to be swept under society's rug. But a priest rescued him. Father Edward Murphy took an interest in the quiet man with the menacing profile and taught him how to box. And then how to be a man.

He got out of prison in 1952, having served two years, and started his career, the first that wasn't illegal in his life. On Sept.3, 1953, he knocked out Don Smith in the first round. Fifteen days later, he won a four-round decision over Ponce DeLeon.

Nine years later, he knocked out Floyd Patterson at 2:06 of the first round and became heavyweight champion.

On his television show, Bob Hope quipped, "I was going to invite Sonny Liston and Floyd Patterson on as guests, but the last time they were together, they almost got into a fight."

In the rematch 11 months later, Liston destroyed Patterson again. This time he needed 2:10 of the opening round to retain his title.

Now the challenger was named Cassius Clay, a windmill of energy with an unorthodox style and a big mouth. One night, two men walked up to Liston's home at 3395 Monaco Parkway. Liston responded to the knock by peering out the peekhole in his door.

Howard Bingham, a friend of Clay's, said, "Hey, Liston, somebody out here wants to talk to you."

Liston, who learned a long time ago to watch where he walked, grumbled, "If he's as ugly as you, I don't wanna see him."

A shouting match between Clay, Bingham and Liston ensued. Police were called. It was all a big publicity stunt. At the time, it was the only way promoters figured anybody would get interested in a title fight involving the skinny loudmouth and the sullen Liston.

He was invincible, said the experts. Rocky Marciano went on radio and said there was no doubt Liston would put away the challenger in the first round.

The fight was set for Miami Beach, February 1964.

Liston saw doctors for a sore shoulder in the months leading up to the fight. Noted boxing historian Hank Kaplan maintains that Liston and his people went to the boxing commission and asked for a postponement.

"They told Liston to take a hike," Kaplan said.

For six rounds, Liston stalked the quicker Clay. His frustration was obvious. Clay danced away and flicked punches off the face of

279

the man he had dubbed The Ugly Bear. And then it was over. Liston sat stoically and refused to answer the bell for the seventh round. A new champion had been crowned because the old one didn't get up off his stool.

The official explanation was that Liston had damaged his shoulder in the first round and steadily became unable to use it. Films, however, showed Liston throwing lefts as late as midway through the previous round.

Marty Marshall could not be reached for comment.

"The emotion licked him," Angelo Dundee said a few days ago. "He didn't know what a great fighter he was facing. Liston had one of the great jabs of all time but Muhammad had the range and flexibility to stay away from it. He got caught up in the emotion, then he just got frustrated."

Chris Dundee, who put on the bout that night in Miami Beach, said "Liston became an old man in the ring in one night."

The Miami Herald ran a picture of Clay throwing a punch into Liston's shoulder, claiming it was the blow that caused the damage and eventual technical knockout.

A ringside observer told another paper that Liston had thrown his shoulder out by himself, lunging and throwing wild punches at the backpedaling Clay.

"Naw," said Schoeninger. "Sonny's legs gave out on him. He got beat up pretty good. His face was all cut up. I was there."

Kaplan said Liston was ahead on points when the fight ended.

Then there was a rumor that the Black Muslims, a religious sect that was courting Clay and trumpeting the eventual arrival of Muhammed Ali, also visited Liston before the fight. A gym rat named Chappie Roberts started the rumor. The Dundees say they've heard the stories and consider them "pure trash." Whether or not threats or bribes were offered isn't clear.

All in all, it's just another brick in the wall.

Champions are supposed to die hard, the critics said. Sonny Liston came home to Denver in disgrace. He immediately started talking about a rematch.

The end had begun quickly and accelerated. On Christmas Day, 1963, Sonny Liston held a party for underprivileged children at his home. On Christmas Day, 1964, he was arrested for drunken driving and spent several hours in jail. On Christmas Day, 1965, he put his home up for sale.

Seven months earlier, he squared off against Ali and was knocked out in the first round. It was a fiasco. Referee Jersey Joe Walcott lost track of the count, had allowed the two to resume fighting when he was told the count had reached 10 and the fight was over. The punch was suspicious.

Jimmy Cannon, a veteran boxing writer, said it didn't pack enough wallop "to squash a grape."

But it had floored Liston.

Now the state of boxing reeled on the ropes.

The country cried fix. More rumors erupted. There was a Muslim threat on his life. A man with a satchel of money had reached him. Sonny Liston just didn't care any more.

There was also Ali's version, who maintained the legitimacy of the phantom blow.

Angelo Dundee insists the punch had done damage. "I went over to console him and he was staring right through me. Liston was out of it, the punch had really hurt him."

Kaplan has a theory as to what happened.

"Maybe he was uninspired. He didn't suddenly become less of a man. The single most important factor in boxing is motivation. It was a case, I believe, of losing motivation."

Whatever. Sonny Liston left Denver for Las Vegas. He bought a home on the golf course and started roaming the casinos and living the good life.

He started training again in a few months. He won 11 straight fights — all by knockouts. In March of 1969, he won a decision over Billy Joiner in St. Louis. Then knocked out two more forgettables.

But the people who rate boxers took no chances. In 1964 he was the No.1-rated challenger. By the next year, despite his string of knockouts, he dropped out of the top 10.

Liston liked the bright lights and relative freedom of Las Vegas. He liked being able to get up early and run with Davey Pearl. He liked his new manager, Johnny Tocco. He and wife Geraldine and their adopted son, Danille, were enjoying life at last. The irony was almost too much.

His next to last fight was against Leotis Martin. Martin knocked

281

him out. Liston forgot to put in his mouthpiece for the final round.

"Things were going smooth," Tocco remembered. "I told him if I'd been at the fight with Martin, he never would have lost. Christ, he beat Martin up pretty good anyway. The kid never fought again. Detached retina, I think."

Regrouping, Liston trained hard. He agreed to fight Chuck Wepner in a tiny boxing club in Jersey City. Liston weighed in at 216 pounds, the lowest in several years.

He cut Wepner to pieces. Later, Wepner would require 58 stitches in his face. Tocco tried to get the fight stopped earlier. Finally, in the ninth round, it was over.

A reporter asked Liston if Wepner was the bravest man he ever saw.

"No, but his manager is," Liston said, the menacing mask back in place.

That Christmas Eve, Liston and his family spent the evening at Pearl's house.

"We always spent Christmas Eve together," said Pearl, now a boxing referee and an employee at the University of Nevada-Las Vegas.

"Everybody had him figured wrong. He was a loner and he was suspicious of people. But once he saw you were sincere with him, you had a friend for life."

There were plans. Liston had just cut a record — rock music. A couple of fights in England were talked about. Then another fight with Patterson. Tocco had a New Year's Eve party planned.

"He told me he'd be there for sure," Tocco said. "Things were going great."

The day after Christmas, Geraldine and Danille left for St. Louis. Her father was ill. Four nights later, Charles Sonny Liston fell as he was apparently getting ready for bed. And died. Five days later, after getting no answer when she called home, Geraldine Liston found the decomposing body of her husband, the former champion of the world.

Lt. Bud Gregg of the Las Vegas Police Department investigated. A quarter-ounce of heroin was found in a balloon in the kitchen. A half-ounce of marijuana was found in the pocket of his trousers.

There were needle marks on Liston's arms.

"I never saw Sonny take a drink around me," said Davey Pearl. "And he was in too good of condition to be messed up with drugs."

Tocco said, "Sonny was afraid of needles. Hell, he was afraid to stand up in an airplane. I seen him have a glass of vodka once in a while. But he wasn't no drinker. And he was afraid of needles."

So was John Belushi.

On his dresser were three objects: a rattlesnake tail, a small wooden cross, and a loaded but unfired .38 caliber pistol.

Geraldine Liston demanded an autopsy. The circumstantial evidence suggested a drug overdose. She couldn't believe it.

Dr. Herman's findings were heart failure. Liston had been in a car accident on Thanksgiving Day. His head had gone through the windshield. He had been back to the doctor a couple of time for chest pains.

The world will believe what it wants to believe. The people close to Sonny Liston have scattered. Geraldine Liston worked in Las Vegas until recently, when she moved. Some people say she has returned to Denver. Another source says she is in Philadelphia. Mel Grebb, a matchmaker in Las Vegas, refused to talk about his late friend.

"Geraldine once threatened to sue if I talked about Sonny. She wants to sell things. And she wants to get paid for talking."

Sonny Liston's funeral began at the Palm Mortuary. Then it detoured down the Las Vegas Strip. Liston had told Geraldine that if something ever happened to him, "his fond wish would be that he go down the strip for the last time."

As the procession made its way past the big casinos, people took time off from the gaming tables and slot machines to watch the former champion go to his resting place.

At Paradise Gardens, celebrities and nobodies stood shoulder to shoulder. Ed Sullivan. Ella Fitzgerald. Roosevelt Grier. Doris Day.

The Ink Spots sang "Sunny."

Father Murphy told the throng, "We should only speak good of the dead . . . Sonny had qualities most people didn't know about."

A few days later, the Las Vegas Sun reported that the last man to see Sonny Liston alive was an undercover narcotics agent. No other specifics were given.

And nobody cared enough to follow it up.

Hank Kaplan said it would be a long time before the world sees another Liston.

"He had one of the greatest left jabs in history. He didn't flick it. He shoved it and it went right through you. He also was one of the greatest two-fisted punchers in history. He had a great chin, too. He was one of the five greatest heavyweights of all time."

"People don't know what a great person he was," said Pearl, "because he didn't like bragging. He used to get all these gloves and speed bags and stuff mailed to him by sporting goods companies and he'd always give them to the Carson City, Nev., Penitentiary. There was a lot about Sonny Liston that nobody will ever know."

Pain is easily forgotten. It is the reason women have more than one child. It is why grown men choose to be boxers.

The grave is like all the others. And it is true that most people couldn't tell you Sonny Liston from an arborvitae bush. But in the gyms around the country, with the percussion of the speed bags going and jump ropes scraping on floors and the stench of a thousand failed careers in the air, every once in a while, someone will walk up to Johnny Tocco and say, "Hey, this kid can punch like Liston."

And Tocco will take a look and watch for a minute, and then with a look of disdain that quickly turns to reflection, say, "Not a chance. Nope, not a chance in hell."

Charles "Sonny" Liston
1932–1970
"A Man"

Ali: Dim twilight is haunting The Greatest
Jan. 8, 1984
The Denver Post

The days seem to trip over each other. Just like his words. Muhammad Ali once was a poltergeist, with hands and feet and mouth so swift, and cunning so perpetual, that he redefined the art of heavyweight boxing. We thought he would last forever. So did he.

But now, the whispers are prolonged and they say Muhammad Ali put his brain cells on the line once or twice too often. He is almost 42 years old. He is middle–aged beyond repair. It is all too real.

You never beat the timekeeper.

He was the center of it all. He was boxing. Now he is history and "Johnny Carson don't call no more." Ali says he doesn't mind. You watch the latest film clips and listen to the rare and brief interviews and memories of Khrushchev wandering in his garden of exile come forth. Maybe Brando's Don Corleone fumbling at his desk. Certainly not Apollo Creed.

Definitely not Ali.

The poetry has gone out of his life, zapped like a cockroach on D-Con.

"They figured I fought more than 15,000 rounds," he told reporters in New York City in September. "I took punches from the best punchers of my era. Wouldn't you have a little change in your speech if you got hit that many times?

"How 'bout if I hit you just once? Would your speech change?"

To look at him, according to his friends, the face still is smooth. His nose doesn't look like a stepped-on biscuit as many ex-fighters' do. No scar tissue. Just puffiness and bloated features. And sad eyes.

Sometimes his hair is flecked with gray. Sometimes it is dyed. He weighs considerably more than when he fought. He still moves like an athlete. He breathes like an ex-athlete.

So say his friends.

Ali has said that things are not so bad as to make him out to be some sort of modern Elephant Man.

"I'm not big and sloppy. I think straight. I'm still pretty. But I'm tired. I need to rest more. I'm tired of walking through the masses, being around people all the time, talking with them."

Those still close to him differ on why Ali seems changed from the wondrous phenomenon he once was.

Angelo Dundee, Ali's trainer for the two decades that saw the great fighter go from matinee idol Rocky status to midnight movie Rocky Horror relegation, says Ali's problem is hypoglycemia.

"That means he got low sugar in his blood. And it also means he gets tired easy," Dundee explained by telephone. Then Dundee added, "But the only thing wrong with Ali really is he ain't a part of boxing no more. He's off stage and the spotlight's turned off. He don't feel no need to be Ali. That was always an act, anyway. He ain't no loud man. Now, he's just being what he's always been."

But you just wonder . . .

According to people who have been to his home in Hancock Park, an area of Los Angeles reserved for the Very Rich, Ali has a most comfortable shelter from the storm. He lives in a 30-room mansion of rococo design. It is ornate and filled with antique furniture and always guarded. Once you get by the posted men at the stations around his house, you confront several grumbling Doberman Pinschers.

The obligatory swimming pool is there as much for ornamentation as anything else. A chocolate brown Rolls and a gold Stutz Bearcat are in the garage most of the time. The place reeks of big money.

But then, five million dollars an hour makes for some compelling arithmetic. That's what Ali made when his orbit was highest. And we all remember (because Ali told us) that Allah gets all the glory. But Ali got the big bucks.

So, where does the second-rate Warhol come in? When did the magic get anesthetized by other people's fists? When did Ali-babble evolve into Ali-bi?

The questions jab against an unmoving target. The answer is simple. Time. The checkpoints are immaterial. When doesn't matter.

It happened, that's all.

Those who have been lucky enough to gain interviews with Ali at his home in L.A. say the mahogany-paneled walls inside are peppered with fight posters and fine art clashing into each other. The decor of Muhammad Ali's home has been an apparent tug of war between himself and the beautiful Veronica, his wife.

A painting of Ali done by LeRoy Neiman hangs over a couch that Ali told a reporter in Los Angeles cost $20,000 "and ain't nobody allowed to sit on it."

Then he adds, "The painting was free. It was a present."

There is a cape given him by Elvis. On a table is a bible Oral Roberts gave to Ali. Ali wears a watch with a floating arrow indicator in it that always points toward Mecca, focal point of the Muslims. A prayer watch.

The king of Saudi Arabia gave him that.

The carved tiger in the den was a gift from a high official in China.

The president of Egypt once offered Ali his daughter as a wedding partner.

"I'm the most famous person in the world," Ali says constantly, both in public and private.

But what he says no longer has impact. It's how he says it that shocks and chills and disappoints. Ali still proclaims himself The Greatest but now you don't believe it.

Ali often walks into a solarium filled with exotic birds and flips on a light switch and a platoon of parrots and macaws screech, "Ali, Ali, Ali . . ." He says he doesn't like all the squawking but fame is a pretty tough thing to go cold turkey on. Sometimes you need reminders.

Muhammad Ali, the champ in retirement.

Dundee talks about the old days. He lives in Miami, on the other side of the continent. They stay in touch. The old days dominate the conversation.

Dundee remembers Ali the movie star.

"Yeah, it was back when he was still Cassius Clay. Remember the movie with Anthony Quinn playing Mountain Rivera? Yeah. *Requiem for a Heavyweight*, that was it. Well. Muhammad was the young kid in the movie who knocked out Mountain Rivera in the end."

Dundee pauses then adds, "Kinda funny, huh?"

Then another pause. "I think I get a royalty check for $6 every time that movie gets shown somewhere."

Ali has said in the past that boxing wasn't real. He recently said that although he conquered the entire world "I didn't get no satisfaction. This life is not real. Boxing was just a way to introduce me and get me ready for my real mission."

Which is working with Wallace Muhammad. The goal: to remove racism from religion. Ali proudly says there are 50 Muslim mosques now — one for each state.

"Life begins at 40," he has said. "I'm ready to live and work for my people. And the white power structure is worried. They're worried about my power with the people."

And right about then, you expect Bundini Brown to pop from behind a curtain and start chanting about who is the greatest and who floated and stung. And yeah, Muhammad Ali is the People's Champ.

But the butterfly's wings have been pinned to the wall. Brown is gone. And the people know better. Ali is enduring the first days of the rest of his life and they are strange.

It has been much more difficult to learn how not to be a boxer than how to be one. Just as it is easier to look backward than forward.

In 1960, Cassius Clay was in Rome, preparing to fight for the gold medal in the light heavyweight division of the Olympics. A crowd of autograph seekers besieged him. He signed them all, including one for a man who seemed older than most fight fans. Also more gentle.

Last year, Ali ran into the man again. Like the fighter, he too had changed his name since that meeting in 1960.

He is now Pope John Paul II.

Ali's ascent turned into a star, then a comet, then a blur. He became world champion. He was drafted into the Army. In 1967, Ali told the government to stuff the 1-A classification and draft notice. For religious reasons. In turn, the government told him with only Justice Thurgood Marshall abstaining that he had five years of jail time and a fine of $10,000 to pay. For official reasons.

His insufferable immodesty compounded his marketability. Love-hate popularity ensued and then Muhammad Ali's career turned into a series of gambits. Ali has always jousted with the world's gullibility tolerance. For a long time, he won.

He once announced to a New York writer, "My personality attracts the world. I realize that everybody's watching. I have to attract the poets, the militants, the rednecks, the Moslems, the Jews, the Catholics, the blacks and the whites. I'm the only human being in the world that when I move, the world stops. I'm unemployed but here I am the most powerful and recognized man on earth. I can walk on the street in England and stop traffic. In the Arab countries, millions shout my name. People line up, they jam, they have wrecks. Every nation, every color. Here I am. I am The Greatest."

Today, the rumor is the tongue is slow. The eyes sometimes wobble and sometimes they glaze over. There is no fire. It would be difficult, say many people close to him, for Muhammad Ali to mouth the words to such testimony again.

Even if he wanted.

But the present notwithstanding, the triple crown winner from Louisville, the thoroughbred who was always furlongs ahead of the field, inhabited his kingdom with unprecedented flair. His adoring public was numbed. His image was distorted by myopia.

And always there were the idiosyncrasies. Remember when he was going to fight Wilt Chamberlain in the Astrodome? But he cautioned Howard Cosell and a national TV audience that Chamberlain had to shave his goatee first "because I ain't fighting no billy goat."

He was offered a chair of poetry at Oxford. He fought a wrestler in Japan. He fought Lyle Alzado, a professional football player. He offered to exchange himself for the Iranian hostages. He put up $400,000 reward when Atlanta's black children were being murdered. He talked a man out of suicide on a ledge on the ninth floor of a building. He threw out the first ball at a polo match.

An airline stewardess told him he had to fasten his seat belt. He told her he was Superman and didn't need one. She told him Superman didn't need an airplane.

It has been a romp.

Not since 1835, when Phineas Taylor Barnum reportedly hired a woman named Joyce Heath and passed her off as the 160-year-old former nurse of George Washington has the world seen such hype.

Ali became the consummate pitchman. He predicted outcomes with outrageous poetry. He mounted his opponents' heads with nicknames.

The Bear. The Rabbit. The Spanish Omelette, The Acorn, The Vampire, The Gorilla.

Indeed, the Gorilla, Joe Frazier. Smokin' Joe Frazier.

Ali-Frazier. The hyphen fits. Theirs was a historical entry. Three fights, historic ordeals, really. Ali won two. Nobody really lost.

The Thrilla in Manila endures as the classic.

Oct. 1, 1975.

"It'll be a killa, a chilla, a thrilla when I get the gorilla in Manila," chortled Ali. His sheep, the media, gobbled it up.

Frazier countered by saying to crowds of reporters about half the size that Ali drew, "I don't want to knock him out in Manila. I want to take his heart out."

Two great boxers headed for Quezon City, the Philippines, to fight for the heavyweight championship of the world. Both left their youth overseas. Neither realized it.

Ali, in retrospect, has said, "It was like death, the closest thing to dying that I know of."

The rest of Muhammad Ali's boxing life became a concession to deterioration.

Ali's doctor, Ferdie Pacheco, kept getting curious information which confirmed a gradual decline. A urologist's test results were startling. Blood in the urine. Stuff like that. But how do you tell the man sitting on top of the world that he's starting to slide?

A fighter named Leon Spinks, with Marine–issue false teeth and seven pro bouts to his name, upset Ali.

Not to worry. The champ came back and beat the champ. It was crowning glory again. But the heart of the laborer did it. Genius or physical ability had little to do with it.

Pacheco grew more and more concerned about the champ's

physical condition. He consulted Herbert Muhammad, Ali's manager. He consulted Dundee. He consulted Veronica. His advice was for Muhammad Ali to find another line of work.

"Some of his people couldn't find their conscience. They were too greedy," Pacheco says. "They fooled themselves."

Pacheco quit as Ali's doctor in 1977. He claimed there was extreme danger of brain and kidney damage if Ali continued fighting.

Ali's assessment of Pacheco?

"He's a horse doctor," Ali told The Miami News.

Pacheco and Ali remain friends. They talk to each other on the phone regularly. No hard feelings, either way.

Ali, says Pacheco, is a victim of those around him.

"It's similar to the U.S. government. Ali willingly supplies a lot of welfare. But the people who need it are too weak to get it. And the hustlers are the ones shoving their way to the front of the line."

Pacheco bites on his words before saying it will be difficult to find anyone who will agree the former champion is a physical mess.

"Ali represents an industry to them. Without him they're nothing. They're very guarded as a result."

Asked to make a personal assessment, Pacheco backs off.

"I performed a medical service a long time ago and have not made any recent examinations. Muhammad is probably the most likable man I ever met. He's a rare human being on this earth. He has a childlike mind, guileless. He's not a great judge of character — remember Harold Ross Fields Smith? — and he's not a good reader. It's constantly sending instead of receiving."

And if he did have some disease or injury involving the brain or kidney, could Pacheco, using his medical background, make a prediction of behavior?

"As the years go by, a relentless downhill pattern will evolve. It won't be pretty at all."

Purely hypothetical, you understand.

Hypoglycemia or kidney damage? Retardation in the pumping of blood to the brain or apathy? Only Ali could get in such a predicament. Anyone else would be just another stiff from the ring wars. And quickly forgotten.

291

Ali emerged again in 1980. This time to fight Larry Holmes in Las Vegas. The week before the fight, Ali showed up and boasted of losing 40 pounds in four months. The world was blinded once more, giddy over their master of space and time. Ali had done it again. Oddsmakers actually made him a favorite to win the fight.

Las Vegas is a perfect place for boxing to be held. This is where Howard Hughes used to live and counted his money and let his fingernails grow. Evel Knievel jumped motorcycles over statues in Las Vegas. Las Vegas is hedonism and sensualism and narcissism and capitalism. There are dope and whores and gambling and imagination and misfits and lost souls and fakers and foul balls and dreamers. All in Las Vegas.

The show girls wearing sequins and feathers atop their heads and nothing on their bosoms never have any problem knowing when their careers begin to sag. The great Ali had no such luck.

It was nolo contendre.

He climbed into the ring and flicked jabs and tried to shuffle around the ring. And stumbled while he was being introduced. In the end, with his gallant fighter barely conscious, Dundee leaned over a gasping, wheezing Muhammad Ali and said softly, "It's time."

An entire generation felt as old as its symbol slumped on a stool.

It wasn't a moment to celebrate. It was a moment to reflect. Holmes said at the press conference, "Ali does not owe boxing anything. Boxing owes Ali everything it is possible to owe. Without him, there would be no million-dollar paydays and no Larry Holmes as he is today. I love Ali and truly respect him."

Ali, head bowed and looking like a dog that had just been scolded, suddenly blurted, "Then why did you whip me back there?"

Then Ali went back to his suite, ravaged with pain and fatigue. And then he passed out. The weight loss had been due to thyroid medicine. Santa Claus really was dead.

In December 1981, Ali compounded the insult in something billed as The Drama in Bahama. He fought again. Somebody named Trevor Berbick recorded a unanimous decision. The scene was abysmal.

It was lounge act stuff and far from the big time. The fighters on the undercard had to share gloves. A cowbell was used for the time keeper's bell. Ali was light years away from where he used to be. Yet Dundee and others insist it was important — that last fiasco in the ring.

"He had to prove something. To himself. And he did it," Dundee says. "He proved he couldn't do it anymore."

The resurrection of boxing was done. His rod was rusty, his magic ordinary. And it hurt every time he went to the bathroom.

It just happened.

If there is a footnote to it all, it might have something to do with illusion. His own. Ali once told writer George Plimpton that when he got hurt in the ring he saw a door swing open, and inside, there were neon, orange and green blinking lights with bats blowing trumpets and alligators playing trombones.

Perhaps that's why he slurs his speech and seems so tired. It's hard to hear yourself speak or get any rest with that damned music going all the time.

He's still "The Bird'
Sweet summer of '76 forever follows Fidrych
May 13, 1986

NORTHBORO, Mass. — The pickup truck is almost blue, if you wash and scrub it, promises the tall man, opening the door. But no rust, look for yourself. The truck also has taken the place of a baseball. In the parking lot of the tiny tavern on a New England Saturday night, Mark Fidrych begins talking to it.

"Come on now, start. I'm going to put the key in and you're going to fire up and take us home. And no swerving off the road either, you hear me?"

His slight smile turns into a wide grin as the truck rumbles to life.

"All right, we're outta here," Fidrych says, flipping on the radio.

The fog outside is common for this time of year. The warmth of the spring day collides with evening's cool at a pace too fast to meteorologically cope. The farther you go into the fog, the easier it is to get disoriented. A man could have trouble grasping where he has been, and even more of a problem determining where he is heading.

Not Mark Fidrych, The Bird who fell back to earth.

"I'm going home," he says.

As always, uncluttered, unspoiled, the un-Cola guy if ever there was one.

It is Ten Years After. A decade. A professional lifetime. Yet, because of the terribly swift ascent, the horribly sudden descent, and that spontaneous joy throughout, Mark Fidrych seems ageless. Still the 22-year-old gawking, squawking treasure who made baseball a game again. But if he is 32, as he claims, that means the world is 10 years older, too. Clinging to such youthful memories can only lead to an eventual head-on crash with perspective. Mark Fidrych says he was caught up in that melancholy ride for a while, constantly feeling cheated out of those ensuing 10 years of glory and riches. But that particular fog evaporated.

"I'm still really (angry) it's all over. So I can't say I got no regrets, you know?" he says, tapping his fingers to the rock 'n' roll song that is making his truck speakers vibrate.

"But see, I never thought it would ever happen. Not really, not like it did. Then it happened and, wow, I never thought it would go away. I was so surprised by everything. But man—it was a real hoot, every day, every second. I was a big-league ballplayer. Wow."

In the half-light of a truck cab, driving along a foggy road 40 miles from Boston, two miles from home, the man-child suddenly catches up in time with his shadow. The hyper spirit remains, the twitchy personality that will forever be ruled by impulse intact. But as the truck wobbles homeward, its driver—shadowy and mute, ringlets of golden-red curls falling around his emotionless face— flicks off the radio. Once, he was driven by the moment. Now he simply drives, just another member of the working class, spinning

294

his wheels on his day off. The mood in the truck is like an empty ballpark. No game tonight.

Finally, a break in the heavy silence. Still looking straight ahead, both hands on the wheel, Mark Fidrych says, "For one year, I guess I had baseball in the palm of my hand, huh?"

Then he laughs. A real hoot. His words have played back and he realizes his metaphor.

"Hey, get it? A ball in the palm of my hand . . . aw, what the hell. I gotta laugh anyway."

Up ahead is the house. His parents are asleep. The 121-acre farm has rolled over, also gone to bed. "Wanna beer? I got a few inside," he asks in a whisper. "Me, I'll probably pass. I guess I'm a farmer now, got responsibilities. But mainly, I gotta get up early."

His two dogs rush to him, tails wagging, mouths open, eyes tilted upward. Mark Fidrych stands in the yard, reaching out to his adoring fans. He can do no wrong; everything he says brings more adulation. Once the entire country fawned at his feet the same way. Seeing no symbolism in any of this, Mark Fidrych walks into the house and turns out the porch light.

The next day, standing atop a hill where the earth seems to roll away into a gentle yaw, Fidrych says, "I love this place. Look at the view. It's not exactly the Cartwright Ranch on *Bonanza*, but I think it's pretty nice. All paid for, too. Cash. See, that's what I'm saying about baseball. It didn't seem like I got the fair shake. But now, I look at things and see what it got me. I got a taste and then I got the fever. It was like candy, I wanted more. I didn't get it. But look at this place. Baseball saved me also from digging ditches; I ain't no yard ape. And it saved me from having to go to college. I ain't going to complain no more."

His hands hurt. All farmers' hands hurt. Fidrych says there isn't much money in farming. Raising pigs, he says, isn't going to get you rich. Canada has the market cornered. He says he doesn't need much money.

"There's the land taxes and little stuff. But every dollar you own, you own a problem that goes with it."

He looks back out at the expanse of countryside and adds, "Just something to keep busy. Occupied. Hey, farming is an honest trade. A lot of them are going down, broke. But it's something to do."

Ten Years After. He still looks like a cross between Roger Daltry of The Who and Bill Walton, the pro basketball player. His face still looks vulnerable but full of mischief, too. No scars on the surface.

"I only have wrinkles when I smile," he says.

Ten years ago . . . Mark Fidrych's rookie season in the major leagues. It was 1976, the American Bicentennial. Nixon was gone, Carter not there yet. The country felt like celebrating. In Detroit, it found all the reason it needed.

In spring training, Fidrych was the big story whenever he pitched. He talked to the ball—"I used to throw any ball that someone got a hit off me back to the ump. So it could rub up against the other balls. Then maybe the next time it would come back out as a pop fly"—and gave the mound a manicure between innings. He shook hands with his teammates at the end of innings and made crowing noises for no apparent reason.

At first he was issued uniform No. 62. When Tigers Manager Ralph Houk realized his kid pitcher might stick with the big club, the No. 20 was offered as a substitute. When he received word he was going north for the season opener, Fidrych scrambled around the clubhouse.

To borrow a dime. Then he called his father. Collect.

"Dad, I made it," Fidrych said, beaming with pride.

His feet rarely touched the ground after that. His first start turned into a 2-hit victory over the Indians. There was a cautious hesitation by Houk. He wanted to make sure all this sparkle and glitter was the real thing. At the end of May, Mark Fidrych had a 2-1 record.

At the end of June, he was 10-1. Detroit could no longer hoard its find.

On June 28, with 47,855 piling into Tiger Stadium and millions watching on *Monday Night Baseball*, Fidrych did his thing against the Yankees. The 5-1 victory was impressive; Fidrych's fastball and slider were never more nasty and darting. But it was the universal appeal of the pitcher—his antics, his twitching, his innocent charm that was the big news. The stadium rocked with the chant of "Let's Go, Bird, Let's Go, Bird" and Fidrych accommodated every cheer with a reaction. Kids just wanna have fun. The world had forgotten such things. When the game ended, the standing ovation would not go away. They wanted to see their free-flying hero. An encore.

He stepped from the dugout, lifted his cap and all those curls, that smile, that spirit, flashed coast to coast.

On July 3, he shut out the Orioles on 4 hits. The next day America celebrated its 200th birthday. Life was good.

"Life was perfect," Fidrych says. "I mean, I met President Ford. I got Walter Matthau's autograph. I even got to start in the All-Star Game. Man, I didn't know what was happening."

His 19-9 record included 24 complete games. His 2.34 earned run average led the American League. He was rookie of the year, runner-up for the Cy Young to Jim Palmer.

He even made the cover of Rolling Stone.

The unspoiled hero was clutched to the bosom of an adoring public. He drove a Dodge Colt, discovered the world. How sweet. He made $16,000 in salary. How quaint. Mark Fidrych became a teddy bear for the masses, a national puppy love.

The following spring, back in Lakeland, Fla., Fidrych could only guess things would get even better. He said he wasn't worried about any sophomore jinx because he breezed through that year in school. First and second grades (which he repeated) were another story.

The only question was whether Dave Rozema could become another Mark Fidrych.

Then—on March 22, 1977—the sweet bird of paradise was no more.

"Yeah, I still remember what happened that day," Fidrych says, annoyed by the familiar question. "I was in the outfield, me and Rusty Staub were standing together. And here comes this fly ball. Nothing to it, right? I go over and jump up and when I came down, something didn't feel right in my knee."

Nobody knows how high he jumped or how long in the air he stayed. And it is only now, Ten Years After, that the conclusions can be made. Mark Fidrych went up in the air, the prize commodity in American sports. He was there but for a wink, a blink in time. When he came down, nothing would ever be the same.

"Big deal. I got hurt," Fidrych told reporters the day he was to undergo surgery on his left knee. "Big deal. I'm not dead. I'll be back."

Then, when he was alone, waiting to be wheeled into the operating room, Mark Fidrych cried.

His stay on the disabled list was a countdown of national interest. Banner headlines trumpeted the day of his return.

A week later, something in Fidrych's right shoulder popped.

If it made a noise, nobody heard it. There was nothing that showed up on X-rays. Fidrych insisted something was wrong.

He tried to pitch anyway.

The sporting world is filled with athletes who play with injury. Ask any doctor and he will tell you pitching is an unnatural act in itself. You do what you can do anyway. What you feel like you have to do.

Johnny Bench, the Cincinnati catcher, says he caught a pitcher named Gary Nolan for 10 years and "I don't think he ever threw a pitch that didn't hurt his arm."

The tale of Tommy John getting a tendon from his right forearm transplanted into his left elbow is testimony to the extremes a player will go. Ray Miller, manager of the Minnesota Twins, gives another example of how desperate things can get.

"I pitched 10 years in the minors. Never made it to the major leagues," Miller says. "Now I see all the success that these split-fingered fastball pitchers have and one day, I got to thinking. Why didn't I have my middle finger amputated? I bet I could have thrown a pretty good split-finger that way. I honestly thought about that one day."

Mark Fidrych knew something was wrong with his arm. But he didn't let the general public know. He kept taking the mound, smoothing and patting the dirt, talking to the ball, the same wonderful routine of individualism the world went crazy over in 1976. But when you're not getting batters out, when you can't get the ball over the plate, those antics are nothing but a tired shtick.

A personal hypnotist was hired, all sorts of miracle cures tried. A special "shoulder manipulation expert" yanked on The Bird's wing.

Others had similar problems. Frank Tanana and Dennis Eckersley discovered their fastballs had depreciated. They scrambled for alternate pitches, techniques, knowledge. Anything to keep them on the mound. They made it. Others stumbled. Steve Busby, author of two no-hitters before the age of 26, battled a losing cause. Don Gullett flamed out. Win a few, lose a few.

The Tigers waived Fidrych goodbye in 1981. The Red Sox picked him up, hoping at least to capitalize on his residue fan appeal. The ordeal of chasing after yesterday was painful; it hurt almost as much as his arm.

Finally, in June of 1983 and laboring for the Triple-A Pawtucket Paw Sox, Fidrych — owner of a 2–5 record, a 9.68 earned run average — surrendered.

"I knew that was it, it was over. So I decided not to let them release me. I retired, " Fidrych says.

And he made another collect call home.

His lifetime major-league record was 29–19. Through at 28. Imagine. Picture Phil Niekro retiring at 28 — that would be two decades ago. How many victories has he posted since then? The other day, Tommy John, 42, won a baseball game for the Yankees. Bill Lee, The Spaceman, still pitches in a semi-pro league. Chasing yesterdays.

It's been done. Rocky Bleier came back. Ben Hogan came back.

"Naw, not me. Last summer the doctor cut on me and told me that I had a torn rotator cuff, all along. That was a relief; it made me know I wasn't crazy. I know I'm young enough that I still could be pitching. But I won't push things back. I'm engaged. I got a farm. It's not going to happen again, though, in baseball. I tried as hard as I could. Man, I was taking 10 aspirin every morning. I got my shoulder shot with cortisone. I really tried. It was a one-in-a-million thing anyway. I got my chance. Let someone else have the next one."

Mark Fidrych, a shade of nobody else, a chip from the block never seen before, a child who raised the ceiling of his sport to include the fancy flight of a soaring spirit, has let go. Once upon a time, the player grabbed the ball. Then he realized the ball had a grip on him. Now he has let go. Not all the stories are nice, not all the endings happy.

299

But the view is spectacular. Miles and miles. Springtime in Massachusetts. And time for a cold one.

"Wanna beer?" he asks with a puckish grin. "I've got a few left."

Looney's search for peace
Ex-football renegade travels globe, finds truth begins at home
Nov. 30, 1986

ALPINE, Texas—"Looney's place? Joe Don Looney?" said the man at the service station, looking down the ribbon of Southwest Texas interstate highway. "It's down that way a bit. Just follow Highway 118. But it's back, off the road a good ways. Best I know to tell you is count the TV satellite dishes. The houses ain't so stacked out here; there's maybe five miles between some of them. So look for those satellite dishes. I'd say you go, oh, maybe three-four satellite dishes off to your right, down 118.

"Then, when you come to the windmill, stop. That's where Looney lives."

The Mexican border is 70 miles away, the surrounding Davis Mountains look close enough to touch with a good stretch. They're really five miles off. Out here it takes you all day to outrun your shadow.

Like the windmill, the house with the dome is wooden and handmade. The landscape is barren; no trees. Across a rolling basin is the majestic sight of Cathedral Mountain. The stark topographical contrast is too perfect. This is where the zigging and zagging world of Joe Don Looney has pitched camp. The restless man no longer runs to daylight. He no longer swivel-hips establishment and stiff-arms conformity. He has quit tilting at the windmills and built one for himself. Joe Don Looney finally is free.

He lies in a trampoline, staring at the sky.

"Catching rays," he says softly. "Be with you in a minute."

300

Five minutes later, he sits up and lets loose a smile that Norman Bates would understand and jumps down.

Joe Don Looney is 44 years old. Once, it was his destiny to be the greatest football player who ever lived. He probably was. But not in this lifetime.

He lives in splendid seclusion. For years, he told coaches he wanted to do it all by himself. Now he does.

His eyes are deep-set, shiny, almost black. His hair is laced with silver, the only apparent concession to age. His smooth face is gaunt. He weighs 180 pounds, 50 fewer than when he played for three college teams and five pro teams in the span of one turbulent decade. And he has a habit of answering any questions with a smile before he speaks. The smile is neither friendly nor false. Simply his.

Looney pulls on a T-shirt and there is no silk-screened message. No ad for a favorite tavern, although once upon a time he had plenty of those. No logos for a favorite sports team, even if he could fill a small closet with them. A plain T-shirt.

Looney walks with a swiftness into his house. Inside, the room is almost dark. There is no electricity. On a table is a book on agriculture and a cassette by Carole King. On the wooden floor is a TV Guide. But no television set.

Joe Don Looney sits on the floor, legs crossed, back straight, wearing nothing but a T-shirt and a pair of sweat pants. And he chants. It is a low hum, unintelligible to anyone but himself. His eyes close, the smile softens and 20 minutes pass.

A housefly buzzes his head. He ignores it at first, still chanting. Then the fly lands on his nose. Looney's eyes flash open and the smile revs up again. He deliberately crosses his eyes, staring at the fly and turning on the high-beams of his grin. A comic rapport between man and insect.

"Look—the state bird of India," he says before blowing the fly off his nose.

"Or maybe it's the FBI, still checking up on me."

Suddenly, he changes field, stutter steps his attention span somewhere else, and says, "If I just am, I have sweetness. If you make yourself your friend, you don't need any others.

"When I played football, the only thing that kept me sane was

301

not selling out. If I did, next thing I knew, I'd be doing a beer commercial."

Bad times are coming, he says.

That's why he moved here. Looney used to live in Diana, Texas, where he indulged himself with such luxuries as a refrigerator, TV ("I became a Raiders fan") and a pyramid.

The pyramid had an underground think tank. Looney explains he used to climb into a concrete hole and pop up through a trap door at the end of the tunnel. In the quiet and blackness of the hand-crafted temple, Joe Don Looney manufactured his own visions.

"Usually farm scenes," he says. "I want to grow my own food. I moved here. It's a start."

But even here, he is not invisible enough.

"They found me. Know what I got in the mail the other day? My first NFL pension check. Listen brother, if the end zone is where happiness is, I would be there. I'd live there. It was not my life's calling to be a good football player. Only a famous one. Everybody knew Looney. I had a reputation—a fruitcake, right?—but I liked it.

"It was easy to get a check cashed."

Suddenly, he rises and walks back outside. He stares once more at Cathedral Mountain and urinates.

Joe Don Looney may not play football anymore. He still is almost impossible to grasp. He was given to violence and adventure. He butted heads with authority constantly, whether for refusing to tape his ankles for practice or getting caught with an unregistered machine gun and a pound of marijuana in his possession.

Once he slept in a Baltimore graveyard and complained "somebody snored all night." He washed elephants for his beloved swami in India. He served for the U.S. Army in Vietnam. He was in a Peruvian cocaine-cutting house when it blew up. He gave up heroin and carbonated soda on the same day he cut off his pony tail. He lived several months in a Japanese massage parlor. He bought a 50-foot sailboat in Hong Kong so he could begin a Voyage to Nowhere and wound up abandoning ship before it ever left harbor. He climbed one night into a pro wrestling ring to help the good guy because the bad guy "was cheating like hell."

And he forever slumbered in the cruel world of unfulfilled promise.

He was 230 pounds of power and speed. He could catch passes, saw defenders in half with blocks, punt well enough to lead the country as a collegian. The complete package. Almost.

His talents were so obvious that until his knees finally disintegrated in 1970 in his final tryout — with New Orleans — coaches were always willing to look beyond his eccentricity to that vast potential. But the wild horse never could tolerate the saddle; Joe Don Looney never was broken. His NFL career statistics show a paltry 206 carries and 644 yards.

"Three yards and a cloud of dust," he says, giggling and walking back inside.

He lights some incense so strong the smoke almost sticks to the walls. Looney says he doesn't mind talking about the greatness that eluded him. Or was it he who eluded the greatness?

"One day, I climbed outside my body and saw myself as I was. My helmet, my pads. I was an alien. What's going on? I knew I was a slave of society. How could I do that? Another time, I was fighting another man. We came to blows and I wondered what the value of life was. The thing of value is the thing you can do without least. And brother — it takes a true genius to starve."

Looney says only the things necessary should be refined. The air, water, soil, food, the spirit.

"The search isn't going to last much longer. Not on this planet. The world monetary system is doomed to collapse by 1987. I truly believe the human race will be wiped out by 1993."

He is at a sink, washing his hands and feet, explaining they are the portals to the soul and the only places on the body that need constant cleansing.

"I don't mind extinction so much. What bothers me is when things get really perverse."

And his laugh is a cackle.

On a nearby wall is a picture of the Indian swami to whom he turned his life over in 1975.

"Muktananda. Baba. He saved my life. I investigated several religions and sects and found most of them were overrun with politics and hierarchies. People were joining them to get their ticket punched so they could get some permanent ride on a cosmic tilt-awhirl or something. Baba was different; he taught me the light. The love.

"He died in 1982. I chanted for 30 days, almost nonstop. I chanted so hard I got chapped lips."

His eyes close. He holds his head as if a migraine is coming on. Then he smiles.

"Baba was wonderful. He wore an orange beanie and red socks. And he carried a wand called a shaktipat that was made out of peacock feathers. He was the greatest man I could ever hope to know."

It's time for a nap.

"Come back later. Tomorrow. In the morning. We'll sing some songs."

Asked what time, Looney says, "I get up at 4:30."

His father was a football player, a wide receiver who caught many of Davey O'Brien's passes at TCU. Joe Looney also played for the Philadelphia Eagles, and then was a respected NFL referee for several years. He named his only child Joe Don.

When his son was 6 months old, Joe Looney put a tiny football in the pudgy baby's hands, took a picture of him and sent copies to friends and relatives with the handwritten message. "He'll be the greatest gridder ever."

Joe Don's mother, who hated football and worried about the injuries, rebelled. She tried to shelter, to protect, to baby her only child.

"Mr. and Mrs. Looney needed twins," Joe Don says.

A childhood friend talked him into lifting weights after school. The compulsive personality of Joe Don Looney took it from there.

"I can remember after he got his own weights that we'd be begging him to quit for the night. It might be 1 in the morning and he'd still be clanging those barbells," his father once said.

That friend, says Looney, "probably feels like Dr. Frankenstein. His name was Monty Morris. Last I heard, he was some kind of banker."

Monty Morris is a high-ranking officer at the City National Bank in Fort Smith, Ark. He remembers his buddy as "someone who wasn't dangerous or anything like that. He was quiet and he was serious about things. It was the late '50s and we were into the beatniks and stuff like that. The coffee houses. Jack Kerouac. I never saw any antisocial tendencies in him. He wasn't a weirdo or anything. He wasn't a follower, either."

Looney played football only one year at Paschal High in Fort Worth. Monty had a track scholarship to the University of Texas. Joe Don followed him, enrolling at Texas, paying his own way.

Morris remembers, "I asked Joe Don to come out for the track team. He was reluctant. Our coach, his name was Clyde Littlefield, couldn't believe Joe Don. He was so fast. I think he did a 9.9 in the 100 first try. He got it down to 9.5 with a little work."

Looney quit school at the end of the semester and enrolled at Texas Christian University. At the end of that semester, he quit again. And went to Cameron Junior College in Lawton, Okla. And went out for the football team.

He was an instant sensation. Cameron won the national junior-college championship. Joe Don Looney was its star. One day Looney was told someone wanted to meet him.

Bud Wilkinson. Oklahoma was the resident bully in the country at the time. A few years earlier, it had a 47-game winning streak. It was a constant contender for the national championship. Its coach, Wilkinson, wanted Joe Don Looney to run with the football.

In 1962, Oklahoma running back Joe Don Looney was fifth in the nation in rushing. He was America's top punter. He broke long, spectacular runs. But the routine and discipline of football bored him.

"I was in good shape and I knew all the plays," Looney says. "I didn't understand why I couldn't be by myself to lift weights."

In October 1963, a few days after Oklahoma had been stunned 28-7 by Texas, trouble exploded. Rumors of dissension were everywhere. At practice, a graduate assistant charged Looney was not hustling.

"We came to words, then I guess I punched him out."

Wilkinson asked the team to decide what should be done. The players voted to kick Looney off the team.

But a funny thing happened in the NFL's college draft of 1963. The 12th pick, the one belonging to the New York Giants, was Joe Don Looney. He had played one year of high school, one year of

305

junior college and one year and three games of college ball. And he was a first-round draft choice.

An even funnier thing happened on the eve of the season opener. The Giants traded their first-round draft pick to the Baltimore Colts after 28 days of training camp. Giants coach Allie Sherman said the problem began when Looney refused to shave or tape his ankles.

"I know my ankles better than anyone else," Looney told reporters.

Sherman said Looney was undisciplined, that he refused to run the plays, that he wouldn't run where the plays were designed.

Looney's reply was, "A good back makes his own holes."

At first, he refused to leave, claiming "I can't leave my record player and albums." The Giants boxed everything up for him. Looney then stated, "I'll go, but I'll have a bad attitude."

The coach of the Colts was a young disciplinarian named Don Shula. Now dutifully anointed as one of the NFL sages and the coach of the Miami Dolphins, Shula remembers Looney as "someone you just had to take a chance on. He could do it all. Every coach thinks he can be the one who gets through to the problem players. It's an ego thing. Looney started off well for us, but something happened."

In his first game, he ran 56 yards for a touchdown that helped beat the Bears, reigning league champions. Then, on election night, Lyndon Johnson defeated Barry Goldwater. To Looney, Goldwater was a hero. Looney proceeded to get drunk with each primary report. Then even drunker, whereupon he and a friend went looking for female companionship. Arriving at the apartment he thought belonged to a girlfriend, Looney heard a party going on inside. The man who answered told Looney he was at the wrong place. Looney knocked down the door.

The arrest and court appearance resulted in a $100 fine. Shula also fined Looney $50. And before the next season, Looney was traded to the Detroit Lions.

"You could coach a lifetime and never see a player with his ability," said his new boss, Lions coach Harry Gilmer.

On Aug. 3, 1965, at 3 in the morning, in an argument over $3.35 worth of hamburgers, Joe Don Looney was arrested at an all-night pancake house in Royal Oak. Training camp was due to open later that morning.

Later, there was an incident at a bar, where a brawl started after a woman threw a drink in Looney's face and he reciprocated. And finally there was the now-famous blowup with Gilmer in the third game of the 1966 season when Looney refused to re-enter a game. He was suspended at halftime and watched the second half, sitting in the Tiger Stadium bleachers.

Traded to Washington, the familiar pattern resumed. Coach Otto Graham said he anticipated no problems with Looney. Great talent, tremendous potential. Meanwhile, Looney got married, declaring he had a new outlook now that he had a wife. But two months into the season, Looney was released. He had complained of tremendous headaches for more than a year. Skeptics said the trouble was not in his head but in his mind. His marriage also was hurting.

Looney's Army reserve unit was called to active duty. The fighting in Vietnam was escalating. Suddenly, he was part of a war, stationed in a Viet combat zone, guarding an oil tanker.

"I believe Vietnam really screwed Joe Don up," Joe Looney says. "He wasn't the same boy when he came back."

The nine months overseas may have altered his outlook. It did not affect his ability to give the greatest first impression in football history. Looney got out of the Army on the 4th of July, 1969, got a tryout with the Saints on the 13th, signed on the 19th, and Coach Tom Fears told reporters on the 22nd, "I've got one hell of a football player in Joe Don Looney."

In October he was released. Both his knees were injured.

"Football has given me up," Looney said that day.

Two days later, his wife and their daughter left him.

Looney traveled the world. South America, the Orient. At last totally free; even the ropes tying him to that ungodly burden of potential had been cut. Looney drifted into drug abuse. The maverick who became a renegade became a vagabond and, ultimately, an outlaw.

The boat in Hong Kong was a turning point.

"I was sitting on the deck with a friend. We were stoned and I had been fasting for more than a week. I realized everybody was insane. I was empty inside. I couldn't pretend anymore. It was worse than the football."

In 1975, at an airport in Houston, he met Baba. And immediately rushed to join his ashram in Ganesphuri, India. Looney was given the duties of taking care of a 2-ton elephant named Vijay. Feeding time was 3 a.m. Cleaning time was whenever Vijay needed a bath.

"One morning, I was washing Vijay and he swiped me with his trunk. I don't know what came over me, but all my anger jumped back inside me. I screamed and punched Vijay. I didn't know all the hatred was still in me. It didn't hurt him. But that was how I got transferred to work in the garden."

Looney married again and went to upstate New York to another ashram. When Baba died in 1982, they returned to Texas.

At 4:30 a.m., long before the day has bummed a light, Joe Don Looney washes his hands and feet. He does stretching and Yoga exercises for 20 minutes. He does deep-breathing exercises for 10 minutes. He meditates for an hour. Then he eats breakfast. Two oranges.

He brings out a guitar and plays. He smiles.

"Brother, join in if you know the words," he says.

After several songs, none of them top-40 numbers from my era, Looney stands up and says, "I'm going for a run now."

Maybe a mile later, several circles of his property anyway, he quits. He walks in the house and lights some more incense.

"Lunch," he says softly.

He mixes some rice and sprouts and lentils and green pepper and some dark sauce of some kind into what looks like a flour tortilla. He is asked what it is.

"Burrito."

Afterward he will work in the garden a while, do some reading, do 202 sit-ups and 191 push-ups and go outside.

"To catch some rays."

Joe Don Looney no longer plays anyone's games. His goal, he says, was to become a millionaire before age 30 and then retire. He didn't make it. He retired anyway.

"The world gives value to power, beauty and athletics. To a lot of people, I was all three. I was priceless. But brother, that's just another word for useless. The dove flies with the crows and he's supposed to be afraid of Mr. Scarecrow, too. People wonder how I made do out here. Somebody's always asking me if I miss the rest of the world.

"Brother, if you're inspired, you can do anything you want."

And the laugh is another cackle.

A curtain call for Pistol Pete
Before the Magic, there was Maravich
Feb. 7, 1987

SEATTLE—Who can see the revolution before it begins? How do you know yesterday's showboat will become tomorrow's Hall of Famer?

Watered-down beer is the rage. It's hip to be square, nerdy, punky, androgynous. Why, there's even a woman playing for the Harlem Globetrotters these days.

And those funky blueprints that Pistol Pete Maravich brought to basketball, the ones that had anarchy stenciled all over them once upon a time—that's tomorrow's script for the NBA on CBS.

A gust of wind used to ruin a hairdo; now it establishes one. And really, who ever would have foreseen how chic it would become to go into a trendy restaurant and order your fish raw? Raw fish? Men wearing earrings? A beer for weight watchers? Get real.

NO—get sushi.

Hey Pistol, they're playing your game. How could we have known?

It is this hindsight, this wrong-end-of-the-telescope curiosity to find not where the rainbow ended but where it began, that focuses upon the check-in counter of a stylish Seattle hotel on the eve of the NBA All-Star Weekend.

"Reservation for Maravich," says the slender man with the

sparse mustache. He is holding hands with a small boy, Jaeson, his 7-year-old son.

Pete Maravich was named to the Basketball Hall of Fame earlier in the day.

"Could you spell that, please?" asks the clerk behind the front desk. How could she know? How does anyone? With all the sky-walkers playing basketball these days, who's going to get excited just because Yoda is trying to check in?

"M-A-R-A-V-I-C-H."

Pistol Pete. Once he brought a Flair pen to the game of basketball and scribbled excitement everywhere. He was such an innovator that he was perceived as a rebel. His moves and shots and passes were so outrageous, so avant-garde, so, ah, revolutionary, the purists considered him terminally afflicted with the most terrible of athletic diseases. A hot dog.

"I remember you," says the bellman standing behind him. "You were great. All that fancy stuff you used to do, it made basketball more . . ."

And there was a struggle as the right word was sought. A second, maybe more, of silence.

". . . More fun. You really knew how to turn on the crowd, Mr. Maravich."

The smile is immediate, but subdued. A smile of shyness. Can it be? Has the guy who blazed new paths of showmanship, who sent out the crackling vectors of excitement every time he touched the basketball, become a half-stepping member of the silent majority? A part of the madding crowd?

Pete Maravich will be 40 in June and he looks it. The wild mop of hair has been tamed, even styled, and is precariously close to a spiked look. And there are flecks of gray. He still has the slouched shoulders and the prominent beak of a nose that make him a walking caricature. But the eyes are framed with creases and wrinkles. Mortality has set in.

Check his socks, check his socks. Has he turned in those beautiful floppy gray good-luck socks, the ones that needed rubber bands to stay up? Has he traded them for the stretchy nylon, black, talk-show socks of establishment?

"Those gray socks wore out a long time ago," Maravich says in a mixed slur of North Carolina twang and Louisiana drawl. "I threw them away finally. But I still wear sneakers and I still wear athletic socks."

But the Italian loafers currently on his feet are almost indicting and certainly conspicuous. The tweed sports coat doesn't help. This is the guy who bucked the hoops establishment?

"Showtime is pretty much a thing of the past," he says. "The world has forgotten about Pistol Pete. I went into a dark closet and that's fine with me. I'm proud to get into the Hall of Fame. It's the Oscar of basketball, the ultimate earthly honor. And there are so many I share it with — my dad, the only hero I ever had; my family; teammates; coaches; the fans. And of course, my Lord and Savior."

Maravich helped make the game more permissive, thus expanding its boundaries. He was middle man in the fast break's transition. Bob Cousy was in one lane, representing the first vestiges of imagination. And Magic Johnson in the other, a figurehead for a new generation of free-form entertainers. Pistol Pete was the bridge, the once forbidden cross-court pass. And the one who endured the growing pains.

People used to boo Maravich for doing the same things that get Magic and Isiah and Bird and The Doctor and Air Jordan standing Os. Pistol Pete was branded a hot dog and today's players are anointed as creative artists for the same stuff. The right stuff.

And yeah, Pee Wee Herman, the undisputed king of the nerds, is a movie star, isn't he? The ridiculous truly has evolved into something sublime.

In his room, Maravich is asked if he feels any ancestral pride. He nods cautiously. Then he says behind-the-back passes were around before he was. Same with 30-foot shots.

"But they only counted two points back then."

He did not invent the tools. Only the spirit. He openly confessed he was influenced by the crowd; his were the biggest rabbit ears in the land. The phenomenon of Showtime became almost a calling.

And now, the clones are everywhere.

"I kinda feel like I was a seed, and a lot of things grew out of it," he says. "The world has changed; Pete Maravich certainly has."

Maravich averaged more than 44 points a game in college. But it was his showmanship, his dribbling ability, his stunning passes and slight-of-hand playmaking that startled the sporting world. He'd put the ball between his legs, behind his back, behind his defender's back. He threw passes from every angle, the trickier the better. Anything to turn on the crowd.

"It's just a feeling, a sense of performing, I guess," he says. "More than just playing."

Maravich was the third player picked in the 1970 draft.

The Harlem Globetrotters also wanted him to become their first white player.

"A million-dollar deal," he says. "I was really proud just getting the offer. But I wanted to play in the NBA. I wanted to win a championship ring."

The Atlanta Hawks drafted him, and maybe for all the wrong reasons. They wanted someone who would sell tickets and fill seats in a football-crazy state. And his whiteness was indeed a valuable marketing device.

The result was, although Maravich proved he was a terrific pro player—he averaged more than 24 points a game for 10 years—he had trouble getting people to take him seriously as a team player. He had this aura that he was more an entertainer than a player. Like a Globetrotter or something.

But lately a Slinky-toy effect has brought the world to where The Pistol used to roost. He has become appreciated after the fact.

"It hurt a little," he says. "It probably distracted me some, too. Before Showtime ever takes off, there is the competitiveness. The will to win. I'm here to play in an Old-Timers Game. But I want to be on the winning team. Anytime I get near a court, the competitiveness takes over. First and foremost, I always wanted to win the game."

Can it be? The consummate individualist, the drummer so different, placed team above self? The irony bounces off the walls.

"No championships," he says. "I wanted a ring so bad. I never got it. I could have played five more seasons. I was only 31 when I quit. But at the time, I was spiritually bankrupt. Really searching. I had tried every avenue for happiness there is. I looked into most of the religions and a lot of the vices, too.

"I got into vegetarianism (Imagine that: A hot dog who didn't

312

eat meat.) I was maxi-dosing on vitamins. I tried hypnosis, yoga, you name it. Transcendental meditation. I was buying secret healing mud from Europe, pills that guaranteed I'd live to be 150. One time, I fasted for 25 days. And at the same time, I was out there partying all night."

When he retired in 1980, he says, "It was like an addict trying to give up heroin."

"I was in shock for six months," he remembers. "Basketball had been my life. My whole emphasis was basketball. My priorities were all out of whack. There wasn't anything else but basketball."

There hadn't been for a quarter of a century. At 7, basketball already had become his magnificent obsession.

He wore out a pair of shoes a month. Every other month, he needed a new ball, the old one also worn slick. Maravich would dribble a basketball while he rode his bicycle. He would take a ball with him to the movies, always sitting on the aisle so he could practice his dribbling.

He'd walk to a gym two miles away, dribbling the ball all the way, play for seven hours, stopping only to eat lunch and dribble back home. After dinner, he'd go to bed and lie on his back and "practice the spin on my shot" by shooting a ball toward the ceiling for an hour.

"I used to make my father drive me around the neighborhood in our car," he recalls. "I'd roll down the window and dribble the ball. He'd get it up to about 25 mph sometimes."

Suddenly, someone tosses Maravich a basketball. Instincts take over. He doesn't catch it; instead he transfers it over his shoulder, a no-look pass that bounces off the wall behind him and returns just as he stands to catch it.

Maravich flips the ball behind his back, twirls it behind his head. Oh wow—the Human Pretzel, one of his favorite routines. He spins the ball on his fingers, rotating from digit to digit, bounces it off his elbow, his knee, slaps the ball to keep its momentum. It obeys. Then he rolls the ball across his back, down an arm, flipping it back. Spinning it on a finger once more. He bats it back and forth, then bounces it off his head.

"You never forget something you've practiced so much."

Then he throws chest passes at a wall. It is the most common of

313

all basketball passes, but Pistol Pete still can execute them with special zip and unique style.

Then the ball changes course. Instead of heading back to the wall, back where Maravich's hands seem to be pointing, it hits a mesmerized sportswriter in the chest.

The wrist pass. Hands go one way, the ball another. So fast, too fast. Showtime. A flick of the wrist, deception, misdirection. The hand is quicker than the eye. The thrill is never gone.

"You never forget," he says again, laughing.

Then he puts the ball down, drops it on his bed. The thrill is never gone. But the passion is.

Maravich begins talking about his Christianity. He has none of the street-minister babble. His quick sermonette is nonaggressive. No push, no shove. No harm, no foul.

"Hey, there is no way I can make someone become a Christian any more than I can make him into a Corvette," Maravich says. "But I read the Bible every day and I realize all my goals I ever set were earthly ones. I was more concerned about retirement than eternity. But I finally have a peace. And it's not only permanent, it's eternal. No more of this twinkle-my-toes-in-the-stream-and-have-my-margarita-and-make-like-Peggy Lee. You know the song—'Is that all there is?'

"I thrived on my God-given talent. But I didn't give Him any of the glory for a long time."

Maravich, his wife Jackie and sons Jaeson and Joshua, who is 4, live in Louisiana. He has real-estate dealings, banking interests. He runs summer camps in Florida, Houston and North Carolina for Christian vegetarians.

"A lot of camps are nothing but tuna fish and Kool-Aid," he says. "We bake our own breads, we have a 22-item salad bar. We drink only spring water and fresh-squeezed juices. We unplug the soda machines. Christianity, nutrition and basketball. It enables optimum growth."

His children have never tasted red meat or canned vegetables "with the exception of a little veal that Jackie puts in spaghetti once in a while."

He is neither bragging nor complaining when he declares, "I lead a very disciplined life these days."

314

"I'm happy," he says. "Happier than I've ever been. I don't need the cheers anymore. I really don't."

Somehow his life has been wrist-passed. Showtime has closed its curtains. Pistol Pete plays to a higher crowd these days.

Dean of the Court: Heels' Smith retains ability to blend legend with reality
March 19, 1987

Up close, nobody's perfect. The devil shard of hair always falls out of position, a nonconformist curl that has never done things the Carolina Way. Dean Smith disciplines it. Quietly, efficiently. A simple swipe with his free hand.

"This isn't supposed to be about me, is it?" asks Smith, the 56-year-old king of the mountain castle that is North Carolina basketball. "I don't do those. This about the team, right?"

And then he looks at his watch.

Distance. The image needs distance. Actress Joan Collins says her beauty cannot stand close scrutiny. Closer you get, older she becomes. But, keep the public at a safe distance and she holds onto her vivaciousness. Could this be why Dean Smith gives everyone a look at him but never a good one?

"Like I said, I don't like to talk about myself," Smith says, smushing a cigarette into the huge ashtray that keeps a running score of his two-pack-a-day habit. And he looks at his watch once more.

He sits silently, politely, his hands folded on his desk. His face is a basketball. But it's a football of a nose. And the smile forces his eyes into blind alleys and he rarely flashes his teeth. Dean Smith looks like every caricature every newspaper artist ever attempted. A gnome at home.

He often is asked about image—his, his team's, his university's. He lights a cigarette and cups it in his right hand.

315

"I owe it to the university to maintain a certain image. I try to be careful what I say. I always say something nice about the other team and the other coach. And I really mean everything I say."

And then, as always, comes the zinger.

"It's just that I don't say everything I'm thinking."

And the smirk, the classic basketball face with the football nose, the uneasy quiet and the folded hands all take on a different dimension. And when he looks once more at his watch, it is almost a peacemaking gesture.

The ghost is friendly, after all.

"Aw, that damn Dean ain't never gonna be one of the guys," says Lefty Driesell, the former Maryland coach. "He don't even stay at the same hotel as the rest of the coaches at conventions. But that's not the reason some coaches don't like him. It's 'cause he's good. If he'd quit whipping up on everybody he'd be a whole lot more popular."

Smith would rather the records speak for themselves. But they are too loud. His Tar Heels have won more often than any college team in the last two decades. In his 26th season at North Carolina, he averages eight victories out of every 10 games his team plays. He has won an NIT championship, an NCAA title and an Olympic gold medal.

This is the image of a winner. But the shadow of Dean Smith is much longer than simply success. It jumps into the area of decency and nobility that is too good to be true.

"Coach Smith is the only saint I every knew," says former North Carolina player Walter Davis, now an All-Star guard with the Phoenix Suns.

Eddie Fogler, a former Smith assistant and now the coach of Wichita State, adds, "Dean Smith is the finest person I've ever seen. And nobody else is even close. He just cares so much."

Yet there are those who say the halo droops. His critics claim he manipulates officials, has too much power, controls too much time, keeps too much distance between himself and his legend.

And the simple truth is that he probably should be stacked somewhere between the Wizard of Oz, who did it with mirrors and an intimidating sound system, and the Wizard of Westwood, who did it with All-Americans and whose system also was quite sound.

"I am required to smoke," Smith says, holding back a laugh. "It's all part of the stipulation for an endowment given the university by Sir Walter Raleigh."

And the few seconds of silence are so his visitor can laugh.

"Of course, I'm joking."

So many dead ends, so many contradictions.

Mitch Kupchak remembers the day he had his first back surgery. Junior year at North Carolina. The Tar Heels had a road game.

"I wanted to stay up and listen to the game on the radio," says Kupchak, now in the front office of the Los Angeles Lakers. "But the anesthesia . . ."

The next thing Kupchak remembers was the pressure on his shoulder. A hand. Kupchak woke up in the recovery room early in the morning. And saw Dean Smith, standing there in a surgical mask and gown, touching his shoulder with his hand.

"After the team got back home, Coach Smith came right to the hospital," Kupchak says softly.

Doug Moe laughs.

The coach of the Denver Nuggets also played for Smith.

"Dean likes to tell everyone how great all his players turned out," Moe says, still laughing. "How smart they were and how everyone got a degree and is now a doctor or a lawyer, right? Well, ask him about me."

Then Moe proceeds to tell the story of the math test.

"I'm flunking out, right?" Moe says. "I had this math test and if I don't pass, I'm outta there. So guess who shows up to help me study? Dean Smith. We pull an all-nighter.

"And I get a 15 on the test."

Moe laughs one more time, this time for several moments, allowing the memory to splash all over him.

"So, I'm gone. I get a job selling insurance and that's it, right? Nope. Dean calls me one day and says he's arranged an interview and tryout with Elon College. And then he reminds me to wear a sportscoat. Then a few years later, he gets me a tryout in Italy. Then he gets me an ABA tryout. I wouldn't be in basketball if it weren't for him. He even got me my first coaching job. He's a great guy, one of the best. But I'm sure he feels funny about me. I mean he was a math major in college. I'm sure he wonders what kind of grade I would have pulled without his help that night."

Once, his Tar Heels rallied from a seven-point deficit against Duke with 17 seconds remaining and won. Another time, he refused to let his team shoot and went into half-time trailing the Blue Devils 7–0. They later rallied once more and won a 12–10 dubious achievement in conservatism.

But he's a raging liberal. He privately detests Jesse Helms. He contributed to George McGovern's 1972 presidential campaign, signed petitions at various times calling for the end to the Vietnam fighting, abortion and nuclear weapons. He once refused to join a country club because it wouldn't allow blacks. He abhors mandatory drug testing yet wept privately when the news of Len Bias' death reached him. Forget about image. It's hard enough getting the man to match the man.

He says he'd like to become less visible. But he does so much coaching during a game. So many moves and decisions that bring the spotlight on him. He is constantly offering the world a new improved blueprint from which the perfect basketball game can be built. He gave the world the four-corners offense, the run-and-jump pressure defense, the foul-line huddle. Even Air Jordan, albeit in a more saddled and subdued version.

Frank McGuire owns the only other NCAA title ever won by the Tar Heels basketball team. That came in 1957 in the famous triple-overtime epic against Kansas and Wilt Chamberlain.

"But whenever I give a speech, the biggest applause I get is when I tell everyone that I'm the one who brought Dean Smith to North Carolina," McGuire says.

McGuire left for the pros and Smith moved up from his assistant's job in 1962, taking over a team beset with probation problems.

A few years later, returning home from a loss to Wake Forest, Smith and the Tar Heels players encountered a nasty banner and a crude dummy likeness hanging from a tree. Believe it or not: Dean Smith once was hung in effigy at North Carolina.

"The man was real upset," says Billy Cunningham, an ex-NBA star who was a forward for Smith that season. "I cut it down, but it really bothered him."

Two nights later, the Tar Heels clobbered Duke and Smith was asked to speak at a postgame pep rally. He refused and the legend goes that he explained he had this "strange tight feeling" in his throat.

Cunningham says he doubts if Smith has ever forgotten or forgiven the incident.

"He's such a competitor. He hides his emotions well. I don't know a more intense person than Dean Smith during a game."

Smith is asked if this year's team can make it to the Final Four — it would be the 10th time Smith has been that far. He is reminded that the Tar Heels have never made it in the year in which they didn't win their conference tournament. And North Carolina State beat them in the ACC championship game three weeks ago.

"I'm not a historian; I'm a mathematician," Smith snarls. Talk of disappointment rankles him. He talks of unreal expectations, of pressure that does not belong.

"I'm the only one who was here for all the failures you talk about. So I guess it's my fault," he says, his mood softening with every word.

"I just wish people could be satisfied with the fact we win a lot of games and our players graduate. Expectations are unfair and really hard to gauge. Do you know that our freshman J.R. Reid's father was a junior high coach who once cut David Robinson from his team? Or that Michael Jordan didn't make his high school team as a sophomore? It's very difficult to tell who's going to grow and who's going to develop. It's especially unfair when the judgment comes from outside, from someone who doesn't really know the way things are."

It is the final look at the watch.

Smith stands and smiles and extends his right hand, buttoning his sportscoat with his left at the same time. It is a reflex move, born from a thousand final buzzers. A tidy habit that allows him to accept the other coach's congratulations while looking his best. Sometimes the evil curl even keeps its place. The man has slid into the image. Or maybe it's the other way around.

At any rate, afternoon practice awaits. Dean Smith, the face of basketball, the picture of rehearsed control, walks swiftly, the image and man once more in step.

319

And the visitor squeezes the remnants of a cold handshake. They play great defense at Carolina. No penetration, no second shots. Dean Smith knows how to play the game.

The King
Petty: American pie with scoop of grits
June 13, 1986

Richard Petty's face, a jagged piece of Americana, seems at half-mast. He rides in the courtesy van from the Detroit Press Club broadcasters luncheon to the local station outlet of the CNN empire, neither tranquil nor animated. Tired eyes hide behind the trademark sunglasses. His cigar went out 10 minutes ago. Long day at the office for The King.

A long time ago, Petty allowed a monster to be created. It still runs too fast to jump off.

Just eight minutes, the man at the station promises. A few questions for a national hookup. It seems Petty, the Dixie Christ of stock car racing, the racingest and winningest driver ever, has had his life divided into slices of either eight minutes or 500 miles every week since 1958.

"The bigger stock car racing gets, the bigger Richard Petty gets," he says, fixing his gaze from outside the van window to his snake-skin cowboy boots. "There's lots of times you got to grit your teeth and hug some drunk gal and shake her husband's hand and a whole lotta other strangers till your fangers get cramped. But you do it for your sponsor and the sport. And for yourself. I love racing and it's all part of it."

On Sunday, he crashed at Pocono; it has been almost two years since he last won a race. He went to a county commission meeting back home Tuesday, still fighting the encroachment of "massage parlors and other trash that dripped over from the next county." On Wednesday he bounced back into the glare of NASCAR, where another chance for victory No. 201 awaits. So does another barrage of media and fans, well-meaning strangers in the court of The King.

Petty clearly brings it on himself.

The poet Kipling once wrote of the special person able to walk with kings and yet keep the common touch. He didn't know he was describing Richard Petty. And Petty never realized his kingly simplicity would be so popular and demanding.

The silent ride ends outside a nondescript downtown brick building. A glass door opens and a receptionist asks what the name is.

Richard Petty.

She looks up suddenly and the wraparound smile that blinds like high beams mesmerizes her.

"Oh . . . yes. We've been expecting you," she says, standing up, swiping at a rebel curl in her hairdo. She doesn't think about a curtsy, although it wouldn't be the first. Instead, she nods nervously.

"How you doin'?" Petty says, now grinning fiercely, somehow regenerated. It is as if he has fed off the energy of his celebrity. It is no front or act; the booster shot of adrenaline is unexplainable. His cowboy boots make regal noises on the polished floor of the TV station as he walks down a corridor into a studio.

"That was really Richard Petty? He seems so . . . nice," the receptionist says. "I don't know anything about car racing. But everybody's heard of Richard Petty."

Twenty minutes later, he's finished. So long Detroit, hello Indiana, where it all starts over. The dogs bark but the caravan moves on. The big race isn't until Sunday.

Petty has been playing down the inevitable until he is now face to face with it. Sunday, at Michigan International Speedway in the Miller American 400, Petty will start his thousandth race. Nobody else is even close. He shrugs at the historical significance, insisting "starting them suckers ain't near as tough as winning 'em."

Then he turns on the toothy headlights again and adds, "But to win No. 1,000, man, that'd be a sweet deal, a real sweet deal."

Petty and NASCAR racing. They practically grew up together, for a while, one and the same. All his records—the seven grand national championships, the seven Daytona 500 checkered flags, the seven Rockingham 500 victories, the four Dixie 500s, the four

321

victories at MIS—are but a part of his legend. Everywhere he has raced—Texas, Virginia, Delaware, New York, California—he has won. He has career winnings of more than $6 million. Yet almost as important as his success has been his acceptance by the masses. He's been voted most popular driver on the circuit nine times.

They say Richard Petty is American history, and there is a car in the Smithsonian Institution in Washington to prove it. When Petty won No. 200 at the 1984 Firecracker 400 in Daytona, his Pontiac was doomed to eternity. A curator from the Smithsonian asked if the car could be donated to the museum's American History division.

And thus, that day-glo blue and red car with the "43" on the door is conspicuously nestled alongside the desk where Thomas Jefferson penned the Declaration of Independence. The original star-spangled banner, the source of inspiration for Francis Scott Key's composition of the national anthem, hangs overhead. The Spirit of St. Louis is there. And the Wright Brothers' airplane. It is in this repository of American history that Richard Petty was asked to find a parking place for his car.

"If I don't win again soon, them people from Washington might get me stuffed by some taxidermist and prop me in that museum, too. I'll be history," Petty says, at least half kidding.

Then he gets half serious.

"I didn't change the world," he says. "I just went along with it a little bit. I'm real proud to be in that museum 'cause there's some good 'uns in there. And every cat that visits that museum can't help but see that car. They might not know who Richard Petty is, but that car is there for a long time."

Then he laughs.

"I had some high school reunion—back in Randleman (N.C.)—and this old boy comes up to me and says, "Richard, Richard, I was in Washington and I seen your car in the Smithsonian.' And I said 'Lee Roy, you been living five miles away from me for the last 30 years and you went all the way to Washington to see my car?' See, that museum is what makes it all so special. It just ain't race cars; there's real heroes in there.

"I only had one hero growing up. My daddy. Every little boy should have the same hero. All them idols kids have nowadays—in sports and music and stuff, maybe including me, too—that's not your real deal. Your daddy's your only hero."

Petty resists the image of hero the same way he resists his millionaire status.

"I just drive race cars to make a living. Been doing it for 28 years. It's all I want to do. All I ever wanted to do since I was 10. All these athletes in the other sports who put their time and money toward getting to where they can do what they really want to do— that ain't me. I'm doin' what I want to do right now."

He looks back at the boots and adds, "And as long as I can crawl through that winder, I'm gonna keep on. I don't feel my age yet; racing's really a mind situation. This 1,000-race thing makes me think. If a boy is a raw rookie today, he's got to run every race for 33 1/3 years just to get to 1,000. That takes some doing.

"The 200 victories is something else, too. The Winston Cup is probably as even as it's ever been. Look at the stack. This year looks like (Dale) Earnhardt's year. Last year was (Bill) Elliott's. But it don't look like any of them's gonna stretch it out for two or three seasons like it used to be."

Like it used to be. Back when King Richard ruled NASCAR like a third-world dictator. Like 1967, when Petty won 27 races out of 48 starts, including a staggering 10 in a row. Or 1970, when he won 18 times. Or 1971, when he roared to 21 wins.

When he won his 100th race in 1969, Petty was asked his immediate goal and he brashly said, "To go after No. 200."

When he got No. 200, at Daytona in the Firecracker 400 in 1984 (with old pal President Reagan in attendance), Petty was asked the same question. This time he stated meekly, "We'll start working on No. 201."

The record seems to be stuck on 200. The whispers that sometimes start whistling in the shadows when a veteran driver runs into a period of winless frustration have not begun. Petty can still win, they say around the garage areas. He just hasn't done it for a while.

"I think we're still real competitive. And me—I think I can still cut it too. Drivers sometimes lose their want-to, know what I mean? Your reflexes go too, but there ain't nothing can be done about that. But also, the longer you race, the better you get at anticipating what's goin' on out there. You build on that experience. This week, they've paved the track new at MIS. That means it's gonna be a fast race. And that means the groove is gonna be just about anywhere you want it. People say my experience won't help me because it'll sorta be a new track. But I see it as I've got a lot more experience on new tracks."

There have been slumps before. Streaks of winlessness. Fans used to send him good-luck charms.

"All kinds of stuff. Rabbit's feet and lucky dollars and scarves and even a pair of red underdrawers. Heck, that rabbit ain't so lucky if he's only got three legs and the other one's on a little chain. But I don't get so many things like that no more. The American public don't seem so superstitious. I know I'm not. Luck's involved and I had about 20 out of 28 years' worth of good luck. But I don't think you can mess with things like that. You just gotta race and take what happens."

It hasn't always been good. The broken bones (including the neck twice) are too numerous to mention. The time he wrecked at Darlington, S.C., and the national wires ran a picture of an unconscious Richard Petty hanging out the window of a demolished car is all the evidence needed to show that not even the special ones are immune to the obvious dangers.

Petty had his gall bladder removed last year. More than a third of his stomach was taken out several years ago when ulcers flared out of control. He wears hearing aids in both ears. And despite his royal presence and ageless charm, he will be 49 years old July 2. His peers from the early days—the Fireball Robertses and Lee Roy Yarboroughs and Junior Johnsons—are either long gone from competitive driving or dead. How much longer will he race?

"I don't know. They keep making things easier for me. They got power steering just about perfected. Maybe power brakes is next. The cars are safer and safer. There's a lot braver drivers in the game than me. I think the whole thing is to win as slow as you can. They don't pay nothing extra if you win by 10 miles instead of 10 inches. Sometimes, racing is touching the other guy, bumping and squeezing each other. You can do that in NASCAR. But those Indy cars, they disintegrate if they touch each other. Twice this year, I was in bad wrecks and was able to climb back in the car the following week."

Petty never eats the day of a race. In 1964, while going through tire tests at Daytona, he and a bunch of drivers took a lunch break. Later that day, one of the drivers blew out a tire, ran into a wall and, even though he wasn't scratched, died because he drowned in his own vomit.

"I haven't eaten on race day since," Petty says.

The cowboy hat with the plumes of ostrich feather, the boots of exotic skins ("Armadillo might be my favorite"), the cheroot, the dark shades, that smile. If you close your eyes, you still can see Richard Petty.

He is grandfather four times over and a county commissioner getting ready to run for his third term. He gave a nominating speech for Ronald Reagan at Joe Louis Arena at the Republican convention in 1980. He considers Jesse Helms among his closest friends and "maybe the only cat more conservative than me."

Friends of Richard Petty are everywhere but on the track.

"We're competing for the same buck, for one thing," he says, "and the other thing is you don't want to get too close to race car drivers just because of uh, circumstances. That's the deal with racing. You try to control all the circumstances. I don't think I've ever been scared on the track yet. Things I can't control—they scare me. Riding as a passenger, I sometimes close my eyes. And those things that go loopity-loop at the fair . . . you can't get me on them."

The ferris wheel frightens him. But not the wall where the blue paint—Petty blue—is often left like a calling card. He says he is not a daring driver, but he drives a tire inside of everyone else. And Sunday, Richard Petty races for the thousandth time.

It will be 140 degrees inside his racing uniform with all the sponsors' decals sewn on it. And three hours nonstop behind the wheel. His only coolant will be the ever-present damp wash rag, another Petty staple.

"You sorta get immune to the heat. You're thinking about other things. More important things. Racing things."

The ominous history drafts on him wherever he goes. He can't outrun it. It hasn't been able to pass him by either. The milestones of Richard Petty are not milestones. Or even speed bumps.

Ask him about the lure of his racing passion and he'll break into stories of innocence in rural North Carolina. Of days when a policeman waited at the dirt crossroads for young Richard Petty and his " '56 Dodge with the '57 Oldsmobile engine with three carbs and the whole deal lowered 'bout that far off the ground.

"Oh yeah, that cat would chase me, and because of all the dust, we could never see each other. But we knew there was a chase going on. It was kind of like a fox and hound deal. If he cornered me, he'd let me go most of the time. But it was the racing, see, that's the big deal. Racing."

Richard Petty. American pie with a scoop of grits on top. History.

Full Circle: From Pershing High School to the pros, Spencer Haywood had the world in his hands and couldn't hold on. Finally, he says, he's got a good grip.
Jan. 15, 1989.

"Oh, precious God, look at that baby's hands. This boy is blessed, this boy is special. He's got them healing hands." — Spencer Haywood's aunt in 1948, when he was born.

Spencer Haywood looks at his hands now, almost marveling himself at their size. He closes them, opens them back up and says, "Big as they are, when the time came to really grasp the important things, I sure enough let a lot slip through. I had the world in these hands. Had it all a couple of times. And couldn't hold on.

"But I have a good grip now."

Haywood leans his head back and laughs. His eyes close and the laugh subsides but the smile stays on. And the hands are fists. For several seconds, he takes a silent inventory. It is the full circle of a man.

Spencer Haywood, onetime basketball superstar, ex-cokehead and now inner-city businessman, has come home.

"I was driving on the west side," Haywood says. "It was several months ago, and I see this big funeral procession. And there are kids running to the side of the street, waving. Mothers are holding their babies up so they can see. I stop to see what's going on. And it's the funeral for Maserati Rick. He was a big drug dealer in Detroit, and somebody finally caught up with him and shot him dead. And he's got this fancy casket with a Mercedes grille and turn indicators built in it, and it's going through the neighborhood. And I can't believe what I'm seeing.

"I walked over to a couple of mothers and said, 'You should be throwing rocks at that scumbag. He's the one murdering your children. You honor the thieves and pimps and drug dealers. It's all wrong, ladies. Believe me I know.' "

The streets are filled with children in Reeboks carrying little plastic bags filled with yellowish rocks called crack. Some of them carry small pistols. Boarded-up buildings and abandoned homes are the marketplace. Supplies are gone in a matter of minutes.

"I can tell you all kinds of horror stories," Haywood says. "Mothers with babies two months old, babies that don't even have names 'cause she never took the time. Cocaine takes away everything. It is Satan at his ungodliest, and, believe me, working on that plantation back in Mississippi wasn't near the slavery you have when you're hooked on drugs. Believe me—I know."

There is a big construction deal to close on later in the afternoon. His TV show is taping the next day. The book deal is set. He signed a contract the other day for the movie rights to the Spencer Haywood Story. The business world into which he has thrown himself has been increasingly receptive.

He goes to nightly meetings, talking about his problems, speaking openly about the despair and weakness he found in himself while he struggled to overcome his sickness. He regularly goes to schools, "elementary to college level," and talks to children about the danger waiting on the corner, in the alley, next door. There are not enough hours in a day, he says.

"I'm still playing catch-up with civilization."

But Spencer Haywood never hit rock-bottom, either. He never

327

scraped up next to poverty; he never spent time in jail other than the prison cocaine builds around its slaves.

"I saw my problem and tried to do something about it myself," he says. "It took me a long time to get here. I still have a lifetime to go, and there are no free tickets or guarantees. There's no statute of limitation on being an addict. You're always trying to get better.

"But I am still here because I sought the help. If I didn't, I would be dead, I'm sure. I sought the help; I chose to make it public because I think people should know about this thing. But my forthrightness has certainly caused some doors to slam in my face, too."

And the easy smile tracks slowly across the long face, and the eyes sparkle as he says, "But that's OK. I'll deal with that. I'll wear the tag until it falls off."

Silver City, Miss. The beginning of the rainbow. Haywood remembers riding on his mother's cotton sack when he was 3, maybe 4. At 6, he was put in charge of the chickens at home, swallowing hard at his mother's warning: "If those chickens don't survive, we won't eat this winter."

Haywood laughs and says, "I took that responsibility and made it like the gold medal or the world championship. Those chickens were fat. We ate good."

As good, anyway, as a fatherless family of 11 could eat on a mother's $10-a-week job as a scrubwoman, the weekly welfare check of $11 and whatever could be scraped up by working the cotton fields.

John Haywood was a carpenter, a hard worker, devoted to his family. He died three weeks before Spencer Haywood was born. Eunice Haywood was not due to deliver for almost two more months. Relatives say the shock of her man's death induced the premature delivery.

When they got a look at the baby, they shrieked in wonderment.

"Facially, I guess I looked just like my father," Haywood ways.

"And my hands were big. Some of them thought I was his reincarnation, that John Haywood had come back to life."

When he was old enough, little Spencer was sent to a house where someone had "the arthritic poisoning."

"I'd sit and rub their knee or wrist or whatever was hurting for hours," he says. "Then they'd get up and walk away and say it was a miracle. They really thought I was blessed. Next month, when the pain came back, I'd go over and rub some more."

When he was 10, he hit the fields with everyone else. Fifty hours a week, 300 pounds of cotton a day, 6 cents a pound.

It was not all drudgery and labor. There was free time, and along the Yazoo River a child's imagination could run barefoot and carefree. There was even basketball.

"Well, sort of basketball," Haywood says. "My brother Andrew would get a hoop off a barrel and rig it on some tree. We scrounged up a ball. It was almost round. Mother didn't like us playing. She said it'd make us too tired to work. Sometimes she'd get the ax and chop down our gymnasium. But there were plenty of trees in the woods and we'd just set up somewhere else."

There were times, Haywood adds, when things seemed so idyllic "it was like Huck Finn all over again.

"But then some days, when we'd be out rafting and we'd spot some boy who'd disappeared couple nights earlier, floating face down in the Yazoo, we'd know the Klan had been out on the prowl. Blacks were, you know, target practice, in a lot of ways. Some of us kids used to go chase lost golf balls at the country club and the rednecks would drive balls at us. One boy caught one on the side of the head. It killed him."

Haywood shakes his head. "It wasn't exactly like Huck Finn, I guess."

Then he changes the subject and is comfortable again. He says his mother was enormously strong in spirit:

"She's still on my shoulder, too, whispering good sense in my ear. There have been times when I didn't listen; there have been times when I was so zonked I couldn't hear. But how she did what she did — raising six sons and four daughters in Silver City, Miss., in the early '60s — I'll never know such strength."

The cancer that afflicted her finally spread so badly that when

Eunice Haywood died in 1983, her son Spencer did not recognize the body at the funeral home.

He was 15 when his mother said she had a bus ticket for him. He had to go. Find a real life. His older brothers had done the same thing. One was playing basketball at a small Midwest college.

"I headed for Chicago," Haywood says. "I painted on a mustache and became a busboy at some restaurant. I was alone, the world's tallest busboy, with coat sleeves that stopped just below my elbow—a country bumpkin loose in the big, bad, Windy City."

His brother Lee Roy invited him to come live in the college dorm. One weekend they played basketball, and Spencer Haywood impressed everyone.

"Lee Roy, you gotta get your brother to meet Will Robinson," said one of the players. "He's in Detroit. Spencer can play. Coach Robinson can make him great."

Will Robinson was basketball coach at Pershing High, one of the more respected teachers and handlers of young people in the country. A meeting was arranged. Be at the Kronk rec center Sunday afternoon.

It was a long drive. Haywood remembers being tired and nervous, and "when I saw this man in a golf sweater, looking me up and down, I couldn't stand it hardly. I was thinking my whole life was banking on this one day. But then I started thinking, 'These are Yankee boys, Northern boys.' I got geeked. My ego went on the ceiling.

"We played all weekend and I turned 'em out, just dominated everybody. Will Robinson finally said he had to find me some place to stay. I'd made it."

Then Robinson found out his young protege could not read.

"I was illiterate. I wrote like a 6-year-old. I couldn't speak decent. I was embarrassed. He just hugged me and said if I wanted to work hard, we could catch up with the rest of the world."

Haywood leans back and says softly, "It was like more than a friendly hug. It was like the way a father hugs his son."

Haywood's mother agreed to let Robinson become Spencer's legal guardian. Robinson found a couple, James and Ida Bell, who let Haywood live with them at their home a couple of blocks from Pershing High. A tutor was arranged, four hours a night.

"When I went to the school," Haywood says, "I couldn't believe it. I thought I was in heaven. Libraries, integrated classes, teachers who cared. The Bells were wonderful. They made me feel part of the family. I even remember the first book I ever read."

The Autobiography of Malcolm X.

"The initiative was mine. But the outlets were there for me, too. It was all Will's doing. He was tough love. You hit the books. You went to class. He screamed. He demanded things. Couple of times I was ready to run away, head back to Mississippi. The pressure to please that man, be what he wanted me to be . . . "

Robinson used to take Haywood for rides around Detroit. "See that guy, that boy there on the corner?" Robinson would ask. "He played for me. Great athlete. But he had no discipline about himself. Now he's an outlaw."

And Spencer Haywood would stare. And nod understanding of the unspoken message.

"There was a lot of fixin' on the street," Haywood says. "Drinking, sex for sale, heroin, weed. I sneaked away a little. But Will's basic training stuck with me for a long while. I wasn't going to mess up. And drugs — drugs were poison. All I wanted to do was play some ball."

The Pershing Doughboys were great during Haywood's junior year. And even better his senior year.

"In 11th grade, we had Granville Cook and Ralph Simpson, both 6-4, playing guard. John Lockard was our small forward at 6-7. Then there was Jim Connally at 6-8 and me — I was 6-8, 230 pounds."

But despite a terrific record, the Doughboys lost every important game.

"I remember well the education Larry Moore of Mumford gave me. Really dusted me good. And Curtis Jones of Northwestern—still the best guard I ever saw. All the talent we had that year and we didn't win any championships.

"The next year we won it all."

That was the Pershing team everyone called All-Pro. That was because Simpson and Haywood wound up playing pro basketball, fellow starters Paul Seales and Glen Doughty wound up in the National Football League, and Marvin Lane became a major-league baseball player. Pershing won the Class A championship of 1967.

"At that point in my life," Haywood says, "there was nothing I ever knew like that night. Champions."

Living with the Bells, trying to please Will Robinson, Haywood was a child within a man's costume. It was Detroit and it wasn't Silver City. And the freedom was smothering.

"I still was basically the hick from Mississippi. I had confidence in myself as a person, though. Dealing with other people, with strangers—that still was to come. That was the next horizon."

He and Robinson talked about the future. He still did not have the grades for a major college, and Robinson suggested Trinidad Junior College on the Colorado-New Mexico border.

"It was too far away to come home when you got homesick, and if you didn't study, you died," Haywood says. "There was really nothing else to do but study, go to class, play ball. . ."

Then, he recalls, came the assassination of Dr. Martin Luther King. Haywood struggles, chews on his words.

"Remember, it's 1968. I'm not 18 yet. The black movement was building. I have always had a tendency to be out front with stuff. But I was in such a regimented environment, living with the Bells and having a white tutor and a lot of white friends, I was confused. The white world seemed a lot better than what I left in Mississippi."

Riots broke out all over the country. It was a pivotal time in history. Also a divisive one.

UCLA All-American Lew Alcindor had announced he was boycotting the Olympics in support of the black movement. Other top players also declined invitations.

"But when I got an invitation to try out for the U.S. Olympic team, I never hesitated," says Haywood.

Haywood was sensational at the trials.

"I'd come downcourt, take off near the foul line, the ball cocked behind my head, and wham! You could almost hear everyone thinking the same thing: 'Who's that?' "

Dr. Harry Edwards, an activist and spokesman for the black movement, "wanted to know how I could turn my back on my people. I wanted to tell him that three years earlier, I was picking cotton in Mississippi. Now I had a chance to play for the United States of America. When I got my passport, I was so proud I had to call home to tell my mother."

In Mexico City, site of the Olympic Games, Haywood was invited to a secret meeting. Track star John Carlos was there, Tommie Smith, too. They talked about demonstration, making a statement. They held up these little black gloves everyone was supposed to wear.

The closed black fist was our symbol of power, togetherness.

"But then Wilma Rudolph got hold of me. She was a former Olympic champion. She also was from Mississippi. She told me to try to remember how it was in those cotton fields. She told me if I joined the boycott, I'd be right back on those fields in no time."

Critics said the U.S. entry was the weakest men's basketball team ever to play in the Olympics. The team consisted mainly of no-names. Especially at center—an 18-year-old junior college player from Detroit.

In the gold-medal game at Sports Palacio del Mexico City, Team USA scored 17 straight points in the second half en route to a 65–50 victory over Yugoslavia. Spencer Haywood, battling flu and diarrhea, had 21 points, 10 rebounds and five blocked shots.

Afterward, Yugoslav coach Ranko Zeravica said flatly, "Haywood is best player I ever see in amateur basketball."

When the gold medal was put around his neck, Haywood could not keep back the tears. The playing of the national anthem made him cover his face.

"I knew then I had made the right decision, to play and everything," he says. "Then when I got back to Detroit and they held a parade for me, I cried again."

The matter of resuming college became a national issue. His grades were now acceptable.

"The riots had taken a toll. Will thought if I came back to Detroit, it would help build some bridges back. There was talk that U. of D. Coach Bob Calihan was leaving after a year. The school told Will he would be the man. We'd all rally around Will Robinson. We had a plan: U. of D. would be the UCLA of the Midwest."

The Detroit Titans opened the 1968-69 season in December by humiliating Aquinas College 105-40. The game was stopped when, with 6:31 to play, Haywood blocked a shot, dribbled the length of the court and slammed a dunk shot with such force that it tore away the rim and shattered the glass blackboard. Both coaches agreed there was no point in continuing. Haywood finished with 36 points and 31 rebounds.

Detroit won its first 10 games, then lost seven of the next 10.

The changing world and the changing man could not stay in step with each other. A game with the University of Toledo was coming up. At least that would bring out his best, for he would be going up against an old buddy from Hamtramck, John Brisker.

What he did not know was Brisker had just been kicked off the team.

"I went to visit him on campus, and he filled my head with all kinds of nonsense. He told me I had to stand up for him. He'd been wronged and he said it was all a racial thing. Well, I flex my muscles and I'm arrogant and when I get on the court, I'm out of control. I lost it."

There were 17 minutes left in the game. Haywood already had 24 points when he got in a shoving match with two Toledo players. Referee George Strauthers tried to pull Haywood away from the battle.

Haywood wheeled and swung.

"I just reacted," he recalls. "No, I didn't hit him. I was lucky. I just grazed him. I apologized as soon as I did it."

Haywood was suspended for one game, which the Titans lost by

334

37 points. There were rumbles, whispers, rumors. Will Robinson really wasn't going to get the coaching job next season.

"They reneged on Will," Haywood says. "I was upset. I had this offer to play in Belgium for $150,000 a season. I got confused again. Will came to my rescue. People later called it his revenge. But he did it all for me. Because he cared."

On Aug. 23, 1969, Haywood, a consensus first-team All-American who averaged 31 points and 21 rebounds for Detroit, signed a contract with the Denver Rockets of the American Basketball Association. The National Basketball Association screeched that the infant ABA was trying to get enough good players to cause a forced merger.

His contract was negotiated by Will Robinson. It included a signing bonus, a nice apartment and a new car.

In his rookie year, barely 20, Haywood set the ABA afire. He was the leading scorer, leading rebounder, rookie of the year, most valuable player. On April 15, he scored 59 points in one game, a league record.

And he demanded a new contract.

"I became a spokesperson for contract negotiations. I said I would take care of myself. I didn't need Will Robinson. I didn't need anybody."

The $1.9 million deal, spread over five years, made him the highest-paid basketball player in the country.

"Then someone read me the fine print. I got explained what all those fancy words meant. And basically what came of it was my $1.9 million was worth $510,000. There was this thing called an annuity fund, and I couldn't draw on the money that went in there until I was 40. Well, that was 18 years ago and I'm just now 40. The contract had no guarantees I'd get paid if the franchise or the league went under. How long has the ABA been out of business now, anyway?"

Haywood looks down and adds. "I wanted out. Fast. I stood up and fought back, and suddenly I was everybody's favorite radical."

Seattle owner Sam Schulman decided to challenge a league rule that prohibited the signing of undergraduates. On the last day of

335

1969, he signed Spencer Haywood to a contract with the NBA's Sonics. The league promptly filed suit.

"That meant I was being sued on three fronts," Haywood remembers. "The ABA, the Rockets, the NBA. I truly spent more time in a courthouse than on a basketball court."

The Supreme Court finally allowed Haywood his right to play basketball. Playing for Seattle meant playing for his childhood idol, Bill Russell, the Sonics' coach.

"I was an all-star; I averaged 25 points a game. But Russell worried about me. I was a vegetarian. He begged me to eat a steak. I was into yoga; he'd come into the locker room and I'd be standing on my head. He'd shake his head and walk out the door. But all in all, I loved the man."

In 1972, Haywood slipped on a wet spot at the Seattle arena. He needed knee surgery.

"The wonderful world of superstardom," he says. "The roof leaked and I almost ruined my career. I came back a little too early. Then I got traded to New York."

At first it seemed like paradise, his kind of town, frantic with excitement.

"My knee was still bothering me. I got off to a slow start. I was immature, still. Angry, still very confused about my life. I was living a lie, still trying to deny that I was a country boy from the banks of the Yazoo. I bought a '76 Rolls Royce. To be on the Knicks at that time, you just had to have a Rolls."

And the memories revulse and he lets his eyes shut and spits out the words.

"I hate that damn car. It's the perfect symbol of everything I became. Everything I hate. I never drove the thing except to impress somebody."

The changes in his personality were striking. He couldn't hear his mother in his ear anymore. He burned his money. He bought a townhouse on Park Avenue "because that's where all the beautiful people lived." He dated women he didn't even like "but they were famous and they looked good on my arm."

Then he met a model named Iman.

"She was the most beautiful creature I'd ever seen. She was from

Africa, Somalia. Very worldly lady. She was the perfect extension of my vision. She was everything the new Spencer wanted."

In his neighborhood, Haywood convinced himself he had found the perfect roost. All he needed was someone to show it off to.

"The whole thing became totally unreal. Iman was not to blame. I was living in my dream world before I met her. She was just as naive as I once was."

Haywood began modeling, doing free-lance shows with Iman, ebony Barbie dolls in a dazzling world of high fashion. And ignoring his basketball.

"Basically I had done a total change. And the world around me was evil. Yeah, there were drugs, but I was all into health. Still, I'd smoked a joint now and then, but put a straw up my nose? Never. The stuff was all around, though. The parties were wild."

He married Iman. She bore him a daughter. It was not a total disaster in New York—"just a plain run-of-the-mill disaster."

He was traded to the New Orleans Jazz, with rumors of his being a malcontent preceding him. Half a year later, he was traded again, to the Los Angeles Lakers.

"L.A., oh L.A.," Haywood says. "Yeah, my kind of people. Optimism. Caviar for breakfast. I thought I'd found the land of milk and honey at last. What I really found was the front door to Hell."

In New Orleans, Haywood averaged almost 25 points and 11 rebounds a game. He came to the Lakers, and everyone thought he would be the perfect power-forward complement to Jabbar.

"At first it was great. Kareem and I spent a lot of time together. I really liked this rookie player from back in Michigan, Earvin Johnson. My juices were boiling again.

"Then the devil got hold of me."

Haywood says most of the NBA was experimenting with drugs at the time. At a party given by a former teammate from his Sonics days, he says, "this guy hands me this glass thing and says try it.

"I look at him like the country bumpkin I still was. Smoking cocaine? Oh, man—California. Got to be the hippest, the most trendy and avant-garde, you know. He tells me it's organic. It's healthy. We go in the kitchen and he cooks some up. He gets a

337

razor blade, chops it, drops it in the pipe and *bubble, bubble, bubble. . .*

"Oh, man, it was like having 50 points at the half; my team's up by 35 points. I felt so good, so confident, so cool. I think I was hooked the first time I did it."

If you put a graph up on the performance of Spencer Haywood in the 1979–80 season, you would discover that the line starts high, drops rapidly and finally disappears. His play disintegrated. He didn't rebound, hardly scored and barely played. Teammates resented him, his arrogant attitude.

"Before," he says, "I was always the first one on the court. But then I was showing up later and later, and then I would sprint to make it there a minute before practice. I used to stay after practice and shoot 100–150 free throws. I started leaving after two or three. No doubt about it, I was hooked on cocaine."

He climbed inside a glass pipe and blew bubbles. Inside, the years would fall away, and the mistakes and failures were wiped clean, and there were no contract squabbles or court dates and no fine print. There were no jealous teammates, and everything was a 10-minute dose of uncut escape.

"No reality," Haywood says. "Just an hour, a day, a week out of a lifetime—wasted, doing nothing but faking yourself out. Fools getting fooled is what it is. And I was the damnedest fool of all.

"All the while, I'm getting more and more filled with fear. I'm thinking Magic Johnson's putting a special spin on his passes, deliberately trying to make me look bad. I'm putting the blame everywhere but where it was. I blamed white society. I blamed blacks who were jealous. I blamed people for being noncommittal, colorblind, ignorant. Everyone but me. Me and my friend, the pipe."

Came the playoffs and Haywood could feel the old urges. He had been in pro basketball 10 years. He had everything but a championship.

"I decided I wasn't going to do any cocaine. I even unplugged my phone so none of my 'good friends' could reach me. I wanted to stay straight; I really did. I wanted that (championship) ring bad. Then one day after practice, somebody nudged me on the shoulder as I walked off the court. It's my old buddy.

"I was only gonna do a little. Me and a couple of guys. Then next thing I know—damn, it's midnight. At 3 in the morning I said, 'Well, might as well stay up now.' I'm all wired, shaking, squirming. They say 'Take this' and hand me a big fat Quaalude.

"And I zonk. But I get up and I'm almost at practice; I'm in my Rolls, stopped at a red light. And I just nod out at the wheel. People are banging on my window. I make it to practice; we're on the floor doing stretching exercises and I lay back and crash again. Reporters wrote that I had put myself into some Far Eastern trance that I could not get out of. Yeah, I was in a trance, all right—only the trance came from South America, and I'd smoked it all night long."

Coach Paul Westhead sent him home. The next night, in a game with the Philadelphia 76ers, Haywood never left the bench. In the locker room, he got in a shouting match with a couple of teammates. Next morning, Haywood went to see Westhead.

"I have a problem," Haywood said. "I'm messed up. I've been doing drugs. Cocaine." If it had been 1988, Haywood would have been sent to some rehabilitation clinic with the blessing of his team and the NBA. In 1980, however, the Lakers suspended him. Three games away from his championship ring, he was gone.

"I went off the deep end," he says. "I had my excuse. I had begged, got down on my knees and asked for another chance. It seemed like Paul Westhead was smiling at me when he told me I was gone. I left, swearing revenge. But first, I had to get high."

Today Paul Westhead coaches Loyola-Marymount in California. He prefers not to talk about the incident but does say, "I had no idea how deep the problem was. I doubt anybody on the team did. At the time I did what I felt I had to do to help the team."

Meanwhile, Haywood slipped further into craziness. One night, alone with his pipe, he decided to murder Paul Westhead.

He called some friends in Detroit, gangster types. Then, one night in the spring of that year, three men in Los Angeles passed the glass pipe and talked of murder with mystery. The plot took all night and several thousand dollars' worth of cocaine to hatch.

"We were gonna mess with his brakes, the steering on his car," Haywood says. "It never got beyond the room, a bunch of junkies talking trash, and I don't think it ever would have gone anywhere anyhow. But then the phone rang."

It was his mother, calling from Mississippi. "Something bad's goin' on, isn't it, Spencer?" she said. "What's goin' on?"

Haywood almost dropped the phone.

"It scared me — scared me bad," Haywood says. "I didn't know what to tell her. I couldn't hardly make sense anyway in my condition. I just told her nothing bad was gonna happen. Everything was fine."

At any rate, his mother called some other friends — some of Spencer's real friends, Vern De Silva and Wiley Davis, a couple of Pershing classmates who had gone to junior college with Haywood.

"They came over and yanked me out of my stupor. The other guys went back to Detroit. I threw away my pipe once more."

The Lakers won the championship. A month later, Spencer Haywood was released from the team for good. Teammates voted him only a quarter-share of the playoff money.

"And all the while I couldn't see it," he says. "I couldn't see what I had become."

He spent the next year in Venice, Italy, playing in the pro league. It was a drug-free year. He played well, and the Italian people warmed to him.

But the following year, after calling his old friend Gene Shue, he joined the Washington Bullets in the NBA. Reunited with his wife and daughter, determined not to fall into the trap of cocaine, Haywood started the season enjoying himself, playing well.

Then a friend from Detroit, Sonny Dove, himself a pro player, died. And Iman was in a terrible car accident and required surgery.

"I had done maybe two lines of coke all season," he says. "I promised I wasn't going to get messed up again. Then Sonny died. Then Iman got her face all messed up. I came home to New York and I couldn't stand the pressure. I got high. Then I announced I was retired. I did it over the phone. I probably had my pipe in the other hand."

He knew it was wrong. Iman got out of the hospital and he started seeing a psychologist.

"Then after three months, for who knows what reason, I got

stoned. I stayed high for a week. Excessive use, thousand dollars a day. Of course, I'm still drinking my carrot juice. Still getting my oranges fresh-squeezed because I'm into health, right? Meanwhile my daughter's telling me while I'm in the bathroom blowing bubbles that she thinks I've changed. I'm a mess, the living dead. And I still know it's all wrong. But maybe I realize I'm not strong enough to whip it alone. Spencer was a no-good SOB; I couldn't trust Spencer. I needed help."

He checked into one clinic, then another. He started going to meetings.

"I got carried away," he says. "Iman and I were having troubles at home. She'd been through a lot. I told her I was sick. I was scared."

The marriage dissolved. Iman wanted him to come back to New York, where her work was. He wouldn't. He couldn't. He decided to come back to Detroit.

He patched things up with Will Robinson. He found he really did have friends who cared. He continued going to his meetings, continued his struggle to stay away from drugs. But he could not shake the feeling that he could still play basketball. He decided playing for the Detroit Pistons would form the perfect symmetry of a life gone full circle.

He asked for a tryout. OK, said Jack McCloskey, the Pistons' general manager. Show us what you have left.

"He was in incredible shape physically," McCloskey recalls. "All the reports were good, that he no longer used drugs. He was worth a chance. I really rooted for him, too."

But according to Coach Chuck Daly, McCloskey and several of the Pistons, Spencer Haywood simply could not play anymore at an NBA level. A pulled muscle hindered his comeback.

"They only gave me a few practices before they told me I couldn't help them," Haywood says.

"I couldn't believe it. I've never been told I wasn't good enough. Nothin' before ever was wrong with my game if I was straight. I got in my car, dazed, still unable to believe what had just happened."

The Pistons train in Windsor. Haywood drove slowly over the Ambassador Bridge, headed back to Detroit and remembers:

"I was sitting at the wheel crying out loud. I looked down at the water and I slowed down. I thought about driving the car right off the bridge. After a few minutes, I drove home. My hands were shaking. I was dizzy. I was about to hyperventilate. I gasped for breath. I needed air. Something was slamming me. Squashing me. Pinching my heart."

When he got home, he walked to his bookcase and reached for a Bible. He read it out loud for an hour. He tried not to think about what he always thought about when things went sour in the past.

"Hell, yes, I wanted to get high. But I couldn't. Not this time. I started calling friends, real friends. Not my doper friends. I had to talk to people. I had to reinforce myself. And by God, I really felt if I didn't get high that night, I probably won't ever again."

The twinges to play ball still come back. Last summer he shopped around a little, mailed out videos of him playing. Pride is a wonderful defense mechanism.

———

No time for remorse. Spencer Haywood, businessman, is attacking once more. The target now is Detroit's urban blight. He is president of a company that renovates abandoned or rundown property and turns it into low-income housing. It is sold to families who care.

"Some of the property is excellent," Haywood says. "It's funny: When I inspect some of the burned-out dwellings, see all the neglect and abuse, I see a person. I see somebody who let himself go, wasted himself. Yeah, I look at those old, boarded-up buildings and I see a man.

"I'm that man."

When he sees men sitting on the torn-out seats of abandoned cars or plopped on some sidewalk, he stops. He tells them to do something about themselves. Get up. Be somebody. It is not street-corner preaching. It is those hands attached to the erector-set arms, still reaching.

"The Colombian is the plantation owner now," he says. "His slaves are in deep trouble because cocaine ain't cotton, you know. I have been lucky enough to re-evaluate things. I got that second chance even though I might not have deserved it."

There is his TV show on Channel 50, a half-hour a week. There is a four-hour weekend radio show, playing jazz and crossover be-bop records on a local radio station. There is the development company. He has basketball camps for kids. He stays busy, and when he goes to sleep, he says, he rarely dreams. And it's better that way.

"I want to go back to the University of Detroit. Be a student again. I don't have any eligibility left, but I'm going to support it any way I can. If I get a degree, that'll validate my ticket, too, make me more legitimate, more qualified to reach people who need help. I need credibility. Too many people drew their own conclusions about me. I'm here to say they're wrong."

It is the full circle. It is not a rebirth. The manchild with the strong hands decided his old life was not worth a damn. He started over. He prays for strength of a different kind. He seeks safe passage all the way until tomorrow. And nothing else.

Last June, while the Pistons were in the championship series with the Lakers, he finally received the championship ring that had been in storage since 1980. An hour later, he drove to the Loyola-Marymount campus, where, in a small office, Paul Westhead and his problem player hugged and held a tearful, forgiving reunion.

"What do you say to someone like that? 'Sorry, I was planning on killing you?' Sorry? He said he was glad for me. We hugged and cried and I really believe we respect each other a lot now."

He stares at the ring on his hands.

"It looks good, doesn't it?" he says, squeezing a fist that makes the ring stick up. "It means a lot to me. A lot of things still do."

His daughter lives with Iman. He wishes things could be different. Right now, they can't.

"I have to re-establish credibility all around, I guess. I'm working on it, though."

He talks to school children regularly, goes to their schools, plays rap music, tells them cocaine is No. 1 on the most wanted list.

"Put it on your most-hated list," he says, eyes burning, words stinging. On purpose.

His dignity has returned. The drugs are at arm's length; he says they'll never get any closer. He plays basketball still, in pick-up games, in old-timers games. All the mirrors of illusions are gone. The self-gratification he used to seek was inside all the time.

"Right here," Spencer Haywood says slapping his chest with his enormous hands.

He looks at his watch. Got to talk to a school in St. Clair Shores, he says. Got a meeting after that.

"I love it," he says, walking quickly, applauding for no obvious reason. And whistling. It is impossible to whistle and be unhappy. Spencer Haywood whistles all the way out the door.

The Human Contradiction: Oilers' Glanville a blend of coach, jester, enemy, friend
Nov. 5, 1989

HOUSTON—There's this tree a couple of blocks from the Astrodome, big, tall, majestic, big around as a pregnant elephant. Jerry Glanville says it used to be the local hanging tree, for horse thieves and rustlers, a hundred years ago. It's a little out of his way as he drives to work but Glanville likes to cruise by and look at that tree. For inspiration.

"I'm always a game away from a hanging," Glanville says, squeezing at his neck. Then the coach of the Houston Oilers, the little tough guy from the streets of Detroit, pro football's newest Man in Black, the guy who thinks life should be lived the same way he drives his stable of muscle cars, namely 100 miles an hour, and that football is a smash-mouth proposition any way you look at it, says with an oozing drawl, "I just love it all. Every bit."

It's a simple game plan: Knock 'em naked or someone's gonna steal your lunch money. Hit the beach with trained killers and Happy Hand Grenades, to everyone. See, that's how it's gotta be when you're a gunslinger who feels everyone's gunning for him. It's always boiling point for Jerry Glanville. He's the coach and in his head, it's always fourth-and-one. Everyone's leaning forward, expecting, waiting, leaning so far out you can feel them on your back, Sunday morning coming down for sure, and it's comfortably uncomfortable. And Glanville loves it.

It's one contradiction after another. It's the dream and the nightmare both come true. You get a good seat on the luxury liner and then you happen to notice the ocean's on fire. And you grin. Hang on buckaroos; you're out there alone. The rodeo chute is open and you'd better nail that bull before he gets momentum. You're on the edge and you force yourself to live on that edge because that's what lets you know you're alive.

"People say I dodge a lot of bullets," Glanville says and his chest seems to puff. "But I don't. Not really.

"I'm actually bullet-proof."

And he swallows his laugh. His football team is said to be the NFL's dirtiest; they lead the league in personal fouls and yellow flags. And they are said to be created in the perfect image of Jerry Glanville.

But that's all part of living on the edge, too. He disagrees, his players disagree. In fact, they believe there's a conspiracy. Everyone's out to get them. Chuck Noll, Sam Wyche, Marv Levy. Everyone wants to get them because they're afraid of them. Paranoia can be a tool, your protective shield, when you're backed up against it. And Jerry Glanville never wants to be anywhere else but up against the wall.

"I do my best work when the alligators are biting me on the butt," says the 48-year-old Glanville.

Not to mention the water moccasins. When he and wife Brenda went for a walk a couple weeks ago and the searing pain suddenly stabbed at his foot, he dropped and rolled over and cursed the cheap shot. It wasn't until he was at the hospital that a doctor told him a poisonous snake had got him. And yeah, that figures, doesn't it? Day before a big game with the hated Steelers and Mr. Chuck Noll, Glanville gets snakebit. Come on world, is that the best shot you have?

"I was on the sidelines the next day. That snake had just eaten a mouse or something. Maybe a Houston sportswriter, I'm not sure. Anyway his venom wasn't any good — the snake's venom, I mean. I

345

made it to the game though. Jerry Jeff Walker, the great American poet (and country-western singing legend), sang to my team before the game. We shut out the Steelers.

"Then all this talk starts that I never got bit by no snake, that it wasn't a water moccasin, that I was just trying to grandstand.

"Life's wonderful, huh?"

But that's living on the edge. When you get down on all fours to watch the game-winning field goal, or run down the sideline almost as fast as your wide receiver sprinting for the touchdown that helps beat the almighty Chicago Bears at Soldiers Field, the very same place you used to love to watch George Halas wearing those dark glasses, chase after referees, or when you just about double over and faint dead as a beaver hat from the third Cleveland Browns flea-flicker that finally beats your team, well, that's getting involved. That's living and coaching at the same time.

You force yourself to reduce life on the football field to gut level, to the wonderful challenge of standing up to the bully and either kicking his teeth out or spitting your own venom back at him while he's standing on your chest. If you're Glanville, that's when it's all worth it. Somebody else keeps the won-loss records. You look at the effort and the passion and the feeling. You see a man with one shoe and someone else wonders where the other one got lost.

You suggest maybe the man found a shoe.

"Ever listen to Kris Kristofferson, another of the great American poets of this century?" Glanville asks. "His song, 'The Pilgrim?' "

And the shrill blue eyes, Oiler blue eyes, sparkle. Glanville shakes his head and recites: "From the rocking of the cradle to the rolling of the hearse, is the going up worth it, knowing that you're coming down?"

Glanville closes his eyes and his head drops, but only for an instant.

"It's like the fighter pilot aces sitting around the bar the night before the big mission over Germany. Some of us just aren't going to make it through the war. One of these days, I won't be coming back. That's coaching. About every 1½ years, six coaches get fired. That's the way it is and that's the way I like it. Coaches are like General Custer; we wear them arrow shirts. We lose a game and we stand up and it's our fault and that's the way it's supposed to be. I don't care. But we do have security guards at the press conferences and nobody with a bow and arrow is allowed in.

"And I just checked that hanging tree today. There's no rope slung over the limb. Not just yet.

"You gotta understand this—I ain't gonna change. I don't teach dirty football. But I love the running and chasing and tackling. I also don't go for the hairspray and wingtip types who want a bunch of robots in the league. I see a miracle a week but because they don't happen enough on the football field, some people want to get rid of me. And that's OK so long as my boss isn't among them. But don't ask me to change. You ask a 17-year-old to change. You don't ask a 48-year-old to change."

Someone asks him what do you do with a 48-year-old? And Glanville licks at his smile as he says, "You replace a 48-year-old, of course."

And the contradictions explode all around. He does care. The arrogance, the struts, the Napoleonistic airs, are all genuine— everything about Jerry Glanville is genuine, "except the parts of me that are flat-out, complete lies, some of which I invented myself"— but they are only a sliver of all that is the modern gunslinger, the talking, walking, swaggering contradiction.

Last season as the man in black heard the final gun of an impressive win over the hated Cincinnati Bengals and Mr. Sam Wyche last season, he turned and ran, galloped like the linebacker he used to be, and took the handoff from the man in the stands and pulled the frail little boy onto his shoulders and headed for the locker room. The boy, who had been sneaked out of a hospital where his diseased kidney was dependent upon a dialysis machine to keep him alive, laughed out loud all the way to the door and it was like music to Glanville.

"I told him if he'd come to our game, we'd win. He had a great game for us; we gave him a game ball. And do you know what else? I saw him and his father at training camp this year. He got a kidney transplant. He's going to be all right."

Yeah it's worth it. And yeah, he cares. On Wednesdays, during his lunch hour, Glanville heads to the Children's Hospital. This particular day, lunch was meeting a nine-year-old cancer patient.

The boy's hair was almost all gone; he was weak and painfully skinny. But Glanville held him in his arms and noticed the tear roll into the boy's smile. It could have been the coach's tear. He's not sure. Does Glanville care? He also talked to a little girl who might not live through the week. She had tubes and wires coming out of both arms so he introduced himself by shaking her big toe.

"And she giggled," Glanville says.

"It ain't me that makes them feel good. It's the job. The coach of the Houston Oilers is visiting them. That's one reason I won't ever take myself so serious that I get overly impressed with my likeness in the mirror. I know we're all here just for a hiccup and then we're gone. Those kids remind me of that. When I was in elementary school in Detroit, one of my best friends died on the playground. It was an accident and I couldn't understand why. I still don't know why but I understand that it does happen."

And he remembers the kid he met last year. The boy was the high-school manager of the baseball team. Another cancer kid. He made it through the cobalt treatments, the monthly series of chemotherapy. Then just when everyone thought he was going to get better, he got the measles and died.

Glanville knows the score. You look at the hanging tree but you better be ready for the snake too. Nobody said life was fair. Nobody ever denied that death wasn't. And everything between is only valuable if you make it worthwhile.

"You just better have some fun along the way," he says softly.

Fun, of course, does not compute with robots. It's like hard-nosed football all subject to public interpretation. Facts are easy to compile and analyze. Fun—what's that?

Glanville says his eccentricities often are nothing but attempts to have a little fun. He once left a pair of tickets for Elvis Presley when the Oilers played an exhibition game in Memphis. Just for a smile. All hell broke loose. Half the world loved it. Another portion took it seriously. Glanville in typical fashion threw a bucket of oil onto everyone's range fire.

Says Glanville, "I left them because Elvis is alive. I know this because I read it in the National Enquirer, I know this because I once visited Graceland and I could smell Elvis. He was in the kitchen making peanut butter and banana sandwiches. He is not dead he's alive, although the last time I saw him, he looked like an offensive lineman."

And the eyes twinkle and mischief is all around his smirk.

But the matter of leaving tickets for celebrities took off in the national attention span. Who'd Glanville leave tickets for this week? Inquiring minds wanted to know. For a while, Glanville complied. In Dallas, Buddy Holly. In New York, The Phantom of the Opera. In Seattle, D.B. Cooper. In Cincinnati, Loni Anderson. In Philadelphia, he was going to leave a pair of tickets for W.C. Fields but he was afraid Ed McMahon would claim them because Glanville's not sure they're not the same person. In Indiana, Glanville left tickets for his personal favorite idol, James Dean, the original Rebel Without a Cause who preceded Jerry Glanville into the spotlight.

"Just having fun was all it was," Glanville says. "But some people thought I was trying to show off or something. I don't leave tickets anymore for famous people but it's not because somebody told me to quit."

And that's important for everyone to know. He's his own man all the way. That is until the contradictions set in once more. He's his own man until Oilers owner Bud Adams tells him to do something. Hey, if Adams suddenly decides he doesn't like the all-black wardrobe Glanville wears at games, Glanville will head for the dressing room. Quick as a hiccup. If the boss wants rainbow pants, polka-dot suspenders or push-up bras, that's what he'll get. There are a lot of reasons to get fired and Glanville's aware of every one of them. Wardrobe will never be one of them. There are only 28 jobs like his in the world. He knows all about the vultures, the hanging trees. They're out there. He knows Jackie Sherrill, the man most often mentioned as his successor, is out there somewhere, waiting.

He'll think about individual freedom and being the gunslinger who can withstand just about anything and he'll be the rebel and play the free-wheeling Jerry Glanville image to the hilt. But he'll also think about those kids in the hospital. And he'll also think about the day in eighth grade he boasted to friends he was going to grow up to be head coach of the Detroit Lions. Or the English paper his sophomore year in high school when he re-affirmed his intentions to coach the Lions. Or the motto he wrote in his high school yearbook that "Life without football is not life." See, he wants to live within society's city limits, even be part of the NFL's exclusive condominium. He really wants to be a coach and really wants the standard ration of success, wealth and happiness.

But if you don't mind, he'll live on the outskirts of town. Out on the edge.

A Houston writer tells him that Harvey Salem, a former Oiler now with the Detroit Lions and also a player who clashed vehemently if not violently with Glanville's philosophies while in Houston, said even Bozo the Clown could coach a team with as many great players (seven Oilers played in the Pro Bowl last season) and No. 1 draft picks as Houston has. Salem says Glanville is "an evil little toad."

The writer wants Glanville's reaction. Glanville once ripped Salem's nameplate from his locker and stuck it on a toilet stall when the big offensive lineman was holding out for more money and a new contract. And there might be the reflex impulse crouching somewhere inside to say Bozo the Clown is too busy trying to play offensive line for the Lions to be a coach. But instead Glanville says only, "Aw, I don't think any less of Harvey than I ever did."

Glanville grew up on Detroit's east side, lived in a federal housing project near Eight Mile and Kelly, across the street from where the Eastland Mall is today. He says, "You always knew where the boundary lines were. And you got a great sense of team feeling ground in real early in life. I used to deliver The Detroit News when I was a little boy. My route was in a pretty bad area. Twice I got robbed while I was delivering papers."

Then comes a sneer that would make ol' Elvis proud. Then the tough guy says with words that sting, "I got my money back both times."

And that's got a lot to do with football and the way he coaches it, he claims. You gotta establish yourself. That's why all the stops he's made in coaching, from coaching the women's bowling team at Western Kentucky, to taking over the Detroit Lions' special teams, starting the Gritz Blitz with the Atlanta Falcons and now painting the villainous House of Pain picture, it all starts with aggressiveness. And gang rule. Establish yourself. Like it was back in the projects of Detroit.

Get them before they get you and make sure you outnumber them. That's coaching.

His father sold Fords. As a result the family car had a rear speaker for the radio, "which was a big deal in those days. We used to climb in the backseat and listen to the Lions' games. If my father would have sold a few more Fords, we might have been able to go see the Lions live, in person. But it was enough back them. I loved the Lions when I was growing up. Charlie Ane, Jimmy David. Lou Creekmur. Joe Schmidt. They were . . . tough."

Football's important. It's not a lifestyle. It's a life. Yearbook mottoes endure. Glanville was an overachiever who blew out a knee in college but that only allowed his coaching aspirations to come more clearly into focus.

Glanville confesses there have been plenty of times where he let the game gain too much control of him. Like that time when he was an assistant for Bud Carson at Georgia Tech and the game was lost in the final minute and Glanville was thunderstuck, almost physically ill with disappointment. His wife Brenda beside him in the front seat as he drove home. Glanville constantly slammed a fist on the steering wheel, his frustration unable to subside. He was speeding.

Brenda tried to console him, saying, "Jerry, honey, calm down. It's only a game."

Glanville remembers the moment. It was somewhere out on Interstate-75, 20 miles from home. It was already dark as he slammed on the brakes, pulled onto the shoulder of the road and said flatly, "Brenda, take a hike."

Glanville smiles and says he's obviously glad Brenda didn't get get out of the car, "she usually never takes me serious anyway. It definitely was not my finest moment. I felt just about the same way after the Cleveland game last week."

And that's another thing to know and remember and even admire about Jerry Glanville. He's irreparably human, prone to mistakes, susceptible to stubbornness. He awards toy army helmets for the Hit of the Week and probably never met a black eye he didn't admire and his ardent love of the blitz—Jerry Glanville

351

would have enlisted in the Japanese Air Force if they would have promised him Kamikaze duty — and constantly pressuring the quarterback has blown up in the Oilers' face more than a couple of times.

"That's not true. Hell, I was only two years old back then," he says and the smile that can hiss like a snake this time escapes like a gentle breeze.

Sure he takes chances — who can ever forget the Stagger Lee play in the AFC semifinal game against Denver two seasons ago when his gimmick play from the Oilers' 4-yard line resulted in a Bronco fumble recovery at the Oilers' one-yard line? And he does seem to have more success coaching average players instead of great ones. And you'd like to assume he's seeing himself out there in uniform, the little overachiever making snap decisions from the gut instead of the brain. But you'd be wrong. He knows he can adjust and adapt and not be stubborn. Just as a football coach must be able to do.

When Buffalo's Jim Kelly burned Oilers blitzes twice in a row with touchdown passes and Houston lost in overtime earlier in the season, Glanville was heavily criticized for so nakedly exposing his cornerbacks. But when the same Oilers defense patiently and impressively smothered Miami and the noted savant of the forward pass, Dan Marino, in a totally blitz-less game, nobody seemed to notice the newfound restraint. They noticed the snuff job on Marino but no credit came his way for having the hands of a jockey.

"That's just how coaching is," Glanville says. "We've had a lot of success with that Stagger Lee play over the years. I still think if (Mike) Rozier catches the ball cleanly, he goes for about 60 yards. But that one didn't work. It ain't gonna make me change my ways. It's a learning experience, something to build on, I suppose. Next time I might be a little more conservative down near our goal. Then again . . . we might put some happy hand grenades on Marino every chance we can."

It's his job to be right, to win, to take the Oilers to the promised land of the Super Bowl. Some say he be will dumped if that does not happen this season. Glanville puts his arms straight out at his

352

sides and makes the sound of a fighter plane in trouble. Better drink up, enjoy yourself. Someone might not make it back.

"All I can do is work hard. I know how to do that. I've always known how to work hard."

His parents divorced when he was about to start high school. Glanville got a quick and stark jolt of reality. Nobody but your Momma and Daddy are going to flat-out give you anything. The rest you gotta earn yourself.

Glanville toted 100-pound bags of flour for General Mills. He once worked 12-hour shifts at the Chevy plant, wearing bulky asbestos gloves and yanking red-hot car transmissions out of the blast furnace. He can't unlearn those lessons and now that he's a supervisor of sorts, he expects everyone to punch the same kind of clock. Of course, since icons like Lombardi, Shula and Halas shared similar thoughts on work ethics, this is not considered part of a rebel image.

"I got a pickup truck that'll get 120 mph. I got a Corvette that'll scream, just flat-out scream, and you crank up Jerry Jeff on my stereo system and it's all real relaxing, going real fast and the music real loud. But that's not how some people think I ought to act. They don't like my dressing in black, even though the entire Cincinnati staff did it too that one year. Hey, Coach Lombardi wore a big furry Russian hat when he was on the sidelines. What does that mean? That he was showing off? I'll tell you what it means. Nothing. But what if I wore one of those fur hats? Is it any different than my dust coat?"

And anyone can tell it really chaps his hide, the hypocrisy, the small-mindedness.

"Bunch of robots."

Once a week, any homeless person in Houston is invited to come out to the Oilers complex and have a nice, hot shower. He figures everyone deserves that much. He, his wife and seven-year-old son (Justin) pass out blankets on the Houston streets right before winter. The compassionate side, the giving side of Glanville is obvious. And yet some complain that he does such stuff not for the right reasons. He's a hog for publicity, they say.

But the blankets are getting passed around regardless. The sick children are getting visited no matter why someone else thinks

Glanville volunteers so much of his time. The Oilers have become one of the most colorful teams in the league, owning a roguish reputation much like the Oakland Raiders of another era. And it's more than a little bit because of their gunslinger-tough coach.

Don't say too many nice things to his face though. He might let his guard down. Somebody's gonna sucker-punch him then, sure enough.

His father told him to always go first class, stay half as long and have twice as much fun. This prairie logic has stuck with him. But he has to beware the calm.

The Oilers' 4–4 record isn't worth an anthill. The Oilers are either one game out of first place or tied for last, depending on how you look at it. Someone either lost a shoe or found one. Glanville seeks the dangerous side, the one out on the edge. He makes himself and his team see that precarious picture. Too many first-class rides numb the survival senses. There must always be that sense of arousal, of perked ears, of imminent danger, of bullies and Jackie Sherrill and Chuck Noll all wanting to step all over you because they simply don't respect you.

Glanville laughs and says he often generates that defensive nature just by thinking about the public address announcer at Three Rivers Stadium in Pittsburgh.

"He calls me Gary Grandville . . . Every time we're there. I love it. It gives me cold chills. Goose bumps. I don't know why that is — me liking to feel like the underdog all the time. It's just living on the edge, I guess.

"I'll tell you one thing, if Elvis was a coach in the AFC Central, then he'd have a good reason to play like he's dead. It's right out there, far as it goes where great challenges are concerned. It's a fight every week, like it was back in Detroit getting off the school bus.

"Last week, did you see the game? We lost to Cleveland on tricks. Gimmick plays. We could play them straight up but they beat us with tricks. That one really hurt. See it's just not a game at the time. Oh, I can put it all back in perspective in about two days. But losing like we did — that's tough going for a while.

"I won't ever feel good when we lose."

Then he shakes his head. "But I feel pretty good right now.

We're in shape to make a good run. We finally have some home games coming up. This week it's the Lions and I sure hope they don't get everything fixed by Sunday. Like New England did against us."

No you don't ever get over losing. Not the one the week before or the one the month before. Such contradiction. He feels good this day and that's not good. He's different because he won't change. Apprehension cheers him up. The forlorn look comes back. Fear of the unknown, the only thing anyone has to fear is the imaginary stuff. Those guys on the other sideline — that's nothing. That's the enemy. And that's just fine.

On Wednesday, the Oilers could not practice in the Astrodome because there is a championship tractor pull scheduled. The football team had to go outdoors. Not only that, it started to rain, a drizzle that got harder and harder. Nasty weather in which to practice football. A miserable climate when you have a job to protect. And a perfect day for an Old West hanging.

"I love it," says the Man in Black, sneering at the weather, double daring it to get worse.

"Did I tell you I got a letter from Elvis yesterday? Hand-written. No, this time I'm serious. Stop by my office in about an hour and I'll show it to you. I'm going to get in a little running now. It's gonna get interesting the rest of this season. You know the NFL doesn't run away from you, it sort of waits for you to catch up.

"You just better be looking in all directions too."

And Jerry Glanville walked away, whistling, actually whistling, as the raindrops attacked, probably in self-defense.

THE SHARK
Lost amid the controversy and the outlaw image is that the man can flat-out coach
Dec. 14, 1990

LAS VEGAS—The battle is constant and futile. The image of the Unviersity of Nevada-Las Vegas basketball team is always first to arrive. The team plane always lands later than its reputation. It's got a lot to do with those nicknames.

If it were the Gladiators or Eagles or something more conventional from the team mascot rack, things might be different. But no—it's the Runnin' Rebels, and it's a perfect fit.

And if Jerry Tarkanian, their beleaguered coach who is always looking in the rear-view mirror and always spotting the NCAA posse hot on his trail, could be known as anything but Tark the Shark, things might be different, too. Nobody would snicker if he were Tar the Lark. People wouldn't get overcome with prurient suspicion if he were Tark the Spark. And how could you say anything bad about a little bald man with big ears and hound-dog eyes called Tark the Aardvark? It's that shark thing and what it insinuates.

Nicknames are a problem. So is the college town they come from. Or at least the perception of that town. Las Vegas. Right away, bells ring, don't they? If you tell someone you're from Appleton, Wis., or Hacienda Hills, Calif., or Pleasant Valley, Tenn., the euphemism Sin City doesn't automatically appear in thought bubbles. But Vegas? The neon city created so that the visage of Sodom and Gomorrah might not be forgotten?

Yeah, you can get sidetracked whenever the UNLV basketball team slithers, er, shows up at some local gymnasium. It's a shame from a one-dimensional standpoint. For these are the Outlaw Kings of college basketball, defending national champions, the ones who turned The Big Game against Duke in April into a feeding frenzy, winning by 30 points. When the waters had stilled and the fish had all been eaten, the kingdom was ruled by the sinister knaves the palace guards had been trying to throw into the royal dungeons for years. Fear and Loathing was rampant at NCAA headquarters.

356

Strictly from the standpoint of basketball, the Runnin' Rebs make everyone else seem like a bunch of amateurs.

And now, just when you thought it was safe to go back into the gym. . .

Saturday at The Palace of Auburn Hills, Tarkanian and the Runnin' Rebels play Michigan State. Early word is the monster is more hideous than before. Four starters return, including a couple of unholy terrors who will be NBA lottery picks. The bench is deeper, and that defense, the howling coyote that caused the rest of the country to shudder in the night a year ago, seems hungrier than ever.

Naturally, their hides are thicker, toughened with the gristle of the latest Controversy du Jour.

Actually, the feeling among them is one of reprieve. The rope already was thrown over the lynching tree and the program already was declared ineligible to defend its championship. It was the result of a complicated legal battle between Tarkanian and the NCAA for a variety of offenses, which occurred when most of the current Rebs were 6 and 7 years old. Then in a manner similar to a pit boss at a casino saying, "Hey pal, we'll take back that card that just busted you and give you another one; your choice," the penalty was lifted and an alternate was administered.

The Rebs have shown their appreciation thus far by chewing up every team in sight. Last weekend, against its cousins at the University of Nevada (formerly Nevada-Reno), UNLV won by 50 points. Explanation for the massacre was twofold: Nevada played a zone, hoping to keep Larry Johnson, the Rebs' 6-foot-7, 250-pound All-American power forward, from going wild inside, and his teammates responded by nailing a staggering 21 three-point shots against the packed-in defense; and the team was highly aroused by a newspaper quote suggesting the boys from Reno were just as good as the Vegas horde.

Hell hath no fury like UNLV on the attack. That is why its image has grown something on it that looks like a disclaimer. When you see the Rebs play with such passion and loose-reined discipline, when you see that defense, when you see them run together, dedicated, organized, yeah, even civilized, redeeming qualities shoot far beyond the arena floor. Their coach, battle-scarred and field-decorated as the result of the ordeal he describes as The Twenty Years War, seems to settle somewhere in public perception between comic book character and crook. Often overlooked is his ability to coach basketball.

The man the NCAA considers a flagrant cheater, maybe the worst ever, has a blank stare he uses for a game face. But it serves him off the court as well. Because when he stands there, shoulders hunched, drooping eyes gazing upward, he looks like a harp seal, wondering when everyone's going to stop clubbing him. You can't help it—you feel sorry for Tarkanian, a 60-year-old survivor, if nothing else.

For years his battle with the NCAA smacked of a witch hunt, of McCarthyism. This thing started in 1977, when the NCAA read off a laundry list of violations and demanded Tarkanian be suspended. The charges came in the wake of similar accusations that surfaced right after he left his job at Long Beach State. Tarkanian believed that the hot breath of inquiry should be aimed at his accusers; investigate the investigators, he said. He took the NCAA to court. For the longest while, he won. His basketball teams followed suit; Tarkanian is about to lap Clair Bee as the college basketball coach with the highest winning percentage.

Then in 1988, the U.S. Supreme Court, between hearing arguments about the constitutionality of burning the flag and whether or not newspapers in Detroit should have a joint operating agreement, ruled 5–4 that the NCAA did not violte Tarkanian's constitutional rights when it tried to suspend him in 1977.

At about the same time, the NCAA gleefully announced it was looking into new alleged violations involving the recruitment of Lloyd "Sweet Pea" Daniels, a Brooklyn street legend who went to four high schools, graduated from none, but somehow was admitted to UNLV. Daniels never played for Tarkanian; he was arrested shortly after arriving on campus on charges of attempting to buy crack cocaine. Forthcoming are the findings of that investigation— horror stories abound of cash payments, free apartments and a motorcycle, as well as a payment for Daniels' drug-rehabilitation program by a UNLV assistant coach who actually became Daniels' legal guardian. Daniels, who is illiterate, has since proclaimed that the NCAA offered him a bribe if he would help it nail Tarkanian.

Truth may be a scarce commodity; surely the burden of proof of either accusaiton will be heavy and difficult. But the outlook for UNLV hoops could be bleak.

That is why the deal Tarkanian offered works so well for this team. The Rebels can defend the title this season. Next year they are banned. But they probably were going to be anyway.

Tarkanian once said, "I never did anything illegal that I knew was illegal," and those sad eyes suggested that ignorance was indeed bliss. But the pattern is conspicuous. He can complain that the NCAA is out to get him, that the governing body of college sports locks into him like a heat-seeking missile, that because he has been so outspoken and unwilling to march to the NCAA cadence, that because he believes every lost soul and problem child deserves a chance at the college experience, that because he admits some of his sins are committed in the name of human compassion, he is the Perennial Prime Suspect.

But funny things keep happening. Like the "irregular bookkeeping" explanation that is being offered when it was discovered recently that 400 tickets for every UNLV home game last season cannot be accounted for. Tarkanian himself gets 233 tickets each game, but he says what he does with his tickets is nobody's business. Then there's the latest complaint that two Rebels, Chris Jeter and Anderson Hunt (a Detroit product), were spotted sitting in the $1,000 ringside seats for the Douglas-Holyfield fight. Or the little misunderstanding that came up in August when Stacey Augmon, the sinewy, sullen superstar whose sweltering defense has deflated the auras of the likes of Danny Manning, Sean Elliott, Mark Macon, etc., was accused of beating up a woman. Augmon's alleged rambling during the incident, "You know who I am? I own this town; I can kill you and get away with it," did not help matters, and it also threw fuel on the fiery rumor that Augmon had tested positive for drugs during the '88 Olympics in Seoul.

Tarkanian blames the image. The charges have yet to be substantiated. The rumors have been denied. The program has been described as being under more scritiny than "bacteria under a microscope," but the fact remains: Nothing ever seems to get a chance to die and fade away before something else arrives. Like everything else in Las Vegas, reality is not so easy to hold onto.

Are you kidding? When you can get married at the same chapel in which Joan Collins and Peter Holm tied the knot and have an Elvis impersonator perform the ceremony, where is the truth to be found? This is the place that boasts in huge neon letters of Nudes on Ice and Trained Orangutans and just down the street, a fake volcano erupts with Swiss timing precision every 15 minutes and the busiest star on the strip is Steak and Eggs $2.99. Liberace lived here. So did Howard Hughes. Wayne Newton still does. Liars' poker isn't a game, it's a way of life. This is the town where nobody goes to sleep the same day he woke up, where fools rush in where other fools have been.

Conventioneers wearing baseball caps that declare "Lost Wages" or T-shirts that bemoan the Mustang Ranch has gone belly-up are the constant neighbors of this basketball team. How many other schools have folks such as Frank Sinatra "praying for you cats to go all the way" or Helen Reddy singing the National Anthem amid an indoor fireworks storm before their games? How many others have a giant white shark hanging from the ceiling, the trademark towel hanging lifeless in its menacing jaws? How many schools play before crowds that are peppered with folks who sit regularly on Johnny Carson's couch? The best seats are called Gucci Row and that's where Don Rickles, Diana Ross and all of Tark's Close Personal Friends and Beautiful People gather. You look around the Thomas and Mack Arena and you only wonder why they didn't go all the way and put in mirrored ceilings. Maybe a little video poker in the restrooms would work, too.

Ah, but how they play the game!

After watching his Duke team get shredded in the championship game, Coach Mike Krzyazewski said softly, reverently, "I don't know if I've ever seen that kind of tenacity; it was one of the greatest exhibitions of total defensive domination, maybe ever. They were. . .unbeatable."

Added a man named John Wooden, who has 10 NCAA championships, a former coach of some note: "Their performance against Duke was one of the better ones in the championship I've seen. And I've seen a few."

Now the word is UNLV is even better. The emphasis, of course, is on athleticism, running and jumping. But someone makes the great athletes into great players. Someone herds the motley crew into the framework of a team. Tarkanian ducks from all the rotten tomatoes of abuse everyone throws at him, but when he gets you on the basketball court, you bow in the presence of greatness. He becomes an all-knowing Yoda, one of the great defensive teachers of the game. And you understand where the players get all that tenacity.

But hey — Tark's used to playing defense. He's one of the great rebounders ever.

"Winning wasn't sweet revenge; it was just sweet," he says. "The distractions made us tougher. I learned a long time ago you can't please everybody. All I care about is the game and my kids. You see them play and you can't help but love them. And I know what everyone thinks. But if you expose a kid to college, to the routines of the campus, to the whole experience, he comes away a better person. Even if they never get that almightly piece of paper (a degree), they're better off than they were.

"Some of them surprise you, too. They change their priorities. I was like that when I went to school; I wanted to play ball and party. But I wound up getting a master's degree. I just won't give up on the ones who are confused. I see too much of myself in them a lot of times."

Tarkanian's logic is a good sell. But he gets help from unexpected sources. The sports sociologist, Dr. Harry Edwards, once went to UNLV to study the situation, fully prepared to blister Tarkanian for exploiting children so that he could win basketball games. Instead, Dr. Edwards became a Tark fan.

"It is no worse at UNLV than most and better than many," Edwards said. "You have to use a different yardstick — he takes the athletes no one else wants. . . You're not going to turn it around overnight. One day they've got no grades, the next day they aren't going to be Phi Beta Kappas. I say it's better they trade their basketball skills for that than being on the street, where they're going to knock you and me over the head."

Edwards said Tarkanian is perpetually in hot water because "he falls in love with his players and he'll do anything for them. He tries not to break rules. But then an inner-city kid comes in with teeth so bad it looks like someone set off a hand grenade in his mouth.

NCAA rules say you can't help him get them fixed. Tarkanian may let common sense overrule the NCAA."

Bob Knight is a friend; so is Jud Heathcote, Saturday's enemy coach. Tarkanian has many admirers among his peers. And despite the long rap sheet, things do seem to be getting better. Players are even graduating. In fact, they're graduating at a higher rate than the national average. Tarkanian contends accurately if he got the kind of students that Notre Dame and Harvard get, all his players would graduate. There'd be no jokes about changing the nickname to the Run-In Rebels. And the NCAA would go absolutely insane with boredom.

"But I take some chances," Tarkanian says. "I really think I couda helped Lloyd Daniels if he didn't get messed up with drugs. I tried about the same time to recruit a kid who was in reform school for armed robbery. Hell of a player, rebounder who'd run all day for you. He didn't make it either. But they deserved the chance. That's what I'm saying. They deserve the chance to try."

Yeah, you can tell the pathetically sad story of Richie Adams, a former UNLV player, now serving time in Riker's Island for sticking a pistol in the face of a woman at an automatic bank machine and demanding money. Adams wasn't hard to find, police said later. The victim described the robber as "about 6-foot-10, having no front teeth and wearing a UNLV sweatshirt."

Like the Daniels' fiasco, some of the gambles fail. Tarkanian admits that and he says whenever it happens, the program gets blamed. It's not such big news when someone like Sidney Green, a former Detroit Piston now playing for the San Antonio Spurs, goes back to UNLV and gets his degree in his off-season. Nobody cares about the positives at UNLV unless it's a drug-test result. The Rebels make news when one of them checks out of a hotel and doesn't pay for the movie he watched in his room or reimburses the mini-bar for macadamia nuts he took.

"We don't have any rocket scientists maybe, but we don't have ax murderers either," Tarkanian says.

The coach shakes his head. Ever hear of Shawn Kemp, he asks. Plays for Seattle in the NBA now, used to be at Kentucky until all hell broke loose there.

"He applied to come to UNLV. We couldn't accept him. He

couldn't get in here but he got in somewhere else. We would have been a pretty good team last year with Shawn Kemp. Lloyd Daniels was a big risk, but Syracuse, St. John's, Kansas all were willing to take the same chance I was. But because we got Las Vegas on our shirts, we're singled out. Stacey Augmon wore a shirt that said USA and everyone cheered and waved American flags at him. He came home and put on one that said UNLV and they booed. That's what I'm talking about."

Probation for this current bunch of Rebels would have been unfair. It would have been like someone moving into an apartment and discovering the power won't be turned on until someone pays the bill the last tenant left behind. Tarkanian says he has better players this year than last. In January, a 7-foot transfer becomes eligible. The epidemic of "distractions" of last year that ranged from chicken pox to suspensions for punching out the coach of an opposing team to those ominous visits — nine in 10 months by the NCAA scratch-and-sniff squad — won't repeat themselves, Tarkanian insists.

"I got great kids, kids willing to make commitments. All that stuff going on last year and we won 21 of our last 22 games. You saw us. We put on a hell of a show. We played the Russian national team last month; their coach told me he was impressed with our style and discipline. We got a lot of heart and I just wish people would take us for what we are and not get hung up with false images and reputations we don't deserve."

The round peg in a round hole. If a man can overlook the six bare-chested women in glittering Statue of Liberty costumes and listen to the song "God Bless America," he's a focused person. If he doesn't hear the siren of the slot machines when a big payoff is a hit, if he can't see the danger of leading the weak into such temptaiton for corruption, maybe no blame can be tossed. He says his team is arrogant enough and also talented enough to make you play the game at their pace, at their style. Their Way. Sounds like a Sinatra song. But it's really the Rebel yell of college basketball's most outrageous and outstanding team.

And their coach, Tark the Shark — Is he Don Quixote or Willie Sutton? — just stares at you with those eyes that never seem to blink. The eyes of a mannequin, the eyes of a shark.

363

9.

COLUMNS V

Heroes must beware of fiery 'Rocky'
June 6, 1990

FLORENCE, Italy—At 4:30 in the morning, the new day has not yet bummed a light. At this time, the only people out wandering the cobblestoned streets usually are the homeless and the desperately lost. It is too early for the garbage trucks, and the *puttane* who sell their honor and share their bodies with strangers have all gone home to get some rest.

But somebody in the alley is singing.

"Io non voglio essere solo. Ho un infinita fame d'amore. . ."

From the darkness came a short man, his face like an egg, neither tender nor hard, his thick hair slicked back, not a Presley but a Valentino come back to life, singing what sounded like that most sorrowful country song imaginable.

But the man wasn't wearing any pants.

Only a pair of beige boxer shorts, a white sport coat still fresh and smooth, a white shirt, unbuttoned almost to his navel, shoes that shone like ebony glass and stretch socks pulled high over his calves, like Adrian Dantley used to wear them.

"I burn my pants couple hour ago," the man says. "I hate them; they were no good. I throw them away and set them on fire."

Hell hath no fury like a jilted lover. But when you proclaim yourself the World's Greatest Lover and things turn so sour you can almost hear the nearby church bells toll twice, once for the birth and once for the death of love in the warm Italian night, well, some songs just aren't sad enough.

"I also burn my pants one other time before. When a woman told me we would go to Rio de Janeiro and then we did not," the man says.

And what was the cause of this latest spontaneous combustion?

"I will not talk about it."

Somewhere in the alley is a trash barrel that became a flaming pyre of torched trousers. There may be no better symbol, synthetic or otherwise, for faded love than a polyester meltdown that yields the ashes of a great lover's pants.

"I am fantastic lover; I treat my women so good, very excellent. I treat them like movie star, like a queen. I write them the poems. I send them flowers. I speak six languages. I have a driver's license. I even cook for them if that is what they want. But they must understand something. When it is time for us to be apart, it is time. I cannot wait."

He sticks out his hand. Happy to meet you. He smiles when you ask his name.

"If you are a French woman, I am Rene. American—call me Eric, please, or maybe Matthew. For an Irish woman, I will be Danny Boy. One time I was with Oriental lady, from Hong Kong. Very rich. She called me Rocky.

"The Italian Stallion, huh?"

Then he smiles and says, "My real name is Luca Fiordi."

He shakes his head. He acted in impulse. The pants were almost new. The woman, from England, divorced "only two months," was here on holiday. They had gone out twice. Then tonight, when he called her hotel . . . "like I said, I do not want to talk about it."

Luca has a spare pair of pants in the trunk of his car, a Fiat that is several years old. He says he wants some coffee. There is a place nearby. Open all night.

"You are here for the soccer, right?" he asks, stirring his coffee with his finger.

You explain that this is the biggest sporting event in the world.

Billions of people will watch the games on TV. Billions. There is nothing like the World Cup.

He interrupts and says, "The Italian team has given up sex."

Yeah. A vow of celibacy. They say they want no distractions whatsoever. Nothing can get in the way of their quest to win the Cup. They saw what happened to Mike Tyson, who admitted spending too much time thinking about women and not enough about Buster Douglas.

"They are fools," Luca says, clearing his throat and spitting out his disdain. "I will steal all their women, their wives, their girlfriends, all of them. Especially if they are Italian women."

His confidence is back. Not that it ever wandered very far. Luca waves to the waitress. More coffee, *per favore*. He stares at the middle-aged woman as she approaches. His smile starts innocently, grows into a grin, then as the waitress starts blushing from his flirtatious glances, erupts into a rehearsed laughter that allows all his perfect, straight white teeth to make a standing ovation. He says something in Italian.

As the waitress walks away, looking back once to smile, he says, "Women need to be loved. If their man, their soccer hero, will not love them, then I will."

He yawns. The caffeine will not kick in; it's just too late. Like all great athletes, he needs his sleep.

"Yes, I am an athlete. I dance magnificent. I can ride horses. I ski. I have no fat. And I am fantastic lover."

He still doesn't want to talk about the one that got away. Yet, La Bella Luna works in crazy ways. Maybe tonight she will be back?

"No, never with me again. I am too proud."

Fiordi is not evil or irrational. He just gets a little moonstruck every now and then. If you must blame somebody, blame that woman from Verona who last week left him a sterling silver Zippo lighter on his pillow.

He says he hates it when someone asks if he is a gigolo. He is not. He has few mercenary thoughts, he claims. Everything is in the name of love. His calling in life is to make women happy. He really believes that. He's sensitive, vain, preoccupied, and oh yeah how old are you anyway, Luca?

"I am 33. Very experienced."

And, um, how tall are you?

"What difference does that make?"

You seem short. Maybe 5-foot-2?

"I am 222 centimeters, 5-foot-4 at least."

Narcissism distorts space and time anyway. When you are in love, you also are younger, taller, more beautiful. Besides, as the great philosopher Groucho Marx once said, you are only as old as the girl you feel.

Luca Fiordi does not want to sound unpatriotic but he thinks his countrymen soccer players are "a bunch of crazies. But I also hope they win a lot of games. I am serious. As long as they keep winning the soccer games, the more chance I got at stealing their women."

He pulled out several lire to pay for the coffee. He leaves a nice tip, then writes his phone number on one of the bills and throws that smile at the waitress one more time.

Sometimes La Dolce Vita is about as sweet as a yellow strawberry. Sometimes you can't tell an abstaining soccer player from the world's greatest lover if all you're looking at is the great scoreboard in the sky.

But all the time there is a new day. And more games still to play.

True act of glove allows man to toss aside cares of world and follow baseball's solo flight of fancy
Sept. 18, 1990

The world escapes from view. Nothing but you and the ball. And your glove. When life swamps you a little bit, when you fret that it is not the bean-counters who run the games of sport who are running things, but the bean-counters who play those games, when you ache with the virus that immobilized your youngest son all weekend, when there is a column to write and nothing has strode into the on-deck circle, you know what to do.

On the bed, staring at the ceiling, you enter the stadium of the mind. You caress the baseball. What an exquisite fit, a baseball and a man's hand. Right away you know what to do with it. So you flip it toward the ceiling.

You never hit the ceiling anymore. Are you kidding? That's rookie ball. Over the years you've learned just how much velocity it takes to heave the ball upward in a tantalizing arc, almost scraping the raised red seams against the ceiling, but always allowing it to reach its soaring crescendo unscathed, before plummeting back to earth to the safety of your oldest friend in baseball, your glove.

The Wilson A2000 that has a permanent home in your little cubbyhole office in the basement is eight years younger than you. And the best birthday present ever. There is so much irony in an old glove. With age they become smooth; their users take on creases and wrinkles and squint lines. We seem to head in different directions.

Once upon a time the name "Carl Furillo" was burned into the pocket, beneath the signature. But everything else remains. Particularly the string of leather that bears the teeth marks of a million breathless diamond dramas.

As the ball disappears into the pocket of the glove and it snaps closed, a leathery vise operated by the knowing hands of the dreamer, the process begins. Some call it daydreaming. But that's too vague, too encompassing. It's just a game of catch you play with yourself when you need to clean the cerebral closets of psychic trash and baseball paraphernalia.

The ball goes back toward the ceiling, the practiced, expert toss a monotonous exercise in perfection. And you notice the slight spin, those haunting seams paralyzing the outside world. How many are there? You tried once to count but got confused and quit because that's something a bean-counter would want to know.

You refuse to be so narrow. The baseball is the center of the universe in such moments. The only foul lines are in the corridors of imagination. And all you can think about right now is the slow rotation of the ball as it drops toward you.

A knuckleball. Hoyt Wilhelm. Reggie knocking Charlie Hough's into the center-field bleachers in the World Series.

Jim Bouton.

The cap always flew off Jim Bouton's head, free as the spirit inside the head that tried to wear it. Remember his book—*Ball Four*? Remember his prairie logic; you spend an entire career trying to get a grip on the baseball and then one day you realize it was the other way around all along. There may be no greater truth than that.

It's still gripping Jim Bouton. He's still pitching for somebody, anybody. Senior leagues, city leagues, Stan Musial leagues. And for the right reasons. Years ago Bouton invented Big League Chew, which is bubble gum shredded to make it look like chewing tobacco, the kind the big leaguers jam into their mouth. The invention has made Jim Bouton a wealthy man, a millionaire. So he doesn't have to pitch baseball for money. He can do it for fun.

The ball makes a nice soft pop as it re-enters earth's atmosphere. People say the best baseball sound is the crack of the bat, but any pitcher will tell you it's that pop of the mitt.

Your kids once asked why you still kept the glove. And they were still a little young to understand priceless family heirlooms. So you told them the story of Satchel Paige.

He was 42 when he finally got his chance in the big leagues as Bill Veeck brought him up with the Cleveland Indians in the late 40's. For years you told your children that until you were too old, you would not officially announce your retirement from baseball just yet.

Then 42 was in the rear-view mirror.

Damn, can't lose concentration about such mortal nuisances. That hasn't stopped Nolan Ryan, has it? When you're flat on your back, having a game of catch with yourself, you don't have to play by the rules of the calendar.

Ah, Bill Veeck. Why isn't he in the Hall of Fame? Why isn't Eddie Gaedel's jersey? Gaedel was the midget who, aside from Babe Ruth's called shot, probably enjoyed the most famous at-bat in major-league history. He walked on four pitches—good eye, Eddie. When you're 3-foot-7, your strike zone is about the size of a can of corn.

Remember when a can of corn was an easy fly ball? Remember when you got caught in a pickle, or hot box? Rundown doesn't have nearly the lovely charm. And remember your first pair of spikes, and the way you folded the toe just so, just like the big leaguers?

Somehow you don't feel so bad anymore. The fever seems down. The problems of the world are back at arm's length. You're drifting . . .

Oh no. The column. The guys at the newspaper are waiting for it. Your boss will be calling anytime now. You'd better get up, go to work and write a column.

But the feel of your hand inside the glove, warm and friendly, lingers. And that ball, nestled so preciously in your other hand.

Sorry, folks, no column today. I hope you understand.

World has passed them by, but, say, is there anybody who plays basketball not from around here?
Feb. 8, 1991

GAFFNEY, N.C. — There was nobody at the cash register in the little service station in the piney woods. There were plenty of live bait and girlie magazines and milk and beer and those frozen burritos that always seem like such a good idea late at night but usually suggest otherwise by morning. But no hired hands in sight.

The wrong turn that got us off the main highway hadn't been all bad. The little twisting two-lanes cut through the mountains and forced a gentle pace. And it was nice seeing all the mailboxes on the side of the road with a yellow ribbon on every one. The road seemed safer.

But now I needed to pay for my gas and get on down the road. To Charlotte, the big city. I walked around back, and there they were. Two men shooting hoops at a rim and backboard nailed to a wall.

"Sorry, sir. Didn't hear you."

I blinked. Two men, but the same face. Twins.

"I'm Earl. This here's Eugene. Bet you can't guess who's oldest."

371

They don't wait for my answer. Earl is, by seven minutes. Sorry about the delay, Earl says. Not many customers during the winter.

"We pass the time playing H-O-R-S-E, one-on-one, stuff like that."

Their father, Herm Mayfield, used to work at the same service station. Assistant manager. Back before the interstates stole away all the business. He and the boss man, Junior, manned the place. This used to be a service station. Got that—service.

"That was awhile ago," I say.

Gene points, "See that antique drink box in the corner? Old-fashioned one, where you lift a top and could help yourself to the Nu-Grapes, Nehi Orange, Royal Crown. Those old boxes used to keep 'em cold, too.

"Well, our father used to keep a baby alligator in the box. Got it from some guy, who got it down in Florida. He put ol' Honest Ed in there to stop the folks from helping themselves when nobody was looking. Lots of times, either Dad or Junior'd have their head under some hood or something. They lost a lot of soft drinks until Honest Ed got to be about 3 feet long, and he wasn't scary no more. He was flat dangerous."

Times have changed, they add. It used to be every kid around here wanted to work on cars and drive fast, like Richard Petty or some of the other NASCAR big boys.

"Now everyone's into basketball. They all want to be Michael Jordan. Even me and Earl. Hey—you ever play?"

"I'm here for the NBA All-Star weekend. I'm a sportswriter."

"For real?"

"Yeah. That Jordan's something special, isn't he?"

"Wilmington. That's where he's from. I saw him when he played for the Heels at Chapel Hill. Almost got his autograph once," Eugene says.

Earl frowns. Not even close.

"He froze. Jordan walked right by him. He just stared," Earl says. "Eugene, you're just like those jerks down at Western Sizzlin' telling everyone Sleepy Floyd and Akeem Olajuwon came in there to eat once. You gotta have proof."

Earl tells about Ray Isom, a traffic cop who once gave Richard Petty a speeding ticket. He then told Petty he was going to tear it up. But he had it framed. It's on his living room wall. Now that's proof.

"Hey, mister, is James Worthy in the All-Stars? He's from Gastonia, you know. That's only about 20 miles from here."

They have an alligator thirst for the game. I tell them about the three-point shootout, the slam-dunk contest, the Legends game. The Big O is going to be there, Rick Barry, David Thompson . . .

"David Thompson? He's from Shelby. That's about five minutes from here."

"That's my name."

"David Thompson?"

"No, Shelby."

"For real? Now ain't that a small world."

And we shake hands. This little spot in the woods doesn't get much business anymore. The interstates came, and Junior and Herm sold out. Earl and Eugene work part-time and practice their jumpers.

Basketball in the Carolinas. Small world, indeed.

10.

FAMILY

Holding hands an hour, remembering the Star of Christmas
Dec. 24, 1988

"Won't you please just sit and hold hands with me this Christmas Eve, just for an hour, and let's listen to the world."

And The Old Cracker Woman, which is what my grandmother used to call herself, would take me and my brother out to the little porch and sit us on her lap and get the old wooden rocking chair going just right, where it'd creak gently, comfortably and we'd take in the sights and sounds and smells of a not-so-silent Florida night.

My brother and I always used to hate that hour.

It was corny, sitting and listening and trying to hear crickets and frogs and armadillos skittering in the palmetto bushes. The smell of orange blossom was strong and it was hard to detect anything else. Unless it was the pungent odor of burning cypress wood. And since it was dark, we couldn't see anything anyway.

Her real name was Laura but we'd always called her Nana, and my brother liked to tease her and call her Banana. And she always laughed so hard she jiggled all over.

Christmas in Florida wasn't what Currier and Ives had in mind. Picture, if you can, a world with no chimneys. Santa Claus used to ride a surfboard ashore every year and hand out bars of surf wax to all the kids who'd been good. That wouldn't inspire any Hummel plates. Snow? That was like a one-horse sleigh. The stuff of dreams. This was what Christmas in Florida was.

Nana said Florida really did have snow. And she'd get out the ladder and we'd go up on the roof. There was nothing there except patches of rusty orange pine needles that fell from the huge Australian pines that shimmered overhead.

"Florida snow," she said, slowly revving up her grin until it reached jiggle stage once more.

"Imagination," she'd say. "Christmas is all around us. If you let it. When I was young, we'd sit on the porch and hold hands and try to hear silver bells. Back then the mosquitoes were so thick there would be this loud hum and you really had to try hard. But we always heard the bells."

She was a hard woman, a worker all her life. A widow for 20 years. She didn't like the idea of toys for Christmas. She thought toys were frivolous. It was fine to exchange gifts — "In honor of the baby Jesus," she'd say — but make them practical. Nana used to give us kids clothes. One time she gave Bibles. Lots of times, we'd pull away plain white wrapping paper ("All those bright colors don't seem right") to find a book on trees. Or animals.

On Christmas Day, the last present usually opened was the one from Nana.

My Dad, her son, told me he got a red wagon for Christmas one year, the first toy he ever owned. Next Christmas, his present was the same wagon with a blue paint job. In her mind's eye, explained my father, "It was like a new toy."

He explained that the Great Depression was in full stride then and money was scarce and he couldn't remember how many nights in a row dinner was the same fish and grits specialty of the house. But, my father added, "She is just stuck in her ways. She grew up in a different world, a different Florida than you boys."

And as my brother and I got older, each Christmas Eve, she took us farther and farther into the Florida woods during our hour rocking on the porch. She'd pick up a carambola fruit, cut a cross-section and we'd behold a star apple.

"This is God's way of letting Floridians know it's Christmas," she'd say, offering us a bite of the delicious fruit. "See the star? Remember the star."

The shrubby pomegranate and the leafy green banana tree and the breadfruit and the lychee nuts put a tropical glaze on Christmas. What about something red?

"How about a snapper? Or a red bird? Or a hibiscus?"

The Old Cracker Woman told us stories not of partridges in pear trees but of someone's runaway parrot that used to hang out in the mangrove swamp, screeching the essence of yuletide carols to the night. She broke open a sand dollar once and she told us the legend of the seven doves of peace inside. And we remembered that time she pulled down a handful of Spanish moss and ran her thumbnail against it, peeling away the outer layer to the thick, black cord beneath.

"Indian hair," she'd say softly, her eyes dancing with mischief. And we'd try to figure if it could possibly be true. The wide eyes of children were her favorite stepping stones. A young chest thumping with excitement was accompaniment to her songs of freedom. She'd turn over a horseshoe crab and the ugly underbelly with wiggly tentacle legs scared us. And she said God had a reason for making something so ugly. But He has never explained why.

"Like an avocado," she'd say. "Why is the seed so big?"

And she'd start jiggling once more.

When I was 11, she took me shrimping. The lantern and the big long net and the bait bucket were all we needed, she'd say. And we'd go to some secret place that only she knew about, a little wooden bridge that seemed a million miles away. And we stayed all night. And we brought back almost 1,000 shrimp. And I never had so much fun working.

"Working? That was playing," she said. "Those were toys we played with. Working is cleaning all those shrimp we got."

And she smiled and walked to her room, holding a back that had stiffened on her.

She was the one who taught us about the stone crab and how you can pull one of its claws off and throw the crab back in the water and it will rejuvenate and actually grow a new claw. But don't yank both off. It kills the crab. She taught my mother how to make key lime pie from scratch. Once my father rented an airboat and we all went sailing across the grassy inland swamps and saw all kinds of birds and flowers and creatures we'd never seen. But Nana could name them all. And when we spotted a big bull gator sunning on a fallen cabbage palm, Nana started making this scratchy sound with her throat and the alligator turned its head and its big red eyes flashed on us and my father made the airboat roar and there was a great fantail of water flying as we made our laughing escape.

The thing about human nature is eventually things that were foreign and hated suddenly become wonderful and fascinating. But then they also become taken for granted. My brother and I spent less and less time with The Old Cracker Woman. Like her lap, the woods started shrinking. Paradise was going the way of the surfboard, becoming more streamlined and also smaller. Pot bales started floating to shore. Time-sharing condos started blotting out the view of the banyan trees. Oil slicks ruined the oyster beds. Nobody hardly ever saw a crane anymore. The clams weren't as sweet as they used to be. Nobody had brought in a really big trout in years.

And Nana had cancer.

At first, it wasn't so bad. She could still tell stories of sea turtles laying their eggs and make you feel right there on the dunes with them. She could still sing the old Baptist hymns she loved. And she could still laugh until she jiggled all over. But then she'd start coughing. And she couldn't stop and someone would run and get a drink of water.

One day my mother went to visit her in the hospital and she'd written out her recipe for conch salad. She'd never told anyone how to make it and we all thought she'd take it to her grave.

I brought her a hibiscus blossom and pinned it in her hair, what was left of it. She struck a pose and said, "Betty Grable, eat your heart out." But when she started to laugh, her eyes suddenly closed and her teeth gritted from the pain inside.

My brother and I made her a Christmas wreath—with a lot of motherly help—of pine boughs, with sea shells and sea grapes decorating it. In the middle, on a piece of plain white paper, I wrote the word, "Imagination."

And she smiled weakly and said, "Been shrimping lately?"

A week later, it was Christmas Eve and there was a big dance party at a friend's house. The whole gang was going to be there. Including my girlfriend.

I was at least an hour late.

We sat in the hospital room, holding hands on Christmas Eve, that Old Cracker Woman and me. There was no rocker but it was a Florida Christmas anyway. There was the story of the hideous moray eel and its pointy teeth. And describing how to smoke a mullet and how poisonous the beautiful bougainvillea bush is. And how to make your own gig and how to throw a cast net. There were a couple of times when we hummed songs together. Old Baptist hymns. And even though I was the one doing all the talking this time, and even though her eyes were glazed over from all the medication, and even though she had a tube in both her arms, she still told me all the beautiful things there are to tell about family and Christmas. With her imagination.

The next morning, leaning up against a wall, was a present for me.

A shrimp net with a red bow around it. At last, a toy from Nana.

We never made it back out to that secret spot though. She never got well enough. And now, 20 years after we put her in the Florida ground she loved so much, imagination isn't so necessary. Living in Michigan, there are snow and sleighs and toasty fireplaces and plenty of avenues for Santa.

But tonight, just before it gets dark, my children and I are going to hold hands just for one hour. And we'll all listen as I tell them stories of The Old Cracker Woman from my Florida childhood. And yeah—we'll remember the star of Christmas.

Mom always batted cleanup
TODAY, Cocoa, Fla.

It was a sound that shall never go away. The sloshing noise of the washing machine was like a siren going off to my 11-year-old ears. Disaster was imminent.

My jeans were in the washer, dirt caked on each knee, as usual. And precious — no, priceless baseball cards were in the right rear pocket. One of the more monumental trades in the history of the neighborhood was about to become a soggy wad of sloop.

Mickey Mantle, Warren Spahn, Ernie Banks. Soon to become indistinguishable, illegible, worthless. All because of a frivolous error of omission.

The panic was so real, the disappointment so looming. A month of negotiation, 20 cards of lesser significance and several days' lunch money were undoubtably being washed away.

I ran full speed through the house, screaming, demanding the cursed Maytag be stopped. I slid on my knees, pulled open the washer door, dumped both hands into the hot, soapy water and began groping for my jeans.

"Are you looking for these?" asked my mother, reaching into the sanitary pocket of her sterilized housecoat, and pulling out the baseball cards.

It was the first time I ever kissed her without being asked.

Good ol' Mom. Steady, dependable, covered a lot of ground. Batted clean-up. Sacrificed a lot. Great team player. She'd have made one hell of a shortstop.

Which, of course, she was. It was during the time I was infatuated with the notion of becoming another Nellie Fox. I always wanted to be a second baseman. But before I got up the courage to ask Dad to work with me on the double play, I asked Mom. She became Luis Aparicio.

The routine was simple. My brother would tap a ground ball to my mother. She'd scoop it up and flip it kind of ladylike to the vicinity of the dish towel we used for second base. I would try to catch the ball, drag my foot across the rag bag and throw to my brother, in Nellie's image. By then, he had discarded the bat, picked up his glove and transformed from hitter to first baseman with only

380

a twinkling of imagination. It was 6–4–3, if anyone was keeping score.

My throws were awful, my form ridiculous. More often than not, the dish towel would get tangled in my rubber cleats and I'd trip. My throw, already off balance, would go straight down and bounce inches from where I soon collapsed.

Whenever that happened, the shortstop became a mother again. First aid, sympathy, whatever was needed. She wasn't a good athlete, only a good sport. But Dad liked sports and Mom was Dad's wife. This was back in the days when ERA meant earned run average and Title IX didn't mean anything. What it really meant was the TV game of the week took precedence over the romantic movie she loved as a kid. It meant sitting with the family, folding socks or underwear, reading a magazine and occasionally asking who was winning and what was the score.

Mom managed the clubhouse. The team came first. She wanted it that way.

There was the time I decided to chew tobacco in Little League. Nellie Fox chews it, I argued. No deal. I knew it was futile. I'd secretly experimented with a chaw once. It was awful. So I found a substitute.

Turtle food.

It looked like tobacco, smelled bad enough to be tobacco and, if mixed with gum, formed a nice semi-lump that made my cheek stick out. Just like Nellie's.

An hour before gametime, Mom discovered my intentions. She laughed at the thought of turtle food being in my mouth. Then she fretted. Then she suggested the magical qualities of Tootsie Roll as an alternative. Wad up one of those babies, slip it in and . . . perfect.

I jumped on my bike, making allowance for the extra ballast crammed into my disjointed jaw. I almost didn't hear the stern warning, "I'd better not hear of you doing any spitting."

Then, as always, she added, "And have a good time, honey."

There was always a special meal that had to be cooked because someone had an early game and someone else a later one. There was only one way to put an ouchless bandage on a skinned knee. And only Mom knew how to do it.

There was only one Mom.

I don't remember if I always told her thanks for playing hurt so often, for supplying emergency sew jobs and last-second pep talks. Or if I always told her I appreciated the uniforms, which were always clean, the bleacher support, which was always positive and the coaching, which was always by the rules.

I think I forgot to do all these things because I thought Mom was like Lou Gehrig and would always be in the lineup. But it's been 15 years now since I realized nothing is forever.

It is a fine day to brag about mothers. I just did.

Now, it's your turn.

Throw of long ago wedged in history
Dec. 25, 1987

"What'd you get?

"These shoulder pads. A microscope. Some clothes."

"I got this helmet."

"I got a bike. And a new bat. Yogi Berra."

All around the group, the same questions. Christmas Day. What were the gifts of Christmas? We had to know. A bunch of kids in a big back yard. Getting ready to play football. Soon as enough showed up.

Just a snatch of time in a lifetime. Three, maybe four years. Just kids, from my brother, who was 8, up to James Poe, the bully, who was 13. Sometimes a lot of us, sometimes not so many. Rarely were the sides even.

That's where my brother came in. He was, umm . . . little. A runt even for an 8-year-old. And when it came time to pick sides, he would squirm. He already was figuring the teams, the sides, how many and who's left. No doubt he would be the last picked. Or would he?

Our dog had developed this peculiar and annoying habit of running beside whoever had the football. And nipping at the cuff of his jeans. And sometimes causing the ball carrier to trip and fall. This feat was, of course, something my brother would never be able to accomplish. And for the past several games, when the sides were evenly numbered, alas — my brother was banished while a canine replacement filled the last spot on the roster.

Yet this particular Christmas Day, he was determined not only to play, but to excel. To be the star. And he had a bright red jersey to accentuate his dream.

"Oklahoma," he announced to the naive and uneducated. "It's just like the kind Oklahoma wears. Except it doesn't have a number. My mom said she would make me one, though."

The gazes of admiration made him grow at least several inches in stature. Because not only was he wearing a new football jersey, but also a semi-new helmet.

In fact, my old helmet.

See, I had a new one. White with green and orange stripes and a double bar of the finest plastic available through Montgomery Ward. The chin strap was real leather and everyone knows what a great smell that can be. And it was smooth; nobody chewed on it yet. It was hours old. Fresh off the sleigh. When you put on a helmet like that, strap up and look in the mirror . . . well, there's just something about a man in uniform.

Although Darwinism had little to do with it, the sight of the new helmet that so excited me had a similar effect on my brother. In a twinkling, ownership had evolved. My old helmet was now his.

But that old helmet, hey, it had taken me through a lot of wars. Big games. I remember when I got it. Gold, the colors of Louisiana State. With the number 20, the number of Billy Cannon, my favorite player, painted above each ear hole. And a homemade face mask, a single bar of wood, whittled and sanded and then screwed onto the helmet by my father, who also scripted the numbers. It was a long time ago in a small town in Florida and the helmets in the sporting goods stores did not have face masks. My father's handicraft vaulted me into a special spotlight. The envy of the neighborhood, for a while. Then everyone had a helmet with a face mask.

Except my brother, of course.

But that was two Christmases ago. I was older, more mature;

383

after all, 11½ is a huge pivotal point in a man's lifetime. And I needed change. I needed a new helmet. And now I had one. And my brother had one too.

The big game on Christmas Day was not an exhibition. There was nothing frivolous about it. It was football, hard-nosed and bitterly contested. And you know how that goes. There may not be a bigger event until Little League season.

The Florida Christmas is not the easiest to notice. Snow, as far as we knew, did not exist. The only one of us who had seen it was the guy who used to live in Boston. And he talked so funny, nobody ever believed a word he said anyway. On Christmas Day, most of the time at least, the sun shone. Sometimes bright enough to make the aluminum, mildew-free Frosty the Snowman on our garage gleam with majestic brilliance. Other times, just a dull humid glow that forced the neighborhood to purr with the sound of window air conditioners. And that snowman turned into just a shadow of its former self.

But on the day I got my new helmet, it had rained. There were puddles. And mud.

"This is neat," I thought, splashing through a post pattern while someone lobbed a semi-spiral in my direction. The pass was a bit long but I never hesitated diving. The delightful landing was compounded by a slide of ecstasy. Glorious mud.

Already, before the opening kickoff, I was dirty. Normally, nobody would consider a lunge or dive. Not with the nests of green sticker burrs that decorated the yard like a minefield. In reflection, the games were not exactly macho affairs. Arm tackles were the norm. It was nothing to see someone carrying the ball and three or four of us along. There once was one of us who made a diving tackle. And wound up with a broken collarbone. And a scar.

We called him Frankenstein after that.

"All right, we got 12 here," someone said. "Let's choose."

There was a rainbow effect in the group. Helmets, jerseys, shoulder pads, some football pants but mostly jeans. Tennis shoes, either black or white. All high-tops.

"Who's captain?"

"First pick, I got first pick."

"How come? You got first pick last week."

"But you got first pick last Christmas."

Somehow, the rationing of talent began. The fact someone was your best friend could taint your judgment. You'd pick him instead of someone better. Hey, that was one of the determinations for best friendmanship in the first place.

It didn't dawn on me at first what was happening. I never thought about it until it was too late.

Then I realized I would have last pick.

The dilemma: My dog or my brother? What price victory?

Hey, it was Christmas. My brother's eyes danced with joy as I declared him my final draft pick. If he had had a tail, he would have wagged it.

My dog wagged hers, anyway.

The game began with the usual counting of potatoes to see who kicked off. Then the surprise. A real kicking tee had been made in shop class by the older brother of a member of the opposing team. At first there was an argument over whether to allow both teams equal access to the tee. There was something suddenly primitive about ever using a pile of dirt again to hold the ball in place. Another checkpoint in the road rally to adulthood? Nah — just sticking up for your rights.

The game was a classic. Actually, a close game. Some of the plays were ingenious. The triple flea-flicker with the standard hook-and-ladder option worked as well in execution as it looked drawn up on the sandy floor of the huddle. I had, as captain, naturally appointed myself quarterback. And some of my passes actually spiraled more than wobbled.

One time I was forced out of my pocket, consisting of the fat guy who always played center and my brother, who was told to stay along the line as a decoy. Suddenly finding myself in the open field, the goal line beckoning, I ran to daylight, fame and everlasting glory only a few strides away. I never saw my dog.

The tackle was nothing special. Again, a simple mongrel nip at the heels. A loss of balance. But while I fell, all I could think of was how I should have thrown family loyalty into the dumpster. I should have picked my dog. That way I could have leashed her to the big palm tree. And I could have scored.

But the passion of competition soon overcame my disappointment and second-guessing. Too swiftly, I switched from offense to defense, from QB to DE. The game raged for at least an hour more, with neither side able to stop the other consistently.

"Trial hike," I bellowed, swallowing my pride. This always brought a storm of protest, especially since the fat guy never made a mistake in centering the ball. In fact, the move was little more than another opportunity to flex my authority. I was the damn quarterback, Christmas Day, 1950-something.

In the late afternoon, when the sense of fatigue and boredom was mounting and the hunger for Christmas dinner began barking on both sides of the line of scrimmage, it was decided the next touchdown would win the game. This is how most pickup football games are decided.

I nodded, along with my team. After all, we had the ball.

In such circumstances, the three-complete-for-a-first-down rules are waived. As are any notions of running the ball. It became bomb's away until somebody connected.

"OK, here's what we'll do. . ."

"Throw it to me down the middle."

"No me, I can beat my man on the left. Pump fake. I'll button-hook, then take off."

"Shaddup. I'm the quarterback."

I assigned all sorts of pass routes, involving vectors of strategy that air-traffic controllers might only dream about.

"On two," I said as the huddle broke.

Then I spotted my brother. He had not complained. Playing had been enough for him. To be a part. That was all that counted. His shoulder pads were much too big, but he had stuffed several beach towels into the gap, solving the rotation of pads and also making him look rather beastly.

The helmet, my helmet but now his, still looked good, I decided. The scratches and missing paint gave it a heroic glow, the battle scars of a warrior. But the wooden bar across the front . . . well, it drooped.

The screws had come loose and the bar had shifted several inches south and it swiveled up and down whenever my brother ran. With his terry-cloth build and lack of stature, he looked like a tub of laundry suddenly possessed with a mind of its own. But the Oklahoma red and the LSU gold were sobering reminders. Somewhere inside and somewhere off into the future, there was a football player lurking.

As we walked to the line of scrimmage, I whispered to him, "Be ready. I might throw it to you if nobody else is open."

Like I said, it was Christmas.

He nodded, twisted his chin strap back and forth and pushed at the face bar until it was almost eye level again.

"Hut one . . . hut two."

Oh what a lovely concert football is. The snap and the response to action. The collisions. The artistry. The dog charging through, tongue flapping, saliva flying, teeth bared.

I held my elbow just right, cocked perfectly, my right hand spreading wide, then wider. The laces felt wonderful as I perched the ball behind my ear and sought a receiver.

And the pass was my finest ever. It might scrape a cloud, I feared. I surely had overthrown everyone. It would land in the street, in the ocean, on some distant shore. The ball rose with a majestic grunt and hissed in the warm December sky. Not a rainbow, but a missile launch. Lift-off. Nearby Cape Canaveral was the symbol then of exploration, of conquest and victory. My pass would be picked up by NASA on radar. First ball on the moon.

I watched along with the defender who had tried to distract me with his falsetto screams and waving arms. It seemed an hour before the ball began a downward arc. The world, I was sure, would never be the same again.

One of my receivers reached for it and the ball continued its scorching journey, unmolested.

Then a defender tried for the interception. But failed in like manner. Also unable to lay a finger on it.

And the gloom of the apparent incompletion had already materialized. Because I never saw what happened.

"He caught it."

"What? Who?"

"Your brother. He caught the ball."

"Who? My brother? How?"

Everyone ran into the end zone, where my brother, still lying on the grass, was yelling. "Yeah, I did it. We win. Yeah. Oklahoma. Yeah."

Only his voice was muffled.

First there were the shoulder pads. They had heaved upward, lifted beyond my brother's neck, jaw and mouth. And upon impact with the ground, the pads succeeded in making it appear a person with no neck was prone in a muddy hamlet.

The helmet and that rascal face bar had become disjointed and slapped upward. The chin strap had snapped. One of my brother's ears had become pinned in the ear hole, an extremely painful predicament. While the pass was in flight and his equipment began failing, my brother had looked up, become disoriented, lost his balance and fallen backward. The face bar had slipped again, this time looping downward and locking up upon impact with the shoulder pads.

And the ball arrived.

And stuck in the helmet. Point first.

Had his head not turned from the pain of the jammed ear, the ball might have struck his nose and bounced incomplete. Instead, he formed a perfect resting place, a human manger of sorts, for this descending star from the sky. A miracle on the day that specialized in such things.

An argument broke out concerning the validity of the touchdown and how much manufactured help my brother had received on his way to becoming a hero. I noticed the subtle appearance of my dog upon the scene. Still lying down, the ball still wedged into his face, my brother giggled as the dog licked his one good ear and tickled whatever portion of face that could be reached.

The epitome of sport, I thought. The sweet, innocent song of Christmas.

And, of course, the original version of the Immaculate Reception.

Breathe, Baby, Please Breathe
June 13, 1982 St. Petersburg Times

Kenny Strother, oblivious to anything symbolic, looked at the small cake with the solitary candle, and tried to mash it with his hand. Everyone laughed. He was hamming it up, smiling and waving his arms and playing peek-a-boo with himself. Making the unintelligible sounds all babies do. Sitting in his high chair and staring at the crowd around him, the guest of honor was confused by all the attention. He loved it. Every gurgle or grunt brought a roar from the crowd of friends and relatives around him.

None of them was thinking about the time there was a sterile, plastic tube running down his nose and into his lungs. I was, though. I remembered when a machine kept him alive. And that's why, while everyone else was laughing and acting silly, I stared at the candle on the cake and hoped it wouldn't go out. I couldn't help it. The memories are still too new . . .

———

"You're going to have your baby tonight," the doctor told my wife, Kim. We weren't prepared; the baby wasn't due. Not for at least another month. Yet, whatever it is that makes babies get born when they do wasn't going to wait for us to pack the suitcase and bone up on the Lamaze book and let the boss know I wouldn't be in for work the next day and leisurely receive a new baby.

No big deal, we said, shrugging. Our other son had come three weeks ahead of schedule. Who cares if this one wanted to squirm into the world five weeks early?

For a while, nobody did. We even joked about it. "A Whine Before Its Time," I announced in mock seriousness as we drove to the hospital.

As the clock in the birthing room at the hospital in Cocoa Beach wound past midnight, the contractions got closer and more intense and my wife groaned and panted and tried to remember her breathing techniques. It went fast, faster than before. A few minutes

389

before 3 in the morning of May 19th, 1981, this gorgeous blob of blood and mucus and human being popped into existence.

A boy.

The doctor, my wife and I all laughed and cried and shook hands and kissed and praised each other for a great natural childbirth. And talked about getting some sleep.

I left to make some phone calls, letting relatives and friends know of our good news.

But while our new son — Kenneth Jack Strother — lay on Mamma's stomach, going through the bonding process of mother and son, she noticed his chest lurching, heaving in and out. Instead of the normal whimpers and sighs, the baby was grunting. Gasping.

The agony began.

He was taken from my wife and put in an incubation unit. For observation, then for tests. Six hours passed. My wife should have been sleeping; she couldn't. I stood at the window of the incubation unit and stared at my son and watched his rib cage heave in and out. He should have been sleeping; he couldn't.

My wife and I were afraid to talk. He looks fine to me, I lied. She nodded and said she wasn't too worried. Another lie.

Finally, some news. Our pediatrician, who had been on call at the hospital that night, walked in. He was frank with us. He suspected our son had been born with a respiratory problem called Hyaline Membrane Disease. It's a common problem with premature babies. The lungs weren't fully developed yet. Sacs inside them, which secrete a fluid called surfactant that allows the lungs to open and close easily, weren't producing yet. Without the fluid lubricating the lungs, the reflex of breathing was as difficult as trying to blow up a wet balloon.

The doctor likened it to trying to breathe underwater through a very long straw. I nodded. I mentioned an old cowboy movie I'd seen where Alan Ladd had slipped by the Indians by breathing through reeds in the river.

"This is a little more severe," he said solemnly.

The problem was easy to understand. Our newborn son wasn't strong enough to force his lungs to work for very long.

The doctor said there was a better place for him to be than Cape Canaveral Hospital. There were special wards called neonatal intensive care units set up specifically for premature babies. There were several of these places around the state. Calls were being made.

"Your son is not in any life-threatening situation right now," the doctor said. But the look on his face told us something had to be done fast.

The closest place was in Orlando. But it was filled. Medical centers in Pensacola and Tampa luckily did have room. Our pediatrician recommended Tampa. A special transport unit would come and take our baby there, he said.

"You'll feel better when you meet these people and see how special they are," he added.

The transport team arrived and immediately began to prepare our son for the trip. I could only watch from a distance. For two hours they worked, stabilizing his vital signs, getting him ready to safely make a 145-mile trip. There were four of them, counting the driver of the modified ambulance with the special equipment for the special passengers.

They pushed our son into the room where we'd been waiting. My wife was ragged. She'd delivered a child eight hours earlier. We were numb, all cried out.

One of the crew smiled and pointed out Kenny was larger—five pounds, seven ounces—than a lot of premature babies.

"That's a big plus in his favor," she added.

Then she asked us to kiss him for good luck.

"Please reassure him. Let him know you're not afraid and he shouldn't be either."

I know babies don't have such capabilities at the age of eight hours. But I eagerly walked over to the bubble-top configuration where our son was strapped. I bent over the table and grimaced when I saw the tube going through his nose and down his throat and into his lungs. I flinched when I saw wires and electrodes attached to his chest and arms and legs. I looked back at the transport crew team, confused.

"Please don't worry about the way he looks now. It's really not as bad as it looks. Most of the wires are only monitors so we can watch his vital signs."

One of the other transport crew members nudged me and said, "Please be confident. Your baby's going to be all right."

I smiled and wanted to believe them. Then I bent over and kissed my son's forehead and hoped I wasn't saying goodbye.

The neonatal intensive care ward is on the second floor at Tampa General Hospital. Room 240-B. There's a sign that has neat stenciled lettering: "No Visitors Except Parents of Patients." Visitors have to wash and scrub their hands with high concentrate surgical soap, then put surgical gowns on over their street clothes.

We washed and dressed and pushed open the double doors andwalked in.

Futuristic machines were everywhere. You'd have thought you were in the blockhouse for the Shuttle launch. We later found out NASA had designed and developed a lot of the equipment in this 240-B at Tampa General. With buzzers and alarms and the steady drone of machines perking our ears, my wife and I walked past each station looking for our son.

I counted 12 babies in the ward. Ours was at station No. 9. We were relieved he'd survived the trip.

My wife noticed a piece of construction paper stuck on one of the machines with tape. There was a drawing of a clown and a space ship on it. And the message, "Hello, my name is Kenneth Jack Strother and I'm from Cape Canaveral."

It was our first clue to the atmosphere of 240-B at Tampa General. We smiled when we saw the sign someone had taken the time to make.

The smiles faded quickly. He looked no better; his chest was still heaving.

"Hello," said someone from behind. "My name is Linda and I'll be the nurse in charge of getting your baby well."

She wore the basic blue uniform and white sneakers of the intensive care worker. Her hair was short. She looked neither young nor old. She spoke swiftly, confidently. The best thing was she smiled as she talked.

"I'll be glad to answer any questions you have at any time, unless there's an emergency and I'm needed at another station," she added, still smiling.

I looked around and saw an intravenous feeding rack, a sinewy tube reaching from a bottle of sugar water into my son's arm. Ugly. I saw some of this space-age machinery flashing numbers that meant nothing to me. Confusing. Mainly I saw that little chest heaving up and down. Agonizing. Yes, I had plenty of questions.

For the next several hours, my wife and I picked the nurse's brain, learning all about Hyaline Membrane Disease. She never hesitated to answer, never seemed to grow tired.

The ward is staffed with uncommon compassion 24 hours a day. Nurses work eight-hour shifts. Well, they get paid for eight hours; usually the one getting off duty sticks around an extra hour or so to brief her replacement. And be with her patients.

There's also a doctor pulling the same duty.

If we chose, my wife and I could have stayed around the clock with our son. If we left, we could call and get an update. If there was some significant change — good or bad — someone would call us.

We brought along a medical encyclopedia that belonged to my mother-in-law. And read all about Hyaline Membrane Disease. It's a killer, the No. 1 cause of deaths involving premature babies in the country. President Kennedy lost a baby to it. Kenny Rogers, the singer, had a baby born with it who survived. There are complications that can arise — blindness, retardation, digestive system problems, etc. The encyclopedia wasn't encouraging. It was a mistake bringing it with us.

"He's in good hands," I said, repeating how impressed I was with the people in the ward, trying to put what I'd read out of my mind.

"He's getting the best care possible," my wife said.

Then we sobbed ourselves to sleep.

Things were worse the second day. Linda had warned us they probably would be. Kenny had to be put on a respirator. That meant he couldn't breathe on his own. He was getting pure oxygen pumped into his lungs. His chest no longer lurched. But the machine was doing his breathing for him. There's a danger there. If it's not regulated perfectly, it can cause that blindness we were reading about. Of course, if he were to require 100 percent oxygen to stay alive, being blind would be preferable to the alternative.

"I just want my baby to live," my wife said.

There also was the problem of dependency. Our son was doing

all right on the respirator. However, he would need to start breathing on his own soon. In one of the cribs to the left of Kenny was a little black girl who had been on the respirator for almost six months. There was little chance she'd ever breathe on her own, without the aid of the machine.

Waiting for Kenny's lungs to mature had become a race against time.

"I just want my baby to live."

We noticed something else too. Our son was strangely quiet. The tube that went in his nose and down his throat had to also go between his vocal cords. He couldn't even cry.

The throbbing ache was worse. We needed something good to happen.

The next day, we went in the ward and there was another piece of construction paper taped to another of the machines.

"Hi Mommy and Daddy. I did real good last night and my oxygen requirements went down to 50 percent. I love you," was printed on the card.

There was also a tiny footprint.

The nurses and doctors were watching. We both blinked back happy tears.

We met some of the other parents. Not all of them, though. Some never came to visit.

On the third day, we walked in and my wife screamed as soon as we reached our son's crib. A large needle was stuck into his head, near the temple area. The needle was attached to a tube. Something was either being forced in or out of his head.

"I just hated to do that," Linda said apologetically. "But being premature, his little veins aren't fully developed yet and they keep collapsing in his arms and legs. We had to shave around his head because there's a good vein there. Really this is nothing at all to worry about. It's only an IV to give him nourishment, that's all. Really."

We gasped relief. Then she handed us an envelope.

"It's the hair we shaved. I thought you might like it for a souvenir. You know, his first haircut."

We were settling into a routine now. Three visits a day, usually three hours per visit. We tried to come at times Kenny would be awake, when we could change his diaper. Wash him. Act like parents.

Most of the babies in 240-B are so small that regular diapers, even the ones for newborns, are too big. So they use surgical masks for diapers.

One morning, standing over him, taking inventory and inspecting fingers and toes and ears, we realized we had no pictures of him with his eyes open. There'd been no time back in Cocoa Beach. Because of the bright lights of the ward in Tampa, Kenny had scarcely opened his eyes, except for frightened peeks at his strange new world called life. Which, so far, was definitely no bargain.

One of the nurses suggested he might open his eyes if the overhead lights were off. So, after an announcement the lights were being turned off for some parents to take pictures of their son, all the nurses at the other stations simply inched closer to the respective patients, squinting in the darkness.

I said to my wife, "I wonder how many other places of business would be so cooperative."

She nodded, then looked concerned again. She was worried about the flash attachment. A doctor suggested we not take any straight-on pictures but added anything else would probably be all right.

Our instamatic clicked several times. We knew the pictures would shock most people and would look strange in a baby book. But they were there for posterity and that counted. His eyes, we discovered, were dark blue. Just like any other baby less than a week old.

We were almost enjoying ourselves now, each visit more promising than the last. My wife, thinking out loud, said she wished she could hold her son again. She'd been able to hold him for only a few minutes after he was born.

No problem, said Linda.

All the machines had to be pushed forward so the wires and tubes could stretch down to the old wooden rocker that was brought to our son's station. My wife sat in it and the nurse handed her our baby. The Mother and Child Reunion was exquisite.

"Kenneth recognizes your voice, you know," Linda said. "When he was still inside your belly, he could hear you talk. He knows you're a friend."

I was intrigued by the rocker. It was old and its arms were worn and the seat shiny from lots of use. I wondered how many tears had splashed upon it, how many hearts had melted in just such situations. As I stood and contemplated previous embraces between mother and child, my wife delicately held our son.

"Hi honey, it's Mama."

Then it started. "Look," Linda said, pointing. "Look at his signs."

The machines were going crazy. Oxygen levels improving. Heart beat stronger. All his vital signs were going up.

It wasn't a miracle and it was only temporary. But we were convinced. Life is love.

That night, back in the motel room that had become a temporary home, my wife pulled out a notebook and a box of stationery.

"I'm going to write my thank-you notes for my baby shower," she declared with a smile. "I think we're going to be using all those gifts after all."

A social worker talked to us the next morning. She told my wife that, although it'd be awhile before Kenny could have it, breast milk could be taken and stored. Frozen until he could take food regularly. With the help of a breast pump and some small containers and a refrigerator — all supplied by the hospital — we were able to stash a week's worth of dinner for him.

"They must feel like he's going to make it," my wife said. "Everybody's so up, so optimistic."

We were thinking positively now too. Too positively. Kenny had been taken off the respirator and was improving. But he still required an incubation unit and oxygen was still being pushed toward him. And there was still a chance he could have a relapse. The people in 240-B are positive thinkers. But they're also realists. We were told not to think about a certain day we could take him home. When he was ready — sure — but not before.

Our spirits drooped a little.

One of the other nurses told us about the little boy who was in 240-B for more than a year. He was a favorite, under two pounds when he was born. But a fighter, a real battler.

"Last week, he celebrated his third birthday, his second at home," she said, smiling. "And he's soooo big. You'd never even guess he'd ever been here."

Did she tell us that story to cheer us up? Probably. But it probably cheered her up just as much. The babies of 240-B with happy endings to their stories are the ones you think about.

There aren't that many. There was one baby who had been in the ward for nearly a year. Room and board for one of the cribs in 240-B costs about $900 a day. The mother had no insurance and was looking at a bill which would amount to hundreds of thousands of dollars.

She put the baby up for adoption. She signed the papers that put her own flesh and blood in the custody of the state and she did it because the state of Florida would then pick up the tab.

Then she stood in front of the crib and looked at her child and cried for more than an hour. A few weeks later, the baby died.

There are lots of horror stories. Tales of babies wrapped up in newspapers who had been tossed in garbage dumpsters. There was the story of the girl who had a legal abortion, paid her money and left. Then someone noticed the aborted fetus was alive. Both babies survived. Miracles, for sure. Also exceptions. At best, the children in 240-B are underdogs.

A baby who weighed 18 ounces at birth was brought in and put in the crib next to Kenny's. By comparison our son looked gigantic. This littlest of lives was three months premature. It was hard to believe something so tiny could make it.

The baby, a boy, was not given a name. He died. He never really had a chance. One of the nurses cried anyway.

The little black girl who had become dependent upon the respirator also died. Her nurse sobbed and said a prayer and pulled off the crib sheets and prepared the bed for another patient.

Kenneth Jack Strother survived.

He stayed in 240-B almost two weeks. The day before he was discharged however, we were told he needed an operation. His circumcision.

We laughed. We knew they'd never perform such optional surgery if he were still in danger.

We checked our son out of Tampa General in the middle of the afternoon of a dreary, rainy day, 12 days after he was born. It was anticlimactic. We were strangely quiet as we drove home.

Six months later, my wife took our very fat, very healthy son back to Tampa General. For a visit. Everyone came over to see him. They all gushed about how good he looked.

"He's soooo big. You'd never even know by looking at him now that he was ever here," said one of the nurses.

My wife asked how some of the other babies were doing. Most of them, she was told, had died.

That night, at dinner, she told me of her visit. She said Kenny was the only one in the ward either still alive or not totally dependent upon a respirator. I shivered.

Kenny Strother got his first tooth later than normal, started crawling later than normal and still has a little bit of a bald spot where his head was shaved. But he has five teeth now, is just about ready to walk now and has long enough hair every where else now that we can comb over his artificial receding hairline.

Sometimes when he's asleep, I'll stand over his crib and just look at him, listen to him breathing normally, watch his pudgy hands wiggling and admire the perfect serenity a sleeping baby offers.

———

"All right now, everybody ready to sing Happy Birthday?" asked my wife Kim, anxious and smiling and loving every cornball moment. We sang and cheered and made a wish upon the candle and the little star it represented. And he banged on his chair and got excited all over again, still not sure what was going on.

We all blew out the candle together. It was insignificant now. Just like any hurdle or obstacle, no matter that it's the tallest and most difficult to scale, once you've gotten past it, it's behind you.

A little star finds a sport
Jan. 14, 1984 The Denver Post

He's 6 years old and in the first grade and bored. Christmas has passed but the break from school hasn't. The weather's been lousy and the kiddie shows on TV have been consuming him.

I was worried. My little boy was becoming a drone. Couch potato is the term, I believe. His old man, the sports writer, had forgotten how important it is to have a father around to do things with. His old man had been too busy lately, it seemed, watching someone else's children play games.

Time for a change, I told him. We'll do something sporty. Together. His eyes told me he was excited before he ever said Yippee.

But we hit an immediate snag. What to do. We were newcomers to snow. I could teach him to ski. If I only knew how.

We got silly. We'll ice a puck, I declared. He looked at me funny. Daddy, we can freeze anything without even trying, he said. I agreed, looking at the garden hose.

We started grasping. Buy the world a coke. Nope, not on my salary. Pray for surf? In Colorado? Skip a flat stone across a pond? We could find neither.

I had an idea and went into the house and came out and handed him a football.

"Carry this like a loaf of bread," I said with a giggle.

Then I ran back into the house and returned. Carrying a loaf of bread like a football.

He wasn't amused.

We tried counting the dimples on a golf ball but lost track when we came to the sliced part. I told him if we were fishing we could spit on our bait and he said his teacher told him it was bad to spit anywhere.

Milk the clock? Punch our way out of a paper bag? We were set to take a long walk on a short pier but the walk to the nearest pier was too long.

"Scoobie-Doo's coming on soon," he said, easing toward the door.

399

How about if we sent in the clowns, I asked, again trying to prompt a grin.

He started to cry. I relented. And Scoobie-Doo turned into He-Man and the procession of cartoons was endless. Maybe even mindless as well. I voiced my concern. My son's brain, I moaned, was being controlled by cathode rays and extra-terrestrial heroes. He was escaping from his boredom by climbing inside our television set. Pretty soon, I feared aloud, "he'll be a prepubescent veggie."

My wife had an idea.

"There is some activity thing available for children his size and age," she said. "I read about it in some paperwork he brought home."

She took a bite of dinner and added, "It's a program that teaches wrestling."

I almost spit out my food. "Wrestling! No way. He'll get hurt."

My wife snapped, "It was just a suggestion."

OK. We'd try wrestling.

The room in the gym at Smoky Hill High School was filled with athletes. Fred Bunegar toyed with the whistle around his neck and observed the flurry of motion about him. Larry Jackel was on the padded mats barking about safety and how important it is to keep your head up. Kathy Jackel was roaring encouragement as two 40-pounders were entangled in eye-bulging strife.

Conditioning, fundamentals and fun. These are the goals, accent on the latter. Lining the walls were parents. Some were even out on the mats, helping out. The sports writer was amazed. Community belonging really does exist.

"This is true sport," he said to himself.

Indeed. Something called a two-armed takedown looks just like a form tackle in football. In principle, they are the same. With the constant supervision that's always there, it's safe. With proper vigor, it's glorious.

But just then there was a shriek that sounded like pain. A boo-boo. The victim rubbed his sore elbow and retreated, on the advice of coach Jackel, to get some water from what must surely be a magical fountain. For when the gladiator returned, the pain and tears had vanished.

Finally, it was my boy's turn to wrestle. His opponent seemed larger, more aggressive, more seasoned. I thought perhaps my son was in over his head. Maybe I should intervene.

Too late. The match began. The other boy immediately escaped from my son's clutches by standing up and turning around. He then dropped my boy with a tackle or two-armed whatever. I frowned.

Desperation set in. I yelled, "Put the sleeper on him, Tommy. The sleeper."

The man next to me whispered, "Hey, this is real wrestling."

By now, my son had maneuvered his opponent onto his stomach and the coach was yelling for him to apply a hold called a half-nelson.

He did it. I let loose a rebel yell. The two rolled over and little legs wiggled furiously, trying to gain leverage. No threat to clutter up a roster at the Olympics. But world-class effort all the way. When the whistle blew and the two separated, the first thing they did was look around for the judgment of their parents. Then they smiled.

Winners need recognition. Losers need consolation. Even the littlest of trees need an audience when they fall down. Or stand up. Or execute the first half-nelson of their career.

Father finds son ready to go man-to-man
November 26, 1990

The rim is about four inches too short, said the boy. Not regulation height, agreed his father. They were going to shoot some hoops.

It had been a grand gesture, the digging of the hole, the cement being poured, the pole erected. A family affair. Mom deciphered the instructions, affixed screws and bolts where they actually belonged. And the orange rim became a part of the clear Fiberglas backboard, which became a part of the thick metal pole. It was a stirring moment when the entire family, the father, mother and their two sons, grunted and strained and everyone pushed and tugged to lift the backboard to the roundball heavens. Or at least the end of the pole, where it belonged.

For one bright and shining moment, a picture appeared in the father's mind. Iwo Jima. That famous picture, those soldiers raising the flag, the everlasting image of teamwork. Only this was a basketball hoop in a backyard, a million miles away from something so harsh and . . . real.

The backboard reached an apex that coincided exactly with how far the father's fingertips could reach as he stood on the small stepladder. There was a quivering moment as he struggled to bear the load while his wife frantically turned the wrench and tightened everything. This is important, he thought to himself. This is a big step, both for his children and for him. His property has appreciated with a backyard hoop. Important step.

Best of all, a safe step. Home is a shelter. Always. Now it could also be a playground.

Too bad about the cracks in the driveway, though.

Names were printed into the cement. The date as well. The red, white and blue net was carefully looped onto the rungs of the orange rim. That's when the terrible discovery was made.

"Dad, the rim seems a little low," said the boy, his voice squeaking.

He's 13, somehow a teen-ager. Just the other day, though, he was a baby boy with an open mouth smile. Yeah, it was when? Nineteen seventy-seven? Has it really been this long? Thirteen years?

His father looked at the rim, bounced the basketball a couple of times and flipped up a shot. It banged off the backboard.

"You're right, too low. We'll have to raise it. When we find a taller ladder."

The boy bounced the ball and shot. His father rebounded. A couple of shots later, the boy swished one.

"Good shot, yeah," his dad shouted.

Basketball has not come easy for his son. His most recent growth spurt has shot him to that blessed/dreaded plateau — tallest kid in the class. Change has been swift. There has been turmoil, confusion. Coordination has not been so quick to keep in step. Last year he played sparingly for the school team, the sixth-graders. He was scoreless for the season.

That was one reason for the backyard gym. Practice may not make perfect but it definitely would help his chances of escaping the bench. His dad, suddenly and once again, had become enough of an authority to seek out wisdom.

"Son, lift off both feet for the jump shot," he had said.

"You don't need to shoot a hook shot from that far out."

"Be ready to receive a pass. Reach for the ball. Expect it."

There were not enough afternoons together. Not yet. The boy still struggled with his skills. He tried to dribble with his head up. Sometimes the ball went off his feet, which also were growing at an alarming, not to mention expensive, rate. But he was working, competing, trying to do something that did not come easily. And that pleased his dad.

"Dad, I want to change my name. Would you call me Wild Thing from now on?"

His father's look was all the answer he needed.

"OK, how about the Rebounder from Hell?"

And their smiles melted into each other. The boy's braces on his teeth had been a social dilemma earlier in the year. He'd weathered that, however, and no longer tried not to smile.

"Rebounder, eh? Still having trouble shooting?"

His dad blinked almost daily at the growth. Such progress. Even maturity. It had nothing to do with basketball. When did his little boy discover the lilting strains of Guns N Roses? When did he care if his jeans were stonewashed? And girls? He has a girlfriend now?

There was even one day last month when the boy had asked, almost in a whisper, "Dad, could you show me how to shave?"

A close inspection actually revealed several hairs on the upper lip. The operation was painless, a rite of passage that was dutifully recorded on the ol' Instamatic camera. He immediately asked if he could borrow some after-shave lotion. The times were a-changing, no doubt about that.

Wild Thing's range on the court was now about four feet, tops. His shooting form was still crude but also starting to resemble a basketball player instead of a shot putter.

The father felt good. Safe passage was underway. Through the perilous straits of puberty and hidden rocks of adolescence. It is a time when lifetime values are being formed. There is trial and error and glorious experience. The father felt good that basketball was a part of his son's journey.

He liked that his boy's favorite Pistons were Bill Laimbeer and Vinnie Johnson. His son had said, "They play for the team. They play to win."

He was grasping things. But he also was staying within his range. He was aware of the cracks. He was trying to stay away from them. He is growing up.

The Birds and Bees talk cannot be very far away. And yeah, his son said one day, he'd like to learn how to drive a car soon. But he can wait.

The father did some math, realized in three years his son could own a driver's license. Suddenly that backyard seems more important, more of a shelter, than ever before. Out there, everything's safe, everyone's still a kid, even if the rim is too short.

One day last week, though, Oz crumbled into dust. Disneyland was condemned and boarded up. Funeral arrangements for Tinker Bell are pending. Peter Pan filed for Social Security.

The boy asked his father about the Persian Gulf.

What's that all about, he wanted to know. On TV he had seen some of the soldiers.

"Some of them look like they've never shaved," he said.

And his dad gasped. Why would a kid, a child, think about such things?

"Dad, are we going to war?"

The backboard could have shattered into a million shards and it would not have been as scary. The real world had invaded the backyard. His boy no longer could shoot at the same goal.

What can you explain to the children? How can you stunt their perspective? They cannot be corraled between the fences of innocence when they notice what is happening around them. They have awareness and that is good. And that is also bad.

"It's not a war," the father said.

"But President Bush keeps sending troops there. We learned about it in my current events class."

And there was nothing to say.

They shot baskets and chased down the rebounds in silence. There is a wonderful bond, an umbilical cord lassoing the two together. But the world had trespassed on them.

The boy still wants to raise the rim to the right height. And that will get done, his father has promised. But what will race through his mind by then? What will stick and infest and alter? What distractions will interrupt his thought process as he tries to refine his athletic and social skills? And what rage will his father sense?

Youth is issued wonderful resiliency.

"Dad, I have a joke. Do you know where the king of Iraq belongs?"

And his smile was still sweet and still decked out in temporary metal. But his eyes seemed sharper and more wise as he said, "In a Hussein-Asylum."

He giggled and asked, "Get it?"

The father's laugh was forced. The shots at the hoop clank as often as they swish. But there is progress and there is growth and just the other day, he came home and announced and described and lovingly told about the basket he had scored that day in his game. A four-footer, he figured.

They all get better, if they are allowed enough time.

The father cannot help thinking about his own field of experience, childhood surrendered, innocence lost, in another place, another time, another faraway gulf. Who remembers a saying from his years of encroaching awareness, "Old soldiers never die . . . young ones do."

And he hates the memory. Haven't we learned from mistakes already made, from sins already committed? Must we sacrifice another generation of mankind? Isn't there some unwritten contract between consenting adults that guarantees their children immunity from prosecution for crimes their ancestors committed? Can't we ever patch the cracks? It sounds like leftover turkey but can't we get our act together? Backyards should not become somber think-tanks. Thanksgiving should not be sullied by threat and fear. Children should not surrender childhood so suddenly.

Come on world. Let's prove there really is a Sanity Clause.

There used to be, the father said. Back when he was a kid.

Sometimes fathers can throw us a curve
TODAY, Cocoa Beach, Fla.

We played catch almost every afternoon. My father and me. The ball popped back and forth and I asked the same question.

"Dad, teach me how to throw a curveball."

The answer was always the same.

"No, you're still too young. You'll ruin your arm because your muscles aren't fully developed."

One day, I made my boldest plea. Teach me how to throw a curveball. I demanded. I pleaded. I persisted. He grew impatient. I pouted.

My father looked at me, then down at the ball nestled in his glove, then back at me.

He said, "I don't know how to throw one."

Time is a father's worst enemy. His children begin their lives thinking he's the greatest man who ever lived. He can do it all, whip anyone. Then time exposes him, unravels his coat of shining armor. When it first hits, when you first realize the man who brought you into the world isn't perfect — it's a crusher.

We didn't play too many more games of catch after that.

I learned to ride a bicycle when I was 8. I learned in spite of my father, who refused to buy me training wheels. He set me on the seat — my legs barely reached the pedals — and he started running and pushing the bike.

I remember the wind blasting against my face. And I remember my father's heavy breathing. Then he told me it was time to let go. I screamed. He let go anyway. I made it several yards before skidding out of control.

After examining my skinned knee, he said, "Let's try it again."

Despite my protests, he put me back on the seat and started pushing once more. This time I fooled him. I didn't fall down right away. I even managed to turn around and ride by him in triumphant disdain.

I told him I didn't need his help anymore.

"Good. I'm proud of you. You learned fast."

When Little League season arrived, I knew it was time for the

Three-in-One ritual. They call it mink oil these days. That's a horrible name for Three-in-One oil.

We headed for my closet where my baseball glove had been stored since last summer, removed the rubber bands that held the ball in the pocket of the glove. And commenced with the annual rubdown that salvaged that glove from one season to the next.

"Don't ever leave it in the rain, or abuse it or throw it and it'll last a long time," Dad said. "It'll last through junior high and high school and the whole nine yards."

We took care of that glove — me, my father and that can of oil. I used to think that's why they called it Three-in-One. It was a great glove. I still have it. It's in my closet, with a ball in the pocket, rubber bands wrapped around it. And the whole nine yards.

My father was 53 years old when his heart gave out. That was 13 years ago. He still seemed stubborn and set in his ways and he was no closer to being perfect than he'd ever been. But something had happened.

I grew up, I think. Just like that time when I had no training wheels and I had to go it on my own. My father was behind me all the way, pushing for me. Then suddenly, my daddy was gone.

I've since come to realize the impressionistic period in a boy's life is that span of time that starts the first time your father lets you beat him in arm wrestling and lasts until the eventual day when you ease up and continue to let him have his way in arm wrestling.

A father calls 'em as he sees 'em. He gives pep talks and forks out for footballs and bats and boxing gloves and required physicals and jock straps and rubber cleats and steel spikes and kicking tees and victory pizzas and consolation pizzas. He joins the booster club because he wants a good seat to watch his children play. He supports the Little League because he wants his son to have a good outlet for the release of youthful energy. He agrees to get up early on Saturday to mow the grass at the field and he comes out of the stands to help umpire when somebody doesn't show up. He knows how to share disappointment and hide embarrassment. He's got just the right look for the son who sat the bench all season. He has a handshake that's heavier than a bowling ball. He blows up the ball when it needs air. He picks up chins from the floor, knocks someone off the high horse he's been riding and lays clubhouse rules that work. He believes the team comes first. A father teaches his children it's only a game and then reminds them never to forget how important that is. He teaches them the game, then gets them ready for bigger ones.

I woke up the day of his funeral and realized I never knew that big man. I never realized all his good coaching and strong support. But one thing I did understand—it's all right to be callous and negligent because fathers seem to understand those things. Some things don't need to be said. A father will take his lumps for his children. He'll let them receive the same hard knocks if there's a lesson to be learned.

We returned from burying that old soldier. It had been a long day at the cemetery. One of my father's friends and some of my friends sat around the gloomy, empty home, trying to drink ourselves into better moods.

A man who'd grown up in the same neighborhood with my father approached me. He'd driven from Miami to pay his respects to a man he hadn't seen in 30 years. He was tired, his clothes were wrinkled. But he smiled.

"Know what I remember best about your old man?" he asked.

Without waiting for an answer, he blurted, "He was the best damn ballplayer around when we were 12 or 13 years old. Still the best pitcher I've seen for someone that age. My God, he had a curveball like you've never seen. That thing would drop like it had fallen off a table. I got him to teach me how to throw it. But hell, it was too much strain on my elbow. Look here, I can't straighten it no further than this."

I went to get another beer. I sat in the kitchen and had a good cry and then a good laugh. And then another beer. It was a cold November day and it was 13 years ago and I was thinking about my father who'd just been placed into the ground. I smiled.

I still smile when I think of him.

And his grandsons—my boys—are getting older and stronger. I think I'd like to play some catch with them.

AFTERWORD

We were in New Orleans, headed to one of those cattle-call press conferences that precede the Super Bowl. Something like 1,500 folks with media badges were about to descend on some four dozen Denver Broncos who were scattered across the Superdome's football field.

As our over-loaded bus joined the caravan, my pal Shelby leaned over and half-whispered an amazing tale about Tony Lilly, the Broncos' defensive back with the tough-guy image.

"I got a heck of a story that none of these other guys know," Shelby confided. "In the off-season, Lilly was out hunting with some fellows when he stumbled into a bear trap. The thing clamped around his leg, but as he lay there on the ground writhing in pain, he gritted his teeth, pried the trap's steel arms apart and pulled his mangled leg free.

"Talkabout a tough guy! After he wiped away the blood and tied his T-shirt around the wound, he kept on hunting. He limped through the woods, came up on that bear . . . and he ended up taking it home as a trophy."

The story mesmerized me. As soon as the bus door opened, I all but sprinted to Lilly's side.

"Tony, tell me about your hunting trip," I said. "The one with the bear . . . you know, where you stepped in the trap, pried out your leg and then shot the bear."

The other writers rolled their eyes. Lilly took a step backwards. I thought he was being modest; he thought I was nuts.

"I just figured that story kind of epitomizes your toughness," I said, pressing him. Before I could say any more, Lilly held up his hands to fend me off: "I don't know what you're talking about. I don't even hunt."

As I shrunk away in embarassment, there stood Shelby, doubled over in laughter.

For a while, I was furious. But the more the hoax sunk in, the more my anger turned to appreciation. I had taken the bait because Shelby had made me feel Lilly's pain and admire his grit.

Such is the spell of the storyteller.

And that's what I'll miss most about Shelby Strother. He was the best storyteller in print and in person that I have ever known.

He was a big man, rumpled and shy and usually wrapped in a Hawaiian shirt. He had a walrus moustache and shaggy hair and, more often than not, a Florida tan. He laughed easily, listened better.

These days, a lot of sportswriters are peacocks. They're forever showing you their feathers. Their favorite pronouns are "I," "I" and "I."

Not Shelby. Instead of a mirror, he used a magnifying glass and showed us other people's plumage. As a writer, he could take the mundane and make it magical. Take the extravagant and make it embraceable.

In doing so, he made the daily experience a little more human for the rest of us.

He treated every day like a kid who runs downstairs on Christmas morning to tear open his presents. He doesn't know what's beneath that wrapping paper, but he can't wait to find out. That was Shelby meeting someone new every day, finding a new situation, hearing a new story, discovering a new place. He loved life's daily surprises.

I had more fun with him than with any other person I've known in my life. And I learned from him about people, writing and, most of all, about friendship.

After his death, Shelby's ashes were returned to his native Florida where they were spread in the waters off Cocoa Beach and Key West. This is the way it should have been. Shelby and Florida were one.

He was the intoxicating smell of the gardenia and jasmine blooming in the summer's night air. He was the sweetness of the stone crab pulled from shimmering tropical water.

Most of all, he was the sunshine. He kept us all warm.

We loved that man.

We'll miss him.

Tom Archdeacon
Dayton, Ohio
April 2, 1991